D0836445

SHADOWS
OF
LEGION

*Who can survive
the shadowed ones at the
edge of the End of the World?*

A Novel by
VERNON BUFORD

© Copyright 2004 – Vernon Buford
All rights reserved. This book is protected by the copyright laws of the United States of America. This book may not be copied or reprinted for commercial gain or profit. The use of short quotations or occasional page copying for personal or group study is permitted and encouraged. Permission will be granted upon request. Unless otherwise identified, Scripture quotations are from the King James Version of the Bible. Please note that Destiny Image's publishing style capitalizes certain pronouns in Scripture that refer to the Father, Son, and Holy Spirit, and may differ from some Bible publishers' styles. Take note that the name satan and related names are not capitalized. We choose not to acknowledge him, even to the point of violating grammatical rules.

Destiny Image Fiction
An Imprint of
Destiny Image® Publishers, Inc.
P.O. Box 310
Shippensburg, PA 17257-0310

ISBN 0-7684-2201-9

For Worldwide Distribution
Printed in the U.S.A.

This book and all other Destiny Image, Revival Press, MercyPlace, Fresh Bread, Destiny Image Fiction, and Treasure House books are available at Christian bookstores and distributors worldwide.

1 2 3 4 5 6 7 8 9 / 10 09 08 07 06 05 04

For a U.S. bookstore nearest you, call
1-800-722-6774.
For more information on foreign distributors, call
717-532-3040.
Or reach us on the Internet:
www.destinyimage.com

DEDICATION

This book is for my Lord and Savior, Jesus Christ.
Also, to my father John.
…Praying for you.

ACKNOWLEDGMENTS

I'd like to thank my family: John, Dorothy, Ben, Priscilla, Faye, Cynthia, and Eric. My Pastor, John Jackson, and Far Hills Community Church.

CHAPTER 1

The funeral procession moved with the slow, deliberate precision of its purpose—to bury a fallen soldier. A black chariot of an old hearse formed the centerpiece of the serpentine line of vehicles winding its way into a national cemetery. The bright light of an early, August morning cut jagged shadows among the tombstones. The sunlight filtered through the trees, fragmenting into glorious rays. God made a beautiful day to lay Warrant Officer Thomas J. Macklin into the earth.

The vehicles in the motorcade came to park within a few feet of the tombs; the mourners departed in somber, sober fashion. Death is the clearest, coldest, most awakening thing. The bright light of the day was a stark contrast to the bleakness of an ended life, and to the shadows resting on the souls and collective consciousness of the mourners.

The pallbearers hoisted the heavy pine casket by its ornate handles, and carried it to the site of the burial. It was easy to find the family of the dead. The Macklins held each other up as they walked to the place where a husband and a father would soon rest.

Kathleen Macklin walked with two of her adult children beside her and the third lagging behind. She wore the graceful appearance of a mournful, strong-willed black woman, her face behind the dark veil. Her high, full cheeks, deep, almond-colored eyes, and willowy expression reminded one of a tree in the wind. It might bend, but it would not break.

As the wife of a career military man, Kathleen had endured endless days and nights of fear and uncertainty throughout his many tours of duty. There was always the packing and moving from one post to another with never any real stability of home or community, only a ceaseless shifting from place to place. Around any established relationships or friendships lurked an aching realization that departure would come soon. The children grew up without a church.

Kathleen Macklin was determined to let no one see that she was not a woman of strength and courage. Cry? Yes, she would cry, but her husband wouldn't want her to make some huge sprawling epic of herself in front of all their folks. No, she would hold her ground and plant her feet firm; she would see her husband off with the dignity she'd shown when he had gone off to the field or on some training exercise. She had always been able to hold back the full deluge of tears when he left. She remembered the day that had been the hardest for both of them, when he'd left for the southeast Asian jungle some ten thousand miles from their home in Clarksville, Alabama. She had cried deeply that day, and so had he.

Clarise Macklin, the youngest child at the age of 26, still she felt the need—especially now—to be held, protected and loved by her daddy. She was his "little girl," and would always be, no matter how she tried to out-grow the title.

She remembered how she hated the way he would often favor her over her brothers, embarrassing them with punishments or by overlooking her faults, while emphasizing theirs. Thomas often lavished all the love and attention on his precious baby girl. Sometimes, she felt it was unfair the way boys got treated differently than girls by their fathers. Now, as she looked at her brothers, she saw her father in both of them.

Clarise felt a sense of fear and uncertainty in her father's absence, not unlike what she had felt in his absence during her childhood. When daddy was gone, things just didn't seem to work right. She remembered the over-whelming sense of security she felt in just knowing that he was in the house, especially at night. His jump boots down the hall, just outside his and Mom's bedroom door, freshly polished in Kiwi boot shine and drying on newspaper, made her feel the presence of her strong, loving father. In the mornings, she complained to herself about the sulphuric smell of the spe-cial shaving powder he used to clean up his tough beard. How it used to stink! But she knew that behind the sound of rushing water and the bath-room radio pulsating an Al Green tune, she was as safe as being wrapped in a warm blanket on a blistery cold day. Daddy was there, and everything was going to be all right.

"Everythang's gonna be all right, Little Duck Duck."

Clarise felt fresh pain warm her chest and tears rolled down her brown cheeks.

"Daddy…" she said, and no other words came.

Robert Macklin was a 32-year-old sales manager at a used car dealership in Montgomery, about 80 miles southeast of Clarksville off I-65. He had often fought with his father over the fact that he hadn't done enough with his life. Though he hated to admit it, his father was right.

Robert was the only Macklin son, though, who had made an attempt to follow his father into the military. When he was a boy, Thomas saw that Robert showed a lot of interest in the Army, and in his father's occupation as a soldier. Robert had spoken fondly of the day when he would one day join the Army, following Thomas's lead.

Thomas had been a motor sergeant in Vietnam, and after the war he did a short stint as a jump instructor at Fort Benning. His MOS changed again when he shattered the metatarsal bone of his right foot in a training exercise. He became a drill instructor.

Robert was always fascinated with how his father could tear something apart and put it back together. He remembered sitting up on late nights in his room reading through Army training manuals on everything from the Bradley Fighting Vehicle to the M-1 tank. Robert watched once as his father took apart the carburetor on a '68 GTO, replacing just a simple, little fuel filter. "Help make it run smoother," Thomas said, with a knowing furrow of his brow, looking down at Robert over the top of his greasespeckled glasses. Robert could never quite muster up the mechanical inclination his father had. It eluded him somehow, but that didn't stop him from wanting to please the man, from wanting to make Thomas see Robert's worth as a son.

Robert joined the Army and less than a year later, with a dishonorable discharge, he was sent home for repeated brawling and public drunkenness. Robert always had an unruly streak, and the Army wasn't exactly a haven for a discipline case.

He had failed his father.

Right now, he didn't want to remember the look of bitter disappointment that had held his father's face, or the way Thomas wouldn't look him in the eye when he came home. All Robert could think about right now was how he had run out of time to show that he could do something to make Thomas proud. The bright sun exposed every bit of weakness, shame, and insecurity he felt. Robert knew that he was going to get very drunk at the wake.

Scott Macklin was sure of what he felt. All he could think of was the day he realized that his father cared about him.

Thomas Macklin had stood with his hands authoritatively on his hips and said something to Scott that he would never forget. "Boy, if you and I end up like me and my daddy, we are gonna be inna sad state!" Scott was nineteen. Afterwards, he had made it his mission in life to bridge the ever-widening chasm between the two of them.

Scott's mother had told him about the tough life she and Thomas had shared growing up in Clarksville. During World War II, Clarksville's economy was fueled by the munitions industry, with a central factory employing practically every able-bodied man and woman who lived there. The town also had a notorious, tawdry side; a deviant mirror image moved in at night.

To accommodate the appetites of the soldiers at nearby Fort Benning, there was a strip in Clarksville called Main Street. There were juke joints and backroom gambling, numbers running, blues, jazz, drugs, and women.

Thomas's mother, at the age of fifteen, had become a lady of the evening. When Thomas was born, his daddy had plenty of reason to believe the boy wasn't his son. His mother beamed when she presented the baby to his father, but he took one look at Thomas, snatched him into his hands, and tossed him out the first floor window. The relationship between Thomas and his father didn't improve much after that.

In segregated Clarksville, the Macklins lived on the Blackside, west of the Chatahoochee River, at 323 Brickyard Road, in Columbus Heights. Blacks weren't allowed to travel east of the river, but on more than one occasion, the Klan staged a hanging on the Blackside.

Kathleen had told Scott how Thomas's father used to hold him down while his brothers beat him. Once, he hit Thomas so hard he was unconscious for a day, and spent a week in the hospital. Despite all this, Thomas somehow believed it was all his fault, that if he'd just do everything right his daddy wouldn't hit him. He often made it his duty to go and look for his dad, if the old man had been drinking and hadn't come home. Usually, he'd find him in a brothel or lying in a ditch or in a filthy gutter. Even when he was older, Thomas had tried to impress his father with his military accomplishments, but nothing worked. After a while, Thomas stopped trying.

When he heard the news of his own father's death, Thomas was 36, and scarcely said a word. He just kept on getting his uniform ready for the next day, kept on polishing the brass, and kept on burning little strings off his fatigues with a lighter. For hours he said nothing, but when he found himself alone he cried bitterly.

Scott had stood in front of Thomas at the age of 19, frail and weak-kneed before a man who had fought in the cloying, dank heat of the hellish jungle. He had watched tears brim in his father's eyes for a son he might lose, as he had now lost a father. Scott had heard his words and hadn't forgotten.

But now, as the pallbearers placed the casket on the straps of the lowering device, Scott could see his efforts toward reconciliation were in vain.

Suicide.

The death of his father was called a suicide; he had driven his car off a cliff in a quarry in Birmingham. It made no sense to Scott or anyone else who knew his father; the man just wasn't the type who would take his own life. To Thomas, suicide would have been the ultimate act of a coward. So why? Why was his car found at the bottom of a 200 foot industrial dig? Why was his body burned so badly they had to keep the casket closed?

An honor guard performed the flag ceremony, meticulously folding and re-folding the flag. Finally, they gave the triangle-shaped piece of cloth to Kathleen, who took it and held it like a baby. The soldier saluted her, and turned crisply on his heel to rejoin the formation.

Kathleen bowed her head to the pastor's voice as he spoke the Lord's Prayer. She felt it coming long before it arrived, a deep yearning for her husband. Kathleen begged God to give her the answer. Why, Lord, why have you left me alone? Why did you take my husband from me?

"Why, Lord, why?"she whispered.

Then Kathleen let out a wail, including everyone in her anguish: Her knees weakened, and her children had to hold her up. She moaned the way the living moan only over the dead. Her husband Thomas was gone.

A few yards away, hidden among the trees, a homeless man in rags covered his mouth and cried at the sound of the woman's voice. Tears rolled down his dirt-covered cheeks. "Oh, Kathy," he said.

Kathleen Macklin's voice carried itself high into the air, hoping to catch the spirit of Thomas Macklin somewhere above the trees of the cemetery.

———•◦•◦•———

Scott realized that Grandma and Grandpa's house in Columbus Heights hadn't changed in the fifteen years since he was last there. The place, among a row of shanty-houses on Brickyard, was so old and run-down the only thing holding it together was God's good grace.

The wake had begun, but the upbeat mood made it seem more like a party. The place was full of people who ran the gamut of black archetypes in a small, southern town. Old churchwomen wore pillbox hats, fanning themselves, watching over the crowd. The Reverend Ellis Tremell, who performed the service; the men, standing in dark suits, talking of things of the Lord, and speaking about Thomas Macklin; children, in their best clothes, having forgotten that someone had died, running and darting around the adults; and families from all around the neighborhood.

Scott, standing in a hallway between the kitchen and the living room, where all the activity took place, believed his family was probably related to everyone in the house, but he intimately knew only a handful of them.

He was holding a plate of black-eyed peas, turnip greens, cornbread, chicken, and sweet potatoes. Normally, the plate would have been quickly emptied, but he couldn't find his appetite. A drunken man whom he knew to be his father's abusive, oldest brother, came up and threw an arm around Scott as if he were a bar buddy. The bourbon on the man's breath assaulted Scott.

Uncle Telvin.

"Boy, I sho' is gonna miss yo daddy. We didn't always get along, now, but I sho' is gonna miss 'im."

Scott read the expression behind the alcohol-clouded eyes as sincere. Uncle Telvin was sixty-two; he had three years on Thomas.

"I know, Uncle Telvin, I know. I'm gonna miss him, too."

Uncle Telvin had a modest job. He worked as a processing clerk at a metal stamping company in the Chatahochee Industrial Yards off the river. His hands were withered and arthritic, but he still managed to keep his job. The knuckles on his fingers were swollen and knotted. He spoke in a humorous tone.

"You know he was proud o' you, now," he said. "Thass right. His boy is a uhm… is a uhm… Whatta you do? What you call yourseff?"

"An architect," Scott answered.

"Now, you know we ain't seen you inna long time. We ain't got too many architects 'round here! No, sir! Thass all right."

Scott nodded his head. "Thanks. Yeah, you're right, it's been a long time. They keep me pretty busy."

Uncle Telvin cocked his head to one side, giving Scott an almost comical look of parental warning. "Now, you cain't get too busy fo' yo' family, now. No, no, no. Don't ever get *dat* busy. You know wha' I mean?"

"I understand, Uncle Telvin," Scott said.

Uncle Telvin smiled with the pride of knowing that someone in his family, a black someone, was making accomplishments in the white world.

"Yeah… A architect. So whatta you do… I mean exactly?"

"I design the interiors and exteriors of buildings," Scott answered pridefully.

"Do what?"

"I make drawings of the insides and outsides of buildings, and they build 'em based on what I draw."

"Yeah, thass right, thass right. So, thass what a architect is?"

"Yeah."

"Yeah, all right, all right, now."

Uncle Telvin turned and announced to the whole wake his newly discovered secret. "Hey, y'all! Tommy's boy is a architect!"

The wake answered with a joyful shout of approval. Uncle Telvin gave Scott a hearty pat on the back and then moved on, beaming through the crowd.

Scott looked around his grandparents' house at the aging memories. He scanned the walls and the mantel over the fireplace; there were fading, yellow-edged photographs, spanning three generations. The pictures were portals of time, slowly closing and locking out the memories of a family that had endured war, poverty, racial hatred, grievous sin, and death. Scott felt the weight of all of it land on his shoulders. How far apart from his people he felt. His life, compared to theirs, had been so blessed. What was his place among them? What would become of his life in Seattle, his beautiful fiancée, and his exalted lifestyle? The disconnection—and the connection—he felt with his people was a soft torture on his soul.

Thomas and Kathleen moved the family from Clarksville after Vietnam, far away from the ghetto. They made visits here and there and during holidays, but after the children grew up and moved out on their own, the visits were fewer and farther between...until they finally never visited at all.

Scott's earliest memory of his grandparents' house was a celebration of the end of the war nearly 30 years ago. What he remembered most clearly from that long-ago day was a stranger... and a warning.

On the front porch there had been swinging, steel chairs which made a wonderful, rusty, musical metallic sound when he and his cousin played on them. The screen door had a tear in the mesh; it had swung and banged lazily against the doorframe with the sticky Alabama breeze.

A junkyard covered a field on the house's south lawn. It was a treasure of adventure for the children, who were everywhere. They found old cars, broken furniture, televisions with their electronic guts spilled, fluorescent bulbs that smoked when you broke them open, tires, rusty refrigerators in which to hide. Inside, the sounds of smoky soul music bounced off the rafters at 323 Brickyard Road.

The adults talked in one room, smoking and drinking. They went over old times, debated all the social-political themes of the day; wondered if the Atlanta Falcons were going to get to the playoffs. Thomas Macklin bragged and boasted about how he had survived Vietnam, and his sometimes-jealous brothers wished they could take him down like they had done when they were children.

The beer and gin were passed to the tunes of Al Green, the O'Jays, the Ohio Players, Patti Labelle, and Marvin Gaye. The children would look in on the adults and see a complicated, loud, and frightening world.

It was 1975.

Scott Macklin was sitting in the TV room, while the other children ran in and out of the house. A news program showed a U.S. Army helicopter being dumped off a ship into the ocean; other footage showed people trying to escape in a second helicopter off the roof of a building. It didn't look like everyone made it. There were pictures of a man in an orange robe setting himself on fire while a jungle burned. Scott could smell it.

A man came into the room.

"What you watchin', boy?"

Eight-year-old Scott didn't really understand the barrage of images coming at him from the small black and white screen. He looked up at the man dressed in a leather coat, with a thick turtleneck underneath. His derby was turned backwards atop a short freshly-picked Afro. The man smiled down on him, holding a can of Pabst Blue Ribbon in his hand. When he spoke the alcohol wafted from his breath, but his words and expression were cold and sober.

"I don' know," Scott answered. "My daddy was over there."

"Thass right, boy, he was," the man said. "It's bad over there. Yo' daddy went through some hell, now. Don't you forget."

"I ain't," Scott said.

The stranger pulled out his wallet and took a one-dollar bill from among many.

"I gotta show you somethin'." He turned the bill over to its obverse side, showing the Great Seal, with the pyramid and eye. He held it so Scott could see it and the boy suddenly felt a latent dread, as if awakening from a nightmare.

"You know what this is, boy?"

"No."

The stranger's expression hardened and froze. "Thass the devil, boy. The devil." He tapped the eye on the seal, then handed it to Scott. "One day you'll understand what I'm talkin' 'bout. You'll be in the fight with us."

Scott took the bill and stared at the seal and eye, transfixed.

"Don't forget, now. Thass evil. It's the devil."

Scott looked deep into the eye, and struggled to read the strange text underneath the pyramid. When he looked up, the man was gone.

Al Green crooned over the record player, asking how to mend a broken heart.

Scott moved to the front door, bathed in the setting sunlight. He held the dollar up, studying it. Thomas Macklin and Kathleen sat on the couch in the smoky living room, laughing with drunken abandon. Thomas's eye caught his son, and he watched him in the light. He saw the bill in Scotty's hand, and he wondered what dark thing his son had just learned.

——•◦•——

The sky was clear blue, azure. An automobile fell out of the fathomless blue; it spun and twisted, the sound of metal creaked as it cut the air. And, it fell...and fell...and fell...

━━━━•◆•━━━━

Scott was in his grandparents' attic, carried there by memory's need.

The sadness of the wake had given way to a more jubilant celebration. From downstairs, he heard the strains of Stevie Wonder. He had opened several trunks and boxes, and had stumbled onto a chest of his father's military memorabilia.

He found a picture of his dad as a drill instructor when they were stationed at Fort Leonard Wood, Missouri. There was a picture of him rappelling across a ravine at jump school in Georgia and a snapshot in Vietnam with his best friend, Mitchell Biggsby, on a hot day in the jungle, leaning on a supply truck with a bright white star on the door. Finally, a picture of Thomas receiving the rank of Warrant Officer, W1, in a promotion ceremony at Fort Bliss. Behind him was a stand with an image of the company logo, a blue devil's head with the motto, "Bravo Company, 9th Brigade, Americal Division. This Will Not Be Defeated." The photo of his father's face bore a look of determination, but the man who swore him in wore an oddly expressionless face, like the dead looks of people in old vintage photographs.

Scott felt a rush of longing for his father, and realized all the sacrifices the man had made for him and his family. He had endured the horrors of a terrible war, only to return to a place where black men where still hung from trees. Scott stared at the pictures, and cried over them.

"Scott?!"

Clarise called him from downstairs. He wiped away tears and sniffed. "Yeah," he answered gruffly.

"Come on back downstairs. Momma wants you."

"In a minute." He composed himself, and then moved toward the ladder, clutching the photos.

He found his mother sitting alone in his grandmother's bedroom. She was still holding the triangle-folded flag in her lap. When she looked up and saw Scott, it was like looking into the face of her husband. It was enough to make her smile. Kathleen Macklin stretched out her hand to him, and Scott took it. His eyes surveyed the dusty room.

"I'm getting ready to go," he said. "I have to get back to the hotel. My flight's leaving tomorrow morning, early."

Kathleen turned her gaze back to the blue triangle. "You can't stay another day?"

"No. I'd like to, but if I don't get back, we're going to fall behind the building schedule for the Washington Lake Project. They commissioned us three months ago, and the steel crews are finishing up now. The building owner's getting nervous about a new tenant who wants to set up a space audit to validate their lease agreement."

Scott was in so many ways his father's son. Kathleen knew how well Thomas had ingrained the virtues of duty and discipline into him. She knew her husband would want his son to get back to work as soon as he could, to not waste a lot of time mourning him.

Scott felt Kathleen's disappointment. "So, are you gonna stay here with Grandma?"

"Yes, for a little while. The doctors say she doesn't have much time. I wanna be here when she goes."

"Are you gonna be able to handle that? I mean, with dad and now her…"

She squeezed his hand. "I'll be all right. You go. Go home and marry that pretty girl and get me some babies. I want me some grandkids." She managed to laugh.

Scott ducked his head, feeling a tug of emotion. He let go of his mother's hand and moved to the door.

"Scott…"

He turned back to her from the doorway.

"Your daddy would want you to make your own life. He needs you to be a man, and carry on like you are. Go build. Go make your family. He may not have told you, but he loved you."

Scott heard his voice crack on the verge of tears. "I know he did. But you know somethin'?"

She stared at him.

Scott gazed out a bedroom window. The evening had come, and the sky was streaked with purplish tones.

"He did tell me…once. Not in so many words, but he told me."

He smiled at Kathleen, and left the room.

———◆·◆·◆———

The wake was clearing out; most of the guests had gone home. Pastor Tremell stopped Scott at the door and gave him an earful of godly advice, laden with biblical verses. Scott barely understood most of it, but thanked the pastor anyway.

He hugged and kissed Robert, Clarise, and Kathleen, climbed into his rental car, and disappeared down Brickyard into the late-summer dusk.

Near the house, a man in rags watched the taillights fade into the black. He hoisted a green duffel bag on his shoulder, and followed Scott's departure. No one at 323 Brickyard Road saw him at all.

Chapter 2

Arthur Calvin Baron sat in the study of his beach house, and read over some text from a private database. He picked up the phone to make a call.

"This is Baron," he said. "Locate Prichard, and deliver the Los Cruzado dossier."

The sun set outside his home in a fiery orb as he hung up the receiver. A cool wind cut across the New England bay.

———•◆•———

Douglas Prichard took in the smell of herbicide glyphosate as it rained down over the brightly flowered poppy fields. Three U.S.-paid Turbo Thrush crop dusters buzzed the Colombian sky, wingtips glinting with the clarity of the noonday sun.

Prichard watched the AH-64 Apache gunship patrol just outside the perimeter of the 100-acre field. The helicopter edged close to the green hills near the village of *Sandvika*, 50 kilometers north of the Peruvian border. It had been quiet all morning, but Colombian Army Intelligence knew there were guerillas in those hills.

Three squads of Copes Commandos cordoned off a crowd of about 200 peasants and farmers. They protested and cursed in Spanish as the planes sprayed the heroin fields, killing their cash crop. The Colombian government was afraid of an uprising similar to the mess in the *Caqueta* state some years back, when similar tactics were used to cut into Colombia's drug production. But, so far, the throngs of peasants were only a mild distraction compared to the potential threat of the FARC leftist rebels hiding in the mountains.

Doug Prichard had been surrounded by death since graduating from the School of Americas in 1978. He gained prominence as a protégé of Calvin Baron in 1979, working as an advisor for the U.S.-backed Contras in Nicaragua. The blood of countless men, women, children, clergy, and other innocents was on his head and stained his hands.

Many condemned him as they brought judgment with the Tower Commission, but they didn't understand the will and drive of a man who was a soldier with nothing to fight for except his country. He engaged in a personal war for what America could be, certainly not for what it had become.

Doug Prichard knew that most Americans had no idea what was happening to their country. They were liberals who cared more for the rights of murderers and drug dealers than for those of law-abiding citizens. They judged him as he organized and led a Copes Commando raid against the notorious drug kingpin, Pablo Escobar, systematically executed his lieutenants, then slipped into Escobar's bedroom and cut his throat while his son slept next to him. The Escobar Cartel gave way to the Cali Cartel, creating yet another war. They judged him as he trained young Columbian men to kill and, if necessary, die without question—young men who would have been farmers, pastors, or priests.

As the world edged closer to the New Millennium, the war grew worse.

Three Columbian Marxist armies expanded with support from the Cali Cartel. The largest of them, the Revolutionary Armed Forces of Columbia (FARC), routinely taxed and regulated cocaine and heroin to subsidize its war effort.

The Colombian government had begged the Clinton Administration for aid, but the U.S. hesitated to hand over millions to a country with a history of a corrupted military, judiciary, and police force.

Prichard was now an advisor to the Colombian military, part of a 900-troop, U.S.-trained battalion making a push into a FARC, guerrilla-infested region called *The Putumayo.*

Prichard, the other advisors, and the Copes Commandos fought with what little aid they had, amidst rumors, and some factual evidence, that the CIA had long been shipping drugs into the U.S. for their own purposes, undermining their efforts in the dizzying, political circles of Washington.

Prichard's gaze turned from the gunship to the angry, jostling peasants. One man broke through the line, charging a Commando. The soldier drove the butt of his AR-15 into the farmer's chest and dropped him. Prichard jumped off the jungle-dressed Humvee, running and cursing at the young soldier in Spanish. The Commando scooped the man up off the dirt; with gentler movements, he handed him back to the crowd. For a moment, it seemed they would all rush forward, but when the Commandos aimed their assault rifles, the peasants subsided.

Prichard let out a long, exasperated sigh. At first, he didn't notice the sound of heavy blades beating the heated air. When he turned, he saw a UH-60 Blackhawk helicopter approaching from the north.

One of the Turbo Thrush planes dropped another load of herbicide.

The Blackhawk landed on the dirt road that led to the village, several meters distant. Doug could barely stand against the wind of its spinning blades.

"Well, what now?" he spat in a faint Virginia drawl.

Dolby Sikes jumped out of the helicopter with all the grace of a politician or an ad executive. He kicked up dirt with his Gore-Tex hiking boots, careful not to get any on his cargo shorts and light denim shirt.

Sikes was Doug's liaison to the State Department, 20 years his senior. He had an irritating way of acting like Prichard's mother.

"*Bien manana*," Sikes greeted, with his arms wide.

Prichard regarded him like an insect that he thought he'd killed, but which had somehow managed to scurry out from under the kitchen sink.

"What are you doin' here, Sikes?"

"Just delivering a message, *mi amigo*."

"Drop the Spanish, you sound like an idiot," Prichard snapped.

The peasants were louder now as a Turbo Thrush buzzed low overhead. The pilot taunted them, dipping his wing.

Doug turned and walked back to the Humvee and Sikes followed. In black fatigues and a jungle hat, Prichard's lean frame contrasted to Sikes's, who looked like he was late for a board meeting.

"Playin' errand boy, again?" Prichard asked. "Got no time for your message, so here's *my* message. The fields north of Sandvika are almost saturated. We're heading into *Leticia* tonight for crop eradication to begin by 0600 tomorrow. But if they want us to keep back FARC, the ELN, and the bloody EPL, we are gonna need more support and we're gonna need it now. We'll also need to get more troops for crowd control. Now, if they won't send us more support, then you can tell them to expect some civilian losses. These peasants don't like the idea of growing coffee or cotton when they can live off drug money."

Prichard was referring to the Colombian government's plan to switch farmers over to alternative crops once the coca, poppy and marijuana plants were destroyed.

Sikes grinned from behind his Porsche sunglasses. "Well, it's not going to be your problem for a while, Prichard. We need you to go to Nicaragua and pick up a man outta this dossier." He pulled out a manila file and a compact disc. "All the info you'll need is right here."

Prichard snatched the disc and file out of Sikes's hands, scrutinizing the items. The file had a State Department seal on it, so he resigned himself to believe the documents were genuine before he opened it.

They stopped at the Humvee.

"Who gave the order?" Prichard asked.

"Baron."

Prichard nodded, looking around at the rich farmland that had long ago been turned into a heroin field. He jerked his head back towards the Blackhawk. "That's my ride?"

"Yeah," Sikes said. "I'll go with you to Bogotá, but they'll be dropping me there for a flight home. You know, back to the world?" Sikes made sure to rub in the "flight home" bit.

Prichard sniffed. "What world is that, you moron? What about my gear?"

"Don't worry about your things. We'll make a stop at Battalion Command."

They walked back to the Blackhawk. Sikes grinned like a man blissfully unattached to his surroundings; Prichard knew that was how men like Sikes operated. "The Uninvolved," he called them.

"You know, you've been out of it too long, Prich. All this time in the sun has made you complacent, I think. We just figured that we'd left you outta the game, thought you'd like a little side-mission."

"Maybe." Prichard pulled a radio off his belt and barked orders in Spanish. Down the road, two squads of Commandos suddenly pulled out from the fields. Sikes was impressed; he hadn't known they were there. The Commandos searched for any peasants hiding in the crops, using themselves as human shields to stop the planes from dusting.

Prichard watched his troops pull back. The platoon leader's voice broke over the radio in a youthful Spanish. *"El campo indicativo claro."* The field was clear.

"So, what's happening, Sikes? Are they gonna cut us off, are they gonna pull us out? What?"

Sikes looked like a snake eyeing a trapped ferret. "I wouldn't worry about the Commandos; we've got a man from Panama coming in to take over. As far as the operation itself, it's still too early to tell. President Pastrana was just in Washington, trying to get Slick Willy to give up 1.6 billion in aid. But there have been some allegations that the Colombian army has a really sad human-rights record, so they're hesitating. Plus, we're in an election year and Clinton's gonna ride it into the sunset with a bang. I mean, the man survived Whitewater Gate, Monicagate, and every other gate you could think of, leaving the country with an economy that's starting to look like the fifties. No, he's goin' out like Michael Jordan, on top of his game. He's concerned, but not *that* concerned. The problems down here? Well, if you catch Mike Wallace, you may have a story on *Sixty Minutes,* but most of the pushers and shovers on the Hill are trying to stay away from this one until after November. They smell a major war and they're dodging the stink."

Prichard puffed his chest in frustration. "So you're telling me that the most powerful, sophisticated military in the history of the world can't stop a pack of drug-running murderers from underwriting a communist army, right in our faces?"

Sikes shrugged his shoulders. "There's a big problem with that, Prichard—it's called the People of the United States of America. We are a democracy, remember? I don't think the American people are interested in Vietnam re-runs. And if you'll recall, trying to rewrite the Constitution got us into a lot of trouble down here in the eighties. Remember, your job and mine is to uphold democratic principles."

"Since when?"

Sikes held up his hand. "Okay, well, given the historical context of what's been going on down here, I guess the word 'democracy' is a relative term, but, be that as it may, we can't just go intervening in the affairs of the world without at least the minimal appearance of propriety."

"Propriety? So, I'm supposed to believe that we're suddenly worried about our reputations?"

"No. What I'm saying is that the timing isn't right. Our country has had a liberal governmental influence for the past eight years. Not many Americans want a repeat of Salvador, Nicaragua, and the other bloody messes we've had our hands in. Like I said, we're waiting for November, but don't worry, Prich, you'll have your war. Down here, that's an inevitability."

Prichard suddenly looked as old and as worn out as he felt. "Look, I don't want a war, Sikes. I just wanna... never mind. Let's just go if we're goin'."

The Commandos platoon leader, Vasquez, stepped up to give a full report of the field clearing. Prichard put his hand on the young man's shoulder and told him that he was leaving. He placed Vasquez in charge of dispersing the peasants and moving the troops to *Leticia*, once the day's operation was completed. The young soldier saluted him and shook his hand, then turned and marched down the road, talking into his radio.

That was it. Goodbye, I guess, Prichard thought.

He had often known missions to end like this, with nothing too dramatic, just on to the next thing, whatever it may be.

They reached the helicopter and the pilot revved up the turbo shaft engines. Prichard and Sikes climbed on and the bird took to the air.

Prichard watched the dying fields below. "Who's this man we're going after, anyway?" he shouted.

Sikes yelled over the engines. "Not *we*, you! I was wondering when you'd ask! You ran into him once! Los Cruzado! Father William Dante Los Cruzado!"

Prichard flipped open the folder and found a close-up photo of a haggard-faced man in wire-framed glasses. The gray streaks in the man's shoulder-length hair made Prichard feel even older still. It had been a long time since he had seen Los Cruzado.

As the Blackhawk pulled away, Prichard watched the crowd. The dust from the wind kicked up and they shielded themselves. The Commandos hardly moved.

Prichard tried to see the AH-64 gunship. He couldn't hear the sound because of the distance and the noise of the Blackhawks' turboprops, but he saw the muzzle flash from the Apache's chain gun as it rapidly lit the hills near Sandvika with fire.

⎯⎯⎯•◦•⎯⎯⎯

Father William Dante Los Cruzado was digging.

The village farmers were laying the last of the polyurethane pipe for the drip irrigation system. Father Los Cruzado had given it a lot of thought and research—drip irrigation was the best method to use for the village community farm. It had been months from conception to completion, and it was almost finished.

He was glad to see that something would actually grow in his war-torn country.

Northeast of Managua by 290 kilometers, on a high plateau at the foot of the *Cordillera Isabella* Mountains, rested the home and church built by Los Cruzado and the local Roman Christian Base Communities some 20 years ago. The *Prizapolka* River wound its way past 2000-meter-high peaks as it flowed into the Caribbean Sea.

Vast coffee fields and cattle ranches dominated these high plains of Nicaragua; the church mission had been a haven to the farmers and their families, a community of only a few hundred, for over two decades. Los Cruzado had made this his refuge and place of worship and, at 50-plus-years-old, he had thanked God his days of running were over. The past conflicts in his country, the Somozas, the Sandinistas, the Contras, the CIA, and the fighting within the Roman Catholic Church, were separate from the contentment he felt as he dug in the simple, raw dirt.

This was the place where he was born, a village named after the mountains.

Los Cruzado felt the calluses on his palms as he bent his back and swung the heavy pick into the dry earth. The sweat dripped from his face and spotted the ground. A hot, Nicaraguan sun pounded his back and neck with hellish heat, but he was almost done with the row. The 100-plus-degree tropical air would have fainted most, but he, like his people, was born to it.

There were about 70 meters left to furrow and as he worked, Los Cruzado let his mind take him off the task and into the deep waters of time gone, into the days of social injustice and civil war, days of famine, violence, and conflicts with God in the hearts of men.

In 1972, a dictator named Anastasio Samoza and his family held a murderous grip over the country. Anastasio enjoyed full control over the Nicaraguan economy, the National Guard, and the media. His money came from U.S. backing and investments in land, transportation, and manufacturing.

That year an earthquake hit the country and destroyed most of Managua. Instead of aiding the people, Samoza sent his National Guard to participate in the looting of the city; shortly thereafter, he robbed the country of millions set aside for civil aid.

The people grew desperate.

The Archbishop of the Roman Catholic Church, Obando y Bravo, wrote several pastoral letters criticizing the Samoza regime, stirring the hearts of the peasants and poor in the country. At the time, a young clergyman and writer named William Dante Los Cruzado edited and published the letters. A group calling themselves the *Frente Sandinista de Liberacion Nacional* began an insurrection and a guerilla campaign against the regime, signaling the beginning of the end for Samoza. By 1979, he had fled the country, taking most of his National Guard with him. Soon, the Sandinistas invaded Managua, the capital of Nicaragua, and her citizens celebrated.

Then the Contras came along with the CIA, and political division hit the Church.

———◆———

Father Los Cruzado kept digging…

———◆———

The exiled National Guard resurfaced in 1981, with the support of the CIA, under two main fronts: The Nicaraguan Democratic Force (FDN), and the Revolutionary Democratic Alliance (ARDE). Collectively, they were called the Nicaraguan Resistance, or counterrevolutionaries… Contras.

Washington, D.C., first under Carter, then under Reagan, funneled support into Honduras, where a military outpost called Fortress America was established as a staging ground for paramilitary raids into Nicaragua. The ex-Guardsmen were deeply embittered by the loss of the Somoza government, and they hungered for vengeance and blood.

The U.S. government tried to involve the church, which grew in prominence during the Samoza years for speaking against the dictatorship, and for bringing to light the gross mistreatment of the poor. As the Sandinistas took power, the church incorporated Marxist doctrine with Scripture, distancing itself from the pure doctrine and faith of Christ's teachings, and thrusting itself into the quagmire of South American governmental politics. A branch of the church developed called the Popular Church of Liberation Theology.

William Los Cruzado was impassioned with the struggle of the people and the FSLN. Consequently, he ended his relationship with his mentor and friend, Miguel Obando y Bravo, who criticized the Sandinista government with the same fervor he had used against Samoza.

As the Contra war grew, the Sandinistas became just as oppressive and ruthless as the ousted Samoza. Obando followed the Vatican, but Los Cruzado and many other young priests adapted a radical theology.

The Popular Church had grown out of what was called the Christian Base Communities or CEBs. They were small groups of clergy and laypeople who gathered in rural and urban areas to read Scripture and talk about social issues. Upon splitting with the church, Los Cruzado led a CEB in the village of *Corderilla Isabela*, where he and the farmers enjoyed the support and protection of the FSLN. They built a mission at the foot of the mountains.

———◆———

Father Los Cruzado kept digging…

He swung the pick furiously, as if trying to match the ferocity of the brutality committed on a hot night, many, many summers ago.

———•◦•———

The first scream had come from the women's quarters in the mission, followed by a quick burst of automatic weapon fire.

Los Cruzado had stumbled from his bed and grabbed his glasses off the night table. He heard the shouts and voices of the FSLN soldiers, who were protecting the mission from their barracks, and the night erupted with gunfire.

Palo, a boy from the village, met him in the mission's main quadrangle in a shaking panic. Palo, who took more joy in beating the other village boys in soccer than in reading Scripture, cried with fear. Los Cruzado knelt and shook him, urging him to calm down. He then sent the boy inside, ordering Palo to hide in the kitchen storeroom and lock the door.

The gunfire stopped.

Fumbling in the dark, Los Cruzado had found his way through the main entrance. Hiding just inside the entrance archway, he watched as the FSLN soldiers were taken from their barracks into the entrance courtyard, their hands clasped behind their heads in surrender. The Contras moved behind them, aiming weapons at their backs.

The Contras had surprised the men in their sleep, somehow slipping past the electronic perimeter security and cameras that the FSLN had insisted were necessary. The security had proven useless.

These men were precise and efficient soldiers; they wasted no time in forcing the Sandinistas to their knees for their executions.

Los Cruzado folded his hands in prayer, clutching his rosary. The weight of the steel crucifix dangled beneath his palms.

He walked into the courtyard, both hands held out in front of his body, feeling the power of Christ with him, a sensation of warmth and comfort in the face of death.

"*En el nombre de Dios!* Leave this place in peace!" he shouted.

A Contra soldier smiled... unholstered his pistola... aimed... and fired.

Under sudden darkness, Los Cruzado heard his own voice say, "*Mi Dios...*"

———◆◦◆———

Father Los Cruzado was digging. The rosary slipped from underneath his dirty field shirt. The crucifix swung and gleamed in the sunlight.

———◆◦◆———

The first thing he'd seen when he opened his eyes was a sky blackened with vultures. Daylight had come and the upper right side of his skull felt raw and throbbed with an unbelievable pain. Blood covered the right side of his face.

He squinted his eyes, grimacing, slowly bringing up his right hand to touch the wound. Los Cruzado let out a quiet yelp as the crucifix banged against it. He realized he must have flinched to the left to avoid a shot directly to his face.

There were flashes in his mind of the previous night, of the screams and the gunfire.

He opened his eyes again and the stench hit him. Los Cruzado realized he wasn't lying on the ground, but on something…or someone.

He raised himself up on his left elbow, and felt it sink into a torso. As he sat up, he turned in shock, his right hand clasping a face. Los Cruzado could hardly see; he had lost his glasses, but he could make out the face under his hand, and it multiplied into vast rows of stilled, blank, dead faces. He saw heads, necks, arms, legs, and torsos. His mouth dropped with a gasp of breath; he turned his head to the left and the right, then back again. He was in an endless ditch with piles of the dead—young children, men, women, and the old.

The vultures were feasting on some.

Los Cruzado realized in horror that he sat on the body of a dead woman.

He scrambled, kicking and climbing his way up the side of the ditch, over the bodies, to find himself standing on a dirt road. He bent and vomited.

Glancing around, he was overcome. Some of the dead had been shot, dismembered, burned, disfigured, and tortured in gruesome and cruel ways. The nauseating, gaseous smell of rotted flesh hit Los Cruzado and he felt a rolling wave of shock sicken his stomach, threatening to topple him right in the middle of the road.

"Madre de dios," he muttered, spitting bile.

He wanted to be anywhere else. He composed himself, and limped down the road. The sound of an approaching vehicle stopped him cold.

A military troop-transport truck screeched to a halt in front of him, dislodging a squad of Contras. Los Cruzado stopped, frozen in exhaustion, pain, and fear. Even if he had the strength to run they would simply gun him down. No more running...he was tired of running. Los Cruzado pictured himself in David's Valley of Death. He knelt in the dirt, closed his eyes, and prayed.

The Contras unloaded more bodies from the back of the truck, and tossed them into the ditch with the nonchalance of garbage men. From the passenger side of the truck emerged a Tall Anglo in jungle fatigues. He moved closer to the man praying in the road.

The Tall Anglo stopped in front of the praying man, watching him. The Tall Anglo recognized the words from childhood. It was a lifetime ago when he himself had knelt in a small church, in a small town in America. He remembered the words now whispered from the man's bloodied lips.

"The Lord is my Shepherd, I shall not want..."

Something snapped in the Tall Anglo. He grabbed the Colt MK IV .45 out of his holster, cocked it, and aimed it at the man.

"...He makes me lie down in green pastures..."

The Tall Anglo felt a blood lust rise in him like a tide. The gun in his hand had killed many times; the squeezing of the trigger was like breathing the air or taking a drink.

"...He leads me beside quiet waters, He restores my soul..."

Tall Anglo flinched as something dark and cloying eclipsed his very being, a presence older than man, an evil that hides itself among all men.

He squeezed slowly on the trigger.

A vulture perched on a tree branch and cocked its eye.

"...He guides me in paths of righteousness for His name's sake..."

Tall Anglo's eyes narrowed, fine tuning his focus on the point of death. The Contras tossed another body on the pile in the ditch.

"…Though I walk through the valley of the shadow of death…"

Tall Anglo heard The Voice rise deep from the darkness within him, as if he was a well and The Voice was a bubble; it rose from the fathoms of a water-filled pit and burst on the surface of his conscious. The Voice sounded like a man talking into his ear.

"Kill him," it said.

"…I shall fear no evil…"

The sound of the gunshot blast scattered the feasting, carnivorous birds; the Contra soldiers turned from their work, startled, drawing their weapons.

Los Cruzado's eyes opened and he stared up at the man. He saw his eyes, and they were cold and clouded with death, but yet, there was something else. He saw that a gun was raised over his head; the shot was fired into the air. The man had a name sewn over a breast pocket on his fatigue shirt: PRICHARD.

Prichard slowly lowered the gun. He brought his other hand to his face, rubbing his tired eyes. Something lifted from his body and dissipated into the air. Suddenly, he pointed the gun back at the praying man, yelling at him to get up.

Los Cruzado stood.

Prichard waved him off toward the jungle.

"Sacar saliente de aqui," he said.

Los Cruzado didn't move.

"Go!" Prichard yelled. Some of the Contras sauntered up next to him, grinning, joking, and laughing at the half-dressed, trembling priest.

"GO! NOW!" Prichard screamed, and this time Los Cruzado turned and ran.

One of the Contras raised his rifle, but Prichard turned, grabbed the barrel, and forced it down. He cursed at the soldier in Spanish, then threw a barrage of orders at them. The disgruntled soldiers walked away, back to the truck, sulking like children.

When Prichard looked back down the road, the man was gone.

Los Cruzado stumbled through the jungle, the horror of the ditch behind him. The Voice came to him from somewhere among the trees. It was clear like a whisper and it stopped him dead. The sound was the most terrifying thing he'd ever heard.

"Los Cruzado," it whispered in a low, gurgling, guttural tone. *"LOS CRUZADO!"*

He froze in a fear that was almost purifying, realizing he was not alone and that The Voice wasn't coming from the trees, but from somewhere within him...

———•◦•———

"Padre, Padre! Padre, Los Cruzado! Alto, Alto!"

"Que?" Los Cruzado answered.

Rosa, a girl from the village, was tugging on his arm. "The row is done, it's finished," she said. *"Tu excavar tambien lejano.* You're digging too far."

Los Cruzado shook his head. Glancing down the row, he saw that he had dug past the other furrows by about fifteen feet. The workers in the field had stopped to watch him. They were laughing.

Los Cruzado felt his mind return like a man from sleep. He looked down at Rosa, who was smiling up at him with a beautiful, crooked grin. He smiled back at her.

"Drink some water, Papa," she said, lifting a canteen with her brown hands.

"Si. Gracias."

Los Cruzado took the canteen and brought it to his lips, pausing after a few swallows to remove his hat and pour some over his head.

Rosa giggled as some of the water splashed onto her face. Los Cruzado poured a little in his hands, flicking and splashing her as she laughed and squealed. A group of the children, who were always quick to play, gathered around him. They tugged, poked, and laughed at him, as Los Cruzado splashed after them with the canteen.

He raced after the children. Unable to catch the older ones, he grabbed one of the smaller boys, hoisting him in the air like a rocket. The child, covered in dirt from head to muddy sandals, threw out his arms, flying.

Los Cruzado laughed as he circled the boy against the sky. The dark days had vanished behind him but how he envied this innocent child. He knew he could never fully protect these people from the horrors he had known, and from the horror to come.

He prayed the most for the children.

After a few moments, he began to wheeze; his shoulders remembered the swinging pick from earlier, reminding him of it with a dull aching. Los Cruzado slowly lowered the boy to the ground and watched him run off with the others. Some of the workers scolded the children in rapid Spanish as they trampled across the newly dug rows. A dirty soccer ball appeared and they kicked and chased it off the field, back toward the village.

Los Cruzado realized every joint in his body ached. At 55, time and death were catching him. His heart pounded much too quickly in his chest, the heat had already evaporated the water and sweat from his skin.

His eyes found the sky. The *Isabella Corderilla* Mountains stood like a testimony to God. Los Cruzado held his hand up to block the sun, which was an hour away from setting just beyond those ranges.

That's when he saw the Blackhawk approaching.

The helicopter banked gracefully against the sunset-splashed sky. The children ran towards it as it descended near the furrowed field. As the children got closer they shielded their eyes from the blade-blown dirt.

Some of the workers moved up to protect them.

Los Cruzado watched as several others appeared from the village, racing toward the Blackhawk. The men seemed curious and impressed.

Los Cruzado saw the American flag on the tail.

He had seen these helicopters before of course. They often carried death with them. The villagers seemed so oblivious to historical realities, he thought. He heard them chattering, excitedly, *"Americano, Americano!"*

The helicopter door slid open, and Prichard stepped down on the field. Some of the children broke their parents' grasps and rushed him, touching him and smiling. Their fingers moved quickly over his pockets, but he had already taken the precaution of buttoning down his fatigue pouches.

Prichard smiled down on the children, but pushed passed them to an older looking man named Luis.

"Buenos dias." Prichard said.

"Si?"

Prichard held the manila file in his hand. He opened it and pulled out the photo of Los Cruzado, popping it in front of Luis's face. Luis, a squat, balding man with heavy arms and protruding gut, squinted at the photo. Prichard saw the wrinkles around his eyes, no doubt from years of working and living under the Colombian sun. Luis nodded quickly after a few seconds.

"*Stados Unidos el gobierno.* United States Government. *Padre Los Cruzado. Donde lata yo hallazgo lo?* Where can I find him?" Prichard asked.

Everyone gathered around Prichard pointed downfield. Prichard saw a man standing alone; the mission loomed behind him.

"*Gracias,*" Prichard said. He moved through the villagers. The children hovered around him as they walked across the field together.

As Prichard approached, Los Cruzado absentmindedly stroked the rosary around his neck. He brought the crucifix up to his lips and crossed himself. He remembered the very taste of fear from that day. He wanted to run but faith steadied his feet. Was the work of the Lord at hand? What other explanation could there be for bringing this man back into his presence? Los Cruzado should have died that day but God had spared him. Why? The questioned resonated in his mind as Prichard cast a long shadow over him.

"William Dante Los Cruzado?" Prichard asked.

"*Si.*"

Prichard flashed his government ID. "Prichard. Douglas Prichard. United States Government on official business." Prichard glanced around. The villagers seemed awestruck. "Is there someplace where we can talk?" he asked.

Los Cruzado threw back his shoulders. "These people are *mi familia,*" he said. "Whatever there is to say in secret we can say here. *No secreto.* "

Prichard held the dossier up in front of him. "I don't think you want to openly discuss the contents of this file in front of your... family, Mr. Los Cruzado. Your past political involvements may serve to embarrass you. Again, I suggest we find someplace to talk, in private. Now, I've had a very long flight and I don't really wanna debate this. *Alquilar nos ir.* Let's go."

The villagers watched the two men as if they had come to prizefight. Los Cruzado grudgingly retrieved the pick from the ground and walked off toward the mission.

Prichard followed.

It seemed to Prichard that Los Cruzado had no recollection of what had happened. It had been almost 20 years ago. Maybe he's forgotten me, Prichard thought. He wished his own memory was as shot.

The sun was setting on the two men as they entered the mission.

When they walked into the courtyard, Prichard saw scaffolding erected around what looked like the mission church. Apparently, some type of renovation was happening. The courtyard fountain was at its center, with what looked like a barracks to the right.

Prichard breathed deeply, inhaling the aroma of cooking corn and meat. He hoped he could sample whatever it was they were making. Anything had to be better than the MRE rations he'd eaten for the past few weeks. They passed through the main entrance archway. Etched on the center of its curve in Latin was a simple mission statement: *Sola Scriptura.* By the Scriptures alone. They walked through the archway into the main quadrangle, where another fountain dominated the center. The mission was breathtaking with ornate frescos and a mural covering the south wall, depicting the FSLN resistance against Samoza.

They turned the corner to the entrance of the padre's quarters and went inside.

Dominating the wall behind his desk was a simple crucifix. A book-shelf, wardrobe, nightstand, and bed were the only furniture in Los Cruzado's humble living quarters.

Los Cruzado shuffled behind the desk and dropped into the chair. He felt the weight come off his tired feet and back.

The day had been long.

Prichard stood at ease while Los Cruzado steadied himself in the chair. After a moment, Los Cruzado looked up at him, and wondered if Prichard remembered him at all. His humility had left him now. He sat in *his* chair, at *his* desk in *his* mission. Leaning forward, Los Cruzado folded his hands and wrinkled his face towards Prichard.

"Why have you come here, Mr. Prichard? What can we do for the United States? *Que hacer tu necesidad?*"

Prichard looked at the ground, then back at Los Cruzado, feeling intimidated by the clergyman. Prichard knew he would one day answer to God for a lot of things, but he wouldn't ingratiate himself to this mere man.

"Mr. Los Cruzado, the details of my mission here have not yet been completely revealed to me, as per common policy and procedure; however, I have been instructed to retrieve you and whatever necessary travel accoutrements you may require, and bring you to Washington, D.C., where we will be contacted and given further instructions."

"*Que?*"

"Again, I have been instructed by the United States Government to bring you to Washington, D.C."

Los Cruzado finally absorbed the full meaning of Prichard's words.

"Me? Going to Washington?"

"That's correct, sir."

"*Con tu*? With you?"

"Yes, that's correct."

Los Cruzado paused, then stood up from the desk. He turned and walked toward a window. A cross atop the mission bell tower was silhouetted against the dusky sky. He stared at it. "And why would I be doing that? Why am I going to Washington, D.C.?"

Prichard casually sat in a chair in front of the desk. He felt the favor of the Game of Intimidation shift to his side. This was the time to falsely assume the weaker position, to lull the opponent into a false sense of security. It was something they hadn't taught him in Coup School. "As I said, Mr. Los Cruzado, the full details of my instructions were not revealed to me for reasons that I cannot dis—"

Los Cruzado turned sharply from the window, interrupting him.

"No, no, I heard what you said about your...*instrucciones*, Mr. Prichard. I'm simply trying to understand this. You fly in here from... no place, expecting me to go fly with you to... no place, in your helicopter. And you can give me nothing to explain this, eh? I really don't think I will be going anywhere with you today, *señor*."

Prichard had anticipated some resistance. He shifted in the chair. "Mr. Los Cruzado, you are not in a position to refuse this request. There are issues here that I can bring to light if you continue to press me."

Los Cruzado glared at Prichard.

"You have some issues with me? Issues? This is good, because I have some issues. Here are some of them: This morning, one of our children, a girl, burned herself in a fire in the kitchen, third-degree burns. This is what they wake me up with. I am mediating a dispute among the farmers over irrigation rights in a community that is supposed to be based on a cooperative system, yet they fight like imperialists. Very frustrating, eh? A group of parents is angry because too many fights broke out in a game of soccer, an activity encouraged and endorsed by the church. Who kicked whom, which boy started what, and so on. Some of the cattle are sick. The ranchers think God is punishing them and they want me to do something. Do what? Pray is what I tell them, and I pray that we can afford to inoculate cattle against bovine disease, but money will not fall from the sky like manna. The church renovations are going slowly, because the government of Nicaragua will only pay attention to its peasants when there is a war. And *you* land your helicopter on my field, where I have worked hard for three months! Mr. Prichard, I can tell you that I have some issues! My main issues right now, however, are to bathe, eat, and sleep! Going to Washington, D.C., is not on my agenda! *Maldecir tu y vuestro instrucciones!*"

Prichard tucked in his chin. A bead of sweat ran down his forehead from underneath the brim of his jungle hat.

"Again, Mr. Los Cruzado, you are in no position to refuse these orders."

"Orders? What orders? I am not in your army."

"Yes, however, there are long-standing grievances and unanswered questions concerning you, the Christian Based Communities, and your affiliations with the FSLN."

"The Sandinistas? *Tonteria.* That was nearly twenty years ago."

Prichard squinted at him. "And, as I said, there are unanswered questions."

Los Cruzado threw his arms into the air. "How many more could there be? You won, we lost."

In 1990, the Sandinistas had been finally defeated in an election, Prichard remembered. The National Opposition Party (UNO) supported by the CIA, with its masterful use of propaganda, had crippled any chances that the FSLN could retain power. Washington placed a relentless embargo and 10 years of war against the country, and a group called the National Endowment for Democracy funneled millions into the UNO's campaign. The people of Nicaragua had grown weary of war and voted accordingly. The revolution was over.

According to the dossier, Los Cruzado became a staff writer for *La Prensa* in that same year, and wrote a series of derisive articles condemning the Contras, calling for the people to use all means of sabotage and subterfuge to deter the counterrevolutionaries. His articles had the effect of a hot spark in a dry field of grass.

A U.S. reconnaissance plane had been shot down just over the border from Honduras. The American pilot's body was found in civilian clothes. The U.S. sent in a Special Forces unit to recover the plane before the news leaked to the world media. The U.S. government told the American people that the U.S. was not heavily involved in the war.

Special Forces found the plane; spray-painted in scarlet on the fuselage were the words *"Aqui no se rinde nadie! Viva Los Cruzado!"*

Prichard leaned forward in the chair. "Perhaps we won the war, Mr. Los Cruzado, but there are crimes that have not been answered for," he said.

"*Verdaderamente*. Indeed," Los Cruzado said, irreverently.

"A U.S. reconnaissance plane was shot down in Honduras, killing an American. Your name was stamped on it," Prichard huffed.

Los Cruzado turned his gaze upward, recalling the incident. "Yes, I remember, except the plane was found in Nicaragua. What was the *yanqui* doing, Mr. Prichard, sightseeing?"

Prichard felt his anger rising. "The articles you wrote in *La Prensa* were reactionary and treasonous, constituting crimes against the Nicaraguan people! You were responsible for the life of that pilot and the plight of his family!"

Los Cruzado felt the shame of his radical past creep up like a weed in his heart.

"I did not pull the trigger!"

"No, but we found evidence that the plane was hit with munitions supplied to the FSLN. We recovered reconnaissance photos from the plane showing the area on the night of the incident; there were no Sandinistas in the region. But, a small village was in very close proximity to the crash zone."

"Meaning what?"

Prichard leaned back, ready to deliver his killing blow.

"Meaning, they were civilians, Los Cruzado. Civilians shot that plane down."

"And where is my involvement, Prichard?" he demanded.

"Your words, your incendiary words! You riled those people against the counterrevolutionary force that was put in place to free them! You incited them against us!"

Los Cruzado pounded his fist on the desk. "They needed incitement! The Contras were bloody, ruthless, murderous dogs, eh? You will never convince me that the United States cared about the plight of the poor in this country, at that time or any other time! Your interest and motivations were to uphold your economic power on this continent! You made a mockery of your own democratic principles! Where is the life, liberty, and the pursuit of happiness, eh? At which point did the Contras intend to explain these noble concepts to the peasants they were killing?" he screamed.

Prichard lost all interest in strategy. He jumped from his seat, jabbing his finger in the air like a dagger. "Did your precious Marxism do anything to better the 'plight of the poor in this country?' You communists, you all think the same! You want the whole world equal, I'll give you that, but equality to you is for us all to live drab, destitute lives and call each other comrade! How could you as a priest, a man of God, I *guess*, support a social theory that excludes God? You should have never gotten involved! The church should have never gotten involved! The Sandinistas were just as ruthless as the Contras; a socialist state in Nicaragua would have done nothing to better this country! We made all kinds of attempts to bring a peaceful democratic end to the conflict!"

Los Cruzado's eyes bulged incredulously behind his glasses. "When you were training the Contras in all the ways of torture, I suppose?"

"We supported the Contadora Group in 1983, and in '79, the Central ·American Peace Accords. Your country was never ready for the truly democratic election process that we wanted in any of the treaties that were developed! The communists wouldn't allow it!"

"You mean *you* wouldn't allow it! The Reagan administration never saw any peaceful resolutions! Don't trade political incidentals with me, Prichard; we might as well trade insults!"

Los Cruzado waited for a response, but Prichard leaned away from the desk and placed his hands on his hips. He looked like a frustrated general in the middle of a losing war.

"You're right, Mr. Los Cruzado. Absolutely. I didn't come here to trade insults or to rehash the past; we can leave that to the historians and scholars. This is what's on the plate right now, tonight. This village and this mission can and will be affected by the decision you make in these next few minutes. Now, I will say this as simply and as clearly as I can: If I leave alone on that bird tonight, inside two weeks, my government will initiate a series of directives cutting off any and all support, monetary or otherwise, to this village and to this mission."

Los Cruzado felt a real threat for the first time. "On what basis can you fabricate this? *Que voluntad tu hace?* What will you do, send down more advisors?"

"On the basis that you were and are indirectly responsible for the murder of an American civilian."

Los Cruzado shook his head in disbelief. "I scarcely think that even within the corrupt halls of Washington they would have the time to conjure up such actions for events that took place fifteen years ago. What you have is circumstantial at best."

"We have enough, Mr. Los Cruzado. Believe me, they'll *make* the time. Besides, what makes you think Capitol Hill will have anything to say about it?"

Los Cruzado searched for a bluff in Prichard's eyes, but what he saw was more of what he'd seen before, on that other day...

Prichard reached for his side holster and pulled out the same Colt. The gun's once-polished surface was scratched and faded, but its deadliness, no doubt, had lost no luster. He placed the gun calmly on the desk, leaned on it and looked up at Los Cruzado. "Mr. Los Cruzado, you can either cooperate with us now, or face the consequences. Your choice."

Los Cruzado moved slowly from behind the desk toward the door, as if he was ignoring Prichard. He opened the door and looked into the courtyard. The evening dusk had colored the mission with a comforting glow. "What can you give me to ensure that the mission will be safe, eh?" he asked, finally.

Prichard stood up, holding the pistol to his side. He answered Los Cruzado with his back. "Nothing. But I *can* assure you that if you don't cooperate, inside three years this place won't be standing."

Los Cruzado looked away from him and fingered the crucifix of his rosary. His fist squeezed around the metal cross, and he felt the edges dig into his flesh.

There was the familiar first twinge of an approaching deep pain. He recognized the feeling as the precursor to a regretable, imminent departure.

———◆———

The Blackhawk turbines began with a low grumble, ascending into a high-pitched whine; the blades spun, building up velocity.

As Prichard and Los Cruzado crossed the field, the villagers gathered and walked with them. Los Cruzado carried a garment bag over his shoulder and a tote in his right hand. Prichard strode triumphantly next to him. Prichard sensed the inner hostility of the villagers, but he knew they wouldn't contest this. It occurred to him, though, that the lightly armed pilots provided their only real security.

They neared the copter and the copilot rushed up, grabbing Los Cruzado's bags. Rosa was suddenly there, with her arms around his waist. Los Cruzado felt her face against his stomach. She shook with tears.

"No, no *nina*. Rosa, *por favor*. Do not cry. I will be back soon," he said.

He looked up at the faces of the villagers, his *familia*. How he would miss their tired, dusty faces. God help me. How can I leave them? He thought. He embraced each of them, feeling the flesh of their faces and the warm, wet slick of tears.

Prichard was already boarding the Blackhawk, and half-expected a shovel or a pick in the back. With all the weeping behind him, he thought he might deserve it. After a moment, Los Cruzado broke from them and sullenly climbed on board the helicopter.

As the bird rose from the ground, Los Cruzado caught the steady gaze of the Rocket Boy he had played with earlier. There was no evidence of sadness or remorse on the boy's face. The child stuck out his chest and Los Cruzado saw the man the boy would one day become.

Aqui no se rinde nadie, Los Cruzado thought. The people united will never be defeated.

The Blackhawk flew away toward the mountains, riding on the wind currents of God's hands. North to America.

———◆———

Scott Macklin always flew first class, but his deep sleep inoculated him from the spacious luxuries in the upper levels of the Boeing 777. The dream he experienced was really a nightmare…

The heat was blistering as he ran in the dream and in front of him, Scott saw rows of burning bamboo huts; the flames roared and hissed as they burned. He could hear the bullets cutting and searing the air around him, missing his body only by providence.

He was in a war; he knew exactly which war, because he'd had this dream before.

And there was someone running with him…

The man along his side seemed stronger and faster, more agile. He looked over and down at Scott, but the sun was behind him and there was only the shape of his form.

The man reached his hand toward Scott...

Air turbulance shook the plane, rumbling currents coinciding with the distant, dreamscape boom of exploding mortars echoing in his mind. Scott jerked awake.

In the murky fog of first conciousness, Scott Macklin didn't see the darting glow of power watching him from outside his window, and then vanishing in the cloud cover.

The plane dipped and banked into a dive, heading into the Seattle Tacoma Airport.

Chapter 3

The Day Trader's fingers moved furiously across the keyboard with the zeal and sweaty desperation of a video gamer in a smoky arcade.

The tech stock he monitored on the markct was plummeting and he watched it fall like a wounded bird out of the sky. It was a small California tech company that started a buzz a month ago after its founders established one of the first Internet computing server systems on the market, threatening to dominate the PC and software industry. The company was called Light Net.

What they introduced a month ago was revolutionary. Instead of using a PC, computer users could now use an Internet device that connected them to Light Net's remote server, giving them access to any software program they needed—for a monthly fee, of course. People would no longer have to buy PCs or software, only a simple, inexpensive, proverbial black box, and a keyboard to connect to the server. The giants in the industry, including Microsoft, felt their foundations quaking.

Millions of Light Net ID Systems sold.

Sheila left him and took the children.

He had spent a year counting losses—thousands here, thousands there—on multiple stocks, riding a rollercoaster wave on the shaky tracks of the minute trades between seductive bids. Short-term investments. No gains. Big losses.

Then along came Light Net.

Day Trader never considered the long term until he read about the company on the Web, in the technology section of CNNFN. This start-up had stirred the tech world.

He'd done some research and found that most tech-stock analysts calculated a 50 to 60 earnings ratio for Light Net, when the company announced its plans to market the ID System. Those were very conservative numbers but Day Trader knew better; after all, this company was making even Bill Gates a little nervous.

When the stock hit 100 he bought 1,000 shares—$100,000 worth. The company was new, so there was no way to show profit. After more study, though, he learned the company's first quarter earnings were about 15 million, reflecting a possible yearly earnings potential of *60 million.* In its first year! That meant 75 percent growth. Day Trader figured he'd be looking at just about $175,000 when all was said and done.

When he quit his job as a CPA, she cursed him, calling him a fool. If only she had seen the numbers. But he knew Sheila would be back. By the end of the year, finally, he'd get her back.

Now it was falling.

Day Trader leaned forward and watched the stock fall through the bottom and it kept on dropping. He exited the market like a NASCAR driver hobbling into the pit. And, yes, it *was* a pit where he was going.

Vanished. Gone. It only took him a minute to calculate his net worth. He had just enough left for cab fare back to the hotel. Day Trader sat back from the screen and rubbed his face. He shook with panic and dread. "Oh, my God, no. No, no, no. What am I gonna do, what am I gonna do?" he muttered. His mind and body vibrated with the weight of the takedown. No place to go, no assets left, no family. Just the streets. He knew he couldn't make it out there. He'd die out there for sure.

Day Trader glanced around the office. The place buzzed. The market hummed behind the computer screens of the other traders at their cubicles. An unseen force lurked beyond the walls of the office, like currents under the still surface of a calm sea.

The others. They just kept on trading, oblivious to the sudden darkness into which he had fallen in a blink. They smiled and laughed.

A fool, she had called him…

A bleak thing, a dark thing stole over him and shifted inside him. A swirl of light and gloom struggled. The light faded slowly… slowly… slowly, to a pinhead in the middle of the screen.

The Voice came to him like a friend from childhood.

"Get the gun," it said.

Day Trader froze.

"Get the gun. Get it now."

Day Trader felt cool and lucid. Maybe it wasn't gonna be so bad after all; maybe it wouldn't be so bad because now he could get back at them for all the times they called him an amateur. They never wanted his success. They only wanted his failure because they needed him down, so they'd have somebody to kick. *They* probably did this. It was all of *them.*

"That's right," The Voice crooned.

He would make sure they wouldn't get the chance to kick him again.

"That's right," The Voice repeated in a reassuring tone. *"You get them."*

He smiled, pushing back a lock of oily, matted hair. Reaching under his cubicle desk, he pulled out a gym bag and methodically unzipped it.

The woman in the cubicle next to him saw the gun as he stood with it in his hand. There was no time for her to scream.

Day Trader smiled at her.

Dr. Rachel Walters was stuck in traffic on South Lake Shore when her cell phone rang. She reached past a stack of textbooks, piled up on the driver side seat, knocking her overstuffed purse to the floor. The phone spilled out of it, along with half the bag's contents, to the floorboard. She stifled a curse as her compact popped open, dusting the floor mat with flecks of beige powder.

Ignoring the incessant bleeping, she quickly found a travel-sized pack of Kleenex, and took a swipe at the powder, only smudging it deeper into the carpet mat. Rachel leaned back and stared at the mess for a moment.

"Oh, that's really good," she said aloud. "Good move, Doctor," she finished, self-deprecatingly.

A double horn blast from behind made her flinch in her seat. She turned back in time to see the shadow of a burly truck driver. His cab was so big she could barely see him waving his arm out the window at her as if flagging down a jetliner.

Rachel turned forward and saw traffic moving again. The Greyhound bus in front of her was a good distance off; she saw it through the haze of its own black exhaust smoke.

The truck horn blared again, drowning out the discordant symphony of traffic engine noise and honking, persistent Chicago commuters. The cell phone bleeped and bleeped and bleeped.

"Okay, okay!" she said to the truck driver. She drove the car 80 meters and came to another dead stop behind the Greyhound. Rachel shook her head in disbelief, and finally grabbed the phone from under the dashboard.

"Doctor Walters," she answered.

The voice over the line crackled with interference, but she recognized the assured tone of her mentor, Doctor Charles M. Smithfield. "Doctor Walters?"

"Yes. I can barely hear you," she said loudly. "Sorry I took so long to answer. I had a little accident."

"Where are you? Are you in traffic? Are you okay?" he asked.

Rachel laughed at his concern over her accident with a compact. "Yes, I'm all right. I just spilled my makeup in the car. I'm on South Lake Shore, trying to get home, but this bottleneck…"

Smithfield grunted. Rachel knew that to mean he now realized she was okay, and he wanted to move on to business. The Director of the University of Illinois Department of Psychiatry, Doctor Smithfield was not known to waste time with idle words. She'd known and worked with him since the beginning of her tenure almost a decade ago; she was familiar with his many communicative quirks.

"What can I do for you, Doctor Smithfield?"

"Well, we have a hostage situation at an office building downtown on Wacker Drive. Chicago PD and a Tactical Unit are already on the scene. It looks like a bad one. The assailant is a day trader. From the reports I've gotten, he's killed eight people and badly injured two others."

Rachel leaned back in her seat. "Oh, no." She let the wave of shock roll over her. "Do we have his name? A history?"

"Right. Um…"

She heard papers ruffle.

"Ah… Davis. Alex Warren Davis. Born in Dearborn, Michigan, August 12, 1973. His father is an autoworker, nearing retirement, and his mother a homemaker; blue-collar, middle-class background. Alex studied business and finance at Michigan State, graduating with an MBA in 1994. Spent two years in Detroit with a small accounting firm before he met his wife. They…"

More ruffling paper…

Rachel noticed the truck driver in her rear-view mirror. He seemed to be shouting, but she couldn't hear him over the traffic's din.

"Oh, here we go," Doctor Smithfield continued. "They moved to Chicago when Alex took a junior position with Stebbins, Roth & Associates. A decent firm. Looks like his income was in the lower six. He and his wife bought a house in Northbrook, but they got a divorce and sold it last year. They have two girls. She took them back to Michigan."

"Psychological background?" Rachel asked.

"In high school he was diagnosed with an acute Schizo affective disorder, but showed marked improvement with regular therapy sessions and treatments with Haldol and Thorazine."

"So, there was some delusional and hallucinatory behavior?"

"Right."

"How long a period?"

"It was pretty severe for about two or three years."

"Was he suicidal? Violent behavior?"

"He was hospitalized in 1987 when his father caught him cutting open his wrists with a utility knife."

"Lord," Rachel said.

She looked out over Lake Michigan. It was a clear, warm day in August. Her eyes caught the nautical markings and brightly colored sail of a boat that leaned and rode against the wind, skimming across the water. She wished she could be on that water, drifting away somewhere. She knew, though, that Doctor Smithfield would never call her after she'd left the University unless something grim had happened.

Rachel's gaze turned to the west, from the tranquil openness of the lake to the staggering urban mountain ranges of Chicago. She knew the Lord's will was calling her to the aid of a man named Alex Davis; she knew His power. It was the same power now moving over the lake. It gave direction and it directed action, propelling her. Rachel felt the warm metal of the tiny cross against her chest… and she knew Him.

She looked in the rearview mirror and caught herself in her own tired eyes. Rachel was beautiful. Her glasses framed dark eyes and equally dark chestnut hair. Her face showed hints of a deep intellect mingled with an

Irish loveliness. Rachel was the kind of woman men fell in love with, but then were terrified to tell her.

"Rachel, it looks like they'll need you on this one," Smithfield confessed. "Davis is refusing to talk to their negotiator, and when he is talking most of it is incoherent. They're saying that his speech is highly disturbed. Vague ideations, sweeping paranoid generalities."

"What *is* he saying?"

"He's saying over and over that someone, *them* or *they,* pushed him, stole from him. The police have a recording from one of the security cameras. You'll see more of what I'm describing once you arrive on the scene."

"Are they working on remote or direct contact?"

"I've instructed them that the University does not and will not sanction any action that will put you in harm's way."

Rachel frowned. "Well, it might be necessary for me to make direct contact with Davis."

She could just see Smithfield's protruding lower lip and glaring eye. This was always a sure sign of his deep disagreement.

"And, as I said," he warned, "I do not want you in harm's way. This man is highly disturbed and dangerous. I want you to somehow make an appeal to him, *remotely,* perhaps on behalf of his wife and children."

Rachel looked over the lake. The boat had vanished on the horizon.

"But, Doctor Smithfield, from what you've described, this could be a good opportunity for me to observe the spiritual-psychological manifestations that I believe are evident in every one of these cases."

Doctor Smithfield cut her off with another grunt. "Doctor, I'm well aware of your religious beliefs and how you have precariously incorporated your faith into your work; I do not want you conducting field research to support your theories of spiritual and psychological connectivity. Davis has killed eight people, and I don't need you getting careless. When you arrive at the scene, the police and tactical units will have contingency plans and scenarios for the given situation, as usual. Do exactly what they say and nothing more. No volunteerism. Is that understood?"

Rachel lowered her head, feeling a slight sting from her superior's chastisement. It would have stung deeper if she didn't know that Smithfield was really a good man, but she couldn't help feel resentment at the dismissive way he spoke of her faith. It seemed she was always defending it, if not against the University Psychiatric Department Board of Directors, then against her friends, certain family members, or a stranger on the street.

"Yes, Doctor," she acquiesced.

The Greyhound moved, gaining speed. Rachel looked around to see traffic moving at a reasonable pace, but still jammed.

She punched the gas. "Should I get over to Wacker Drive? From the looks of this mess it'll take about two hours."

"No. Where are you now?"

Rachel craned her neck, searching. Finally, she got close enough to read an exit sign.

"I just passed the East Forty-seventh Street Exit."

"Can you make it to the East Oakwood Exit?"

Rachel could see the traffic bunching up about two miles ahead, near the exit.

"Eventually," she concluded. "But maybe not anytime today."

"Take that exit and go west on Oakwood to the corner of East Lake Park. There's an empty lot. They'll meet you there with some alternate transportation."

"Okay."

She was just about to hit the "End" button, when Smithfield interjected. His tone became softer and less instructive. Rachel always thought he was quietly flirting with her when he sounded like this.

"Listen, Doctor... Rachel..."

She smiled. "I know, I know. I will."

"Can I at least say it?"

"I'm sorry, go ahead."

"Be careful."

"Thank you. I will."

He ended the call.

Rachel put the phone on the passenger seat, then deftly maneuvered her Acura into the far right lane. She was barely able to squeeze in as the lane slowed to a steady crawl. She coasted, seeing a sign for the East Oakwood exit about a mile ahead.

Faith, she thought. Faith had been the driving force in her life since her childhood. One of the earliest lessons she learned attending a small, Methodist church in an equally small town called Kenton, Ohio, was that faith is a cornerstone.

At Bowling Green College, Rachel was drawn to the sciences of the mind, excelling in her studies. She caused a small controversy in the school's psychiatric department when she completed her thesis. The paper highlighted how much the psychoanalytical pioneers Alfred Adler, Erich Fromm, and Melanie Klein had influenced her; it displayed her fascination with the links between the spiritual, the psychological, and the physiological. She was forced to edit the paper because of its religious suggestions. The work was deemed convoluted and unnecessarily complex.

Rachel had left her home and moved to Chicago for post-graduate work at the University of Illinois some 12 years earlier. Her wonder and innocent belief in Christianity had faded with every mile she'd driven. As a child, God and Christ had been a source of comfort and reality to her, but as an adult the complexities of the world and the science that she'd learned to love made believing in God seem juvenile, almost ignorant. The pressures of the world blotted out any real need for consistent faith in her life. Rachel found herself drifting away from the Lord she had once loved. Upon her arrival in Chicago, Rachel resigned herself to concentrate more and more on the science of psychiatry and less and less on theology.

One childhood memory chased her, though, always moving her back to God when she strayed. It was the death of her younger brother, Michael, by his own hand. The wrenching circumstances of her brother's suicide never left her. As she grieved him, she turned her anger against God, but found her love for Him somehow growing.

Soon, her own brilliance, research, and social observation would bring her to some stunning conclusions about violent, suicidal, and homicidal behavior in society. In almost every case she studied involving a disturbed individual, Rachel found there was a psychological pattern. From the Manson murders to the Son of Sam, from Eric Harris and Dylan Klebold to Buford Furrow, there was one common thread. In almost every incident, the participants were all mentally disturbed; something within them took control over their minds and guided their hands in acts of horrible violence. There was a common, devious split in consciousness.

They all heard voices. In the end, Michael had heard them too.

But what *were* these voices? Rachel had wondered. What did they say? Were they simply a by-product of the chemically imbalanced mind, a depletion of serotonin receptors in the brain? Or was it that these individuals, having no conscious or subconscious connection with God, found themselves instead vessels for pervasive, unseen, dark forces at work against humanity? Rachel could only come to one conclusion to the last question: Yes.

The East Oakwood exit finally came and Rachel took it, almost tempted to fly onto the off-ramp, relieved to be out of heavy traffic. As she sped down the ramp, she watched the Greyhound and the semi, the two that had sandwiched her, move lazily with the rest of the commuters. Rachel turned left, heading west on Oakwood.

She saw the Bell police helicopter just as it landed on the lot off Oakwood and Eastlake Park. A bill-posted, graffiti-covered, plywood fence surrounded the block area. Part of the northeast brick wall of whatever building had been there was crumbling away into a jumble of eroded stone. Piles of Styrofoam, newspaper and fast food wrappings blew as the helicopter landed. A moderate-sized afternoon crowd gathered and gawked.

Rachel pulled up and parked just across the street. She looked around the neighborhood. This place was a mix of African-Americans, Latinos, and European immigrants, a collage of the Chicago working class.

Rachel didn't feel like leaving her Acura parked there; she envisioned it becoming a trophy on concrete blocks. Her compulsion to try to save a man, however, overrode her need for self-preservation.

She quickly gathered her purse, books and laptop off the passenger seat, hefting all of it in her right hand, while grabbing the keys and fumbling the door handle with her left.

As she climbed out of the car, the music, noise, and smells of the neighborhood enveloped her. She held the books and laptop to her chest, pushing the door closed with her hip. The movement caused the books to fall, a few of them sliding under the car. This time Rachel did curse, but bit her lower lip afterwards. "Sorry, Lord," she said.

The crowd, gathered to watch the helicopter and rubberneck, formed on the sidewalk and around her car. A Young Hip Hopper yelled, "'Ey, lady! You cain't park dere! Read da sign!"

Rachel glanced around and saw the NO PARKING sign in red, posted on the corner. "Great," she muttered.

The Young Hip Hopper stepped up to her through the crowd with a side-turned, tilted Chicago Bulls cap, and most of his clothes bunching at his feet. The bottoms of his pants were frayed from dragging the ground. He looked at her with a mocking scowl.

"Dats agains' the law, lady. Ya knowwhatem sayin'? NO PARKIN'. Wha', you cain't read or sumptin'?"

Rachel had worked with inner city youth for a good many years, and she recognized the bitter resentment for authority in this young man's eyes. He no doubt had been on the opposite side of the law many times, and it delighted him to see someone like Rachel on the wrong side of it, no matter how minor the infraction. For once, he could play cop.

Rachel smiled on him with Christian patience. He reminded her of a boy she knew from the department's Urban Youth Study.

"Well, if I get a ticket, do you think you could take care of it for me, sweetie?"

"Say what? Lady, you trippin'? Yeah, I'll pay fo' it if you gimme dat computer."

She felt the first real sense of trouble when the quick warble of a police siren startled them both. The police cruiser pulled up bumper-to-bumper to her Acura.

Two officers stepped from the car, a young rookie of Polish or Czechoslovakian descent, and an African-American vet. The rookie moved into the street to direct traffic. The vet pulled his tonfa and pointed it at the Young Hip Hopper, motioning to him.

"Get back up on dat sidewalk now, before you get hit by a car or sumptin'," he said.

Young Hip Hopper twisted his mouth in frustration but moved, grudgingly, back into the crowd.

The vet moved up to Rachel and spoke with a calm, deeply urban, and commanding tone. "Doctor Walters?"

"Yes?"

He touched his hand to his massive chest, which held about a pound of decorative ribbons. "Officer McDonald." Rachel reached out, and he shook her hand.

"Good to met you," she said, impressed.

"Yes, ma'am. My partner, Officer Weckel, and I have been assigned to watch yo' vehicle. You can leave yo' things with me. You need to get on across da street now; they're waitin' on you."

"Thank you," she said, gratefully.

Officer Weckel had the traffic stopped and he motioned Rachel to move. She handed McDonald her computer and remaining books. "Some of my other books fell under the car. If you could get them…"

"I'll get them, ma'am. Go on now," McDonald said.

Rachel smiled appreciatively, catching a glance at Officer McDonald as he reported the situation status into the radio receiver mounted on his right shoulder. She ran across the street.

The copilot waited for her on the corner. He put his hand on her back and they ran through the fence opening to the chopper. "We have Doctor Walters en route. ETA to rendezvous point, six minutes," he said into his radio.

Rachel and the copilot ducked under the blades. She was in flats but one of her ankles turned slightly over some rocks. She felt dirt in her shoes and the wind threw dust in her eyes.

They boarded and the bird took to the air. Rachel saw the skyline of Chicago in a haze on the horizon.

———◆———

Grant Park rose underneath the police copter as they landed. Rachel and the copilot exited and raced away, ducking low from the spinning blades. A squad car, guarded by two bike patrol officers, waited. The copilot opened the door and Rachel climbed inside the back seat. She scarcely had time to settle when they raced off with screaming sirens and flashing lights.

Tailing the patrol bikes, the squad car made a quick right turn, heading east onto Wacker Drive off Michigan Avenue. Rachel saw the clock hands on the Wrigley Building; its full-moon face read 8:35. The sun was hiding among the mammoth peaks of downtown Chicago; the river flowed west from Lake Michigan as they sped to the scene of the murders just a half block away.

She looked at the fast approaching scene through the steel mesh of the patrol car's cage barrier. The patrol bikes pulled away as the car slowed just enough for an officer to pull up the perimeter tape. The media crews craned and jostled for better shots and angles. Rachel saw crews from WBBM, WLS, and the *Chicago Tribune*. They drove through the tangle, parking among some other squad cars from various precincts. From what Rachel could see, it looked like nearly every Chicago police department had answered the call.

They climbed from the car, and the boyish-faced driving officer moved up next to her. "Ma'am, the command post is right over here. If you'll just come with me..."

The cordoned-off area, from Stetson to Columbia, then north across the bridge to Water Street, was crammed with vehicles, police, tactical, EMS, a small village of media, and evacuated office personnel.

The police vehicle lights flashed and bounced off the buildings in crimson and blue.

As they walked to the tactical command post vans, Rachel looked up in time to see the Bell chopper that had dropped her in Grant Park, buzzing in over the river. It hovered, then turned to begin a patrol sweep.

Two fully-geared S.W.A.T.s stood in back of one of the command post vans. One of them was making adjustments on an ornate scope on top of a powerful looking rifle. The man's gaze had Rachel's eye—it was the death stare of a sniper. She prayed he wouldn't earn his pay tonight.

The boyish-faced officer pounded on the armor-plated back door of the second van; it swung open immediately. Rachel recognized the gruff, mid-western features of Captain Macon Ballard of the 20th Precinct Tactical Unit.

"Well, it's about time you showed up. Come on, I gotcha some home videos," he said.

The videotape scan lines wriggled across the screen. Rachel couldn't make out too much of the information, as the images were rapidly fast-forwarding. She could just define some shadows and blurs of figures moving in and out of the camera view. The camera angle was above the office vestibule.

Finally, the S.W.A.T. tech adjusted the control knob closer to the center position, slowing the frame rate of speed.

"Now, right here…", Ballard said.

The S.W.A.T. tech pushed in the toggle on the video controller and the frame froze on the lurking image of a white male in his late twenties: above average height, dark, matted hair with glasses, in a gray, hooded pullover and jeans. He held two automatic pistols in his hands, frozen in a searching, hulking lurch. There was a fist-sized, dark blotch on his right arm. Blood. Probably not his.

"Davis…", Rachel whispered.

The heavy contrast of the black-and-white image looked like an old, German impressionistic horror film, starring Davis as the monster Nosforatu.

Rachel shivered. "What about audio?" she asked.

The S.W.A.T. tech adjusted an audio knob on a portable mixer.

"They've got some standard pick-up unidirectionals on their cameras, so we were able to record some of Davis's conversation, if that's what you want to call it."

"Where?" Rachel insisted. "Let me hear it."

The S.W.A.T. tech worked the VTR knob and the image of Davis vanished as the tape went into rapid fast-forward. After a few minutes, he stopped the machine and hit play. He handed Rachel a pair of headphones and she threw them on, taking a second to adjust her hair. The tech hit another knob and the audio crackled and hissed from a small monitor.

The van was full of S.W.A.T. officers, commanders, and uniformed police from six different districts. The men gathered around to listen. They heard screams and the eerily hollow, echoing pop of gunfire as Davis went on his rampage.

At one point Rachel thought she heard Davis say something as one of his victims crawled across the screen, dragging his paralyzed legs, trailing a line a blood.

"You don't look donc to me," Davis said, stepping into the frame.

Rachel turned her head from the monitor as Davis put several rounds into the man's back. Still, she heard the voice of the victim crying out, and then Davis's voice again.

"This is what happens when you steal!" Davis declared over the dead man. "THIS IS WHAT HAPPENS WHEN YOU STEAL FROM ME!"

Rachel looked back at the screen in time to see Davis staring into the camera, and into her eyes. He suddenly became calm. Then his eyes darted and his face pinched into a mad frown.

"Yes, yes, I know. I'll get the others in a minute. They aren't going anywhere. They know they must wait for their just punishment. See, I know they had no right to do what they did to me. See, I used to listen to what they said about me. They were fools because they didn't think I was paying attention, but I was listening... I was always listening." He said all this to no one, at least to no one she could see.

Rachel watched his manner and facial expressions. He cocked his head in a quizzical manner, glancing around and then pacing as if he were arguing with someone. He seemed to listen, and then answer.

"What are they saying to you?" she quietly asked the screen.

Davis turned back to the camera. "All right, I know. I'll get to the others now. But first I want to say something." He fixed his focus on the lens and Rachel felt a deep chill resonating through her body, mingling with a prickling, repulsive sense of dread and death. "If you learn nothing else from what you see here today, learn this: Beware the wrath of a patient man."

Davis stepped back and walked casually into the office.

The S.W.A.T. tech stopped the tape and inside the van there was silence until Rachel finally spoke.

"Has anyone tried to contact him?" she asked.

The 18th District's negotiator quickly stepped into the van. All eyes focused on him. Negotiation Commander Allen Maldone took one look at Rachel and rolled his eyes in disbelief. "What is *she* doing here?" he asked with disgust.

Maldone had all the arrogance a Harvard education afforded him. He was a brilliant psychologist, having several dozen successful negotiations to his credit. But, two hours earlier, he'd tried talking to Davis before he'd begun shooting. Maldone couldn't decipher Davis's madness and had recommended going to the Final Phase—setting up the team for Close Quarters Combat and moving the snipers into position.

Captain Ballard stepped in front of him. "We requested her, Maldone."

"That's *Commander* Maldone, Captain. Why was she requested?"

"Because he ain't talkin' to you, sir."

"Correct. And what do you think she can do? Davis is beyond our help, gentlemen. He shows all the classic signs of paranoid schizophrenic behavior. This man is not going to be receptive to any type of communicative effort on our part."

Ballard huffed. "I think she can get to him, Maldone. I'd like to avoid another death tonight, if it's all right with you."

"As would I, but I think we'd only be wasting our time."

The Incident Commander of the 18th, Wallace Figgis, a burly native of Chicago and a lifelong Cubs fan, spoke next. His fatherly demeanor lulled others into thinking he was soft, but he had the ability to turn gentleness into a growling manner not unlike that of a grizzly bear.

"People, we are running out of time. We've only got six hostages left, so somebody better convince me why we shouldn't go to Final Phase contingency and eradicate this situation. Mr. Davis has gone way past my caring threshold. I'm ready to put the finishing touches on this thing. One of you better start talkin'," he rumbled. Figgis's heavy body shook like an erupting volcano.

Maldone pleaded his case.

"Commander, I'm in full agreement. Davis has a history of delusional behavior from early childhood, manifesting itself in him as a teenager. I've obtained his medical records. During the most acute episodes, Davis exhibited all the psychological as well as physiological symptoms of paranoid schizophrenia. Davis was given an MRI and Positronic Image Tomography tests, which showed several structural abnormalities in his brain's temporal lobes, basal ganglia, thalamus, and hippocampus."

"Layman's terms, Commander. Spell it out." Figgis grumbled.

"Sir, abnormalities in these regions of the brain give way to hearing voices, plus delusional, abnormal, and violent thinking. Davis was treated, but given his recent divorce and his losses on the market, he has plunged into a mental abyss. Evidently, he believes the only way out is death."

Figgis mulled over Maldone's assessment but turned to Rachel. "Is there any way to save this man and these hostages, Doctor? We seem to be runnin' outta options."

Rachel could only think of One who could save Davis, and she hoped that He would shed some light on the solution. "I agree with everything Maldone is saying, except I think I can offer Davis a way out besides death."

"Now, I've worked with you before, young lady, and I've seen you and Maldone save a lot of people. But this man isn't showing me any sign that we can reach him. It looks like he's gonna kill the last hostages and then do himself," Figgis pressed.

Rachel folded her hands together in a gesture of patience, summoning her mental powers. "I understand, Commander, but I think I can appeal to this man's spiritual side."

"His what? I don't think he needs a priest," Maldone said. "Well, at least not yet."

"Quiet, Maldone, we heard from you," Figgis warned.

"What are you getting at, Rachel?" Ballard asked.

"I'm saying there is a link between the spiritual and the physical. Scientists have not yet been able to explain the cause of these abnormalities, but I believe human beings are acted upon by spiritual forces, resulting in diseases of the mind."

Figgis looked at Rachel with his gentle, fatherly eye. "Rachel, we really don't have time for a Bible study."

Rachel pressed. "Well, can anyone explain the voices?"

"I think I just did," Maldone said.

"Yes," Rachel answered, "but can you explain *what* they say? *What* they are? When you watch that tape, look at Davis's behavior. He seems to be speaking to and answering someone; someone who isn't there, something unseen. Davis really has no control over his actions. The true Davis, the spiritual, essential Davis, isn't in control, because that Davis has been taken over by whatever—or whomever—he is hearing."

Maldone scoffed. "You're not talking about demonic possession are you?"

Rachel gave Maldone a challenging look. She wasn't about to back down from what she was proposing. She had done enough of that her whole life, where her faith was concerned. But not now, not with a man's life at stake. Rachel knew that evil was working against Davis at this very moment.

"Well, that's wonderful," Maldone sneered. "Let's venture back to the dark ages. Bring in the leeches and holy water while you're at it," he finished.

Rachel moved up to Figgis, putting her hands on his shoulders, pleading. "Let me talk to him, Commander."

"What do you think you can do?"

Rachel honestly didn't know. "I'm not sure, but let me make direct contact with him."

Ballard stepped next to her. "Wait a sec. Direct contact? This man's an unstable killer, Rachel. Now, I believe in the Lord, too, but He gave us brains for a reason."

"Apparently, our brains are not invulnerable," she concluded.

"Well, what about your boss, Smithfield, and the University? If somethin' happens to you, the department is liable," said Figgis. He folded his arms across his chest, resting them on his massive belly.

Turning to him, Rachel's eyes pleaded again. "I'll take the responsibility."

"That's a hollow gesture. But I'll take it in the spirit in which it was given. You know you're not in any position to take the responsibility, Doctor."

Rachel felt defeat creep into her bones.

Figgis gave Ballard a hard stare. He looked like a sports coach in the middle of a big game decision. "Captain?"

"Yes, sir."

"Get her a vest."

"Sir?"

"Take her in. If there's a chance we can prevent another casualty, I'd like to make it happen. Do it."

Maldone threw his hands into the air.

Rachel was stunned.

Ballard touched her arm. "Well, as much as I'd like you to just stand there lookin' pretty, we gotta go, lady."

———

Davis heard The Voice and he listened.

"Save the last ones for a while. They are sending someone," it whispered.

"But I'm ready to finish them," Davis answered. "I'm tired of listening to their crying and w-w-whining."

"Yes, yes, I know, so am I. But, let her come. Take care of her, then take care of the rest of them. When you're done..."

Davis interrupted, sounding like a child lost in the street. "I can come home? I can come and s-s-see you?"

If it had a face, The Voice would be smiling.

"Yes," it purred. *"You will come home with me."*

———

The vest and Kevlar helmet only weighed a total of 12 pounds, but it felt more like 50 to Rachel as she and Captain Ballard strode into the lobby of 223 Waker Drive.

The S.W.A.T. captain's need to shield her from danger surged into overdrive. They passed the abandoned security station, and headed toward the elevators. One thought possessed him: He had to protect her, to protect Rachel at all costs.

Being a God-fearing man, but maybe not as strong a Christian as Rachel, was a conflict for Ballard. His line of work put him in a position, on a daily basis, where he might kill a man. His conscience never let up, knowing the eyes of the Lord were upon him. This day, however, had been different.

They entered the elevator and Ballard punched the twenty-sixth floor. Rachel glanced at him, feeling a latent dread as the doors closed forebodingly. She knew that if she had her way, Ballard wouldn't be able to help her. Her eyes fixed upward, staring at the soft fluorescent lights of the elevator. She heard them humming.

Ballard looked at her and tried to reign in his thoughts, since he knew God was reading them. Yes, he would allow Rachel the opportunity to talk Davis down, but the second he suspected that she was in danger, he wouldn't hesitate to give the kill order. If necessary, he'd take the shot himself. He hefted his Hecklor & Koch MP5-PDW assault rifle, resigning himself.

Ballard pulled a radio off his belt. "Sergeant?" he called.

A voice came back. "Yes, sir."

"We're on our way up. Stand-by. Prep the team for possible CQC."

"Team prepped and ready, Captain."

"Warm up the TIR Program. I want a full report on the latest tactical analysis in seven minutes."

"Roger that. So, are we taking down this lunatic, sir?"

"Just do your job, Sergeant."

"Right. Gotcha, Cappy."

The elevator doors opened to the twenty-sixth floor.

A hallway, dimly lit by emergency lights, ran into the lobby of the Larson Trading Company, located about 60 meters to the left. Ballard aimed his weapon and poked his head through the open doors.

The receptionist desk and lobby area was dark and empty; Ballard didn't hear a sound and there was no visible sign of Davis. He saw the body of the man Davis had shot in the back, and the camera that had captured the whole grisly event. He tried not to look at the spackling of blood on the wall and the spread of it underneath the man's chest.

Ballard held up his hand, gesturing for Rachel to stay back. He checked to the right a few feet past the elevators. He spotted three of his officers standing in the doorway of the Baxter Insurance Company.

Ballard motioned and the three officers took up defensive positions in the hallway, two aiming their weapons in the kneeling position, and one standing over them. Their weapons were outfitted with powerful halogen bulb flashlights and laser scopes that shot thin ruby beams down the corridor. Under their Kevlar helmets and protective goggles, there was a deep focus and concentration in their eyes. Ballard was glad to see it; he trusted the efficiency of his team.

Ballard looked back at Rachel. "Come on," he whispered, taking her hand.

They moved quickly. One of the officers jumped up, blocking them from any possible gunfire as they dashed into the Baxter offices. The two remaining officers exited the hallway right behind them in a sequential fashion.

Rachel could see that the 18th Tactical Unit had converted the front office into a makeshift, mini-command post. There were six officers, including Sergeant Nathan Union, who sat at the receptionist desk tapping the keys of his laptop. He sprang to his feet at Ballard's approach. The Captain had a strong confidence in Union, having worked with him for 11 years, so he waved off the Sergeant's formality.

The office windows overlooked the Chicago River. The Bell copter buzzed by in the background.

Ballard pressed a button on the TASC II communications device strapped to the left side of his chest. He spoke into a mini-boom mic that protruded from underneath his helmet. "Eagle One to Nest. We're in. Over."

Commander Figgis's voice boomed into Ballard's ear. "Copy, Eagle One."

"Entry breach in five minutes. Recommendations? Over."

"Proceed on your command, Captain. I don't want any more casualties, understood?"

"Understood, Commander."

Ballard changed frequencies. "Red Team, this is Eagle One. Report."

Tucked just inside the window of an office, in a building directly north of 233 Waker Drive, were Officers Terrance Harper and Donald Ramierez, Sniper and Infrared Thermal Scope Technician, respectively.

"Yes, sir. Red Team reporting. Ramierez has thermals set to full acuity and we're picking up Davis and the remaining hostages a few feet away from him in a mass reading."

Ramierez made minute adjustments to the video monitor that picked up a live feed from the IRWS 1000 Thermal Scope perched atop Harper's sniper rifle. The scope was specially designed to see in the thermal and infrared spectrum; they could literally see through walls or in the dark. The infrared light gave off a ghostly green cast; the forms of Davis and the hostages gave off hues of red, yellow, and orange.

"Davis is obstructed. So far, we've got a negative on target acquisition, unless we can get him to move. The rest of the hostages are on the floor sitting close together. Two of 'em are hurt and he's got 'em pinned down," Harper finished.

Ballard's voice came over their ear monitors. "I copy. We might be able to flush him out and get you a clear shot. But I want you to hold position. No shot, repeat, no shot until I call. Is that clear?"

"Yes, sir."

Back at the Baxter office, Rachel stepped in front of Ballard. "Do we really need them?"

Ballard felt Rachel's compassion for Davis but he couldn't really afford to be too moved by her graciousness. "Rachel, we're gonna give you your chance, but one chance is all you're gonna get. Now, I don't know squat about psychology, or Freud, or any of that other nonsense. I don't know what snapped him, but right now Davis is wacked, and he needs to be taken down. You did catch the body in the hall, didn't you?"

Rachel felt the impact of his words.

Ballard regretted the harshness of his tone. He stepped closer to her. "Listen, for what it's worth, they're not gonna fire unless I give the order. That will buy you a little time. Whatever you think you can say to him, start workin' it in your head now, 'cause we're goin' in three minutes."

Ballard stepped away from her with a dutiful, militaristic turn. Rachel felt the first tinge of panic as it settled like a sickening weight in her stomach.

She watched Ballard as he moved around the receptionist area next to Sergeant Union and then leaned over the laptop. Rachel glanced around the room. The men seemed almost chillingly at ease, not in a casual manner, but with a professionalism bordering on stark coldness. They were well trained and ready. Rachel felt the irrational terror of a small child convinced her bad dream was real.

Voices or no voices, psychosis or not, Davis had killed eight people and Rachel was going in there to have a *chat* with him. She was starting to think maybe she was just a little insane herself, though she had done this a dozen times before.

The fear raced through her heart as she turned to the windows and looked over the Chicago River. The sun had just set behind the concrete and glass ranges of the city when she remembered Him at *His* critical time:

Gethsemane.

Rachel suddenly knew His fear, His dread and His momentary doubt. The way He must have felt that night. Her soul froze. Fear dried her throat and pounded in her chest like a thrashing animal—a fear that was nauseating and disorientating, giving way to an inner ear vertigo that threatened to topple her.

But the Lord kept the cup in front of her, not budging it, not moving it. She prayed and begged, until there was nothing more to do but take it… and drink. The drink was cold and deeply bitter.

"Rachel?" Ballard's voice echoed inside her. She was startled.

"Y-yes?"

He walked over to her, putting his hands reassuringly on her shoulders. "You've got it in your head? You know whatcha gonna do?"

"I think so." Her education, training, and knowledge seemed to elude her, replaced by something more, something better. Rachel felt a shimmering resonance ripple across her entire being. Her horror and fear dissipated, giving way to a deeply powerful sense of serenity edged with the sharpness of veracity.

The Spirit.

"Let's go," she said, almost absently. "I'm ready."

They moved closer to Union at the receptionist desk. Ballard turned the laptop so Rachel could see a layout of the inner office of the Larson Trading Company.

The layout was set up on the specially designed 2000 Incident Response Program used by EMS, tactical, and military. Ballard clicked on the Incident Perimeter page.

There was the lobby and a hallway behind it, cutting across from north to south with two entranceways at opposite ends of the corridor. Those doors led to the trading room. A floor manager's station centered the room with workstation cubicles arranged around it in two semi-circles. There were more cubicles against the walls and along the windows that looked north over the river.

A graphic illustrated the position of the snipers on the outside perimeter; another one represented Davis's and the hostages' current positions. They were tucked between two rows of cubicles near the north windows, with Davis hiding behind a painted concrete column. Sergeant Union was fully geared and ready. He pointed a pen at the laptop screen.

The team gathered near him.

"We'll split into two teams," he instructed. "Hylton, Alverez, you're Blue Team. Williams, Young, you're Green Team. Blue Team, you'll take the south entry. Green, you'll go in with me, the Captain, and Doctor Walters. I'll announce to Davis that we've brought her to talk to him. Alverez, if he cooperates and we get her inside, I want you to flank around the cubicles along the east side of the room. It looks like you may have a shot from at the end of this row. The angle's awkward, but if we can get him to move back a few feet, we'll have him."

Alverez stared at the layout, familiarizing himself, then nodded at the Sergeant.

Union turned to Rachel. "Good to see you again, Doctor. Good work on that Blakley incident a few months back."

Rachel would have smiled at him under other circumstances. "Thank you. I'll do what I can to talk him into disarming. Just give me enough time."

"Will do."

"Thank you, Sergeant," Ballard said. "All right, let's go everybody. Take your positions.

The men started for the door, but Rachel hesitated. "Captain?"

They stopped and turned to her. Ballard walked through their ranks to stand in front of her.

Rachel dropped her head in a gesture of awkwardness. She hated this feeling, and the way it always arose when she needed to express her beliefs. She fought it down, knowing she should never be ashamed to speak of His name in front of men. "I think we should have a prayer before we go," she said.

Ballard felt the slight sting of his own shame, but he nodded. After a moment, he turned to the men. "Let's bow our heads, everybody."

Some of the men did, and some didn't.

Rachel took Ballard's hand, closed her eyes, and prayed.

"Lord, please protect us as we go into this danger. Give us the wisdom, the strength, and the guidance to make the—"

Ballard's radio buzzed loudly, the noise cutting through air with the voice of Commander Figgis. The men snapped to attention.

"Captain, are we ready up there?" Figgis growled.

Ballard glanced at Rachel, who looked away, self-conscious.

"Ah, yes, sir. We're going now."

"Keep all frequencies open, Captain."

"Yes, sir."

Ballard turned back to Rachel, apologetically. "You wanna finish up, Doctor?"

She shook her head. "No, no. I... I was just going to say... amen."

"Amen," he said.

———————

The team moved stealthily down the hallway with Ballard and Rachel in tow. They reached the lobby and took up defensive positions. Union brought a bullhorn to his lips, his voice echoing down the darkened corridor.

"ALEX DAVIS..."

Davis heard Union's voice and jumped to his feet, startled. The hostages recoiled from his quick movements. Two of the six remaining hostages were women. They cried softly.

Davis stood behind the concrete pillar, hoisting one of his pistols, a Smith & Wesson Sigma 40 F. Strapped over his shoulder was an Austrian-made Steyr Aug, with a full magazine of 42 rounds. The ergonomic, futuristic design of the weapon made it look like something from a science fiction movie. It was capable of firing over 850 rounds a minute, going from semi-auto to full auto by just pulling the trigger past a second pressure stop. Davis could empty the clip in seven seconds. He hadn't fired a shot from this weapon yet, but soon he would.

Nervous sweat soaked his brow as he listened to Union.

"THIS IS THE CHICAGO POLICE DEPARTMENT! DO NOT BE ALARMED. WE DO NOT WANT TO HARM YOU! REPEAT, WE DO NOT WANT TO HARM YOU! WE WANT A PEACEFUL END TO THIS SITUATION AND A SAFE RETURN OF THE REMAINING HOSTAGES! PLEASE RESPOND!"

Rachel and Ballard watched intently from behind the lobby. Williams and Young guarded the north entrance to the trading room and Hylton and Alverez watched the south entrance.

There were two more bodies on the floor in the south corridor; a stream of blood had spread near the south entrance door. Alverez made a mental note not to slip on it when they moved for entry.

Rachel could see the body of the man Davis had shot in the back. She noticed one of his shoes had come off; it was curiously tilted on its side underneath one of the chairs along the wall. The tell-tale camera stared down at her.

The stillness and calmness of death cast a cloying fog over her; she wondered if the man had been a Christian.

"ALEX DAVIS, PLEASE RESPOND!"

Davis shook on the edge of panic. They were here. How could they be here? How dare they? But he trusted The Voice. It had guided him through to this glorious vindication. The terror on these faces before me, he thought. How good it is for them to beg for their lives; how good it is to finally have the command over their destinies as they once had command over mine; how good to deny their groveling with a bullet.

But, what now?

"Let them in," said The Voice.

Davis sighed deeply, as if a woman had whispered her love into his ear.

"Tell them to bring her in. We want her. She has denied us many times and she must answer for much. Bring her to us, then you'll come to us," The Voice dictated.

Davis nodded and stepped with a renewed purpose from behind the column, marching over toward the hostages. The women screamed at his movement, terrified and uncertain of when he would kill again. He grabbed one of the injured, a balding man with a bloodstained left shoulder. Earlier, the man had tried to run, but Davis convinced him to stay with a shot across his arm. Blood spotted the man's white shirt and tie; he grimaced in pain as Davis jerked him roughly off the floor, throwing his free arm tightly around the injured man's neck. With his right arm, Davis brought up the Steyr Aug and aimed it in front of himself and his human shield.

Ballard, Rachel, Union, and the team listened as Davis shouted.

"Listen to me! If you can hear me, understand that I am prepared to kill the rest of these p-p-people! All of them!" he said. "I don't wanna have to shoot anybody else, but I will! They shouldn't have done what they did to me, do you understand? I didn't want this! They brought this on themselves! I didn't want it to be like this!"

Commander Figgis and the other officers in the command post van listened intently.

Ballard looked at Rachel and she nodded, indicating she was ready. He turned to Union and gave a signal. Blue Team rushed down the corridor to the south entrance, and Alverez hopped over the blood puddles of the two bodies. They held position at the entrance to the trading room.

Union, Ballard, Rachel, and Green Team moved down to the north entrance. Union brought up the bullhorn.

"WE UNDERSTAND YOUR POSITION, MR.DAVIS! IT SOUNDS LIKE YOU'RE HAVING A TOUGH TIME! WE HAVE SOMEONE HERE WHO MIGHT BE ABLE TO HELP YOU! SHE'S A DOCTOR! JUST BE PATIENT AND WE'LL SEE WHAT WE CAN DO!"

Davis's eyes lit with revelation. This must be the woman they were talking about, he thought. The police are sending someone in to talk. *They* were right, but then again, they've always been right. Ever since he was a boy they had been his guides. For a while they were gone, but they came back to point him in the right direction. When all had left him, The Voice was there.

"DAVIS, WE NEED YOU TO RELEASE THE INJURED! THAT WOULD SHOW GOOD FAITH ON YOUR PART! THAT'S THE ONLY WAY WE'LL BE ABLE TO HELP YOU!"

"Not until they send her in first," The Voice instructed.

"Not until they send in the doctor!" Davis shouted. "And don't send in anyone else! The rest of you stay back! I swear, I'll kill everyone else in this room!" He emphasized his point by squeezing the balding man's neck, slightly choking him.

Ballard signaled to Alverez and Hylton; they disappeared into the trading room.

"THAT'S NOT A PROBLEM, MR.DAVIS. WE'RE NOT COMING IN THERE AT ALL! WE ARE NOT GOING TO SEND IN ANYONE ELSE! WE JUST WANT TO WORK WITH YOU, SIR!"

Alverez and Hylton crawled on the floor along the south wall of the trading room, inching their way to the east wall. There were three more bodies along the path.

"Send her in here, NOW!" Davis ordered.

Ballard, Rachel, Union, and Green Team were positioned by the north door. Ballard looked at her. He whispered. "We're gonna be right behind you. Go slowly, hands high. Give Alverez and Hylton enough time to get situated. I'll be right behind you, Rachel, I promise. Do what you do. Talk him down."

She looked back at Ballard with trusting eyes and a kind of warmth seemed to pass between them. He had only thought of her in the professional sense until just now. Bad timing, he thought. What an odd moment to have a romantic epiphany.

He saw the cross around her neck, and something in her eyes.

Rachel raised both hands in the air, turned, and slowly walked through the north door.

As she entered the trading room, the first thing Rachel noticed was the quiet. Even with the low crying of the hostages, she could hear her own pulse.

She stopped just inside the door, surprised by her composure. Among the cubicles were the tell-tale signs of sudden panic, followed by violence. Documents, briefcases, and purses were haphazardly dumped all around the room. A reader board on the east wall in front of her was still working, the stock quotes sped along at what Rachel thought was an impossible-to-read clip. Splotches of blood and bullet holes were everywhere.

"Davis?" she called.

There was a row of cubicles in front of her to the left, and another row behind that one against the north windows, forming an aisle between them. That's where Davis is holding them, she thought.

After a moment, she heard the sounds of body movement, and Davis emerged at the far end of the row with the balding man. Rachel saw the pain on the balding man's face, and the blood.

She caught Davis's eyes and saw what she had seen many times. His sullen and vacant look was that of a man who was once innocent, but was now given over to a gloom she could scarcely read on the surface. How far into the deep had he fallen? Was there any hope of recovering him? Rachel took one look at the exotic looking weapon in his hand and thought this one might end badly.

"Mr. Davis?"

Davis stared at her.

"Mr. Davis, my name is Doctor Rachel Walters. I'm a psychologist from the University of Illinois. I would like to help you if I may."

Davis shoved the hostage to the floor, eliciting more screams from the rest. He brought the Steyr to bear against Rachel, holding it level against his waist.

The balding man rolled on the carpet in pain.

Rachel brought her hands up higher, speaking rapidly, almost feeling the cut of the bullets. "Mr. Davis, we won't... I won't be able to help you unless you r-r-release some of the hostages. I would be more than happy to talk with you, but you have to let us get this man some medical attention."

Davis broke his stance and started to pace back and forth at the top of the aisle. He took on the mad persona Rachel had observed on the video-tape.

"I told them! I told them to stop but they kept going on and on and on! They kept getting in my head! *Pushing!* Everyday! Everyday! I just wanted to make a little money, that's all! Do something! Get my kids back! AND I'M NOT A FOOL!"

"Yes, Mr. Davis."

"SHE CALLED ME A FOOL! I loved her! She didn't understand why I was doing this! We had two mortgages on that house! The bank was call-in' about the car payments, insurance! I just wanted them to be happy, I wanted my kids in the best schools. I mean, y-you can't send your kids to public school, those places are little prisons! How are they gonna live with-out me? How are they gonna grow up in this hell we call a world? And these people with all their self-righteousness, smug... This is what they deserve for trying to kill a man with their voices! This is what they deserve for twist-ing my thoughts and jumbling them up and mixing them up with their own perverted thoughts! I don't wanna think like they do!"

Rachel felt like she'd found an entryway to Davis's psyche. She felt an inner calm and brought up her most soothing, caring tone.

She slowly brought down her hands, holding up her palms.

"I completely understand, Mr. Davis, and I'm sorry for any pain you've gone through. Please, let me help you. I would really like to talk with you about anything you want to talk about, but first you have to help me. I need to get this man to a doctor, and I would like you to let the other hostages go."

Alverez and Hylton made it to the cubicle row along the east wall. They could see the column, but not Davis, who had stepped just past the cubicle at the end of the row.

Alverez saw the last two bloodied bodies a few feet in front of them. He activated his throat mike and whispered, "Total eight body count confirmed. I can't see Davis just yet. About fifteen more feet."

Ballard was outside the north door. "I copy. Can you see Rachel?"

"Negative."

"Get in kill position."

"Yes, sir."

Davis pondered Rachel's offer. In her presence, he felt some residue of hope that was fleeting, but still there. She looked awkward under the Kevlar and vest, but he was somehow able to see the serenity on her face. She was pretty.

He suddenly remembered how beautiful Sheila had been, and how cruel.

"Who else is out there?" he asked, coldly.

"They're police officers, Mr. Davis."

"They wanna kill me."

"No, no. They don't want that at all. They don't want *any more* killing. The police don't want anyone else to be hurt. If they did, they wouldn't have sent me."

"They don't care if I live or die. I told you I'm not a fool. They only sent you to protect them. These people induce evil with their thoughts. I *told* you. They were trying to kill me and now the police want to protect *them?*" He laughed. "It's backwards, it's all backwards, everything's backwards."

"I agree, Mr. Davis, but could we let them go? I'd be more than happy to talk with you about it."

Rachel watched his posture as he seemed to relax.

Davis suddenly turned to look behind the row at the hostages. They looked at him like frightened children. "Get up," he yelled.

They all stood, huddled and shaking together. Davis impatiently waved them on and they moved hastily past him. As they moved toward Rachel, two of the men picked the balding man off the floor and carried him to the door.

Ballard activated his mic and whispered. "Alverez...?"

"I've almost got it."

"Don't let him take her."

"No, sir."

The hostages disappeared through the north door. Rachel watched their departure and then turned back to Davis.

"Bring her to you. Hurry," said The Voice.

Rachel saw something bleak pass over Davis.

"Come 'ere," he snarled.

Alverez was at the corner of the cubicle row. He slowly brought his weapon to sight. The shot was clean.

Rachel moved down the aisle toward Davis.

Ballard and Union poised for entry.

The men in the command post van were silent, listening.

"Shoot to the left," whispered The Voice. *"Now!"*

Davis turned and opened fire, spraying bullets across the east side of the room. The first volley ripped through the wood and carpet of the cubicle walls. Alverez felt solid heat smash into his collarbone. Hylton fired blindly, then grabbed his fallen partner by the boots, pulling him back. The two officers managed to duck around a cubicle wall to the center of the room.

Rachel dropped to the floor as Davis turned and aimed down the aisle toward the north door. Ballard, Union, Williams, and Young moved through quickly and low; Davis's shots just missed punching the walls behind them. The four officers put their backs to a cubicle. The impact of bullets was deafening.

Ballard cursed.

Davis grabbed Rachel off the floor with animal strength, spinning her around and wrapping his arm around her throat. He shrieked in her ear.

"You set me up!"

"No," she choked. "They were supposed to wait! They were supposed to wait!"

"Get back here!" He pulled her around the end cubicle into the north aisle, but not before firing a few more rounds in the direction of Alverez and Hylton.

Union barked into his radio. "Union to command, we got shots fired, repeat, shots fired!"

Ballard activated his mic, struggling to maintain composure. The last thing he wanted was for this maniac to take Rachel, and now he had her. "Ballard to Harper, respond!"

Harper had his eye on the thermal scope. "Harper, here, sir."

"He's got her! I need a shot, now! Get me a clean shot!"

"Yes, sir. I can see them. He's hiding behind the pillar again. I can't shoot through it. That's gotta be solid concrete."

"What about Rachel? Can you see her?"

"Yes, sir. She looks okay. He shoved her pretty hard to the floor, but she's all right. If she can talk him out from behind that column, I'll have him."

"We should not have sent her in there! Get this thing over with, Harper! You're authorized!"

"Yes, sir. As soon as he's unobstructed."

Rachel sat on the floor rubbing her left ankle. She'd twisted it earlier, running to board the police chopper; now she'd sprained it again trying to keep her balance when Davis pushed her.

She looked up at him with a mixture of fear, loathing, and pity. Rachel sensed the hovering fog of the dark presence that enveloped him. Davis took off his glasses and rubbed the sweat from his face and brow. He placed them back on with both hands in a gesture of childlike humility, but by the time he caught her gaze again, he wore the mask of a killer.

Davis carefully pried his eyes around the column, looking to the window. The blinds were down, but he knew they could see him. He knew because they told him.

He trusted them.

Davis made one last check in the direction of Alverez and Hylton before sitting on the floor, and leaning his right shoulder against the column. He pointed the barrel of the Steyr Aug over his knee toward Rachel, who sat passively with her legs tucked under her skirt.

"I didn't know what they were going to do, Mr. Davis. I'm sorry if they frightened you," she said.

"They don't scare me. Do you think I'm afraid? You think I'm afraid of them or you?" He taunted the S.W.A.T. team. "If you try anything else— anything—I'll kill her! And I'll know if you're coming, you understand?! I'll know! So don't try it!"

Ballard and Union looked at each other, knowing they had run out of options.

"Davis, this is Captain Ballard of the Chicago Police Department. We won't try anything else, but you've got to promise us you won't hurt the doctor. She only wants to talk to you. We wanna see if we can help you."

"I don't need your help," Davis shouted back. "And the only thing I can promise you is that I will shoot her if you try anything else!"

"All right, all right! We're not going to try anything; just don't harm the doctor. Let her help you," Ballard answered.

"Davis?" Rachel asked. He focused on her. "What do you want? What happened to you?"

Davis looked at her, and felt the crushing weight of the past year's losses. His life was a vacuum, sucking him deeper and deeper into the void.

He looked at her and said, "With mercy, God built the walls of Hell. Evil is incarcerated within. God locked the gates and sealed the breach. He widened the chasm against the evil one's reach. With mercy, God built the walls of Hell."

Rachel's jaw slowly dropped.

"You don't want to know what happened to me," he said. "That's why God made hell. So he could trap dead souls like mine. It's not for you to be concerned with what happens to a devil. That concern is what's gonna get you killed."

Rachel was stunned. Her heart thrashed in her chest, and she fought down the impulse to curl in a ball and shrink away from him. Instead, the Spirit shimmered inside of her and courage rose up in her.

"Davis, whatever it is you think you have to do, whatever it is you feel compelled to do, you don't have to act on it. I can see you never wanted to kill those people. You don't look like the kind of man who would harm anyone, and I know you don't want to kill me. There is something compelling you to do this."

"How do you know? What makes you think you know? Do you hear what they say to me? Do you know what kind of power they have? Do you know what kind of comfort they are to me?"

"Who?"

"*Them!* Them. Their thoughts are my thoughts, their words become mine. I can't see them, but I can hear them and I...I can *feel* them."

"They talk to you?"

Davis suddenly became Rachel's patient.

"Yes."

"Voices? In your mind?"

He looked at her with tears in his eyes.

"What do they say to you?"

Davis smiled. "They tell me things."

"What things, Mr. Davis?"

"Everything."

"Did they tell you to kill these people?"

He nodded. "They told me about you, and about how that officer was about to shoot me. They saved me. That's why I stopped taking the medication."

"Because they saved you?"

"Because... I *wanted* to hear them. Sometimes the medication made them stop, but I wanted to hear them."

Rachel folded her hands together and pleaded with him.

"Mr. Davis, they are lying to you. You didn't have to kill anyone. That's what they want, but they need us to carry out their deeds. Please, let me take you someplace where I can teach you to fight them."

Rachel pointed to the gold cross around her neck. "Let me take you to Him."

Davis's eyes clouded over and he simply wasn't there. His mind locked in on The Voice. "Yes...I'll take her to the roof...Yes...Yes, I'll bring her to you...Yes...I know...You've always been there for me...You warned me about them...You've always been there...Always..."

Rachel stood slowly, sensing the tide had turned. "Mr. Davis?"

He dug another magazine out of the gym bag that sat next to the column. Loading the Steyr, he stood up and glared at Rachel.

Harper watched Davis' rainbow-colored thermal image through the column as he stood. "I got movement..."

Davis grinned at Rachel like a jack-o-lantern. "It's time now. They want me to bring you home. Don't be afraid. You'll like them."

Rachel turned to run.

Davis stepped from behind the column after her.

"He's clear," Harper said. He squeezed the trigger.

Davis caught Rachel roughly by the arm just as the sniper's bullet punched neatly through the window glass and tore through the meat of his right shoulder. He grimaced and yelped, but somehow managed to hold her, pulling Rachel closer to his body. Gripping the Steyr Aug, he fired through the windows, shattering and powderizing the glass.

Harper and Ramierez ducked as wild bullets cracked and popped the windows in front of them.

Rachel scratched and clawed at Davis's arm, struggling to wrestle free, but he swung her around with little effort.

Hylton popped in from around the cubicle row, pointing his rifle, but Davis anticipated him. Rachel screamed as the close impact of bullets tossed Hylton against the east wall.

Davis dragged her toward the east wall, both of them stepping over the fallen Hylton. As they stepped out from the aisle, they came face-to-face with Ballard, Union, Williams, and Young.

"DROP THE WEAPON!" Ballard commanded. "DROP IT, NOW!"

Davis and Rachel stopped. They were at a standoff, but Davis knew he had the advantage, and so did Ballard. After what seemed like an eternity, Davis spoke.

"You and I both know that you won't shoot past her. You'd have to kill her to kill me."

Ballard had a shot, but Davis was injured from the snipers and he didn't seem in any way affected. Ballard wondered how much rage was left in the man. He knew it would take more than one bullet to drop him.

Behind Davis, on the floor, Hylton crawled from around the cubicles. He had his nine-millimeter. One bullet had managed to penetrate his vest at close range, and Hylton felt warm blood coursing down his abdomen. Ballard saw him and glared at him. His eyes were enough to let Hylton know not to try the shot.

Ballard held up his hand at Union, Williams, and Young. They lowered their weapons. He looked at Rachel and she nodded. She wanted one more chance.

But Ballard was thinking ahead.

Davis and Rachel moved down the aisle, between the four men, and headed toward the north doors.

Davis found the stairwell doors and they entered.

Ballard jumped on his radio as Union went to attend to Hylton and Alverez.

"Harper, Ramierez!"

"Harper, sir."

"Move your position to the roof! He's taking her to the roof!"

"Roof side's too high, Captain. Too much of a downward angle. We figure four floors up."

"Do it, then!"

Davis kicked, and the roof access door flew open and slammed against the shed. Rachel felt the blast of warm August air. Her stomach wrenched, as her inner ear told her that she was 40 stories off the ground.

Davis pushed her to the roof, and the gravel cut into her palms and knees.

She turned to see Davis pull his Smith & Wesson 40 F. He placed it against his temple. "Time to go home." He pointed the gun at her.

Rachel stood up slowly. The eye of the barrel was death. "Mr. Davis, please, this is what they want. You'll kill me, and then they'll kill you, or you'll kill yourself. I know what it is that's talking to you. I know you've heard them for a long time. And they've been working on you for a long time, haven't they? Since you were a boy? They were with you the first time you thought about suicide, the first time you tried to hurt yourself, and they were with you when you shot those people. I believe you want to be free of them, but they've made you believe they are a part of you and that you need them, but you don't. You need God and He's here, but you've got to open your heart to Him now, before it's too late. This is your last chance, Mr. Davis. If you kill me, I'm ready. I'll go home. But, if they kill you, you'll die without knowing the truth; without knowing Him."

Harper and Ramierez found the perfect perch, four stories up. Ramierez pulled back the glass of the window as Harper set up the tripod and rifle.

The sun was gone and darkness closed in on Chicago.

Ballard, Union, Williams, and Young climbed up the steps toward the roof access door.

Rachel waited for the bullet. She turned away from Davis toward something blue and bright which caught her eye, a force of light on the edge of her peripheral vision. It was a sphere of perfection, a glowing orb of bright power, and the presence of it comforted her with a calm she hadn't known since she was a child. From the edge of the building, she watched it disappear over the river. When it vanished, she felt the rush of the world's tide flooding over her, drowning her…

Rachel turned back to Davis. "Give me the gun." She stretched out her hand to him.

Ballard, Union, Williams, and Young reached the roof access shed. They held at the door. They could see Rachel, but the roof heating and air conditioning assembly blocked Davis.

"Harper," Ballard whispered into his radio.

"She's in the shot, sir. It's not clean," Harper answered.

Davis stared at her from behind the barrel. His eyes shimmered with tears.

"With mercy, God built the walls of Hell. Evil is incarcerated within. With mercy…With mercy…" He turned the gun against his temple.

"Davis!" Rachel raced toward him, reaching for the gun.

Harper's sniper finger squeezed. "Shot's clear, " he announced.

"Hold your fire! She's in the shot, she's in the shot!" Ballard ordered.

Rachel was a foot away from the gun, but Davis stepped back just out of her reach, and pulled the trigger. The blood spattered her and she closed her eyes as she stumbled back, catching the cry in her throat. She felt the impact of the gravel as she landed hard on the roof. Ballard was suddenly there, covering her with his body.

Union, Williams, and Young moved quickly over Davis, pointing their weapons. Once they saw the fatal damage they relaxed their postures.

"Suspect is down, repeat, suspect is down," Union announced over his mic.

Figgis and the other officers in the command post van gave a collective sigh.

Ballard held Rachel by her shoulders. "Rachel? Rachel... Are you all right? Are you hurt, are you shot?" he panted.

Her body vibrated with shock.

She shook her head, then turned to Davis. Union had covered Davis's head and upper torso with his vest. Rachel looked away and dropped her face into her hands. She felt tears stream through her fingers.

Ballard picked her up off the roof and soon other officers and an EMS crew arrived. Ballard made sure she was all right, then went to debrief with Union.

Rachel walked to the edge of the roof, thankful to the Lord that she was alive, but remorseful for the lives lost. She felt the Spirit settle within her, resting now that the danger was over. The Voice came to her like the wind over the river. For the first time in her life, Rachel Walters felt her mind open up to not only the presence of God but also the presence of deep evil.

"Rachel Walters," called The Voice. She froze with a terror she had never felt before.

Fearfully, she called the Lord's name, but the words never passed her lips.

Chapter 4

The sky was clear blue, azure. An automobile fell out of the fathomless blue; it spun and twisted, the sound of metal creaked as it cut the air. And it fell… and fell… and fell…

———◦•◦•———

It had been a long while since Scott Macklin had felt this good on a run. He raced along a path overlooking Elliot Bay in Myrtle Edwards Park on a cool, rainy Monday morning. Scott was supposed to take a couple of days off, at the recommendation of his podiatrist. He had badly bruised his feet in a mini-marathon two weeks ago, but he just couldn't stay away from the road for long. He'd gotten up that morning, wrapped his black-and-blue toes in Mole Skin, and put on double socks. Then, to ward off cramps, he'd hydrated with Gatorade and water.

He exited the park and headed south on Alaskan Way along the city waterfront, past the bayside piers, shops, and seafood eateries that catered to the spring and summer tourists. Farther south were the industrial piers and the giant shipping cranes, looming like steel mantes.

Downtown was barely visible in a mist just to the east of the waterfront, a green metropolis rightly dubbed the Emerald City.

Seattle.

Scott Macklin had come here twelve years ago to study architecture at the University of Washington. He excelled in all facets of the craft, borrowing influences from masters such as LeCorbusier, I.M. Pei, and Frank Lloyd Wright. Scott soon soared to the top of his class with work that gave breadth to the angular approach of design. His drawings often pushed the rules of design logic.

Soon after graduation, he'd joined the architectural firm of Watkins, Porter, and Dallas. He was only a few projects away from becoming a partner, and he'd only been there for 11 years. His current project, the Lake Washington Office Complex, had proven to be a bigger challenge to him than he'd first foreseen, and with all that, the death of his father couldn't have come at a worse time. How selfish, he suddenly realized. As if his father had somehow timed his demise to interfere with Scott's schedule. God, what is happening to me? he wondered.

He didn't know what he would have done if not for the love and support of his girlfriend, Denise. He tried to think more about her and less about the Lake Project as he neared his Lexus, which was parked across from Waterfront Park.

He checked his watch; the chronometer told him he had to knock off two seconds to average a seven-minute mile over his eight-mile course. He took in two huge breaths and sprinted; he felt the strength and tightness in his legs.

For Scott, this was the best part of his run, the last 50 or 60 meters. The air rushed in and out of his lungs, but they didn't burn now as they did during the warm-up miles. He felt the adrenaline release as he pushed hard past his finishing mark.

He slowed to a brisk walk; the stress in his muscles subsided and he stopped just as the car phone rang. Scott took the time to check his watch as he trotted back to the car. He had beaten his time by exactly two seconds. Good, he thought, a good way to start the morning.

Scott opened the driver side door and grabbed the phone; he fought the urge to sit until his heart rate came down.

"Scott Macklin," he panted.

"Missed you."

He smiled at the breathy, waking voice of his love. "Hey, sweetheart. You up?"

"Ummmm… Now I am. Now that I hear your voice," she said.

"How can you miss me like that? I've only been out of bed for two hours."

"Too long, sweetie, too long. Are you coming in for breakfast? I could make us something."

"I'd like to, baby, but I can't. I'm going to the club to shower, then I've got to get to the office. Bryce has left me about 50 v-mail pages. We've got a little trouble with one of the new tenants. They've got a problem with their lease."

"Are you gonna hafta audit?"

"It's starting to look that way."

"You hate that."

"Yeah, you're right. I'd rather be drawing. Can we turn breakfast into dinner?"

"I don't know. Depends on how mad I am for being stood up this morning."

"I'll make it up to you, sweetheart. I'm serious."

"Fine then," she said, coquettishly. "I'll just have to save my love and morning kisses for somebody else."

"Say what?"

"You heard me."

Scott laughed. He loved it when she got into a playful mood. "Woman, when I get home tonight, I'm gonna teach you the first lesson in cell phone etiquette."

"What's that?" she purred.

"Never tease your future husband at a distance from which he can't reach you."

"Well, you could remedy that with a short drive, mister. Besides, you love it when I tease you on the phone."

"Well, maybe I do, maybe I don't."

"I know you do."

He laughed. "Well, as much as I like being tortured, I have to go. I'll cook tonight. You want me to stop at the market?"

"No, we've got some stuff here. I really don't care about dinner; I just want you. We haven't had a minute these past few weeks. We've just been passing each other in the hallway to the bathroom. I've been so busy with preparing my client portfolios... I know I haven't been the best company around here."

"Baby, don't worry about it. We've both had some pressures. Lord knows I have."

"I know. Sweetie, I'm sorry again about your father."

Scott felt a slight sting but tucked it away. "I know. It's okay. I'm all right."

"I'll see you tonight, then?"

"You got it."

"I'm gonna have a busy day, but I'll squeeze you into my thoughts, love. Have a good day and be careful on the job site."

"I gotcha."

"I love you."

"I love you too, Denise."

———⋅◆⋅———

Bryce Watkins, senior partner and founder of Watkins, Porter, and Dallas, sat at his desk in an office in Kirkland, Washington. He had a powerful view of Lake Washington, the 520 Bridge, and the hills of central Seattle to the west.

His office was dominated by rich mahogany and a framed, original schematic of the Columbia Tower and his Prager Award—the equivalent to the Nobel Prize in architecture. He kept his prize encased in glass atop a pedestal made of imported Italian marble.

Another wall held an ultra-realistic painting of a sitting lion, with a crown of thorns on top of its mane and two nail holes in its paws. It looked regal and powerful. It instilled fear and, at the same time, a sense of calm and comfort.

Scott stepped into the open doorway and knocked.

Bryce smiled at his protégé and greeted him like a father would.

"Scotty, Scotty. Come on in. Shut the door, if you please," he said.

Scott moved in and sat in one of the plush leather chairs at the front of the desk.

"Good morning, Bryce," he said.

A devout Christian, Bryce was Scott's pastor, priest, friend, and teacher, all in one. Scott found his sermonizing to be irritating at times, but he realized it was because Watkins was often so truthful. Besides, working for one of the most brilliant architectural designers in the country more than made up for the occasional index finger held to his face, followed by a recitation of Biblical chapter and verse.

Bryce had a slight Scandinavian lilt to his voice. "Hey, Scotty. How's that run, son?"

"Not bad," Scott said, pridefully. "Bruises are healin' up. Got some new blisters this morning."

"Take care of that, son. You were more of a short distance runner in school, weren't you?"

"I used to like the 400 relay. I wasn't that big on milers. But I guess I just got used to longer runs."

"That's good, good. It seems the Lord never saw fit to bless me with any athletic ability, but He made up for it by giving me an artist's hands and a keen eye for talent."

Scott felt the sincerity in his comment. "Yes, sir. Thank you."

"You're welcome. Now on to business."

"I know, I know. Let me guess, Beaumont's Books. They still want that space audit?"

"Well, son, based on BOMA measurement standards, they think they stand to lose a huge amount of money over their lease term. Morgan Properties didn't inform Beaumont's that they'd be charged for rentable space on the building common, but they were probably going to sneak the cost into their lease agreement anyway."

Scott wasn't surprised; it wasn't the first time a big property owner tried to squeeze as much rent as he could out of a tenant. With the new BOMA property management laws, a tenant could be charged for more than just his office and store space. Morgan Properties, the owner of the Lake Washington Office Complex, didn't give Beaumont's an accurate space measurement, and it looked like they weren't going to bother to inform their client.

"They want us to do the measurement?" Scott asked.

"At first, they wanted to hire some outside space auditor, but Morgan wants to save a little face on this thing."

"So they told them we'd do it."

"Right."

"When, today?"

"Today. Reps from Morgan and Beaumont's are going to be on the site this afternoon. They want to look at any findings you come up with. After they see some numbers, they'll decide if they want to stay as a tenant."

"Probably won't be able to afford it after I factor in the common space."

"That's what they want to assess."

"What time?"

"We'll be on site by three. Can you come up with some annotated drawings by then?"

"I see it happening. I'll have to get my gear and laptop. Set up and measurement should only take a couple of hours."

"Good. We've got another problem, also."

"What now?"

Bryce stood up and turned to the window; he enjoyed his view.

"OSHA. There's a crane operator who's got them watching the site. He almost got some people killed last week. Bailey Tower Crane says he's the best they've got, so the general contractor is keeping them on. OSHA's agreed to it, but if they have one safety violation—I mean, no matter how slight—they're going to shut down the site, and fine the GC and Bailey Crane. If that happens, it'll kill our schedule. It doesn't seem like a huge problem right now, but just be aware that they might be there."

Scott knew that if OSHA, the Occupational Safety and Health Administration, was snooping around a job site, it was pretty serious. He wondered what the tower crane operator had done, but he didn't ask Bryce.

"Got it. Anything else?"

"No, thank you, Scott. That's all."

Scott got up to leave but he could sense Bryce wouldn't let him go without dropping some wisdom on him. He almost couldn't wait to hear it.

"Oh, one other thing, Scotty."

"What's that?"

"How's Denise?"

Scott felt the sermon coming. "She's good. She's doing really well."

"How's her career? She's a broker, isn't she?"

"Right, that's right. She's happy with it."

"So, when are you gonna marry her?"

Scott would have rather listened to some complicated life lesson taken from Leviticus or Deuteronomy, or maybe even endured a lobotomy. "Ah...well... we... we're... we'll be engaged soon, sir."

"Yes, yes, but aren't you *already* living together?"

"Well… I wouldn't say that… I mean… she visits… often. I wouldn't say we were living together, exactly."

Bryce smiled.

"Scott. Don't kid yourself, and don't lie to Him." Bryce gestured to the lion painting. "Ephesians 5:25-27 reads, 'Husbands, love your wives, just as Christ loved the church and gave himself up for her to make her holy, cleansing her by the washing with water through the word, and to present her to himself as a radiant church, without stain or wrinkle or any other blemish, but holy and blameless.'"

The words moved him, but Scott couldn't quite grasp the meaning.

Bryce moved from around his desk, stood in front of him and placed his hands on his shoulders. "Listen. Come to my church. I could make arrangements for my pastor to perform the ceremony. You two should be married, son."

"Bryce, I appreciate it, but we're not ready yet. It's just that my father's death kind of set us back a little. We're gonna get to it, Bryce, but just not right now. Not yet."

Bryce stepped back a foot. "Well… I'll let you slide for now, but only because I need you on that audit. But this conversation isn't over."

"Yes, sir."

"I'll see you on the site, then."

"Okay, Bryce."

When Scott left the office, he felt like he had just left a confessional. He thought about Denise's smile, but it was clouded by the nightmare vision of his father's car falling out of the sky.

———◆•◉•◆———

Scott focused his eye on the crosshair as he looked through the lens of the electronic measuring device rotating it as it sat on top of a tripod, until he heard the machine beep. Then, he tilted it vertically until it beeped again in confirmation. He took his eye away from the lens to look at the LCD screen on the unit's computer, which now indicated it was set for measurement.

The Sokkia Powerset 3000 used an infrared beam to measure and record the horizontal, the vertical, and the distance within a given space. The onboard computer translated these measurements into the x, y, and z axis.

He could then download the information into his laptop, and annotate his current drawings of the Washington Lake Office Complex.

He was set up in the middle of the skeletal steel structure of the complex. The site was busy with the activity of the general contractor and the hired subcontractors, as they hustled to bring the project in on schedule. Scott waited as an operator moved a rough terrain forklift across his measurement area. The huge tires on the machine threw dust off the concrete floor of what would become the complex's atrium.

As the machine rumbled by him, Scott turned and followed it through what would eventually be the main entrance. He passed underneath some scaffolding, then turned his gaze upward. Some 30 stories above him, he saw the bright orange color of the load jib on a construction tower crane as it swept across the sky.

Scott waited a few minutes for the dust to settle, since it could affect the accuracy of the infrared beam. He took a good long look at his design as it came to life.

The first four floors of the complex would house 16 retail shops, a bookstore, and a restaurant. The next 20 floors would be prime office space, with the west side of the building affording a breathtaking view of Lake Washington and downtown.

Scott credited Frank Lloyd Wright, and especially his favorite architect, I.M. Pei, for their strong influences on this project. Pei's designs for the Bank of China Building in Hong Kong, the Pyramide du Lourve in Paris, and the East Wing National Gallery in Washington, D.C., all were inspirational factors in the complex's design. Scott incorporated his own sense of flow and space, with Pei's concise use of line and pyramidal, triangular themes, to come up with a unique design. He was proud of his work, as proud as he was sure his father would have been.

He turned his focus back to the measurement area. Checking his watch, Scott saw he had about three hours to get the measurements calculated and downloaded.

The dust was down now, so he reentered the building.

Bryce pulled up just as Scott completed the last calculation on his laptop, which was perched on the hood of his Lexus. He knew, based on what he had found, Beaumont's Books wasn't going to be happy with Morgan.

Bryce parked his Audi A8 next to Scott and climbed out of the car, with the reps from Beaumont's and Morgan in tow. The Morgan rep smiled at Scott in a curious, pleading way, as if he hoped Scott had been able to pull off some face-saving magic with his measurements. The Beaumont rep looked like he had a bad case of indigestion. Bryce smiled at Scott, knowing Scott had gotten the job done as always, but he was eager to be finished with this embarrassment. He introduced Scott, who moved quickly to the point of business.

"Well, gentlemen, here it is. As you know, back in 1996 the Building Owners and Management Association, which we fondly call BOMA, made a significant change to its measurement standards. They added what is called the Building Common Area, which includes any building area that serves tenant customers: the lobby, atrium, concierge, vending areas, and so forth."

Scott tapped the keys on his laptop as the group gathered around. He brought up an annotated CAD drawing of the building, showing Beaumont's space. He pointed at the screen with a pen and shouted above the back-up alarm of the rough terrain forklift as it moved nearby.

"Now, after measuring the building floor, common areas, your core area, i.e. the office and store space, the rentable and core areas by floor and any vertical penetrations into other floors, I came up with a total of 5,327 square feet added to your floor rentable!"

The Beaumont rep frowned and tapped the screen. "This space is all included in our rentable?! All of this?! Over 5,000 square feet?!" he asked.

"Yes, sir! In accordance to BOMA's new measurement standards!"

"Do you know how much that's going to add to our lease over the long-term?! That's ridiculous; we should have known about this! It doesn't say anything in our lease about any common area! Why didn't we know about this?!"

He was looking at the Morgan rep, who stood there with a grin, but his face blotched red in humiliation.

The RT forklift drove on, and they spoke in normal tones.

Scott started to answer, but the Morgan rep jumped in. "Well, it was a very… an extremely gross oversight on our part. I apologize on behalf of Morgan Properties. In all honesty, we thought we could cut some corners on our measurements by doing them ourselves instead of letting the professionals, the designers of the project, Watkins, Porter, and Dallas, do the space auditing."

Scott and Bryce could see the doubting expression on the Beaumont rep's face.

"May I speak to you in private?" he asked.

"Certainly," said the Morgan rep, sweating.

They walked several feet from the cars. Scott and Bryce watched as the Beaumont rep folded his arms, and listened as the Morgan rep further ingratiated himself.

"That man knows he was about to get ripped off," Bryce said.

Scott shut down his laptop. "Yeah, I'd say so."

"I'm telling the other partners: this is the last time we do a project with Morgan. I don't want this firm getting a bad reputation. This business is cutthroat enough as it is, without builders and owners stealing from tenants. I told them from the beginning that we should have done the measurements in the first place, but I guess they figured that they could bleed Beaumont over the lease term. Pretty stupid. Over time, somehow, Beaumont would have found the truth, anyway. The truth always has a way of coming to the surface, one way or the other," Bryce said.

Scott nodded.

The Morgan rep and the Beaumont rep moved back toward them. The Morgan rep looked like he was about to burst from pressure. Veins popped on the man's forehead, but still the Morgan rep managed to smile. Scott wondered how long he could keep it up before he'd actually need medical attention.

The men all shook hands and Bryce loaded the reps into his car. Scott assured the Beaumont rep that he'd send him copies of the drawings by FedEx, delivering them the next morning. It looked like they were going to stay on as tenants, but Beaumont's corporate headquarters would have to approve the audit findings.

Bryce waved to Scott as they drove away.

After loading the electronic measuring device and tripod into the trunk, Scott checked his watch.

Three-thirty.

He'd make a trip back to the office, download the new measurements, print the drawings and set up the FedEx. Scott figured he'd leave the office by six; if he hurried, he'd beat Denise home and surprise her with flowers and a bottle of cognac. Then remind her about that cell phone etiquette. Scott smiled as he remembered their morning conversation.

Scott was just about to toss his hard hat into the back seat, when he took one last look at his building. He suddenly felt it swell his chest; it warmed him.

Pride.

He gazed at the structure of the building and the hustle of the contractors. Despite the usually delays and problems with Morgan and Beaumont's, six months from now, he'd find himself basking in the glow of another completed project. At the age of 34, he had accomplished more than most do in a lifetime, but he knew there was more to living than designing buildings.

Scott thought about his next projects, the biggest in his life: becoming a husband and father.

The 30-story-high tower crane jib swept over the site majestically. Scott glanced at his watch again, and then back at the crane. He wondered what the view was like from up there.

He reached into the car, grabbed the phone off the driver's seat, and called Denise; after several rings, he got her cell phone voice mail.

"Denise, it's me. I'm gonna be a little late tonight, baby. I've got to print and FedEx some drawings for Beaumont's. Anyway, expect me at around seven and be ready. I love you, sweetie. Bye."

Scott ended the call, pocketed the phone, and locked up his car. He headed back to the site, looking for the foreman or site manager. He knew they were close to the end of the day, but he wondered if they'd let him get a view from the crane.

⸻•◆•⸻

The Voice spoke to Carl Jenkins as he swung the tower crane jib through the sky, bringing it to a slow halt.

"The bolts," it said. *"Did you loosen the anchor bolts?"*

"Yes," Carl answered. "I did it last night, like you told me."

"What about the safety overrides?"

89

"It's cross-wired. They won't be able to shut it off without getting killed."

"Good. You are about to have a visitor. Make sure he does not get out of the cab until it's done. Make sure he dies with you."

"All right...."

"They'll have your respect when this day is over, Carl," it hissed. "And so will we."

"I thank you."

"No, friend. We thank you. We all do..."

----◆----

The site manager for the general contractor stood in front of his company trailer, going over some blueprints with two subcontractor project managers. Gerald O'Dell rolled up the blueprints and tucked them under his arm as they brought their discussion to a close. The two project managers stepped away as Scott walked up.

"Are you the SM?" he asked.

O'Dell looked at Scott as if he was expecting to be subpoenaed. "Yeah."

Scott extended his hand. "I'm the architect. Watkins, Porter, and Dallas."

O'Dell relaxed and took his hand. "Oh. You look like a lawyer."

Scott had to shout over a crawler crane that rolled by; it rumbled on its tank-like treads. "What's that?!"

O'Dell looked at his watch and started to move away from the trailer. Scott walked with him. "I said you look like a lawyer! The tie and khakis! I was about to tell you that the child support check's in the mail, but I guess you ain't here for that, are you?!"

Scott was surprised at how casual the man was about his private business. "Ah, no, no. I just wanted to check to see how the project was going, and to ask you a favor."

O'Dell looked suspicious. "You ain't with OSHA?"

"No. I'm a junior architect with Watkins, Porter, and Dallas. I just wanted to see how far behind schedule the project was."

"Not that far, a week, maybe two. We had some equipment problems. A couple of the rental companies got us some really junky gear. And I mean junk. There was some downtime, but that always happens with these subs. So, you designed this thing?"

"Yeah, that's right."

O'Dell looked up at the steel and concrete flooring of the structure. He had been impressed with the building layout when he saw the original drawings. "Not too bad," he said. "It looks pretty ugly right now, but we'll see how she looks when we're done."

"Listen," Scott asked. "Is there any way I can get up in that tower crane? I'd like to get a good look at it from up there."

O'Dell looked at the ground, kicking some dirt with his work boots. "Well, we're just about done here tonight, friend. Everybody's gettin' ready to go home. Besides, I don't think we should let you up there with Crazy Carl. I don't know if they told you boys, but he almost got some people killed with that thing a couple weeks ago. OSHA's been creepin' around here asking questions about him. I was thinkin' they were gonna come back today, but I guess not. Got everybody on their toes."

Scott nodded. "Actually, we did hear something about that. What happened?"

"Ah, he tried to trolley a critical load too fast, and the hoist cable frayed and snapped under the weight stress. Brought down about eight tons of steel on our heads."

"Man. Nobody got hurt?"

"Nope. Shook up, is all."

"Thank God. Why do they call him Crazy Carl, anyway?"

"He's a little odd. Kinda weird. He ain't got any friends. Never likes comin' with the guys and me to put back a few after work. I don't think he's got a lady or nothin', either. Mostly keeps by himself. Won't even eat lunch with the crew. He just comes to work, climbs up in that cab, then climbs back down when we quit. I guess they call him that 'cause he kinda talks to himself, too. I heard him once. He was carrying on a full-blown conversation. Crazy Carl."

Scott wasn't worried. Besides, all he wanted was a quick look at the view. He didn't plan on spending a whole lot of time up there with a guy who might be a little off.

"Well, it's about three-forty now. I figured you guys would be leaving by four or four-thirty. If you can talk him into it, I'd love to see it from up there. I'll just take a couple of minutes."

"I guess that'll be okay, but make it quick. I got a cold one and a Mariners game waitin' on me. Here, let me call him."

O'Dell pulled a two-way radio off his belt. "O'Dell to Jenkins, O'Dell to Jenkins. Come in crane."

Carl sat in the tower crane cab and stared out at the horizon. He was angled facing the west as the sun dipped low over central Seattle. The Cascades glowed with the orange light just beyond the bay.

Nearer was Lake Washington and the affluent suburb of Kirkland. Carl wished they were a little closer to the piers. That would be a spectacular end, he thought, to bring this thirty-three story monster down on top of the boats and into the lake. Now that would get their attention.

But, The Voice had been clear on how things should be done, and he would obey. When all was said and done, he would be remembered. Yes, they would regret the way they had chided and taunted him.

He would no longer be Crazy Carl, the fat slob of a man, but King Carl. King of the World. The Voice had promised him dominion over all the kingdoms of the earth, if he would only worship them. And worship them, he did.

Soon, Crazy Carl would reign.

He answered the radio. "Yesss," he growled.

O'Dell was taken aback by his tone, and shook his head, hopelessly. What a nut, he thought. "Listen, Jenkins, we've got the building architect comin' up. He just wants to take in the view."

Carl spoke, but his voice wasn't wholly his. "I just have a load of I-beams to move for tomorrow. I was gonna do that and call it a day. I didn't plan on any tourists."

"Well, go ahead and load 'em up. In the meantime, this man's gonna come up and ride with you. You got that?"

There was a deep pause, then Carl's voice crackled over the radio. "Send him on," he said, finally.

O'Dell nodded at Scott. "The elevator's over there on the west side of the tower."

Scott started off, but then hesitated. "So… is that thing really safe?"

"What, the tower? Yeah. It's safe."

"What's holdin' it up?"

O'Dell laughed. "Well, to make a short story long, I'm not an engineer and you'd almost have to be to get the finer points, but here it is: First you lay down a network of rebar, then you bring in some special cut material called embed plates for the anchor bolts. The embed plates are cut in the same circumference as the motorized base. You lay that across the rebar and fasten your bolts through each hole in the plates. There's usually about 180 bolts, by the way. With the bolts in the place, you're ready for the concrete.

"After they pour the concrete and it sets, you've got almost 200 anchor bolts sticking up outta the foundation in a circular pattern. Then the motorized base is lowered over the bolts. They use PVC pipe as a guide through the holes on the base, to perfectly fit each bolt. Then you make sure the thing is level and lock it down with two- or three-inch nuts on each anchor bolt.

"And aside from that, the crane is always balanced by the counter-weights on the rear jib. What makes this crane so special is that it has one stationary counter-weight and a *mobile* counter-weight."

"I see. So you can keep it balanced by adjusting the placing of the counter-weight along the radius of the rear jib."

"Yeah. Smart man. See, these cranes are really stable. In fact, it would take winds over 100 miles an hour to tip one of 'em."

O'Dell checked his watch again. "Well, look. I've got to get over there and make sure they get those beams tied down, or we'll be payin' the devil."

"All right, then. Thanks a lot," Scott said, and raced off.

Scott found the access elevator at the base of the mammoth tower. He craned his neck, held on to his hardhat, and turned his gaze straight up. The clouds moved slowly, high over the top of the crane where a smaller service crane was mounted inside the upper tower. It looked to Scott to be somewhere around 400 feet to the very top of the structure. He spotted the operator's cab at the base of the upper tower, just below the jib.

Scott climbed inside the access elevator and closed the metal door. He pushed a green button and heard the whine-rev of the elevator motor starting his ascent.

As he rose, he marveled at how smooth the ride was, how solid the crane felt, over all. He was impressed by the sheer sturdiness and scope of it.

As he rose above the site, he could see Lake Washington. It was spectacular at sunset. Boaters and jet-skiers enjoyed the August afternoon.

Scott noticed the length of the crane load jib, and he estimated it had to be somewhere around 250 to 300-feet long.

The elevator came to an abrupt halt at the back of the operator's cab. Scott pulled open the door and stepped onto a metal platform attached to the rear entrance of the cab.

The wind gusted, and vertigo forced him to grab the railing on the platform. He tried the handle on the cab door, but it was locked.

Scott peered through the Plexiglas window on the door.

Carl Jenkins sat innocuously at the controls.

Scott knocked on the Plexiglas. "Hey! Hey, Carl?!"

After a long moment, Carl moved his hand to tap a button. Scott heard the door unlock and he climbed inside.

The cab was huge, about the size of a small van. Scott's breath was taken by the operator's vantage point. The jib in front of them seemed to extend to the horizon; the workers and crew were toy men beneath them.

Scott walked over to introduce himself. Carl Jenkins turned and Scott was shocked at the look of the man. His face appeared ragged beyond normal fatigue with deep, dark circles that encompassed his eyes, and a three-day peppered growth of beard. He was a big man, out-weighing Scott by about a hundred pounds. Carl barely fit in the control seat. "Scott. Scott Macklin. Watkins, Porter, and Dallas."

Carl stared at him and Scott felt a sudden chill. "Carl. Call me Carl."

"Good to meet you, Carl."

They didn't shake hands. "Have a seat and buckle in," Carl said.

Scott moved back and sat in the other cab chair; he found a lap belt and buckled it.

He felt slightly unnerved by Carl, but content enough to enjoy the view.

Carl activated his radio. "Jenkins to steel crew."

"Copy, crane. Go ahead," came the reply, over static.

"I'm swinging around for critical load pickup and re-position."

"Copy. We're clear."

Scott watched as Carl toggled one of the three joystick controls and the massive tower slowly began to turn, the jib traveling to the left from south to north, to 180 degrees. Scott could see the Lake Washington Building through the front cab windows as the jib spun over it.

The sight floored him; his eyes lit up like a child's.

The base of the crane was built just outside the building's main entranceway. Seeing the structure from above was more than Scott could take. This would truly be his best work once completed.

On the ground, the steel crew made some last-minute adjustments to the hoist cables and tie downs on the I-beams. There were 12 beams stacked together weighing about eight tons a piece, coming to a total weight close to 200,000 pounds. The crane was capable of lifting much higher weight, so this load was dangerous, but fairly routine.

Carl jogged the hoist trolley, which ran along rails underneath the jib, halting it at about 200-feet radius. He then lowered the hoist into the hands of a steel crewman, 300-feet below.

A pair of steel crewmen fastened the hoist hook to the load cable hooks, and cleared the rest of the crew safely back from the load.

"Steel crew to crane," Carl's radio crackled. "Load secured."

"Copy," Carl replied. "We're swinging over to the drop area on the building's southwest corner."

"Copy."

Scott felt a vibration as Carl raised the hoist and lifted the load 100 feet into the air. He jogged the weight closer toward the main tower at about 150 feet radius, then slowly spun the crane, moving the jib towards the drop site.

Below, the other sub-contractors began to wind down for the day. Some of them watched as the crane carried the heavy beams across the sky. The steel crew moved to the drop area, ready to unhook and secure the load. The beams would be used the next day to add the final stories to the building.

Carl lowered the hoist as the jib spun over the drop site. He was under 50 feet when he halted the load descent and brought the tower to a full stop.

The I-beams hung in the air where they swayed gently.

Carl sat frozen at the controls. He felt a dark squeeze on his heart as he became numb with the presence of evil. A bleakness passed through him and settled itself within his mind and spirit; a storm hovered and held steadfastly in place. The thing now inside him adjusted and secured itself in its new dwelling.

Months ago, Carl Jenkins resigned himself to the end of his life, and he closed off his heart; he became a fertile nesting ground for the forces of blight and despair. They hacked and chewed at him until they had rotted away every remnant of Carl Jenkins' soul. He was now their willing instrument.

"What's the holdup, crane? Over." Carl's radio buzzed.

Scott leaned over in the cab chair; he tried to get a glimpse of Carl but the man's back was like a wall.

"Hey! Everything all right up there?" The radio buzzed again.

The steel crewmen stared up at the suspended beams in confusion. They were anxious to be done with the day and head home.

O'Dell stood in the midst of them with the radio in his hand. "What's he doing up there?" he asked, of no one in particular. "Jenkins!" he barked impatiently into the radio. "Look, we're ready to go home! Get that load down here, now! Copy!"

Scott felt an overwhelming sense of dread. Maybe this hadn't been such a good idea.

"Jenkins! Do you copy?!" O'Dell ranted over the radio.

Suddenly, it was there. To Carl, it sounded like The Voice filled the cabin; Scott heard nothing.

"Now," it ordered. *"Do it now, Carl."*

Carl threw his hands into action; the tower spun to the right at full speed. Simultaneously, he lowered the hoist and pushed the trolley close to the edge of the jib. The I-beams built up a deadly swing from the momentum of the tower as it turned; Carl lowered the weight closer and closer to the ground.

O'Dell and the steel crewman watched as the I-beams flew overhead, straight in the direction of some equipment and oblivious crewmen.

As Carl swung the jib and tower at full speed, one side of the base rose off the concrete footing two inches and fell again.

The rough terrain forklift operator sat in the cab of his machine, having just parked it. He reached into his pocket to fish out his last cigarette from a crumpled pack. He didn't hear the screams and shouts of O'Dell and the steel crew, because the cab of the RT forklift was covered with Plexiglas, muting the shouts of the men.

What a long day, he thought, as he lit the cigarette and opened the operator side door.

The shouts of the crew hit him like a wind. They ran toward him and there was O'Dell, waving his arms and shouting. "Get outta there! Get outta there!"

"What?"

He looked up just in time to see the I-beams; they came down as if they'd suddenly fallen from the sky. The RT forklift operator leaped and hit the ground, landing flat on his chest. He felt the rush of air blast from his lungs from the impact and tasted dirt.

The beams passed over him eight feet above the ground and threw a shadow.

The forklift weighed somewhere around 10,000 to 12,000 pounds, but when the I-beams smashed it into the cab the machine was hooked. The force lifted it into the air and flipped it as if it were made of cardboard.

The forklift landed nearly upside down; the other side of the cab was crushed.

Finally, it came to a rest on its side.

"What are you doing?!" Scott shouted.

Carl's hands moved with a mad quickness across the controls. System and operation warning lights flashed on the two consoles, but he ignored them, and Scott.

O'Dell screamed into his radio as the steel crewmen picked the RT forklift operator off the ground. He watched the load of steel as it rose high into the air, headed straight for the north side of the building. There were still a few workers on the eighth floor. "I WANT EVERYBODY OUTTA THE BUILDING NOW! CLEAR THE BUILDING!" he roared into the radio.

All around the site, workers and crewmen scrambled. Vehicles jumped to life and tires spun in the dirt, racing to get clear of the tower which was obviously at the controls of a madman.

Workers on the eighth floor ran to the elevator on the north side of the building. There were too many to make the first load, so some crowded in and a handful of others remained. As the elevator descended, the crane jib swung over them ominously; the cable and hoist whipped the I-beams in at a deadly trajectory.

The men still on the floor backed away from the edge as the beams pounded the steel structure; the building shook with the power of a small earthquake.

The elevator jostled violently, terrifying the workers, but it continued its descent.

Several anchor bolts popped off along the base; they bounced and sparked off the bottom of the tower with bullet velocity. The base lifted four inches off the concrete flooring, held in the air and then dropped...

O'Dell climbed inside his trailer and jumped on the phone P.A. His voice echoed through a network of speaker horns. "CLEAR THE SITE, REPEAT, ALL PERSONNEL CLEAR THE SITE IMMEDIATELY!"

O'Dell tripped a switch and a warning siren blared.

Scott jumped from his seat, turned, and grabbed the door handle to the cab. It wouldn't move. Locked. He was locked in with this lunatic.

Now he understood how Carl had earned his reputation. Through the cab window, he could see the crews making their exits. What now? His mind raced, calculating.

Scott saw Carl operate the door lock, but the switch was up on the console; the only way he could get to it was past Carl.

Scott sized him up. He hadn't been in a fight since he was a sophomore in high school, and this man looked like he could take some punches; maybe he had taken a few already. Could that be what this was all about? Could Carl had been driven to this somehow? Whatever the case, he hoped he wouldn't have to fight him.

Scott mustered up an authoritative but even tone.

"Listen, Carl. Whatever is goin' on with you, or whatever your problem is, I'm telling you this isn't the answer. Now just stop this thing and open that door."

Carl worked the console without a hint that he even realized Scott was in the cab with him.

O'Dell was just coming down the steps of the company trailer when he cursed under his breath, then broke into a run. The I-beams suddenly flew in behind him, battered the trailer, and crumbled and tore away huge chunks of aluminum and plywood.

O'Dell stumbled to the dirt, rolled over quickly to hear the deafening shriek of the metal, and watched as the trailer was jerked off its blocks and tossed, lengthwise and almost fully vertical, into the air. It came down in a mass of glass, metal, furniture, paper, and fiberglass insulation.

O'Dell stared in disbelief at the wreckage and then jumped to his feet. Carl was known to be one of the best crane operators in the state, and now

O'Dell could see why. He seemed to be *aiming* the beams at select targets from 300 feet above the ground. Incredible, he thought.

As much as he admired his skill, though, O'Dell figured it was time to stop his madness.

He raced full speed toward the tower base; he saw the I-beams as they cut across the sky. The jib swung them toward the southside of the building.

O'Dell saw the load suddenly drop as it smashed into the 30-foot-high network of scaffolding along the west side of the building near the entrance-way. Several sections of the scaffolding gave way and fell into a thunderous crash of metal; steel bars of it flipped and spiraled in all directions.

Finally, O'Dell reached the base as it spun and spotted a yellow-painted power junction box attached against the base itself. The massive tower stopped abruptly and he heard the sound of the I-beams smashing against the building again, this time on the southside of the structure. It sounded like thunder. He watched in horror as the base rose off the concrete footing by about six inches and then dropped.

O'Dell's eyes popped as he noticed the pieces of broken metal all around him on the ground. He stooped to pick up a few and felt his heart stop. They were anchor bolts, each one of them cut.

"Oh, my God," he said. "Carl, what did you do?"

The tower base spun again, this time back toward the north. O'Dell knelt at the base and saw what the metal in his hand confirmed: Almost half the bolts were missing from their mooring holes. The base suddenly rose again. O'Dell jumped up, stepped back, and turned in time to see the I-beams ripping into a group of six scissor-lift, mobile platforms. The weight of the load tumbled and flattened the wheeled machines. The I-beams lifted and flew innocently away from the ruined equipment, leaving the machines in a pile of bent metal and spraying hydraulic fluids.

The base dropped again and bounced on the concrete flooring. The ground vibrated under O'Dell's feet; dust puffed up from underneath the circular rim.

O'Dell's senses reeled. She's going over, he thought. God, the tower's going over.

He knew that even with a majority of the anchor bolts missing, the centralized weight of the tower would keep it in place until they found an alternative means of securing it. But if Carl kept wildly swinging that much load...

O'Dell reached to the side of his belt and pulled out a lock-blade buck knife from its sheath. As the base spun, he stepped toward the power junction box and paced with the tower as it turned. He popped the blade on the knife. If he severed the power cables, the gear motors would shut down and cut off from the tower's main engine on top of the base.

When O'Dell grabbed the cable a jolt of fire seared through his hand, arm, and upper body. His feet rose from the ground. At first, he thought that his spirit lifted, floating his body. Maybe he was already dead. Not even enough time to pray or ask for forgiveness or anything. But then he felt the solid impact of his head and back smacking against the concrete.

Scott saw the cab door lock switch on the console and decided he wouldn't have made a very good diplomat. His patience with Crazy Carl had just ended.

He shot past Carl and reached for the door lock release. He saw the blur of Carl's right arm. Scott gasped as the big man's elbow dug into his midsection with a force that knocked him back through the cab. He stumbled backwards, choked for air, and tripped over his own feet. Scott found himself in a pile on the cab floor.

Carl brought the tower to a stop. Finally, he stood and turned toward Scott, who now saw, for the first time, how huge Carl was. He was imposing, well above six-feet, and about 250. The expression on his face was monstrous; his eyes were vacant.

As Scott felt the pain in his chest, he wondered how anyone had gotten away with teasing this man and calling him Crazy Carl. Based on the damage he'd just inflicted below, Scott started to wonder if he'd get out the cab alive.

Carl suddenly loomed over him and grabbed Scott by the throat. He lifted him off the cab floor with ease. Scott gargled and choked. Carl's hand almost fit completely around his neck; he squeezed and the pressure felt unbelievably inhuman. Scott saw black around the edges of his vision; he was about to pass out.

Scott tightened his fist and threw his hardest right punch; his knuckles slicked across Carl's sweaty left cheek with no effect, but connected solidly with the left side of his nose. Carl was surprised by the blow and tumbled back against the control seat. He lost his death grip on Scott's throat as he brought both his hands up to his own bloody, broken nose.

Scott panted, confident his blow was effective. He spaced his legs and brought up his fists in a fighter's stance. Carl pinched his face into a macabre frown. Scott knew the man meant to kill.

Carl charged him with a low growl in his throat; Scott swung first a right, then a left, but neither punch landed. Carl had ducked low under his swings and rammed his shoulder into Scott's chest. Scott felt like he had been hit by a truck made of flesh and bone. Carl caught him completely off-balance; he jammed his right forearm across the right side of Scott's face like a linebacker block. Pain exploded across Scott's cheekbone. Scott's skull cracked against the back of the cab wall; this time, the blackness edged in like a dark tide on a beach at night.

O'Dell came to and winced at the second and third degree burns on his left hand. When he moved, a burning, stinging pain shot up his left arm, stopping at the elbow. He smelled his own cauterized flesh.

O'Dell turned over on his right side, taking the pressure off his left arm. He looked up just in time to see the tower turn again, heading south. The I-beams dangled and bounced; the base began to rock up and down.

O'Dell glanced up at the counter-weight jib, and saw that Carl wasn't jogging the counter-weight to compensate for any of the load movement. It looked intentional. The tower shook and groaned erratically in protest. It was going to come down any minute.

O'Dell checked his arm and concluded that it was useless. Moving a finger caused shafts of pain. Most of the palm of his hand was burned, the skin flayed and torn. His forearm was blackened and cracked, revealing reddish muscle underneath. His head throbbed with a migraine, locked around his eyes.

Carl must have somehow sabotaged the junction box. The cable he tried to cut was insulated, but the coupling connecting it to the box was metal. O'Dell realized he had grabbed it by mistake. A big mistake.

The I-beams swung into the crane tower of the crawler crane that sat abandoned. O'Dell watched as the tower crumpled like a tinker toy and the cab crumpled like foil. Plexiglas exploded outward. The crawler crane tower bent and twisted to the ground, kicking up dust.

He watched the remaining eighth-floor workers race from inside the building, running past the devastated crawler crane. One of them just barely missed being crushed by its falling tower.

That looks like a good idea, O'Dell thought. Time to go. He figured his best bet was to get off the site. When a tower this size came down, he didn't want to be in the neighborhood.

O'Dell stood painfully on his feet and looked around for his radio. It was in the dirt a few feet away. He grabbed it. "O'Dell to tower! Tower respond!"

Carl ignored the radio, but spied O'Dell far below through the Plexiglas flooring beneath his foot controls. O'Dell was on the move; Carl saw him heading for his pick-up truck, the last vehicle left on the site. Carl smiled and worked the controls, slowly creeping the load toward O'Dell.

O'Dell barked into the radio, and moved with his back to the tower. "Carl, listen to me. You haven't killed anybody yet! But, that tower is comin' down, and you might not care about yo'self, or you might be ticked off at me or whoever, but that man up there with you didn't do you any wrong! Power down, climb down from that cab, and let's talk about this thing!"

As he neared his truck, O'Dell heard the faint sound of approaching sirens. He hoped the authorities would know what to do, because he was at a loss. He felt especially bad for the architect; O'Dell knew he shouldn't have let him up there. That man's life would be on his head.

As he neared the truck, something reflected off the rear window. O'Dell's flight instinct kicked in with a surge of adrenaline. When he turned and looked upward, he saw the I-beams dropping down on him.

O'Dell cursed again and painfully jumped into the truck. He dug for his keys, found them, started the engine, and threw it in reverse. He gave himself whiplash as he gunned the engine, but he saw that he had timed it perfectly. The I-beams pounded the ground right where he had parked.

O'Dell felt the vibration from the I-beams as he spun the wheel and whipped the truck around on the dirt. The I-beams lifted, and as O'Dell floored the accelerator, Carl swung the jib. The beams flew after the truck.

If O'Dell had just a few more seconds, he could have easily out-run the spin of the jib. He had his eye on the job site exit when he felt a sensation he'd never imagined.

Through his rear-view mirror, he saw the I-beams on the front end of the load land and pound the bed of his truck. He slammed into the wheel as he came to a dead stop. The weight of the beams lifted the front of the truck off the ground, the front tires spun and kicked up dust, and both rear tires blew. O'Dell bounced in the cab like a doll.

For a moment, Carl held the load down, the truck caught like a mouse in a claw. The load had landed just left of center on the back of the bed, causing it to tilt upward and lean slightly to the left almost sideways. When he finally lifted the hoist, the truck fell over on its left side, rolled, and landed upside down.

The air bag popped and punched O'Dell in the face.

In the tower cab, Carl gleefully licked his lips as he brought the hoist high. He couldn't wait to see what would happen when he brought the weight down on the gas tank of the truck.

He was just about to hit the load drop switch when he felt punches to the back of his head, then to his right temple, then to the back of his head again. He yelped in pain, and turned in time to receive another shot to his already damaged nose.

Carl cried in agony and jumped to his feet in front of the console. Scott stood there, blood coursing down from his own mouth, and with a lump so large on the back of his skull that it felt like he was growing another head.

He took one more shot at Carl, knocking him back against the console.

A console switch tripped, and the load started to fall...

O'Dell managed to unbuckle himself and tumbled to the roof of his upside-down truck. He saw that the windows were closed, and the door on the driver side was jammed against the ground. He would have to turn around and climb out the passengerside door.

The load was dropping...

O'Dell could barely squeeze his feet past the rear window; he felt himself get caught on something...

Carl slammed Scott against the Plexiglas window to the right side of the console. The glass cracked against his weight. Scott reached up and clawed at his nose; Carl screamed in pain and rage. He lifted Scott, and tossed him to the back of the cab.

O'Dell's bootlace on his left foot was snagged on a rear-window latch. He jerked and pulled on it.

The load dropped...

Scott hit the cab floor, and threw his feet up to kick Carl in the lower ribs as he charged. Carl gasped and waddled from the hit. Scott jumped to his feet, but Carl threw a quick hard-left that caught him off-guard. His jaw muscles nearly tore from the solid blow. His knees gave out and he fell.

O'Dell kicked the window latch with his other foot, broke the latch off its frame, and freed his boot. Something told him there was no time left. He scrambled and got himself completely turned around, then grabbed the door handle. O'Dell unlocked it and pushed on it, but it suddenly flew open. He looked up and saw the anxious faces of two or three of the steel crewmen. He reached for them, but he didn't really have to; they grabbed him and pulled him from the truck.

The men got O'Dell on his feet just as the I-beams came down on the truck, crushing it like tin. The gas tank burst and a wave of fire rolled out from underneath the beams. The concussion sent O'Dell and the men to the ground.

Carl stood over Scott, who languished on the cab floor in a daze. When Carl heard the explosion, he ran to the window. He saw the ball of fire and the crew on the ground and he let out a yelp that pierced Scott's ears. Carl stared at the rising fireball like a madman.

Scott moved to get up, but he was dizzy and nauseous. The tower suddenly turned; the movement rolled Scott over on his back. He needed a few more seconds, and then he would contend with Carl.

O'Dell and the steel crewmen got back on their feet and moved quickly out the site exit. The police, fire, and EMS crews had arrived. O'Dell saw the King 5 news chopper circling the site overhead. Other media vans were parked just outside the police parameter. "Well, I'm glad y'all could make it," he said, exhausted and impatient.

The jib swung at full speed toward the north. Carl aimed the I-beams as they swung around and rammed into the steel frame of the eighth floor. The building rocked and the steel beam that took the impact buckled and bent. Carl brought the jib out and swung it back in, hitting the same support beam; it twisted and collapsed.

Carl let out a war cry as the concrete corner of the eighth floor fell in a cascading mass to the ground.

Scott sat up and shook his head from Carl's surprise hit. He felt the bruises on his knuckles and his head pounded. The side of his cheek was swollen and throbbed with each heartbeat; the blood in his mouth tasted like copper. It felt like one of his ribs might have been cracked or badly bruised.

He heard Carl's animalistic cry and hoped he had just enough energy for one more attack. This time, Scott would have to bring Carl down.

Scott stood to his feet and saw a field of moirés accompanied by a wave of vertigo; his body hit the cab floor again, as his legs gave way and he dropped.

Carl didn't notice Scott, but spun the jib away from the building, then swung it back in, pounding the structure. The warning lights on his console flashed and suddenly the cab filled with the repetitive blare of a warning klaxon. One of the console emergency lights glared and a panel read:

OVERTURNING MOMENT IMMINENT

Carl swung the jib away from the building again; the tower vibrated and groaned with the off-balanced load.

The base lifted several feet off the concrete footing, onto the edge of its rim.

Carl leaned back into the seat with an eerie calm; he took his hands off the controls.

Scott could see the horizon through the front Plexiglas of the cab. It tilted insanely. He grabbed the seatbelt strap and held on. "Oh, my God…"

On the street, just outside the site, the crewmembers and a crowd had gathered. They now scrambled farther from the site of the 400-foot tower crane leaning towards them. The police, EMS, and fire crews all shouted and corralled the crowd even farther back, closer to the Kirkland Piers.

The crane tilted toward the west; it threatened to come down at the edge of the piers, but abruptly… it stopped.

Scott and Carl froze.

The base tilted at a 30 degree angle; the edge of the base rim cut a deep gash in the concrete footing that nestled the edge.

The top of the tower and the smaller service crane leaned in the sky.

Scott's eyes darted about the cab, but he didn't dare move.

Carl shook with a sickening rush.

The warning klaxon stabbed at their ears.

The crowd was enthralled at the site of the crane as it just leaned there…

Carl moved his hand slowly towards the control console. His breathing was loud and ragged.

"Carl, no!" Scott shouted. "Stop! What are you doing?!"

Carl ignored him and wrapped his hand around one of the jib controllers.

"That's it, Carl," said The Voice. *"Don't listen to him. Tilt it back the other way. Destroy the building."*

"Yes," Carl answered, barely audible.

Scott looked around the cab desperately; he searched for something to grab or to climb under, but the cab wasn't meant to take a heavy impact.

He wrapped the seat belt several times around his hands.

Carl slowly jogged the load toward the inner radius and swung the jib away from the north side of the building. At the same time, he moved the counter-weight jib to its outer radius. In effect, he swung the load jib toward the lean to keep the tower from tilting the rest of the way.

O'Dell and the crowd marveled at the site of the lopsided spinning tower.

The jib was about to complete its turn; the I-beam load swung closer to the south side of the building. Carl pushed the load trolley toward the outer radius, and the I-beams whipped around as the jib continued its turn.

The tower base slowly dropped down, back on to the concrete flooring.

The I-beams slammed into the steel structure on the south side of the building and the steel edges tore away huge chunks of concrete.

Scott slid and bumped the passenger chair.

The velocity of the counter-weight tilted the base off the concrete footing again, but this time the tower leaned toward the building instead of away from it. Once again the tower slowly stopped.

Carl's eyes widened at the thought of dropping the tower on the building itself. He turned back to Scott with a wry, bloodied smile.

Scott looked at him with panic in his eyes. He knew what Carl was thinking. "Don't do it! You're gonna kill us!"

Carl reached for the counter-weight trolley control.

"CARL, NO!"

Scott heard a motor and turned; he looked out the cab door Plexiglas and saw the counter-weight jib and the counter-weight trolley moving towards the jib's inner radius.

He reaffirmed his grip on the seat belts and hung on.

The counter-weight trolley moved closer to the inner radius on the jib, and the tower crane leaned toward the building closer… closer…

The tilt movement picked up momentum and the giant crane groaned as it toppled.

Scott yelled and braced for the impact.

Carl gripped the sides of his chair but felt a sadistic thrill as the horizon tilted.

The upper tower of the crane crashed onto the top floor of the building with a tremendous, thunderous force. The upper tower itself buckled and bent with the impact.

Scott was thrown toward the ceiling, but he held on to the belts. His feet scraped the roof and the walls, and then he fell, tumbling off the passenger seat and hitting the floor with his right shoulder.

The Plexiglas windows cracked and shattered. Carl was thrown from the chair against the window to his left. He would have flown through it had it not been for his size.

Instead, Carl wracked the side of his skull against the window frame; he went instantly unconscious and fell back, his big body wedged in a tangled heap between the chair and the console.

The crowd gasped and pointed as dust rose from the tower.

Fire, rescue, and EMS crews raced into the site.

O'Dell prayed for Scott.

The base of the tower tilted on its circular edge; slowly, it pushed away from the building as it scrapped across the concrete flooring.

The upper tower buckled and threatened to slip. If it did, the main tower would fall the rest of the way, twenty-five floors down…

Scott felt a dull throb in his shoulder, but he could still move it, so it wasn't separated. He looked toward the console where he could see Carl's bloodied head leaning over the armrest of the seat.

He looked through the broken Plexiglas of the side window, and saw the building floors and a drop to the ground of just under 300 feet.

Scott stood awkwardly and walked along the left wall and the floor of the tilted cab. When he reached the console, he found the button for the door and tapped it; behind him, the door lock made a mechanical clap. Open.

Scott looked at Carl and thought about dragging him out of there; he realized, though, that he would more than likely have to fight him again. For some reason, Carl had wanted them locked in together, and Scott wasn't going to take any more chances with him.

Scott moved through the cab to the door. He felt the tower shake slightly. When he reached the door, he grabbed the handle… and heard it lock.

As Scott turned, Carl sat up in the chair and stared, not just at him, but through him. Scott turned in panic back to the handle; he pulled and jerked on it, but it was locked. He looked back at Carl.

There was no more Carl Jenkins. Crazy Carl stared with a demented look that made Scott take a step back. Crazy Carl held his finger on the lock release button; he held control over the door dividing life and death.

"You don't really understand, do you?" he said. Blood bubbled on his lips.

Scott was dumbfounded.

107

"They're going to come after you now. There is no place to run. You'll only make it harder. They are Legion. They are many."

Scott stood there, not knowing what to think. Carl tapped the button again and unlocked the door. Scott didn't hesitate; he pulled, and the metal door slid open.

Scott stepped precariously onto the elevator platform, balancing his feet along the rail. The tower crane shook and became more violent. Scott saw the upper tower bending; the main tower seemed to slide away from the building.

There wasn't much time.

He poked his head back inside the cab door. "Carl, listen to me! We've gotta climb up! The tower's gonna fall the rest of the way! Come on, man!" Scott offered his hand without going back into the cab.

Carl smiled and said, "With mercy, God built the walls of Hell. Evil is incarcerated within. God locked the gates and sealed the breach."

Carl turned away.

Scott felt the impact of the words, and concluded that Carl Jenkins intended to die. He had done all he could. He turned and quickly climbed the tower.

The base inched farther away from the building and picked up speed.

The EMS, fire, and rescue crews made it to the twenty-fourth floor where they figured they'd have the best shot at a rescue.

Scott climbed the outer tower, carefully maneuvering along the intricate, metal lattices. The tower creaked, moaned, and shook, causing Scott to repeatedly lose his footing. He saw that he had about another 50 feet to the top floor, but the top of the upper tower was moving too quickly. By the time he got there, it would have gone off the edge.

"HEY, MAN DOWN HERE. DOWN HERE!"

Scott saw the EMS, fire, and rescue crews on the twenty-fourth floor.

One of the rescue crewmen shouted; Scott could barely hear him. "CLIMB THROUGH THE LATTICES! COME UP THROUGH THE TOWER AND WE'LL GRAB YOU!"

Scott comprehended, but a deep fear caught his heart, and he froze.

It was a twenty-foot drop to the other side of the tower; if he landed wrong, he'd keep right on falling. He panicked and dreaded death. He couldn't move.

"BUDDY, WHAT ARE YOU DOING?! COME ON!"

Scott held on and gripped the steel rungs with his life. "God, please… don't let me die…" He closed his eyes and waited, until… a sudden feeling of warmth and comfort; his mind cleared and the fear lifted like smoke. Scott opened his eyes and the fabric of space in front of him broke away and opened.

A sphere, undulating with some unbelievable power, emerged with a light that should have blinded or burned him, but didn't. It was so bright, he could barely see his own hands in front of his face. It was ancient and terrifying, yet somehow familiar…

Just as quickly as it appeared, it was gone.

"JUMP, MAN! JUMP!"

Scott swung his legs inward through the metal lattice and down; he hung there a split second, calculated the fall, and then let go. He landed almost perfectly, but his right foot slipped on the metal and he banged his knee. Scott ignored the searing pain and reached blindly. He slid backwards until his hands found a grip.

The EMS, fire, and rescue crews cheered and screamed as he climbed up, now inside the tower, right along-side the service tower.

The tower base kicked up dust as it dragged and banged along the ground.

Scott got to the bend in the upper tower and climbed into it. The EMS, fire, and rescue crews were right there; several hands and arms reached for him.

The top of the upper tower was a foot from the edge of the top floor…

The EMS, fire, and rescue crews pulled Scott through and a few of them tumbled onto the floor. They jumped up, and everyone raced away from the edge, as the upper tower slipped and dropped with a metal screech.

The upper tower nicked the edge of the twenty-fourth floor and knocked away a massive chunk of the concrete.

The crane tower then fell like a slain monster. The upper tower crashed and smashed into each floor; on the way down it shattered more concrete. Finally, it hit the ground with a thunderous roar, shaking the entire site. A piece of the service tower jib snapped and somersaulted straight up in the air, only to come down again; it disappeared in the huge dust cloud that ensued.

Then everything settled. The thunder of the crane's fall echoed in the distance and subsided.

Scott and the EMS, fire, and rescue crews appeared through the dust to the applause of the crowd. Two EMS paramedics escorted Scott; he limped on his right leg, his pant leg covered with a patch of blood.

O'Dell raced up to Scott, amazed and grateful that the man was alive. He extended his good hand and Scott took it. "Hey, man! Hey! Hey! You all right?! You okay?!"

Scott nodded. "Yeah. Banged up a little bit. I think I broke my knee."

"It's not broken," one paramedic assured. "But we're going to have to get it x-rayed."

They reached the ambulance, and Scott was placed on a gurney. One paramedic disappeared through the back of the ambulance while the other worked on Scott's knee.

O'Dell hovered over him. "I'm sorry, man. I shoulda never let you go up there with Carl working six cans short of a twelve-pack."

"I could use one of those right now."

"What, a beer?"

"No. A twelve-pack."

"Yeah…"

Scott and O'Dell both realized how close they'd come to dying; there was a pause between them.

"You got a phone on you?" Scott asked.

"Naw, bud. I just got my radio."

Scott looked around. "Does anybody have a phone? Can I use somebody's phone?"

The EMS paramedic reached in his pocket, pulled out a phone and handed it to Scott.

"Who you callin', man?" O'Dell asked.

"Denise. My girlfriend."

"I remember those days. I'd better go, then."

"Why are you still here, anyway? Why aren't you at the hospital? I mean… that's a bad burn."

O'Dell shrugged. "I just figured that I'd… I dunno. I guess I just wanted to see how everything would end up."

Scott nodded. "Thanks."

O'Dell turned and walked a few feet when Scott called him again. "Hey."

"Yeah, bud."

"Thanks for letting me up there."

O'Dell smiled. "How was that view?"

"It was good. It was… it was good. But, wait a second. Don't you know? Haven't you been up before?"

"Who, me? Whatta you, crazy? You could never get me up in that thing. I hate heights." He headed to the other ambulance, cradling his bandaged arm.

Scott smiled.

He dialed home and got the answering machine. He decided not to leave a message and disconnected; he'd call her from the hospital. So much for a romantic evening at home. At first, he wondered why she wasn't there, but he checked his watch and it was only four-fifty. She was on her way home now.

Scott settled back on the gurney and closed his eyes. The events of the day flashed in his mind in stunning color. He could hardly believe he was alive. He was already trying to forget everything he had seen, but what about that light? Had that been real?

He was haunted by the words Carl spoke; the warning he gave. What did he mean? They were legion? Who? Somehow, he knew what Carl was trying to tell him.

For the first time in his life, Scott Macklin heard a voice inside his mind that wasn't his own.

"You'll have your answers soon enough, Scott Macklin," said The Voice.

Scott was startled. He opened his eyes and shot straight up on the gurney. The paramedic gave him a quizzical look.

"Settle down. Just relax, you'll be okay," he said.

Scott heard it again, but could scarcely comprehend it.

"Soon enough…"

CHAPTER 5

The Greyhound pulled into a rest stop off Interstate 90, near Exit 195, some 40 miles east of a town called Moses Lake, in the middle of Washington State.

The driver parked the bus and opened the front door.

A green duffel bag hit the asphalt; down the steps came a homeless man after the bag. He picked it up, turned, and faced the driver.

The homeless man had a King James Bible in his hand.

The driver glared at him. "Now, this rest stop's got bathrooms. Go in there and get yourself cleaned up. Five minutes," he said, holding up an open hand. "This bus is leaving for Seattle in five minutes."

The homeless man nodded, picked up his duffel, and walked toward the rest stop.

The driver yelled back at the passengers, waving his hand across his nose.

"Open the windows, everybody." Then he peered back at the homeless man. "Maybe that'll get rid of the smell."

The homeless man hadn't eaten in two days, and he couldn't decide what would make a better meal: a Snickers or a Milky Way. He opted for a bag of Doritos.

He dug in his pockets and found the 65 cents, dropped the coins into the vending machine, and got his dinner. The homeless man didn't realize how hungry he was until he tore open the bag, and finished the chips before ever reaching the men's room.

The bathroom was small and unkempt, but hospitable enough for his purposes. He dropped his duffel bag. There was a name stamped on the side of it, etched in a faded, almost unreadable military stencil: Biggsby, Mitchell PFC 1st Class.

He placed the Bible on the edge of the sink, carefully. Biggsby stripped off his field jacket and t-shirt, turning on the hot water to full blast. A silver crucifix hung on a chain around his neck.

Over the years, Biggsby had taken more sink baths than he could count; he'd get relatively clean, but his clothes would still smell. Maybe it would be enough to keep the passengers from tossing him off the bus before they reached Seattle.

He splashed the water on his face, finding his own stare in the mirror, and combed his fingers through a haggard, predominately gray beard. The cracks and lines on his 56 year-old face looked like ancient, dried-up, riverbed tributaries. Biggsby ran his wet fingers through a mane of shoulder-length hair, clotted with street dirt. After washing under his arms and cleaning his nails and hands with a yellow liquid soap, he punched on an air dryer, turned the air funnel upward, and stood over it.

After a moment, Biggsby threw his shirt on, and turned back to the mirror. He looked into eyes that had seen death as vivid as a sunset; he had seen the murderous impulses of men, of his soldier brothers gone mad in the cloying heat of the jungle. His eyes had spilled tears on the dead faces of Asian children and fallen friends. He picked up the Bible and turned to Revelation 6:8. He spoke it aloud. "And I looked, and behold a pale horse: and his name that sat on him was... was..." Biggsby choked, but managed the last word. "Death..."

Biggsby was well familiar with the name of the rider.

He slammed the lid down on the toilet and sat, grabbing for the duffel. Biggsby reached inside and pulled out a thick Army field portfolio, its nylon edges frayed. He ripped back the Velcro cover flap and revealed several pages of military and government documents. Most of them were highly classified.

Someone started to walk in, and Biggsby jumped to his feet, throwing his body against the door.

"Hey, what are you doing, man?" came a startled voice from the other side of the door.

"Occupied," Biggsby said, with a heavy voice.

"Occupied? What are you talkin' about? Look, man I need to—"

"I said occupied!" Biggsby repeated, emphatically banging the door with his fist.

After a moment, he was gone. Biggsby breathed a raspy sigh and quickly moved back to the duffel, concealing the portfolio.

He decided he'd better get back to the bus. This wasn't a good place to inventory his information, his evidence against *them*, the ones who were watching and listening.

The Shadows of Men.

Biggsby threw on his field jacket, pocketed the Bible and grabbed the duffel. As he did, a pile of photographs, bound by an elastic band, fell to the floor. Some of the pictures unwound and spilled. He reached down to gather them, taking a moment to shuffle through the stack.

Biggsby stared in disbelief at the black-and-white images. The first was an image of him and his best friend, a young Thomas Macklin. They laughed, as if caught in a good joke, surrounded by piles of green sandbags. He remembered the day the photo was taken; it was hot that day, but then again, it was always hot. They had spent most of it drenched in seasonal, torrential rains. The underground bunkers were flooded; the day and most of the evening spent filling bags to stave off the rain. Their eyes were tired, but the smiles reflected the souls of two good friends in a very bad time. They were young and skinny. Boys, really.

Biggsby flipped through a few more and found a shot of himself, his wife Karen, Thomas and Kathleen. They were in a bar in Waikiki, holding up beer and exotic cocktails, cheering the camera. The faded ink around the borders of the photo read: "Aloha from Waikiki! Mitch, Thomas, Kathy and Karen! 1972."

Biggsby's gaze locked on the beautiful eyes of his wife and his love for her was a warm, surging flood within him. He had to quickly sift past the picture, had to keep his wits.

Finally, an image of Thomas and his son Scott on Diamond Head that same year. The boy's father hoisted him into the air on his shoulders, and the two of them were laughing. Kathleen must have taken this one, because Biggsby couldn't remember how he'd gotten it. He did remember a promise he had made to his friend, reaffirming the nature of his current mission. The boy's eyes looked like Kathy's, but his face was his father's.

"Scott," he said softly, aloud. He had to find him. He had promised.

Biggsby wasn't used to The Voice. It had become almost like a condition of combat, like something you came to expect in the middle of a war.

Still, when he heard it, it startled him. It had been a few days since they had spoken to him.

"He's dead. We've already killed him," it sneered.

Biggsby calmly repacked the photos. "Liar," he answered.

"How true. But, he'll be dead before you can find him. We've already begun our work on him. We almost had him, but we like to bide our time. It's more interesting for us that way."

" 'Almost' had him? Almost only counts in two things: horseshoes and dancin'. You mean he escaped y'all," he said, a hint of his southwest Texas accent slipping through.

"No one escapes. Did Thomas escape? Did Karen escape? Will you escape?"

"Well, maybe I ain't gonna live, but you won't get Scott. I promise. I'll stop you."

Biggsby's emotions roiled, but he held them in check. He pulled down the front of his shirt so hard that he almost tore the neckline. His silver crucifix shone from underneath his beard. "By the way, just in case y'all forgot, He did escape," he said.

There was no response. It was gone.

Biggsby adjusted the bag on his shoulder and headed for the door. He opened it and then paused, turning his eyes to the ceiling. "Thank you, Lord," he said. "Thank you for helpin' me, Jesus. Let me live long enough to find him. Just long enough..."

Then he went out the door.

As he entered the parking lot, he dropped the bag in frustration. The bus was gone. In light of all that had happened to him, this was really only a minor inconvenience. He shouldered his duffel and moved towards I-90, heading west.

As Biggsby walked, he thought back to a time when he, his best friend and their wives walked along a beach, at the edge of an impossibly blue sea. It was a paradise he knew he wouldn't see again until the end of his life.

CHAPTER 6

The voices had been especially bad on the day Jeanna Dowlin died.

She walked through the door of the DME Thermoplastics Company, found her timecard, and punched it in the clock. It was six forty-four in the morning; she had about 15 minutes until first shift, so she headed for the break-room.

Jeanna moved past the tables and vending machines to the lockers. Third shift was ending, and workers were filing out of the room. She found an empty locker, where she put her purse, and hung her windbreaker on a hanger.

She saw one of the tables covered with newspaper, as usual. Someone would drop the *Dayton Daily News* there in the morning; by afternoon, it was always strewn across the room.

A headline jumped off the front page: "CHICAGO RAMPAGE: MAN KILLS 8, INJURES 1, THEN COMMITS SUICIDE." She realized she had already read it; the paper was a couple of days old.

Jeanna remembered thinking that death by a gun wouldn't be how she'd do it. It'd be too painful, she thought, and besides, what if you didn't die? What if somehow you survived? She couldn't imagine lying there suffering. And, how could this man hurt other people like that? What had they done to him to deserve what he did to them? No, she'd come up with something better.

She walked from the break room and headed to the manager's desk to get her press assignment. The humid, late August air was thick in the shop.

117

She moved down the first aisle, past the rows of plastic injection mold machines.

Jeanna watched the other shift workers come in, but none said a word to her.

She thought about how her life used to be before they told her she was crazy; back when she was 23 and beautiful. A shroud, a fog of sadness and austerity, had overwhelmed her then. Jeanna was far from home when it first happened, when her thoughts had become rushing, uncontrollable, slippery electricity.

Somehow, her mental and visual senses had become more acute; in social and everyday interaction with people, Jeanna was able to detect a behavioral dynamic among them that had distinct and repetitive characteristics. She became more and more introverted and paranoid. And, the voices. Sometimes she could barely squeeze in her own thoughts because of them. They clouded her mind, polluted her dreams, and perpetuated her nightmares.

The nightmares.

Once she had dreamed that a demon spoke to her. It was a strange, dark vision: Lying in bed, her body had felt so heavy with sleep, but her eyes were open and she could see her shadowy bedroom.

Her heart raced as she felt the presence of something, creeping and evil, at a great distance, from the very edge of the universe, but coming closer. A faint sound, a growl, the rushing wind, growing closer and louder and closer still, bringing evil with it.

Her chest heaved and Jeanna panicked, but she couldn't move. The growling, howling wind was louder and louder. The darkness had taken on a shape and a form; for an instant she'd seen it, before it cloaked and jostled her body in the bed. It had hands—cold, strong hands and arms that pinned her to the mattress. Jeanna screamed, but no sound came from her throat.

It held her there as she cried and whimpered like a child.

Then came the pig.

A pig, a filthy, foul animal, with tusks and a protruding, glistening snout lying next to her on the bed. Her eyes had widened with shock, and the pig mocked her expression with a grunt.

Then a woman entered the room. She had dark hair flowing in wisps on her shoulders, covering her face. The woman wore a white robe, revealing her pallid, bare arms. She moved to the bedside, knelt and looked up, displaying a beautiful face with sullen, sorrowful eyes. Jeanna knew the woman was herself.

Jeanna had leaned over and vomited on the floor.

The woman vanished and The Voice broke into the black, like a stone shattering the surface of some placid water.

"You will do exactly as I say," it ordered.

Jeanna wrenched in the bed, but couldn't move a frozen limb. Somehow, she knew what it was that had spoken to her; somehow, she knew that this thing, born in darkness, had always been after her. Now, it had finally, hungrily, gripped her.

"Noooo!" she cried. "Noooo! God, help me!"

"You will do exactly as I say!" The Voice coarsely bellowed.

The hands released her, and The Dark Thing and The Pig were gone.

Jeanna had screamed so loudly the neighbors called the police.

When the cops got there, one of the neighbors told them to take her in and lock her up before she woke up the whole trailer park. It wasn't the first time she disturbed them late in the night. That woman was *crazy,* she remembered them saying.

Crazy. Just like the doctors said.

Jeanna had been a sophomore at Ohio State University when it all started, but as the illness progressed, school became too much to bear. She'd found herself back in Dayton, Ohio, the kind of middle-sized town you'd normally move away from.

It had been 19 years since then. Now, after two divorces, four children who lived out of state, both parents deceased, and a brother who never visited, Jeanna found herself, once again, free for the evening. And vulnerable.

She was among the first to reach the manager's desk; the others straggled in by six fifty-nine. The Manager stood at his desk, and called off names and press numbers from a sheet on a clipboard.

Jeanna was assigned to Press 11, one the oldest units in the plant. You would think that a company that supplies to Delphi Automotive and General Motors could come up with a better machine.

The mold in Press 11 was set up to produce plastic A/C and heating vent grills for the car dashboard. Jeanna's quota was for over 8,000 during the 12 hour shift. She knew she wouldn't make quota with defective number 11.

The machine was running on its first cycle. A greasy, empty cardboard box under the mold caught the parts as they ejected. Before she sat down, Jeanna began to set up a pile of boxes for her quota.

The machine hummed and hissed as the heated melted resin injected into two closed, metal press molds. There was a 15 second delay for the plastic to cool and then the presses opened, dropping the first set of vents into the catch-box.

Jeanna moved to a chair in front of the machine and sat down as the cycle started again. In the back of her mind, she wondered how soon it would be before she heard from *them*.

It usually didn't take very long.

"So, Jeanna. Have you decided what you want to do tonight? Have you decided how?"

———◆———

It was just over three hours into the shift when the manager came by to do a quality assurance check on her parts; he found Jeanna sitting in front of the press, with her face in her hands, quietly crying.

The box under the mold was overflowing with the plastic vents; they spilled all over the floor. "Jeanna?" he asked. When she didn't respond, he let out a frustrated sigh and pulled the full box out from under the machine, exchanging it for an empty one. The manager took a second to check the gauges of the machine, then called to a passing worker. "Hey, Jeff," he said. "Could you get Mike to bring another load of material for the hopper?"

Jeff nodded and walked off, but not before throwing Jeanna a critical look.

The manager turned to her; the embroidered tag on his shirt read: CLIFF.

"Jeanna?"

Cliff watched her shoulders shake softly with sobs, but she didn't turn. He put his hand on her back and she jumped to her feet, knocking over the chair.

"Easy, easy," Cliff said. "It's all right, take it easy. It's just me."

Jeanna looked at him incredulously. "I don't wanna die. I don't wanna die."

Cliff gave her a look of assurance from behind the thick lenses of his glasses, but he felt confused. "Nobody wants you to die, Jeanna."

"They're gonna kill me. They keep talkin' to me. They keep talkin' and talkin'."

"Who? Is somebody in the shop bothering you again?"

Jeanna's face took on a childish frown and her eyes leered around the shop. "They hate me. They hate me because I got sick. Because I have to take medicine."

Cliff suddenly felt protective of her. "Who's bothering you? Tell me who it is and I'll handle it. Now, I told them to leave you alone about that stuff. You're one of my best workers, and I don't want nobody messin' with you."

Jeanna looked shamefully at her hands, wrenching them together. Fresh tears came. "It ain't nobody here," she said. "It ain't nobody in the shop." She reached up, absently pulling at her blue headscarf; it came off and a lock of dark hair, tinged with streaks of gray, fell alongside her face. The hair accentuated a latent youthfulness in her 42 year-old features. "It's in my head again, Cliff, and I can't take it anymore. I really just can't take it. I want them to stop talkin' to me."

Cliff's voice became almost patronizing. "It's in your head?"

She nodded.

"Jeanna, do you think you can finish your shift?"

"No," she said meekly.

"You want us to call your doctor?"

She looked forlornly around the shop. It would be the last time she would see it. "No. I'll call him when I get home."

"All right, then. You go home and rest up. I'll get your quota."

She nodded. "Thank you, Cliff. Thank you."

"No, Jeanna. I told you before. Don't use pills. Haldol and Tegretal, your medicines, may not give us the results we want. You always want to be

sure in these things; otherwise, you defeat the whole purpose. See if you can come up with something better. We know you can do it."

Jeanna climbed off the RTA on the corner of North Dixie and Siebenthaler, just north of downtown Dayton, near her trailer park. The only real businesses nearby were the poor man's used car lots and the bars.

She walked to the United Dairy Farmers convenience store a half block from the bus stop. There was one thing she'd need for tonight's celebration, the night when she'd finally free herself.

Jeanna moved into the store, heading to the beverage coolers. She found a bottle of Mad Dog 20/20, the grape kind. She wasn't supposed to drink and take her medicine at the same time, but since she was leaving tonight anyway, why would it matter?

When she got to the counter, the teenage store clerk snatched the bottle and bagged it. Jeanna smiled at her, but the girl looked at her indifferently.

"Anything else?" the girl asked.

Jeanna glanced around the counter. There were banners, displays, and ads for everything from Ohio Lotto tickets to dip tobacco and ice cream. She saw a rack display of ball caps. One of them had a big, white stylized number six on the front. Jeanna's eyes lit up.

"Martin," she said confidently.

"Huh?" the store clerk said.

Jeanna pointed over the counter. "Martin. That number six cap."

"Oh."

The store clerk climbed on a short stool to reach the cap. She tossed it on the counter, punching the buttons on the register.

Jeanna took the hat, bent the bill, adjusted the head size, and put it on. Wisps of her hair streamed from underneath, framing her beaming face. She hadn't smiled in months. "My ex-husband use to love him," she said. "Martin had 24 career wins in the NASCAR Busch Series. I used to not like stock car racin' but I guess I kinda got addicted because of my husband."

The clerk looked at her impatiently. "You gonna pay?"

Jeanna was embarrassed but dug into her purse and pulled out some cash. The clerk shook her head as Jeanna gave her a twenty. As the clerk made change, Jeanna thought back about her husband and the children; she thought about how happy they were, even though she was sick. He had been patient and loving with her for a while, before things went bad. But, even though they were gone, sometimes, at odd moments, she thought of him and the tears warmed the corners of her eyes.

He would've liked the hat.

———◦◦◦———

Jeanna's trailer park was just off Dixie, a few blocks south, down from the UDF. She unlocked the front door of her trailer and went in. There was one more thing she needed.

"Is that really necessary?" The Voice suddenly spoke, booming like a cannon in over her thoughts.

Jeanna screamed, dropping her purse and the bag of Mad Dog. She covered her mouth and cried. After a minute, she composed herself from the initial shock.

"Y-y-y- yes. It's just a picture. I'd like to have it, p-p-please."

There was a long pause as Jeanna waited in the dark for their answer; she hadn't even a chance to turn on the light.

"Have you decided what you are going to do? And, remember, not the pills."

"I know. I just need my picture."

"We've just learned your thoughts. I like your idea, Jeanna. That's very impressive. Not so original, mind you; many have done it that way, but a good statement. It seems purposeful, with a strong since of completion and finality. Good. Very Good.

"Your choice of location seems a good distance from here. How do you plan to get there?"

"I'll walk," she answered weakly.

"Then you had better get moving."

Jeanna felt like a child talking to a cruel parent. "Can I get my picture?"

"Yes, you may."

———◆•◆•◆———

It took Jeanna just over an hour to walk north on Dixie, east on Needmore, across the Interstate 75 overpass, then down to the railroad tracks across from the Cargil corn processing plant.

She moved in the moonlit evening toward the tracks on the edge of a treeline. The Cargil plant security lights beamed behind her, casting an orange glow across the grassy field. This part of town always smelled like chicken, because of the plant.

Jeanna felt her feet shuffle across the gravel as she reached the tracks. She walked over them until she stood centered between the south and northbound rails.

Jeanna knelt, feeling the gravel dig into her knees. She took the picture from her purse and stared at it.

It was a shot of her husband and children, two years ago. The kids all came home to visit, right before everything went bad. It was the last time they were all together, smiling in front of the ticket booth at Fifth Third Field. It was the opening season at the new stadium for the Dayton Dragons baseball team. The Dragons won that day.

Jeanna felt the tears shake her body with an immeasurable despair. She moaned and turned her gaze to the sky which was a deep black; the stars were gone, wiped away by the glare of Cargil's security lights.

Jeanna cried out to something she wasn't sure she could believe in.

"Lord, please watch over my babies. Please watch over them. Forgive me."

The train was moving in from the south; at first, the engine light appeared no bigger than the beam of a flashlight.

"Lie down, Jeanna."

Jeanna turned and saw the light growing and bearing down on her. She heard the horn and began to shake with fear and hesitancy.

"Lie down, Jeanna. Now."

She was no longer in control as she prostrated herself on the tracks; the steel was hard and frigid through her clothes.

Jeanna panicked and cried out, every nerve sparking and surging with the flight instinct. Suddenly, she wanted to live more than anything. At that moment, no feeling she ever experienced, not even love, could equal this sudden, powerful, forceful need to just simply live.

She started to rise off the tracks when she felt the cold hands. They were invisible underneath her clothes, like mechanical talons, a vice on her arms and shoulders. She couldn't move.

Jeanna screamed, but this time it was as if the wind pulled it from her throat. She made no noise.

The train was a few feet away when the operator saw her and threw on the brakes; it didn't stop until the engine was 50 feet past the place on the tracks where Jeanna Dowlin died.

And, somewhere, in a dark place, the spirit of Jeanna Dowlin was held by cold hands, and her scream went on forever.

———————

Scott channel surfed from his bed, in a University of Washington Hospital recovery room. The morphine numbed the pain in his knee from the surgery to repair a torn ACL. The doctor told him that he wouldn't run again for four months; Scott would have almost rather fallen off the tower crane than be cooped up for weeks.

Denise was on her way to visit and Scott couldn't wait to see her. He needed a spark of life in his day, and Denise was always good for putting a smile on his face.

He flashed through channel after channel, being very careful not to land on the local news. If he saw another report of the tower crane accident, he'd bounce the remote off the screen. After a little more curious searching, Scott gave up finding anything to watch and turned off the television.

He glanced over at a picture of Denise by his bedside. She smiled at him in a black-and-white, professional portrait. Scott reached past the strings attached to the get-well balloons tied to his bed, and picked up the frame. Staring at her image, he knew for certain that he wanted her for the rest of his life. Once he fully recovered, Scott reasoned, he would begin planning their engagement. There was something holding him back, though, and he couldn't quite figure out what it was. Since his father's death, something was slowly moving against his life, like the first symptoms of some grave illness.

Scott looked deeply into the portrait and sensed a rising, forboding tide, threatening to overtake him. What was it?

The Voice broke rudely into his mind, *"I told you that, all your questions would be answered. You just don't have enough patience, do you?"*

The nurse at her station wondered why the pulse reading on Scott Macklin's heart monitor suddenly shot up, and she raced into his room.

CHAPTER 7

The souvenir stands in Washington, D.C., were all the same, and so annoying to Prichard. He hated jockeying through the crowds who stood in babbling circles, deciding which lousy, overpriced t-shirt or postcard to buy.

This particular stand on Constitution Avenue, just outside of West Potomac Park, happened to sell coffee and newspapers. Prichard just wanted a copy of the *Post* and a cup to wake him up, but first he'd have to wade through a group of tourists from Africa, who were speaking in a quick dialect unfamiliar to him.

Finally, the man behind the stand leaned over the counter, pressing his face at Prichard. He was a black man who must've been in his fifties, but he had a curiously youthful face and demeanor. Prichard noticed the black MIA/POW t-shirt he wore, and how he had decorated the booth with Vietnam pins, medals, and Vietnam vet newsletters.

The early morning sun sparkled off the modest silver cross the man wore around his neck. His name was James Dupree; it had been a few years since Prichard stopped at his stand. He wondered if Dupree would even remember him after such a long time, but Prichard wasn't one for emotional reunions.

Dupree recognized him, though, and let a brief smile flash across his face. "Wha' cha doin' up here? I thought you was in Colombia," he said.

"Yesterday, I was in Colombia," Prichard answered. "Got something else going on now."

Dupree cocked an eyebrow. "Ohhh. Anythin' you'd like to share?"

Prichard smiled. "Nope. Too soon. I'm not 100 percent on exactly what I'm doin' on this one yet, Jim."

Dupree leaned back from the counter folding his arms, giving Prichard a mocking, distrustful look. "You wouldn't be tryin' to keep ol' Dupree in the dark now, Prichard?"

"No, no… Well, actually… I was hopin' that you'd know somethin'."

Dupree shrugged his shoulders and averted his eyes from Prichard, glancing around Constitution. The monument tour buses pulled up in herds. Soon he'd have more business than he could handle. "The only thing I know is how ta sell you one a these here *I Love D.C.* or Georgetown sweatshirts and a cup of coffee."

"Well, keep the souvenirs. But gimme a cup, black, and a copy of the *Post.*"

Dupree pulled an early edition of the *Washington Post* from under a brick paperweight and tossed it on the counter. Prichard grabbed it, but before he could open the first page, he had a steaming Styrofoam cup in front of him.

He reached for his wallet, but Dupree held up a hand. "Keep it. From the looks of things, you probably gonna need it."

Prichard nodded, took his coffee, and moved off.

"Hey, Prichard," Dupree called.

Prichard turned back to the stand as the tourists swarmed around. "Yeah?"

Dupree had a look of almost fatherly caution, but he seemed to enjoy his role in the game. "Check the real estate section. You might make a good deal on a beach house."

Prichard watched as the crowds moved in on Dupree's booth, and the vet went right to work as if he hadn't uttered a word.

He opened the *Post,* turning to the travel and real estate sections. His eye found what he'd been looking for. The ad read: SMITH ISLAND. WHERE THE FOXES SWIM. SECLUDED BEACH HOUSE FIT FOR A KING OR BARON. SERIOUS INQUIRIES ONLY.

There was no address or number, but Prichard had an idea the place wouldn't be too hard to find once they got to Smith Island.

"Baron," he said aloud, reflectively.

Prichard folded the paper, looking west down Constitution. He sipped his coffee and watched the morning sun gloss off the Potomac River, through the trees of the park. A cab cut the corner off Twenty-third Street, coming right for him. He hailed it.

———————•◆•———————

Father Los Cruzado knelt and prayed at the foot of the altar in the Saint Matthew Cathedral off North Rhode Island Avenue.

His mind and body were tired from the flight, but long ago he had learned how to speak to God under duress. His pushed all thoughts from his mind, clearing it, and prayed with an earnestness that came from deep within. The world was quiet as the Lord received his words.

He rose to his feet, staring up at the wall statue of the Crucified Christ. Los Cruzado wished that He would give him some immediate answer as to why he was here, so far from his home and village. The last time he was in America was as a small boy. He had family, relatives in southern Texas, but he knew nothing about them.

America was a foreign and alien place; Washington, to Los Cruzado, was the center of all the capitalist pollution in the world. But, this church was indeed beautiful with its buttresses and vaulted ceilings. Prichard had looked at him with an irritated eye when Los Cruzado asked to wait for him in a place of God, rather than at the hotel, but he helped him find this cathedral anyway.

When he left this morning, Prichard stated he was going to "gather information." Los Cruzado wondered if Prichard knew any more about where they were going, or what they were doing, than he himself did. In all his years of dealing with the political intrigues within his own country, Los Cruzado had learned that men often worked in these arenas blindly, under veils of confusion and secrecy.

Los Cruzado resigned his heart to the comfort of the Lord. God would reveal to him what He needed to reveal when the time came. It would probably be sooner than he imagined.

"So, what'd He tell you?"

Los Cruzado was startled and jumped to his feet, turning to find Prichard standing behind him.

129

"It would be awfully good of Him if He'd answer for once," Prichard finished, caustically. He looked up at the Crucified Christ with about the same amount of indifference he'd feel for a discarded shell casing.

Los Cruzado frowned at him, moving toward Prichard with a cautious look on his face. "Where is your sense of respect, Prichard? *Probar una peqeuno respecto.* This is God's house."

Prichard's eyes fixed on the Crucified Christ. Los Cruzado could detect the edges of some conflict within him, but the surface was all he could read.

Los Cruzado moved closer to him. "Did you find your *informacion?* Where are we going?"

Prichard stared first at the Christ, then at Los Cruzado. "The beach," he said, walking down the aisle toward the exit. Los Cruzado followed after him, but not before crossing himself at the altar.

It took them two hours in a rental car to reach the town of Crisfield, Maryland, on the shores of the Chesapeake Bay. It was just after twelve noon; they waited nearly an hour for the ferry to Smith Island.

There was a trail store in Crisfield, and Prichard bought provisions. By the time he was done, they had two back packs, sleeping bags, Swiss Army knives, a cooking kit, a compass, hiking boots, blankets, a Coleman lamp, flashlights, extra flannel shirts, trail mix, dried beef, and water.

When Los Cruzado asked him why they were buying so much, Prichard said, "You never know where we might end up."

The three-thrity ferry pulled into the County Port of Tylerton, Smith Island. The occupied southern half of the island held three ports: Tylerton, Rhodes Point, and Ewell.

Prichard did some fast-talking, and managed to commission a boat to take them to the northern part of the island, which was mostly an uninhabited wildlife reserve.

The craft was a small fishing vessel, which looked like it had seen many years at sea. Los Cruzado couldn't tell which was more weathered, the boat or the captain, a man who claimed to be a direct descendant of Captain John

Smith. Smith had founded and aptly named the island after himself almost 400 years ago.

The Maggie Brown made its way north across a navigation channel called the Big Thorofare, cutting the islands into their northern and southern halves. Prichard moved into the vessel wheelhouse. The captain, McLean Smith, turned and pierced a wrinkled eye at Prichard.

"Are there any foxes on the northern part of the island?" Prichard asked.

"What's that?"

"Foxes on the island. Foxes that swim?"

"Uh... on the beaches. The island is mostly marshes, but the foxes, uh... live underground in burrows on the beaches. Sometimes they swim when the tides come in."

Prichard nodded, ducking his head, thinking. After a moment, he asked, "Where is the most secluded part of the island?"

"Uh... the northwest tip."

"Take us there."

The Maggie Brown rounded the northern half of Smith Island, which was lined with beaches. The sunset cast a yellow glow across the Chesapeake. The cooling, early September air carried a flock of black ducks south across the island.

The Maggie Brown pulled up to a nondescript pier, which lead to a quiet duneless beach.

Los Cruzado and Prichard climbed down from the pier, hefting the backpacks on their shoulders. They watched for a moment as the Maggie Brown pulled away from its dock. Captain Smith told them to be there the next day for a return trip, so it looked like they'd spend the night under the stars if they couldn't find Baron.

Fortunately for them, finding him was going to be the easy part.

Prichard gestured down the beach. "Now how can you miss that?" he muttered, ruefully. "False advertising. Doesn't look so secluded to me."

The house was of a contemporary design, made of two octagonal-shaped sections with high bay windows, painted to perfectly match the sand

and marshes. Baron's home was easily the most impressive structure on the island.

As they moved east across the beach, they saw a man far down the shore. They grew closer and saw him toss a stick into the bay. The man's dog, a tan Labrador, chased after the stick, splashing in the cold water. The dog retrieved the stick, swam back to shore, and raced to the man, who clapped and vigorously rubbed him on the head.

The man looked like a graying old professor. He ignored Los Cruzado and Prichard, who were close enough to hear him congratulating the dog.

"Good boy, that's a good dog. Good dog."

Prichard spoke up with a jilted tone.

"Baron?"

Baron turned to see that he had guests on the beach, then back to toss the stick into the bay. The Lab shot off after it. "Well. It looks like you've made it. I take it that the trip was pleasant?"

Prichard glared at him.

"'Pleasant' isn't the word I'd use, Baron. I was doin' just fine in Colombia. What's this all about, anyway? You know they got this new thing, maybe you've heard of it? It's called e-mail! Why yank us all the way up here?"

Baron nodded, feeling genuinely apologetic.

The lab returned with the wet stick and Baron absently petted the animal. "I regret the intrusive, untimely, inconvenient manner in which you were summoned. Come, then, up to the house. We have much to talk about." He gazed over the bay, watching the sunset. "Yes, many, many things to discuss," he concluded, heading up a set of wooden steps leading to his home.

Arthur Calvin Baron led Prichard and Los Cruzado across the deck area of his beach house into a mini-theatre. The room was impeccably crafted and decorated with walls made from the richest woods, track lighting, and comfortable furniture, giving it a combination boardroom-lounge look. On the far wall was a large HDTV plasma screen that hung there like a blank canvas. The screen was of the latest technology, only a few inches thick. "Gentleman, feel free to place your things there on the floor. Sit down and relax," Baron said, congenially. "Would you like something to eat or drink?"

Prichard and Los Cruzado dropped their backpacks and sat. "Let's just get on with it, Baron," Prichard quipped. "What are we here for?"

Baron dropped onto a couch facing the plasma screen. The three men sat there silently as Baron savored the moment, relishing his control over the situation, but then feeling guilty for it.

He remembered his pledge to the Lord.

Baron began his career as a staff member on Henry Kissenger's National Security Council at the age of 28, back in 1957, quickly becoming a major power broker in Washington.

He was overwhelmingly successful in the development of news leaks to the American media concerning the Gulf of Tonkin Incident, which prompted U.S. involvement in the Vietnam War.

Baron became the consummate propagandist, orchestrating U.S. policies during every major foreign venture, from Cuba to Honduras, Nicaragua, Colombia, and Chile.

Because of his love for his country and commitment to honor and duty, he gained a post on the Council of Foreign Relations in 1976. He became a member of the Trilateral Commission in 1988, attaining a position of prominence and power, along with the elite few who controlled and manipulated the events of the world.

Then, in 1992, he simply disappeared, retreating to a life of seclusion and fear.

Baron told his friends in Washington and the media that it was simply time for him to retire. When one reporter asked him why, he said, "I've found God."

Baron joked to the reporter about disappearing like Enoch in the Old Testament, but the reporter didn't have a clue what he was talking about.

Since then, he lived with the promise of the Lord's return, and the dread of the forces of darkness threatening to devour him.

On this day, he planned to reveal everything he knew to these two men and then soon, God willing, to the rest of the unknowing world.

"Henry said something profound once at a party he was hosting for some foreign dignitaries," Baron said, reflectively. "This meeting reminds me of it. Let me see if I can remember... I think it was... Oh, yes, very clever. Something like, 'You may take the most gallant sailor, the most intrepid airman, the most audacious soldier, put them at a table together and what do you get? The sum of their fears.'"

Los Cruzado wrinkled his face with confusion. "*Que?* Who is Henry, eh?"

"Kissenger," Prichard answered. "He's talking about Henry Kissenger."

"Yes," said Baron. "A very intelligent and influential statesman, as you know, but lacking the whole truth. Henry never really understood what was behind the plight of mankind, though he had so much power over so many. In the eyes of men like him, power should only be reserved for the super intellectual, or those privileged to gain access to the so-called secret knowledge that unlocks the doors to the wellsprings of power. The Illuminated Ones.

"Men like Henry believe that the average man cannot comprehend the events and dominions and machinations controlling their lives. The average man simply lives a self-indulgent, Hellenistic life, while he is quietly destroyed by unseen forces."

Baron stood and walked to a control station behind the couch. His fingers moved fluidly across the panels, the lights dimmed, and the plasma screen jumped to life.

"That is why God has brought you here, gentlemen. There is a saying: 'The only way for evil to triumph is for good men to stand by and do nothing.' Now it is time for something to be done."

Los Cruzado and Prichard found themselves staring at an image on the screen of the Great Seal of the United States as it looks on the back of the U.S. dollar.

They stared at the image, their attention drawn to the eye in the triangle.

"Have either of you seen this before?" Baron asked.

Prichard turned to him. "Yeah, it's the Great Seal. So what?"

Baron smiled. "Do you know what it means?"

"I dunno. The eye is supposed to be God or something, and the pyramid means... well, I mean, I don't know."

"I see," Baron said. "And you, Father?"

Los Cruzado's face was like stone. "*El Diablo.* The eye is not God. It is the devil."

"Yes. And the Latin inscription underneath the pyramid?"

"*Novus Ordo Seclorum.* There are many translations. Some say it to mean 'New World Order' or 'New Secular Order,' which would mean an order without God."

"Very good. I have another translation which you should find very interesting, Father. We will discuss it soon."

Prichard stood up, holding out his hands impatiently. "Wait a second, now hold on a minute. Baron, are you telling me that you brought me all the way up here to talk about one world government conspiracy theories?"

"No, Prichard."

Prichard moved in front of the screen, pacing. "Okay, okay. Then, what are we doing? Are we being invaded by aliens? Don't tell me, the government is really being controlled by FEMA or a handful of geriatrics, plotting away the world in some secret smoky room? I mean it sounds like you have been cooped-up on this island, spending way too much time talking to losers and fruitcakes on the Internet."

Baron ducked his head in shame. "Prichard, if you'll just permit me a moment."

Prichard looked with embarrassment at his former mentor. "For what? You used to have a handle on these things, Baron. I think you've been such a professional liar for so long you're starting to believe your own spin. What happened to you? This country, our principles, and our way of life are systematically being stolen from us. All of our liberties are being eroded away right in front of us. You were the last of a breed of intelligent patriots, and you left us. You deserted."

Baron answered patiently. "First off, I'm not as good a liar as I used to be; second, do not question my patriotism. You don't have the right to judge or criticize me. I was committing my life to this government and its people long before you came along. My friend, you were merely a boy; you only had a dreamer's zeal and desire with no real understanding of the deeper worldly issues, until I taught you. And, little do you know, Doug... it is all even deeper still."

"But, you quit!" Prichard screamed, pointing a finger.

"No. I found the truth, Prichard. His truth."

"What are you talkin' about?! Whatta you mean 'His truth'?!"

Los Cruzado stood. "Prichard. *Por favor.* He is speaking of God."

Prichard startled at Los Cruzado's interruption. He'd almost forgotten that he was there. "What?"

"I remember," Los Cruzado continued. "It was in 1991. You told them you found God, eh?"

Baron turned to Los Cruzado, grateful for an ally. "Yes, but it was 1992."

"*Si.*"

Prichard shook his head in defeat. "So, you got religion. So what? I'm happy for you. What am *I* doin' here?" He stomped across the room, bumping past Los Cruzado to grab his backpack. He jerked it off the floor with a grunt, storming past Baron. "I'm going back to Colombia. You and Quido Sarducci over here have a good time."

Baron glared at him. "Prichard!" he shouted.

Prichard stopped in his tracks.

"Sit down. Indulge me. You claim to love your country so much, but I see you are the one who is running out now. You're right... America is in trouble, but there's much more. We are *all* in *deep* trouble, Prichard. I called you and Father Los Cruzado because I need you. Now please... sit down."

Prichard held his stance for a moment with his back to Baron, but then he turned, dropped the backpack, and plopped down on the couch. He realized he couldn't get off the island for another 12 hours anyway, until the Maggie Brown came back to pick them up.

"Very well, then," Baron said. He gestured for Los Cruzado to sit, and he did.

Baron moved back to the control panel. "I'm afraid I'm going to have to take you back, gentlemen, to the beginning of the Christian Church. This is where all our difficulties began."

The image on the screen showed a dark and moody 1620 painting, by Flemish artist Peter Paul Rubens, of the crucified Christ.

Los Cruzado's heart leaped at the realistic depiction; he could feel the nails.

"Didn't we just leave this scene back in D.C.?" grumbled Prichard, looking away.

Baron cleared his throat and began his lecture. "The Apostle Paul was summoned by the Lord, 40 years after Christ ascended to the Father, and was commissioned to begin his great church-building work.

"The churches were miraculously raised in the deeply pagan territory of the Roman Empire and suffered three major heresies: Gnosticism, Arianism, and Pelegianism.

"Gnosticism held to the false belief that man can come to the wisdom of God through the attainment of certain hidden mysteries or secret knowledge, separate from what is written. Arianism suggested that Christ was a lesser God, denying the Holy Trinity. Pelegianism spread the lie that the will of man alone can overcome evil."

The screen suddenly flickered and flashed with artistic, historical depictions of the troubles within the church, and of the ensuing atrocities that occurred throughout Europe.

"These heresies were all evils against and within the church, culminating in many heinous acts against mankind, everything from the Crusades, to the Inquisitions, to Nazism, and Fascism. These were all attempts of the Evil One to draw man away from God.

"Now let's talk about the birth of a country called America."

Prichard perked up and turned his head to the screen.

A portrayal of the signing of the Declaration of Independence appeared on the screen. Baron finally had Prichard's attention; Prichard gazed at the painting.

"During the same year that we declared ourselves a free nation, a man named Adam Weishaupt, a University of Ingelstadt professor in Germany, began a movement based on Gnosticism, Satanism, and the occult. Weishaupt was a Freemason and, as you may know, the Masons dabbled heavily in the occult. Weishaupt started a new movement among them and invited the hyper-intellectual and the wealthy to join. The stated purpose of the group was to be a fraternal, benevolent order among men, but in truth, their real purpose was to begin the paving of the way for the rise of the anti-christ, as described in Daniel and Revelation.

"The men and women involved in this group considered themselves to be enlightened with ancient powers and secret, hidden knowledge, giving them the privilege, power, and wealth to control the inner workings of our society. Weishaupt named the group the Order of the Illuminati.

"At least three U.S. Presidents have spoken against them. In fact, George Washington, in a letter to a friend, called their plans 'nefarious and dangerous doctrine'.

"After ten years, they were discovered and prosecuted by the Bavarian government; many believed that after that they ceased to exist. However, they continued to flourish, importing themselves secretly into America. In a short time, they were indoctrinating some of the most brilliant minds in the world; they have members now in every facet of our modernized society, from international bankers, to all forms of government, corporations, media, and world organizations. They are collectively known today as the New World Order."

The images on the screen showed the progressive growth of early America, from its humble agrarian roots, to the mighty Industrial Age, climaxing with shots of the United Nations, the European Union, the congresses and parliaments of various countries, central banks, powerful corporations and media giants.

Los Cruzado and Prichard were engrossed as Baron continued.

"Now, then. The Bible tells of a time when a 'man of lawlessness' will come upon the world and deceive it with a false, secular, One World Government. The Book of Revelation describes the beginnings of these events.

"After Christ rose to the right hand of the Father, the devil followed him into heaven, in hopes of defeating Him. No man before had defeated the evil one, and he wanted to make one last attempt to do battle with God. But he failed."

Los Cruzado's eyes lit up as illustrations and depictions of heavenly spiritual battles between demons and angels flashed and dazzled him from the screen. He turned to Baron, feeling the Spirit of Truth stirring him.

Los Cruzado stood on his feet. "'And there was a war in heaven,'" he quoted, eloquently.

Baron stopped and listened, aware that the Spirit was connecting them. His instincts on Los Cruzado had been correct. He was glad he ordered Prichard to bring him.

As Los Cruzado spoke, Prichard watched him, dumbfounded.

"'She gave birth to a son, a male child, who will rule all the nations with an iron scepter. And her child was snatched up to God and to his throne. The woman fled into the desert to a place prepared for her by God, where she might be taken care of for 1,260 days.

"'And there was a war in heaven. Michael and his angels fought against the dragon, and the dragon and his angels fought back. But he was not strong enough and they lost their place in heaven. The great dragon was hurled down—that ancient serpent called the devil, or Satan, who leads the whole world astray. He was hurled to the earth, and his angels with him.'"

Baron nodded and smiled. "That's right. Revelation 12:5-9. Well said. Well said, indeed. Let's take it a little further, my friend. Note verse twelve of the same chapter. 'Therefore rejoice, you heavens and you who dwell in them! But woe to the earth and the sea, because the devil has gone down to you! He is filled with fury, because he knows that his time is short.'"

Los Cruzado moved across the room, holding up a finger.

"*Si, si. El diablo* has been heightening evil on the earth against mankind ever since his defeat at Calvary. All heresy against the church, all wickedness and depravity in society and now, as you say, a *secreto* order, has developed to lead to the creation of a global government."

"Precisely," Baron said. "Revelation 13:7 says, 'He was given power to make war against the saints and to conquer them. And he was given

138

authority over every tribe, people, language and nation.' So, you see, not just a secular government, but a *world* secular government."

"Okay, so… What does all this have to do with the flipside of a greenback?" Prichard asked.

Baron cocked his head and smiled. "I'm glad you asked that, Doug," he said.

He ran his fingers across the control panel and the screen changed back to the image of the Great Seal. "Now, once again, have either of you seen this before?"

Prichard rolled his eyes impatiently. "It's on the back of the dollar."

"Yes, we've established that, Prichard," he said. "What I mean to ask you is, where *else* have you seen it?"

Los Cruzado and Prichard mulled over the question, but came up with nothing.

"I see," Baron said. "Let me see if this will stir your memories."

He tapped the control panel and the screen danced with images of familiar corporate company logos: Ameritrade, CBS, Fidelity Investments, America Online, Time Warner, and at least a dozen others. All the logos were designed with a common, pyramidal shape, having either a stylized eye or line bursts emitting from the top of the pyramid. The similarities and close likeness to the Great Seal were obscure in the design of some of the logos, but blatant in some of the others. No question, though, that a resemblance was there in all of them.

Prichard reached for his wallet, flipping through some cash and finding a dollar. He plucked it out and looked at it as if he'd find something different, but there it was, the Seal with the Eye, pyramid, and cryptic Latin. Los Cruzado leaned over and examined it with him, peering over the top of his glasses. After a moment, the men glanced at each other with a newfound awareness and uneasiness.

They gazed back at the screen and then turned to Baron as he spoke.

"The Eye, as Father Los Cruzado correctly stated earlier, is not the eye of God, as some would have you believe. The Seal was placed on the dollar during the administration of Franklin Roosevelt, who was a thirty-third degree Freemason. The Eye is the Eye of the Egyptian god Osiris or Baal, an ancient pagan god that the early nation of Israel confronted among the peoples of Canaan. The name Beelzebub is a Greek translation of the Hebrew name Baal-Zabul, which over time has become known by the Hebrews as a name for the devil."

"What does the pyramid mean?" Prichard asked.

Baron stepped from around the control panel, speaking and gesturing with his hands in an oratorical style that had been both mocked and admired in Washington. "The Roman numerals at the base of the pyramid translate to 1776. There are thirteen tiers leading to the glowing Eye. Some say the tiers represent the original thirteen colonies, or some type of transcendental ascension to a higher, worldly consciousness. I've conferred with many theological scholars on the subject, and it appears that America has been used as some sort of stepping stone to the upcoming luciferian order."

"How close is it?" asked Prichard.

"Very close," Baron replied grimly.

"You say you have another meaning for the Latin underneath?" Los Cruzado asked.

"Yes, and this will fascinate you. The truest translation of Novus Order Seclorum means, 'New Order of The Ages'. The Roman poet Virgil coined the term around the time Jesus Christ was born. He was speaking not of Christ, but of the Roman Emperor, Augustus, who would bring an era of peace and progress to Rome after a civil war and power struggle that occurred when Julius Caesar was assassinated.

"Now, the Romans deified their emperors to the highest degree and much hope was put in Augustus. Virgil called him the 'present deity' and 'restorer of the world'.

"In the Bible, The Lord spoke in Matthew 24:15 of 'an abomination that causes desolation.' What He was referring to was the detestable act of the Greek ruler Anticochus Epiphanes, who tried to force Greek rule over the Jews. In 168 B.C., he entered the most sacred place in the Temple, the dwelling place of God, and desecrated it, killing an unclean pig and spilling its blood over the altar.

"The Biblical, prophetic apex of this 'abomination' will happen when a man, at some time in the near future, will enter the rebuilt Temple in Jerusalem and stand on the Most Holy Place and declare himself God."

Baron was feeling the Spirit, and an urgency to relay the message. "You see, gentleman, when Virgil spoke of 'the present deity' and 'the restorer of the world,' he was clearly speaking against God. He was speaking of a man who was coming to falsely claim to be God, Caesar Augustus. However, the man who will come in our time, to bring about 'the new order of the ages' will be the anti-christ... the beast. That is why Novus Ordo Seclorum is written there. The New World Order is the one world system that the anti-christ will rule."

Baron finished and paused. Los Cruzado and Prichard were awestruck. After a moment, Prichard asked, "Why would a U.S. President allow something like that to be put on our money? It doesn't make sense."

Baron continued. "Because for the New Order to come about, the sovereign and foreign power of the U.S. has to be weakened. Roosevelt had Masonic ties with the Council of Foreign Relations, which was formed in 1919 by an international group to advise governments on world affairs. Just after World War II, the CFR gained much influence in the U.S. State Department, effectively giving government control to a non-sovereign power.

"Even before that, in 1913, the Federal Reserve was secretly formed, creating a centralized bank in America. The board of the Fed is mainly made up of foreign banking interests that efficiently manipulate our economy to suit the purpose of the coming world order."

Baron moved back to the control panel. "Now, gentlemen, observe the screen. I have one more thing to show you, and then we shall take a short recess."

The screen flooded with image after image, overlapping and transitioning in slow motion, then increasing in speed...

Eyes.

Single eyes from film and video media. Eyes from movies, commercials, television, Web sites, logos, paintings, print media, advertisements...

It was an endless, mind-boggling menagerie, created surreptitiously, manifesting itself through the visual art of man. The Eye was penetrating, permeating, and shaping the minds of humanity into a submissive, collective, subconscious that was somehow being drawn and absorbed by the evil power of the fallen one.

The Eye was subtle, subliminal, yet somehow overt and flagrant.

The Eye was everywhere and all seeing, but nowhere.

The three men were among the few who knew the truth, and it felt like a fog of doom clouding their minds.

They became silent, feeling the weight of it; they added up the sum of all their fears.

The photo of Mitchell Biggsby was taken just after his arrest for arson and murder in El Paso, Texas. He was 32-years old, and his face had yet to take on the gaunt raggedness that prison and years on the streets would give it. The image stared down at Los Cruzado, Prichard, and Baron from the plasma screen.

"Mitchell Biggsby," Baron said. "Finding this man is part of your assignment."

"Who is he?" Prichard asked.

"In the late sixties, Mitchell Biggsby was involved in U.S. Army Psychological Operations in Vietnam. Biggsby was part of a special National Security Agency Black Operations program that was developing very advanced psyops techniques. Not just the psychological use of radio or propaganda, but training men and experimenting in telepathy."

"Que?" Los Cruzado asked.

"What are you talkin' about, telepathy?" Prichard scowled. "You mean hearing other people's voices?"

"Yes. And also being able to transmit your thoughts into someone else's mind."

"That's not possible," Prichard dismissed, with a wave of his hand.

"But, I'm afraid it is. In fact, soon, it will be possible for all of us, not just those with the most advanced minds."

"So you're saying that this *señor* Biggsby could do these things."

"No, but as part of psyops, he knew a great deal about it and had seen it work first hand in the jungles of Vietnam."

"What do you mean by, 'soon, it will be possible for all of us'?" Prichard quipped.

"Well, our government has been conducting experiments in extra sensory perception, telekinesis and telepathy since World War II. Imagine how powerful a country could become if it masters these phenomena. Imagine an Army trained in telepathy. It could conquer a country just by mentally manipulating the will and minds of the people. Not a single shot would have to be fired. Imagine training a soldier to do exactly as he is ordered, with just a simple mental command. And, think of what a global government could do against its people with this kind of power."

Prichard and Los Cruzado were speechless.

Baron continued. "The only problem is that the men who conducted these experiments foolishly thought they could control this dark power; they thought the human mind was evolving to the point where such abilities would be routine, and they wanted to be the first to master it.

"You see, the men who initiated the experiments were men who delved into the ancient ways of the Gnostics and mystics. They tapped into a power that came not from the human mind, but from the dark principalities."

Prichard shifted uneasily in his chair. "The Illuminati again."

"Exactly. My theory is that our minds are being prepared for the New Order; once it arrives, most of the world will be easily drawn to it after these years of early conditioning. Biggsby has official, documented proof of the psyops programs. We lost contact with him just outside of Seattle, Washington, 12 hours ago."

"You want us to locate him?" Prichard asked.

"Yes, I will be making all this evidence public soon, and I must have those documents."

"So, that's why you went into hiding. So you could dig all this up."

"Yes."

"You're not doin' all this alone, though. Who else is helping you?"

"I won't divulge that; it has gotten far too dangerous as it is. Suffice to say that just as there is evil in high places in this dark world, so there is also good. The people I'm working with are Christians, like I am. Very concerned, and very pro-active."

"Well, Baron, why me? Why us? You could've just grabbed someone from one of the agencies."

"Because, Prichard, the thing that makes you so naïve, your garish patriotism, is the very reason I called you. I know you are a loyal man; I know you'll do your job. Besides, there is no one at any agency who I can trust. And, as for you, Father Los Cruzado, your experience in the political upheavals of your country should serve our cause in this arena. Also, of course, you are a man of God. We will need your kind of guidance."

"Have *you* heard these voices before?" Los Cruzado asked

Baron ducked his head, remembering his dark days after he went into seclusion.

"Yes. At first, they were pervasive and vile. Abrasive. There were times when they were simply overwhelming. I was on the edge many, many times. Then I learned to fight them."

Los Cruzado furrowed his brow. "How?"

"You have the answer to that, Father. How did Christ fend off the devil in the desert? He quoted from Deuteronomy. The Holy Scriptures."

Los Cruzado nodded his head reflectively. "Mmm… mmm… *Si*."

Prichard felt convicted by the Spirit; he couldn't remember the last time he opened the Bible. "So that's it, then. The only way to beat it is with the Word of God."

Baron smiled at Prichard like a proud father. "That's the only way. I don't know how much longer I have, but I wouldn't be alive if not for the Good Book."

Prichard sat back in resignation and Los Cruzado felt his own faith fortified and strengthened.

"Eyes on the screen, gentlemen," Baron said.

They turned to see the face of Doctor Rachel Walters, taken from her University of Illinois campus ID photo. Even under that type of photography, she was beautiful. Prichard felt something stir in him. "This is Doctor Rachel Walters of the University of Illinois Psychiatric Department. She has a unique position there as an attaché to the Chicago Police Department. They call her in to negotiate in hostage situations where the police are ineffective."

The screen flashed to the *Chicago Tribune*. The headline shouted about the murders and suicide at the Larson Trading Company. "You may not have see this, but about a week ago, a murder-suicide happened in Chicago. Doctor Walters was called in to diffuse the suspect, but in this case she was unsuccessful; however, in several cases she has proven to be quite remarkable."

"What makes her such an expert?" asked Prichard.

"Well, she has an interesting take on the affliction, suffered by many, of hearing voices, and how the victims often succumb to violent behavior. Doctor Walters has developed a unique theory; she believes there is a connection between the spiritual, psychological, and physiological. She has written some fascinating papers on the subject, but her work has been widely criticized and rejected by the university and psychiatric community."

"What, they don't think her theories add up?"

"That, and the fact that she's a Christian in an unbelieving, fallen world."

"Oh."

"I want you and Father Los Cruzado to find her. Her expertise and insights into how this phenomenon is affecting our society could prove a useful testimony."

Prichard brought his hand to his face with a mad laugh. "Well, this must be really bad if we need a head shrink *and* a priest."

The men all laughed.

After a moment, Prichard regained his composure. "So, we pick her up in Chicago. Then what, go after Biggsby?"

"No. I want you go to Clarksville, Alabama, where you'll meet this woman..."

The screen showed the face of Kathleen Macklin. "She is the wife, or rather the widow, of Warrant Officer Thomas Macklin of the U.S. Army. Mr. Macklin died in a car accident a month ago. Her name is Kathleen Macklin."

The screen flashed an Army photograph of Thomas Macklin.

"*Tu y este hombre asesinar?* You think this man was murdered?"

"Yes. Biggsby and Thomas Macklin met in Vietnam and became close friends. After the war, the Biggsbys and the Macklins kept close ties. Thomas Macklin was buried in Clarksville, and Biggsby more than likely attended the funeral. He may have given the documents to Kathleen Macklin."

Prichard didn't like the idea of traveling to Chicago, and then all the way south to Alabama. "But what if she doesn't have them?"

"Then we have one last option. Officer Macklin's son, Scott."

The screen shifted to an image of Scott from a surveillance photo taken at the ground breaking of the Lake Washington Office Complex.

"We think that The Illuminated may be after him already. A few days ago he was almost killed in a tower crane accident at this Seattle building project site. If Biggsby hasn't dropped the documents off with Kathleen, he is most certainly headed to Seattle, to pass the information to the son of his fallen friend.

"And, gentlemen, we are running out of time. Our enemies know we are working on compiling this information. You must be on your guard. This is a dangerous and deadly organization, which we know little about. Take every precaution."

"And what will you be doing while we're schlepping' across the countryside?"

Baron sighed with fatigue. "I will be busy preparing our indictments against the Council of Foreign Relations, the Trilaterals, the Federal

Reserve, agencies in the U.S. Army, the State Department, the Freemasons, the International Monetary Fund, the World Bank, various national media groups, and multinational corporations."

Prichard and Los Cruzado were thunderstruck. "In other words, you're gonna try to sue the New World Order? Are you insane? You'll never get anywhere near an indictment. You won't even get close. There'll never be a trial."

"I already know that, Prichard. The Bible predicts that the New Order must come before we see the Glorious Return of the Lord. It is in God's timing. As much as we want to stop it, we cannot; it is part of His plan. Our task is to raise the awareness of the people, to stir their hearts and inspire them to come to Christ. The modern saints will be revealed as they move against the satanic order."

Baron tapped a panel and the screen went blank. The lights in the room came up.

He stepped from behind the panel, looking grave yet determined. Prichard and Los Cruzado both felt a new respect for Baron. "Gentlemen, those documents are the last piece in the puzzle. Once we have them, our evidence will be complete. Find them.

"Tomorrow morning, I will equip you with the means to communicate within your group and to me, through my liaison. Prichard, you will be given access to an expense account—a very generous one, I might add. I'm sure your loyalty and trustworthiness will translate into good stewardship."

"Well, I don't know. When we head south, if I run into one of those Stuckey's restaurants, I just might blow the whole wad."

Baron almost laughed. "See to it that you don't. Are you armed?"

"That's a stupid question."

"Good. You'll need to be. Let me know if I can help you in that regard. Any other questions?"

Prichard's eyes narrowed. "Yeah, one more. How do you know so much? I know you've been in the loop—heck, you practically were the loop. But how'd you get in so deep?"

Baron looked at them with trust in his eyes. "Because… I was one of them, Prichard."

Prichard and Los Cruzado gave each other nervous looks.

"Come, gentleman," Baron said. "I will show you your guest quarters. I will not see you in the morning, as I'll be on my early run. I hope you'll get started bright and early, as well."

———•—•—

The sunrise over the bay brought the warmth of morning to Prichard and Los Cruzado, as they stepped down from Baron's house to the beach.

They looked northeast and located Baron and the Labrador, almost a half mile down the stretch of pristine island coast. Prichard wondered if they'd see him again. If this was as dangerous a mission as Baron was making it out to be, they all might end up dead.

"Let's go. We've got an hour to catch the Maggie Brown." He started to move past Los Cruzado, who stood staring at the bay and sunrise.

Prichard stopped and turned. "Los Cruzado."

The Father turned to him.

Prichard felt for the man so far away from his country, and caught up in a mess with the likes of him. "Come on, Father, let's go."

Los Cruzado angled up to him. "Why did you not kill me that day, Prichard?"

Prichard's mind went numb for an answer; he had hoped this subject would never come up.

He walked away, slowly at first, adjusting his boots on the sand.

Father Los Cruzado hesitated for a moment and then followed him down the beach.

CHAPTER 8

The gun in LeShaun Jennings' hand was too big for his fingers to fit completely around the handle. The barrel twitched and shaked—and pointed at Rachel Walters.

The Chicago Transit Authority Red Line train rolled ominously overhead on elevated tracks; Rachel knelt on the cold, littered pavement, where broken glass sparkled in the glow of the streetlights. The Le Corbusier-designed, prison-like project towers rose oppressively around Clybourne and West Division Street in the Lower North Side of Chicago, in an infamous ghetto known as Cabrini Green.

Police units from the 18th Precinct had cordoned off a two-block area, from the corner of West Division and Clybourne. The 20th Precinct S.W.A.T. Sniper Unit was on hand. Officers Terrance Harper and Donald Ramierez were parked in their van some 50 meters east on Division. Harper had an easy shot at LeShaun Jennings, who stood over Rachel, brandishing the gun. Ramierez watched the infrared ghost-image of the suspect on a monitor. Both men silently prayed they wouldn't have to do their work this evening.

Captain Macon Ballard stood in civilian clothes, shielded by a squad car, with the 20th Precinct Watch Commander and hostage negotiator. Ballard was awakened almost an hour ago; he offered the services of the sniper unit, but cringed when they gave him the suspect's description: black male, five-four, 130 pounds, 14 years-old. Fourteen? Ballard had thought. God help us.

When he learned that Rachel was going to be the auxiliary negotiator, Ballard somehow knew she would end up in front of the gun.

His thoughts moved along with a prayer as he activated his radio. "Harper?" he whispered.

"Go ahead, Captain."

"You got him?"

"Yes, sir. Clean shot."

"Not until my signal. We gotta be real patient on this one; he's just a kid."

"I copy, Captain."

LeShaun Jennings' face was enraged as the gun quivered in his hand. The streetlight blanketing him and Rachel was the calm eye of a swirling storm of social conflict in the heart of Chicago.

The Cabrini Green projects, world-renowned for their violence, gangs, drugs, and monstrous depravity, were being torn down. The Housing and Urban Development Department in Washington, D.C., and the Chicago Housing Authority had put together a plan to rebuild Cabrini Green, which sat near some of the wealthiest real estate in Chicago. In doing so, they'd hoped to bring in middle-class and upper-middle-class residents and businesses to give the area a long-needed economic boost. Congress finalized the legislation in 1996.

Over 17,000 units were slated for demolition and reconstruction, after preliminary testing showed it would be more cost-effective for the city to build new facilities than refurbish existing units. CHA had promised to give vouchers to the 12,000 families affected, but the promised monies hadn't materialized.

A new plan was formulated and the CHA authorized the demolition of only 11,000 units, with the intent of building Cabrini Green into more of a mixed-income development. Still, many families were affected. Those who were removed ended up in the sprawling projects of the South Side of Chicago, where the CHA redevelopment had yet to take hold.

The Lower North Side of Chicago exploded with militant community activism and protest against the CHA redevelopment. Several lawsuits were filed. Many residents believed that the CHA was only interested in Cabrini Green because of its close approximation to the wealthy North Side of the city; they believed once the city had completely rebuilt Cabrini Green, redevelopment would stop, leaving the rest of the city projects swaying in the cold breeze of poverty.

Just a week ago, LeShaun Jennings aunt, Carrie Jennings, and his baby brother, Ray Ray, got the notice from CHA. Their building, just west on North Larrabee, was coming up for demolition in three months.

LeShaun Jennings bought the gun from his homie in the North Side Tripps. He was still a Baby G now, just a wannabee gangsta, but the NST had plans to bring him up, he thought. Auntie wouldn't have to work no more for no white people at that drycleaner on Webster, he thought. Once the NST brought him up, he'd get his 'spect and his props and the cash. Nobody would mess with him. But, if they moved, they'd have to go to the South Side. And, if they did that, he'd be dead. Lotta Tripps' rivals down that way.

Just mindin' his own business, stepped off the Red Line and PO, POs everywhere. Now they got him boxed in, and this white lady, who say she a Christian, talkin' about helpin' him. Yeah, he'd like to see wha' she gon' do. Like to see wha' any of 'em gon' do. But, the voices'll tell 'em what to do. They always did.

Rachel didn't know LeShaun, but she'd worked with inner city youth through the UIC Psychiatric Department H.O.P.E. project. She'd had violent confrontations with young people, but she had never encountered anyone like LeShaun.

He had a rap sheet the length of a short novel: armed robbery, burglary, petty theft, arson, assault, and gang-related activity, just to start. He spent two years in the Cook County Juvenile Detention Center, and participated in the SWAP program, designed to reintegrate juvenile convicted felons back into society. Once LeShaun completed the SWAP program and hit the streets again, the Tripps almost instantly recruited him.

The 20th precinct was investigating LeShaun in connection with a drug-related gang murder. He was one of the chief suspects.

He kept the police at bay by pointing the gun to his head, threatening to take his own life.

Rachel Walters searched her heart and found the Spirit. She prayed the Lord would give her the words to disarm this 14 year-old boy, who stood over her with hell in his dark eyes. "LeShaun, may I ask you a question?"

Under a hooded mane of cornrows, the boy's face wrinkled with disgust and confusion. "Wha'? Lady, wha' choo wanna axe me? I ain't got nothin' to say ta you."

Rachel sighed with exhaustion. "I'll do the talking then. Do you know the man named Jesus Christ?"

LeShaun stopped pacing and stared at her. "Wha'? Who? Jesus? Lady, look around. You see any God anywhere? God where? There ain't no God. Dang! I mean, where you think you at? Wha', did God make the projects? *This* is hell, ain't no God."

"But there is, LeShaun, there is. And you're His son. He loves you and wants something better for your life than this."

"Yeah, I see how much He loves me, lady. Buncha rich white people comin' in my hood, tearin' down our homes. I see how much God loves black people. White people always talkin' 'bout God. Why should I believe in Him when there ain't even no black people in the Bible?"

"No, LeShaun, you couldn't be more wrong. God loves your people. In the book of Acts, God sends one of his servants, Philip, to teach an Ethiopian man how to read the Scriptures."

"You say wha' choo want. That's a white boy's religion. Ain't no black folks in no Bible. Um down wit' da Muslims."

"LeShaun, there were African Christian churches 600 years before Islam; Islam falsely teaches that God doesn't have a close personal relationship with His people, but He does. He loves you and cares for your life, but now the devil has you. The devil's leading you down a road you may not recover from unless you turn, right now, to the Lord. Think about your family, your aunt, and your little brother. Do you want Ray Ray to follow your footsteps?"

"Lady, shutup."

"Do you want him out here on the streets like you?"

"Shutup, ain't nothin' gon' happen to Ray Ray."

"He'll follow you and he'll die out here."

LeShaun's eyes lit up with anger and terror at the prospect of his baby brother falling prey to the streets. "I said shutup! Baby Ray ain't gon' end up like this! Thass why Um rollin' with the Tripps! Um gonna make it so him an' Auntie ain't gotta worry 'bout nothin'!"

"But they *will* have to worry, LeShaun. They'll have to worry about you. What good are you going to be to them if you're dead? How long do you think it'll be before you're killed out here, or imprisoned? What good will you be to a family you claim to love?"

"'Ey, I love my peoples! Don' be questionin' me, lady!"

Rachel didn't know if it was her knees that were starting to ache on the hard asphalt, or whether she was just tired, but she decided the soft approach wasn't going to work. "I will question you LeShaun. I think you're selfish, and a coward. You're pointing a gun at an unarmed woman on her knees. You're a coward."

"I ain't scared o' nothin'!"

"Yes, you're scared! How many *brothas* have you killed, LeShaun?"

"I ain't shot nobody—yet!"

"You're supposed to be a gangster and you haven't shot anybody? Have you ever been shot, or even shot at?"

"Thass my business, Lady, my business! Um OG, baby! Straight trippin'! You keep clownin' me an' we gon' see about who a coward!"

Rachel looked at him with a confidence that was beginning to unnerve him. "I see. Well, I'm not impressed. You're not going to shoot me, LeShaun, and you know why?"

He stepped closer to her, menacing. "I'm startin' to wonder why myself."

"Because the minute you do, those police officers will kill you; because even if I die, I'll simply be going home. Do you know where you're going? Do you know where you'll go?"

LeShaun contemplated the question, looking around in the darkness. The brightness of the squad car headlights blinded him, but he couldn't see the S.W.A.T. sniper van. His skin prickled with tension and a feeling that he always carried with him…fear. Uncertainty washed over him like a dark, thundering wave. He dropped his eyes to the concrete and slowly lowered the gun.

"LeShaun?" Rachel asked, gently.

He looked at her and, for the first time, the torment was gone from his eyes.

"Have you ever thought about why you've never shot anyone? Or, why you've never been in a life-and-death situation where you might have to kill?"

He shook his head.

"Because Jesus didn't want you to. He's saving you, even though you don't believe in Him."

LeShaun's expression softened. He looked like the lost fourteen-year-old boy that he really was. "I don't get ya'll, lady. Whass God want wiff me? I ain't nothin'."

"You are something, LeShaun. You're His son. He loves you, your family loves you… And even though I'm just a white lady, I love you, too."

He was shocked at her words.

Ballard and the police were stunned.

Harper lowered his rifle, and Ramierez switched off the infrared monitor.

LeShaun felt something in his chest besides the ever-present knot of rage. Something rolled over him and covered him with a warmth he'd never known. "How you know you love me, lady? You don' know me."

Rachel smiled. "But I do know you. I know what it's like to be lost and scared and unsure. I know you because we are *all* under God."

LeShaun looked around the streets, suddenly drained. He had seen and experienced more hardship than most. He was cold and tired—very tired. LeShaun Jennings simply wanted to go home.

Rachel held out her hand. "Please give me the gun."

LeShaun hesitated. "Dey think I kilt dat boy over on Delaware. Dey'll shoot me anyhow."

Rachel stood on her feet. "No, LeShaun, they just want to question you. They don't want to kill you; they need to talk to you. Did you see who did it?"

LeShaun looked away.

"Then you have to tell them," Rachel said. "Don't you see? This is where you can turn around your whole life. Right now. Give me the gun."

LeShaun's eyes brimmed with tears. "Lady, they gon' kill me."

"No. Walk slowly towards me, give me the gun and take my hand. I'll pull you close. They won't shoot."

LeShaun looked into Rachel's eyes with a mingling of trust and fear. She reached under her coat and sweater, pulling out her crucifix to let it dangle. The light of it glinted with hope and promise.

The night was still. The police officers watched in disbelief and awe as LeShaun Jennings moved toward Rachel and put the gun in her hand. She grabbed his arm and pulled him into a tight, protective embrace. Rachel kissed his head and her heart leaped with joy. "Good, LeShaun. Good. You're going to be okay. It's okay now."

He cried.

Rachel turned her eyes heavenward. "Thank you," she whispered.

Ballard spoke into his radio. "Harper, Rameriez. Stand down. Suspect contained."

"Way ahead of you, Cappy," Harper replied.

The police officers moved in, taking the gun from Rachel and cuffing LeShaun. His eyes watched her and he turned his head to keep his gaze on her as they took him away. Rachel ran to catch up with them. "Hold on a minute, officers."

The men stopped.

"LeShaun. Answer one more question for me. Have you ever heard something in your mind? A thought or a voice in your head that told you to do things, bad things?"

LeShaun looked up at her pensively. "Yeah. Lots at times."

"What do they say to you?"

"Whatever, lady. They say a lot of stuff. They told me you was comin'."

"That I was coming?"

"Yeah."

The officers became impatient. "Okay, Doctor, we've gotta go. Gotta get him to the precinct."

Rachel stepped back. Before she knew it, LeShaun Jennings was in a squad car and gone. She headed slowly past the 20th Precinct Watch Commander and Ballard.

"Can you make a report tonight, Doctor?" the Commander asked.

Rachel didn't look at him but kept walking toward her car. "I'm tired, Commander. I'm going to bed. Tomorrow morning."

"It is tomorrow morning."

"Right, right," she said, glibly.

Ballard watched her with admiration. "Rachel," he called.

She stopped and turned back to him. "Yes, Captain."

"Good job."

<hr />

Rachel was stopped at a light on LaSalle and West Division when a boy no older than LeShaun raced on foot across the intersection. A squad car roared after him, flashing its blue-and-red. Rachel felt overwhelmed by grief. One triumph with LeShaun couldn't overshadow the travesty of life for the youth and people of Cabrini Green, Chicago.

It had been just over a week since the Davis hostage crisis. On the roof, Rachel had thought she'd heard something, but rationalized it away as shock and extreme stress. Then, The Voice filled her head so loudly it sounded like it came from her car speakers. *"Don't worry, Rachel. LeShaun may have slipped past us for now but, as you can see, there are plenty more where he came from."*

She stifled a scream.

———————•◆•———————

Rachel pulled her car into UIC parking lot "J" on the corner of Pauline and Taylor Street. The School of Public Health and Psychiatric Institute loomed over her as she climbed, wobbling, out of her Acura. She tried to stop it, but the shaking had gotten worse; it had worked its way from her hands through her body. She reached into the car and grabbed her laptop, some textbooks, and her purse.

Slamming the door with her foot, she moved over to a parking card access machine. She awkwardly opened her purse, fishing for her card when everything slipped from her quivering hands and hit the pavement. The laptop landed on a corner edge with a loud crack. Rachel cursed, but this time forgot to take it back.

She knelt, gathering everything, her mind reeling with the truth of what she had just heard. It wasn't her own thought; it couldn't have been. Why would she even think something like that? Was it something that crept up from her subconscious? No. There were no events taking place in her life that could lead to the manifestation of such a thought. Where did it come from? Had something invaded her?

Rachel knew what the sensation of hearing voices or having racing thoughts must be like, but was it possible the voices could be as lucid as those she'd heard? More to the point, it really wasn't her voice—was it? God, what is happening to me? She thought.

"*Beunos noches,* Doctor Walters."

Rachel had just gathered everything, only to drop it all again. This time, she didn't hold in her scream, and it echoed across the parking lot. Her flight instinct kicked in, but her feet planted themselves when she saw the cross around the neck of the man who greeted her.

A taller, grimmer-looking man stood behind the first one, both holding up their hands in innocuous gestures.

"*Por favor, Por favor.* We won't harm you, Doctor. *Facilimente.* Easy, easy," the first man said in broken English.

Rachel stood there gawking at them for a moment. "Who are you?" she asked.

"My name is Father William Dante Los Cruzado and this is Doug Prichard."

Prichard moved over and stooped, grabbing up her things, but Rachel snatched them from him.

"I got it, I got it," she insisted. "You should know better than to sneak up on a woman, in the middle of the night, in an empty parking lot."

Prichard threw his hands up, shrugged his shoulders, and stepped back. "Sorry. Just tryin' to help."

"We did not mean to startle you, Doctor," Los Cruzado added. "We are here because we need your help. We are friends."

Rachel could only stare at them, dumbfounded. "What's this all about?" she asked.

"That is the question of the ages, lady," Prichard quipped.

———

Rachel's office in the Public Health and Psychiatric Building was stark and modestly decorated, except for her numerous diplomas and certificates of merit. Her degree from Bowling Green dominated the wall behind her desk. There were plaques from the H.O.P.E. program and pictures of her with children from Chicago neighborhoods like Cabrini Green.

Notebooks and textbooks littered every surface—the desks, the long window sill, and the bookshelves.

Prichard noticed there wasn't a photograph of her with a husband. He glanced at her left hand and found no ring. A couple of photos could have been family, and one photograph was of a young boy.

Rachel sat behind her desk studying the Great Seal on a dollar bill that Los Cruzado had handed her. Prichard noticed that her University ID photo didn't do her justice. The circles under her eyes gave her a worn and fatigued look, but she was still beautiful. Why was this woman alone? And why was an old war dog like him thinking about her?

They had gone over all of it with her: the Seal, The Illuminated, the New World Order—the whole thing. Rachel listened to first Los Cruzado and then Prichard. Now she examined the Seal with the intensity of a researcher.

Finally, she stood up from her desk with her arms folded and moved over to the window. She had a view of the southern end of the campus. The sun rose slowly, casting a wake-up glow.

They talked and poured over all the various dossiers and information provided by Baron for over an hour; the way Rachel viewed life and society was greatly altered, but still, something held her back.

She turned to Prichard and Los Cruzado, and picked up one of the dossiers.

"Gentlemen. All this information is compelling and I must say I'm intrigued. But, I can't just walk away from my life here and chase across the country." She tossed the dossier on her desk. "I mean, what do you expect to accomplish? Do you really think anything can be done against something as organized, far-reaching, and sinister as this, if it indeed is true?"

Prichard was sitting in a chair in front of her desk next to Los Cruzado. He stood up. "That's why we're going after Biggsby. He's had possession of documents we need to finalize a public case against these same organizations."

"But why do you need me?" she asked. "This sounds like something for the government to get involved with."

Prichard shook his head. "They *are* involved—but most of them are on the wrong side."

Los Cruzado leaned forward in his chair. "Doctor, during our travels I've had time to review some of your work, and you seem to have a keen insight into what is happening here. You are a Christian, and you understand that in its essence, this is a spiritual war. These institutions and systems are merely the weapons of this war."

Prichard finished. "As we go forward, we expect resistance, though we're not sure what form it may take. We know they'll use some type of power to attack the mind. We need you to help us through those attacks, to help us formulate a of mental defense against them."

Rachel leaned back in her chair, as if about to go into deep thought, but she came back quickly with her answer. "Gentlemen, I'm afraid the answer is no. I just cannot get involved." She stood, suddenly moving about the office, tidying papers. "I'm sorry I can't help you, but I simply have too much to do here. The fall semester is starting soon and I have lectures and a curriculum to complete. I'm already running late this morning with filing a report for the Chicago P.D. I just can't. I can't. I'm sorry."

She ended with her back to them, standing at the bookcase, pretending to read over some old teaching notes.

Prichard and Los Cruzado looked at each other. Prichard shook his head and gestured for them to leave.

Los Cruzado gathered the files and dossiers off Rachel's desk and moved into the hallway, but Prichard reached into his pocket for a business card. "We're gonna be in town for another 24 hours, but then we've gotta move. Here's my cell number and voicemail. Give us a call if you change your mind."

Rachel turned from the bookshelf and gazed at her desk. She absently took the card from Prichard. "Thank you," she said. "I'm sorry."

Prichard reluctantly left her office.

Rachel sat down and dropped her face into her hands. After a moment, she looked up at the picture of the young boy, Michael, her brother. The feelings of helplessness over his death rose in her again. So, what about Father Los Cruzado and Prichard? Could this be a chance to finally find some real answers or would it be just a tremendous, drawn-out waste of time? And the voice? She'd heard it twice now and it wasn't her own.

She looked around the office. All her work, all these years. Could this be it?

"Lord," she said. "I need your help here. Please help me."

———•◆•———

Prichard's cell phone rang as he and Los Cruzado approached their rented Chevy Blazer in the parking lot. "Prichard," he answered curtly.

"How long do I have to pack?" Rachel asked.

———•◆•———

Television seemed to be Scott's constant companion as he rested on a couch in his townhome, recuperating from the surgery. He found his eyes caught by the flowing color and precision graphics of a Cadillac commercial. There was a beautiful woman framed by a swirling background, smiling confidently behind the wheel, comfortable in the leather and polished wood grain interior of the car.

The camera pushed in on the woman's face, moving closer and closer with the pitch of the music. Soon her right eye filled the screen and held there for a second before the angle shifted to a shot of the car resting on shining, wet pavement against a special-effects generated stormy sky.

Scott fell asleep in front of the big screen, and his dreams were disburbed by the woman's eye framed by a turbulent thunderstorm.

CHAPTER 9

The truck driver dropped Biggsby on the corner of Yesler and Fourth Avenue in Seattle's Old Town, known formally as Pioneer Square. He hefted his duffel and waved at the driver who pulled his rig off into the early morning.

Thirty years had passed since he'd been to the Pacific Northwest. He had stopped at Fort Lewis in Tacoma, some 20 miles south, on his way to the war. He never thought he'd see this part of the world again, let alone come here to search for the son of his dead friend.

The term *skid row* was coined in this city, in this part of town, back in the 1800s. Lumber workers would slide timber along the street, down Yesler, to a wood processing plant on the waterfront. Skid row was exactly the right term to describe where Mitchell Biggsby's life had gone.

Despite losing his family years ago, and now his best friend, Biggsby knew the Lord was going to take all the misery and pain he suffered over the years, and weave it into gold. He also knew the Dark Ones would catch him soon and his life would be over, but not before he passed everything he'd learned over to Scott Macklin.

Right now, he had to find a relatively safe place to sleep; there were at least a dozen shelters in this part of town, and one had his name on it. He'd rest and then begin his search later that morning.

Biggsby walked into Occidental Park, scattering a pack of pigeons as they feasted on the bread and popcorn crumbs spread over the cobblestone. After a moment, he took a seat on one of the ornate Victorian, wrought-steel benches that dotted the park. He ignored the two tourists who jumped off the bench and raced hastily in the opposite direction. Biggsby considered his appearance; maybe he'd shave at the shelter, if they had scissors and a razor. For right now, they'll just have to deal with me, he thought.

He rested a moment, taking in the park. It was early morning, in the middle of September; the sun was already making long autumn shadows through the trees. It was the middle of the week and tourists were moving through Pioneer Square, gawking into antique shop windows, and venturing into outdoor eateries and bars.

Biggsby felt the weight rise off his feet. He walked nearly 20 miles west along I-90 before he'd been picked up by the truck driver. He wanted to curl up on the bench and sleep, but instead he dug in his duffel bag, felt his fingers grace off the steel and wood of the gun, and pulled out his King James.

Flipping through the book, he found a passage that reminded him of what God had done for him, and what remained unfinished. Ecclesiastes 12:13,14 said, "Let us hear the conclusion of the whole matter: Fear God and keep his commandments, for this is the whole duty of man. For God shall bring every work into judgment with every secret thing, whether it be good, or whether it be evil."

Biggsby felt full of a fire of determination; he brought his bleary eyes up from the holy pages and gazed about the park. The city loomed to the north beyond the trees. "Every hidden thing," he said aloud, reflectively.

Every hidden thing, indeed.

CHAPTER 10

Scott Macklin stared in the bathroom mirror, inspecting the bruises and cuts on his banged-up face. The contusions on his ribs and shoulders were healing, but his knee had kept him off the road for over a week. He managed to get plenty of work done from home, but Scott was starting to feel cabin fever.

Scott glanced over at his watch on the bathroom counter. It was almost ten in the morning—late, for him. Since the crane accident, he was under doctor's orders to stay off his knee as much as possible. Bryce had given him two weeks leave, and Denise had been more of a nurse than a girlfriend, catering to his every whim. Scott appreciated all the attention, but he was becoming more and more anxious to get back to the office and to work.

He threw on a robe and padded into the kitchen, his wrapped knee causing him to wince in pain. The timer on the coffee maker triggered a half hour earlier. Scott reached for a cup and poured himself a fresh brew.

He'd check the snail mail first, and then his e-mail. Scott responded to several companies that were looking for consultants on their building projects, and to a half-dozen more inviting him to chair on their studies. Most of the invites were from companies in other cities. He thought it might be good to work on something out of town for a while, until all the noise about the crane incident died down. Besides, Denise had some time off coming up, and he'd like to get her away from all the distractions, to make real to her his intentions for their future. Scott thought that Bryce's recent reminder to him about marriage, and then the way he'd almost lost his life, was more than just coincidental. Something was telling him he had to make his move now. His life's priorities finally aligned, giving a sense of urgency to his need to become a father, and to make Denise Milbourne his wife.

He took a sip and moved into the living area of his contemporary town-home.

Scott's tastes were reflected in the style and decoration of his home. Mammoth schematic drawings lined the walls, along with photographs of all his projects. The living area had a high-tech, yet warm feeling. One striking item was a huge, almost banner-sized, framed poster of the legendary jazz saxophonist, John Coltrane. The caption underneath the image said *Love Supreme*. Scott walked into his open study near the long balcony doors, affording him a view of the apartment and condo high-rises of the Belltown section of downtown Seattle, with Elliot Bay to the west.

He dropped into his chair at his workstation, flipping on the desk lamp and computer. In a few minutes, he was checking and responding to his e-mails, most of them from get-well-wishers, with about a half dozen more solicitations for study groups and projects.

Scott read through a few of them before deciding to check his stocks. He clicked over to Ameritrade and found mixed results on the mutual funds, IRAs, and High Preferred Common Stock he'd invested. He worked on diversifying his portfolio several months ago, and it looked like it would pay off soon. The softening economy was having an effect on the market that was bound to come in an election year, so he wasn't too worried about the losses of last quarter. Still, he hoped the Fed would cut interest rates soon.

Financially, Scott was doing very well, but it hadn't always been that way; he remembered his college days when coming by a meal was often a task.

He'd decided that next year he'd move into some higher risk stocks and investments, like options or commodities. The chances of losing money were greater, but then so were the rewards.

Scott reached to exit the site just as the Ameritrade logo caught his eye. Something about it stirred a cloudy feeling within him. Scott leaned back in his chair and focused on it. It was a simple design really, just a triangle with lines emitting from the peak. He had seen it every time he logged on to the site and, of course, on Ameritrade's commercials. Why was it drawing his attention now?

The logo grew on the screen, searing itself into his mind. Where have I seen that before? he thought.

The front door opened, and Scott heard heels on the hardwood and ruffling shopping bags. "Scott? Baby, it's me."

Scott smiled, snapped out of his trance, and logged off the computer. Denise. He was happy to hear her voice.

He moved toward the hallway, catching her as she turned the corner.

Denise smiled at him and then frowned with concern, glancing at his knee. Scott leaned over and she kissed him sweetly.

Denise was stunning. Scott took in her beauty, remembering when he'd first met her almost seven years ago. They were both students at UW, she was working on her MBA, and Scott was turning heads with his innovative building design work. They were fast-trackers, with no real time for dating or relationships, but soon love made the two of them stop and take notice.

She'd caught his eye at a party for the University Alumni Association. Denise's shoulder-length, auburn hair framed beautiful, soft eyes, round cheeks, and generous, sensual lips. Those qualities were enough to catch any man's attention, but Scott was struck by her quick smile and warmth.

Even at the beginning of the relationship, he'd had his reservations. Denise looked like money—the type of woman who wouldn't date outside her tax bracket. And, besides, he was not about to get himself involved with a white woman—too many complications. Soon, though, they both found that love had a funny way of not adhering to the social barriers and prejudices of the world.

As it turned out, Denise had been in and out of a handful of unsuccessful relationships with the type of men her family would have been happy for her to marry—corporate high-climbers, men whose ambitions made up the essence of who they were. Denise thought that was the type of man she wanted, until she met Scott. His modest background gave him a strong appreciation for the things he was gaining in life; he was able to be an anchor for her even though he also had powerful, hungry dreams and aspirations. It thrilled her to watch how quickly he moved up academically, and how now he was among the city's best in his field.

Scott smiled at her, remembering how she loved him even when he was nothing. He loved her so much; he wanted to give her himself and everything else, too.

"What are you doin' up on that knee, mister?" she asked.

Scott took her shopping bags and Denise hung her coat on the wall rack by the front door. "I just got back from an eight-mile run; what are you talkin' about?"

Denise laughed and moved back to him, embracing him, gingerly pecking his bruised cheeks with kisses. Scott dropped the bags, enjoying the attention.

"Sweetie, you couldn't run eight feet on that knee."

"Okay, maybe I exaggerated. It was more like seven-and-a-half miles."

She smiled. "Uh, yeah, okay. Whatever you say, *Mike Johnson*. But, seriously, I just got home and you're talkin' way too much. What's a girl gotta do to get a decent greeting around here, anyway?"

Scott tightened his arms around her and kissed her deeply. She cooed and sighed.

"How's that?" he asked.

"We'll work on it," she swooned.

"You got that right."

Chapter 11

"Every Sunday after church," Kathleen Macklin said aloud to the photograph. "I'll come see you every Sunday until the day I'm restin' there next to you."

It was an old photo of Thomas Macklin, one from the Army. He was standing at attention in his green, full-dress uniform, with the flag dominating the background. His eyes were serious, almost disturbed. A frown wrinkled his brows and a terse line ran across his lips.

Kathleen knew the man in the picture wasn't really her husband; the Army had done something to him, altered him. Before Vietnam, he'd been someone who laughed and loved easily. She remembered an athletic, confident boy, who chased after her from grade school on, until the day she finally gave in. They'd gone on their first date when they were sophomores in high school. He was so sure of himself, almost to the point of arrogance, but the more he and his friends bragged of their sports exploits, real or imagined, the more she and the other girls loved them. But Thomas had been more than the other boys, she thought. Out of all her girlfriends, she'd ended up with the best man around.

She'd never forget his confidence just before he left for the war. He boasted about what he was going to do to the enemy. He and his other friends—Jimmy James, Bobby Richland, Carter Boyd, Curtis Charles, Michael Baldwin—they all drank and laughed and sang before they left for Vietnam. When Thomas came back on R&R after six months in the jungle, he wasn't laughing or singing or bragging. She tried to remember where she had seen that rueful look in his eyes, the look he had in the photograph.

Now it came to her. It was when he came home on leave late that summer in '72. He had seen the true horrors of war, and they would remain with him for the rest of his days. Kathleen Macklin remembered holding her husband on the hotel bed, feeling his body shake with an incalculable pain, feeling his tears course hotly down her neck. For the first time since she'd known him, she felt something dark and sickly evil creep into their garden; she felt naked...afraid.

She learned of a few things that happened to him through the court martial, but she never truly understood what had gotten inside him and deteriorated his spirit. Now that he was gone, she'd never know. "Oh, Thomas," she cried. "I miss you... Oh my God, I miss you so much." Her tears ran fresh from an endless reservoir as she stood in the doorway of the house.

Scott had protested, not wanting his mother to move into his grandparents' old house after the funeral, but she insisted. She would stay here until Thomas's ailing mother passed. It would be the best way she could honor her late husband. After Grandma was gone, Scott said, he'd move her to Seattle, but she didn't really want to leave Clarksville. For better or for worse, it was her home.

The tears passed and Kathleen Macklin composed herself. She placed the picture of Thomas back in her purse. She reached for a plate of food, wrapped in foil, on a small table next to the door. She had cooked all of Thomas's favorite foods, and every Sunday she would leave a plate at his grave.

Kathleen stepped out the door and into the bright sun; her car was parked next to the house where, for many years, the junk pile had been. Some of the neighborhood boys came by with trucks and moved it all away; the yard was now a plot of red, Alabama clay.

Kathleen checked her watch while walking to the car. "Oh, Lord," she said. There were only three hours left before the Fort Mitchell National Cemetery closed for the day. She quickened her step.

———◆———

Prichard exited off Interstate 185, and drove the Chevy Blazer west on State Route 80 into Clarksville.

"Como muy mas lejano?" Los Cruzado asked from the passenger seat. "How much farther?" he repeated in English.

"Rachel, can you pull up that map again?" Prichard asked, peering at her in the rearview mirror.

"Yeah, hang on a minute," she replied, popping open a laptop computer. In a few moments, her fingers nimbly tapped the keys.

"And hand me that can of pecans, will ya? It's in one of those bags."

Without looking up from the screen, Rachel dug into one of their large travel bags and rifled around, finally producing a can of Stuckey's Salted Pecans. She handed it to Prichard, and opened a bottle of water for herself. "The map's coming up here in a second. Did you need anything, Father?"

Los Cruzado shook his head and kept his gaze out the window as they traveled north of Columbus, Georgia. "Here we go," Rachel said. "We can take exit 22C south into Columbus, then cross west over the Chattahoochee into Clarksville. It looks like we're about twenty minutes away, Father."

Los Cruzado nodded.

Prichard was munching pecans. "What's that address, again?"

She tapped, then said, "323 Brickyard Road."

———◆◆◆———

Rachel rapped her knuckles against the door. "Hello? Kathleen Macklin? Is anybody home?" She turned to Prichard and Los Cruzado, who stood behind her on the porch. "Nobody here, gentlemen. What now?"

Prichard glanced around the street. "Maybe she's runnin' an errand or something. Let's head back over to Columbus and find a hotel. We'll check back tonight."

The three of them were leaving the porch when a neighbor in the house next door poked her head out an upper-floor window.

"Kathy ain't there," the old black woman said, her voice crackling. Her bottom lip was stuffed with snuff. "She gon' over ta see her husband."

Rachel, Prichard, and Los Cruzado stepped closer to the house. "To see her husband?" Rachel asked.

The old woman nodded. "Thass right. It's Sunday. She go over dere every Sunday ta see 'im.

"Over where?" Rachel asked again, smiling.

"Fort Mitchell. At da cemetery."

Kathleen was heading to her car when the Blazer pulled up. Prichard jumped out first.

"Ma'am? Kathleen Macklin?"

Kathleen looked at him incredulously, and then turned her gaze to Los Cruzado and Rachel as they joined Prichard. "Who are ya'll? What do you want?"

Prichard brandished his ID. "My name is Douglas Prichard, ma'am; I'm with the U.S. government. These are my colleagues, Father Los Cruzado and Dr. Rachel Walters."

Kathleen took a step back. "Are you from the Army? Well, what do ya'll want? There ain't nothin' else you can do to him now—he's dead. Now get on away from me. I ain't got nothin' to say to you."

"Ma'am, we're not here about your husband; we're looking for his friend," Rachel interjected.

"What? Girl, I don't know what you're talkin' about."

"*Señor* Biggsby?" Los Cruzado said. "Wasn't he your husband's friend from the war? From Vietnam?"

Kathleen's face lit up with anger. "You listen to me, because I ain't gon' say it again! Stay away from me an' what's left of my family! I don't want to talk to you or anybody about my husband, the war, or anything else! We've had enough, do you hear me? Enough!"

Kathleen's tears rolled as she stormed off to her car.

Los Cruzado followed her. "Ma'am, we know what your family has gone through. "*Por favor*. Please, you must let us help you. Biggsby is alive. We know he didn't start the fire that killed his wife and children. We know who did. They are already after your son, eh?"

Kathleen was in her car, but sat motionless. Prichard, Rachel, and Los Cruzado glanced at each other, and then moved toward her. She sat there, frozen, her eyes fixed ahead.

Los Cruzado knelt at the driver door. *"Señora?* The accident, in the crane? It was no accident. They are after him. We need you to help us."

"Not my baby," she lamented softly. "They can't have my baby."

"Mrs. Macklin, could you step out of the car, please?" Prichard asked.

Kathleen paused for a moment before moving slowly out of her car. She leaned against it, numb with fear. Now that Thomas was gone, she thought all of the intrigue and mystery surrounding his life were gone with him. Now she knew it was far from over. "What do you people want from me? I don't know anything."

"Have you seen Mitchell Biggsby?" Rachel asked.

Kathleen turned and walked. They walked next to her through the park. The words came slowly to Kathleen, but she gave them what she could.

Evening settled on the hilly cemetery. Most of the grave markers were small, simple, white crosses, but there were a few larger, massive headstones. The setting light cast a supple glow among the trees.

Prichard wondered if this woman knew anything useful at all. After the long drive, he was worn out and starting to feel just a little used by Baron. The thought of trekking all the way across the country to Seattle wasn't appealing to him.

He noticed a lone Grounds Keeper on a slope among the trees. He'll probably be reminding us that the park closes soon, Prichard thought, turning his attention back to Kathleen.

"Was Biggsby at your husband's funeral, Mrs. Macklin?" Rachel asked.

"No. If he was, I didn't see him. There were a lot of people. I didn't see Mitch, and I haven't seen him since '82 or '83. That was when they were knee deep in it, him and Thomas."

"Knee deep in what?" Prichard asked.

Kathleen stopped in her tracks, and so did they. She gave them a chilling look.

"Whatever evil followed them back from that jungle," she said, resuming her walk. The three of them followed.

"Did he or Mitch say anything to you about a military program called psyops?" Prichard asked.

"Thomas kept me and the children clear of anythin' they were doin' in the Army. Him and Mitch both had jobs that required high clearance. He wasn't allowed to say anything about it, and to tell y'all the truth, I didn't wanna know. One time, he came home with this briefcase that wasn't his. He told me not to touch it; not to try and open it. Kept it in the house for a month, and was walkin' around nervous and edgy the whole time. Then after that, he took it and I never saw it again.

"They asked him about that briefcase and what was in it during the court martial. They were accusing him of stealing classified documents and passin' them off to the Cubans, but Thomas wasn't a traitor. He loved this country. That thing you were talkin' about, psyops, it did come up during the trial, but that's the only time I ever heard of it."

"So, you don't know of any classified materials he might have left in his things? I mean, tell us anything you can think of, Mrs. Macklin," Prichard pressed.

"Like I said, he didn't tell us anything. He was exonerated, but right after the trial, Karen and the kids got killed and Thomas got even more quiet. That was in '85."

"'Karen and the kids'? You mean Biggsby's wife and children," Rachel said.

"That's right. They died in that fire in El Paso. We all knew Thomas didn't burn his wife and babies, but they sent him to Leavenworth. Yeah, Thomas got real quiet after that. And real scared."

"Did *Señor* Biggsby know who did it?" asked Los Cruzado.

Kathleen shook her head. "No. He wouldn't say much except that it was them." She stopped again and they stood with her.

"Who?" Rachel asked.

Kathleen turned to her and then to all of them with an expression of warning. *"Them,"* she finished.

"WE KNOW WHO YOU ARE, SON OF GOD!" A voice shouted in a high-pitched shriek, echoing through the cemetery.

They were all startled and Prichard's gun was instantly in his hand, so fast that Los Cruzado and Rachel never even saw him draw it.

Their eyes turned toward the slope and there, silhouetted against the sky, was the Grounds Keeper, waving his arms and bellowing like a madman.

"HAVE YOU COME HERE TO DESTROY US?! YOU CANNOT KILL ALL OF US, FOR WE ARE LEGION! WE ARE MANY AND WE ARE STRONG; YOU ARE WEAK AND YOU ARE FEW!"

Prichard raced off to the Blazer. "Both of you stay with Mrs. Macklin!" he ordered. "I need to have a little talk with him."

"No, Prichard! Wait! You don't understand! He could kill you!" Los Cruzado cautioned.

Prichard was already in the Blazer and plowing up the rise toward the Grounds Keeper, who turned and vanished over the hill.

The Ground Keeper jumped onto a four-wheeled utility vehicle, parked just out of view over the top of the slope. He turned the key and the engine coughed to life, just as Prichard came roaring over the top of the rise.

Prichard bore down on the Grounds Keeper as they both rolled down the hill, which was lined with cross markers. Prichard hit the gas, gaining on the slow cart. "Just a little bump," Prichard said aloud through gritted teeth. "Just enough to let cha know I'm knockin'."

The Grounds Keeper turned the cart quickly to the left, but it was too late. The Blazer bumper punched into the back of the cart bed and the cart's wheels skidded on the grass, throwing dirt. Suddenly, the thing tilted and the Grounds Keeper leaped into the air, flying forward on momentum. Prichard's eyes lit up as the Grounds Keeper spread his arms and pulled his legs together, looking like a diver coming off the platform. He flew 15 feet high across the air in total control. The forward momentum subsided, though, and the Grounds Keeper threw his hands in front of his body, hitting the ground in a forward roll.

After several tumbles, the Grounds Keeper sprung like a gymnast to his feet and, without stopping, took off in a full-blown sprint.

The cart spun and flipped out of control, crashing through the grave markers before coming to a dead halt.

"What in God's name?" Prichard marveled.

He punched the gas.

The man was running on foot at an impossible speed, kicking up dirt from underneath his boots. Prichard raced next to him and when he glanced at his speedometer, his jaw dropped. He was doing 40 miles per hour, and this guy was keeping up with him, on foot.

"Oh, my God," Prichard muttered.

The Grounds Keeper, running to the left of the Blazer, glanced back at Prichard and grinned.

The man and the Blazer raced off the grass across a paved road, and then back onto the grass, onto an area with taller, massive gravestones.

Prichard stared in awe at the man's impossible foot speed, but then let out a yelp, jerking the wheel to the left. The stone wings of an angel statue scraped across the left side of the Blazer, breaking off chunks of stone and cracking the glass on the passenger side door. Prichard almost ran right into it.

After he adjusted, he drove between a row of headstones toward a tree-line. Prichard knew if the Grounds Keeper got there first, he'd lose him. Careful to keep his eyes on his driving, Prichard could still see the man running and leaping over the tallest headstones without breaking stride. Impossible. Prichard wondered what he'd gotten himself into.

There was a break between the treeline and the tombstones. The Grounds Keeper took a final leap over one of the last headstones, then vanished over some high shrubs into the woods. The Blazer swerved as Prichard pulled up and skidded to a stop.

He leaped out of the passenger side of the truck, wielding his pistol, throwing his back against the Blazer, using the truck as a shield between himself and the treeline. He moved to the front of the vehicle holding the gun low in a crouch, then popped up, keeping the weapon at the ready. Prichard took cautious steps toward the treeline, when suddenly his combat instincts stopped his feet.

Prichard peered into the dark trees in front of him and saw nothing. A slight wind moved through the brush as a cold front cut in across the sky. It had turned cooler and darker with the clouds. From across a great distance came the sound of thunder.

Prichard calmed himself and drew on his training as a hunter and a soldier; one thing he'd learned to do in the art of catching prey, whether man or animal, was simply to listen. He focused his hearing and became disturbed. There was no sound of any kind, especially not the sound he was listening for: footsteps on brush, receding into the woods.

Where had the man gone? Prichard had seen some incredible things in his life, but nothing like the speed and agility he'd just witnessed. Even so, could the man have simply vanished?

A bird burst from the brush to his left and Prichard turned toward it, almost firing. He didn't see what hit the wrist of his gun hand, but he felt something hard like wood pound into his knuckles with such a force that the gun flew, but not before blasting off a round.

Something moved in front of him, a shape; a blur about the size of a man. He heard and felt the rush of air when it moved against him, and battered him with a shower of fists. He staggered from the hits, feeling the blood run from cuts around his eyes and mouth; his head throbbed like it would explode.

He swayed, struggling to keep on his feet, trying to see, but blood ran into his eyes. Prichard wiped his face, clearing his vision just in time to see the flash and blur of a boot heel as it flew into his abdomen. Prichard's feet left the ground and his back slammed hard against the Blazer; he slid in a painful lump to the ground.

Prichard's wind was gone and he hyperventilated. The pain was unbelievable, searing. His lungs felt like they imploded; he wheezed like an old man, old and terrified. What was attacking him?

Prichard opened his eyes, and the Grounds Keeper stood a few feet from him. He couldn't see the man's face; the wind blew hair across his eyes. There was nothing remarkable about the man, though. He had an average height and build, no real distinguishing features. Prichard was an experienced, worldly combat vet and he had just been put down hard—by a lawn boy.

He flinched when the Grounds Keeper suddenly produced a long blade from underneath a sleeve and brandished it, holding the blade high away from his body in some kind of martial arts stance. It looked like a precursor to another attack.

Prichard decided he wouldn't just lie there and let the man kill him. He glanced around, spotting his gun some 20 feet away in the grass. He knew he wouldn't make it, but what else could he do? He struggled to rise to his feet, but the man was suddenly upon him, his hand like a vice around Prichard's neck, pinning him to the truck. Prichard brought up his hands and feebly tried to remove the Grounds Keeper's grip, but he couldn't move his arm. The muscle around the forearm felt like roped metal. Prichard watched in horror as the man raised the blade, poising it for a killing thrust; the tip of the steel hung in the air, quivering. He grinned.

Prichard closed his eyes, waiting for the stab.

The Voice suddenly rumbled in his mind. *"Withdraw...,"* it ordered.

Prichard's eyes flew open. The Grounds Keeper relaxed his grip and Prichard threw his hardest right cross, connecting to the man's cheek. The Grounds Keeper jumped back from the punch, glaring at Prichard, more irritated than hurt.

"Withdraw! Now!"

The Grounds Keeper growled at The Voice in frustration, but hid the blade. Prichard realized they were both hearing the same thing and he could now see the man's eyes; they were a swirling void. Prichard froze.

"Withdraw!"

The man smiled at Prichard, then turned and leaped back into the woods with only two quick strides. He was at least 25 feet from the treeline.

Prichard listened to the sound of the man's footfalls, which faded in a just a few seconds.

The thunder rolled again, this time closer, almost overhead.

Prichard tried to stand, but his knees wobbled and he slid right back to the ground.

He heard tires screeching on asphalt as a car pulled up and stopped on the road. Soon, he heard footsteps. Rachel and Los Cruzado called to him.

"I-I'm right here!" he managed to shout.

Los Cruzado and Rachel appeared from around the truck, moving to his aid.

"Madre de Dios," said Los Cruzado. "My friend, are you all right?"

He and Rachel knelt next to Prichard. "What happened?" Rachel asked, her voice trembling with concern.

Prichard felt his wind coming back, and the fear subsiding. The sound of The Voice echoed in his head. "I don't know," he finally answered. "But, I think… that… was one of *them*…"

CHAPTER 12

The user tapped his I.D. and password into the log-on field, entering the largest information database in the world: LexisNexis.com.

His connection was fast, and for the small fortune he was paying for the service it had better be. The user selected search sources, and the screen flashed a window and prompted him to enter his search terms. He entered them in Boolean language with an unlimited date range:

New w/2 World w/2 Order.

There was a delay of mere seconds. The screen then showed over a hundred documents, from news sources all over the world, with New World Order as the main search term. He pulled the documents up in full, displaying the complete articles. After a moment of scanning the first few, he found an article titled *New World Order Quotes,* published in the *Independent* out of London. He pulled it up, wondering if he'd see himself quoted here.

> "The Council of Foreign Relations (CFR) is the American Branch of Society which originated in England...(and)...believes national boundaries should be obliterated and one-world rule established." <u>Professor of History Carroll Quigley</u>, Georgetown University, in his book "Tragedy and Hope."
>
> "Some of the biggest men in the United States, in the field of commerce and manufacture, are afraid of something. They know that there is a power somewhere so organized, so subtle, so watchful, so interlocked, so

complete, so pervasive, that they better not speak above their breath when they speak in condemnation of it." Woodrow Wilson.

"(The New World Order) cannot happen without U.S. participation, as we are the most significant single component. Yes, there will be a New World Order, and it will force the United States to change its perceptions." Henry Kissenger, World Affairs Council Press Conference, Regent Beverly Wilshire Hotel, April 20th 1994.

The user smirked at this last one. They had it right up until the date. It was actually said on April 19, 1994. He should know, because he was there. The user laughed to himself, shaking his head, and continued reading.

"The real rulers in Washington are invisible and exercise their power from behind the scenes." Justice Felix Frankfurter, U.S. Supreme Court.

"All of us will ultimately be judged on the effort we have contributed to building a New World Order." Robert Kennedy, Former U.S. Attorney General, 1967.

"For some time I have been disturbed by the way the CIA has been diverted from its original assignment. It has become an operational and at times a policy making arm of the government." President Harry S. Truman.

"The real truth of the matter is, as you and I know, that a financial element in the large centers has owned the government of the U.S. since the days of Andrew Jackson." U.S. President Franklin D. Roosevelt in a letter written Nov. 21, 1933, to Colonel E. Mandell House.

"Fundamental Bible-believing people do not have the right to indoctrinate their children in their religious beliefs because we, the state, are preparing them for the year... when America will be part of a one-world global society

Vernon Buford

and their children will not fit in." <u>Nebraska State Senator Peter Hoagland</u>, speaking on radio in 1983.

"We are grateful to the *Washington Post*, the *New York Times*, *Time Magazine* and other great publications whose directors have attended our meetings and respected the promises of discretion for almost forty years. It would have been impossible for us to develop our plan for the world if we had been subject to the bright lights of publicity during those years. But, the world is now more sophisticated and prepared to march towards a world-government. The supranational sovereignty of an intellectual elite and world bankers is surely preferable to the National autodetermination practiced in the past centuries." <u>David Rockefeller</u> in an address to a Trilateral Commission meeting in June of 1992.

When are they going to get the dates right? the user thought. That was in 1991, a year before he had walked away.

"The Trilateral Commission is intended to be the vehicle for a multinational consolidation of the commercial and banking interest by seizing control of the political government of the United States. The Trilateral Commission represents a skillful, coordinated effort to seize control and consolidate the four centers of power – political, monetary, intellectual and Ecclesiastical." <u>U.S. Senator Barry Goldwater</u> from his 1964 book "No Apologies".

"I believe that if the people of this nation fully understood what Congress has done to them over the last 49 years, they would move on Washington; they would not wait for an election... It adds up to a preconceived plan to destroy the economic and social independence of the United States!" <u>George W. Malone</u>, U.S. Senator (Nevada), speaking before Congress in 1957.

"From the days of Sparticus, Weishaupt, Karl Marx, Trotski, Belacoon, Rosa Luxemberg and Ema Goldman, this world conspiracy has been steadily growing. This conspiracy played a definite recognizable role in the French Revolution. It has been the mainspring of every subversive movement during the 19th century. And now at last, this band of extraordinary personalities from the underworld of the great cities of Europe and America have gripped the Russian people by the hair of their head and have become the undisputed masters of that enormous empire." Winston Churchill to the London Press in 1922.

Finally, he had to smile. Yes, indeed, they quoted him:

"What a blind world we've become. Men and machinations, the elected and the corrupt, have covered our eyes. The world is crying out for the very thing that will enslave us all: a Global Unity – New World Order. Man has always wanted peace and cultural and religious tolerance, but the thing offered will become a falsehood born in the very depths of hell. For me, and my fellow Christian brothers and sisters, I am overjoyed, for today I must say with all exuberance, that I have found God." – Arthur Baron to the press outside of the UN in 1992.

They got it right, Baron thought.

He tapped and clicked, commanding the LexisNexis system to download the documents to his home computer. He didn't have time to read through the rest of the them; he was already late for his meeting with a contact from the National Press Corps.

Baron shut down the laptop just as the waiter brought his check. The Italian restaurant, in the affluent D.C. suburb of Vienna, was a far cry from the more hauteur venues of his old days, but given his current circumstances, it was perfect. Anonymity was more on his mind than luxury.

He checked his Bulova; he had a half hour to get from Vienna to the *Washington Post,* some 15 miles east on I-66 in late afternoon traffic. He was going to be late, but his contact would wait.

Baron paid for lunch and headed for the exit. More ammunition, he thought, gently rapping the side of the laptop. Now it was time to go to war.

CHAPTER 13

Derek "Baal Boy 2000" Cole's ears rang from the death-metal guitar blast. The shock wave of grating chords, and the rambling, hyper-kinetic, pounding of the drums and bass shook his room.

The music from his all-time favorite band, *Cauldrons of Babylon,* pounded his ears in sonic ecstasy. His room was decorated with a gothic black motif; posters of the band and single shots of the pentagram and leather-clad members covered his walls. On another poster was an image of the lead singer sitting in a coffin of blood, sipping on a goblet of more blood that ran down the side of her black-painted lips. Behind her were two humanoid angels with severed wings, strung up on gallows, their throats cut.

A Nazi flag hung on the ceiling over his bed.

Derek Cole was on-line, chatting under his pseudonym—Baal Boy 2000—to some friends in a *Cauldrons of Babylon* chat room. Derek, thin and wiry, had a face covered with piercings and wore black exclusively. As he typed, he bounced his head in time with the reverberating pulse and quickening beat. The singer's voice had been manipulated in such a way that it sounded impossibly deep and menacing. She screamed and raged over the music.

Derek finished typing his last message, letting all his friends know what he had in store for the world. The Voice told him that the mark he would leave must be spectacular. Once his work here was completed, he'd finally go to Raleigh and see *Cauldrons of Babylon* in concert. The Voice told him that he'd actually meet the lead singer Lilia Libertine, which was really no big deal since he'd met her at least a dozen times. The thrill was that The Voice assured him he'd finally get to marry Lilia and join her band. Finally, he'd have the love of the only one who understood him. Her lyrics permeated his soul and spoke to him, comforted him. He had never known anyone who could get inside him like Lilia—not even his mother, or father, or older sister.

"That's why it is so important you get them out of your way," said The Voice, suddenly filling his head.

Derek looked up from the computer, gazing at the ceiling and laughing at the sound of The Voice. He brought his hands to his multi-pierced face, revealing black polish on his nails. He laughed and laughed, relishing in the freedom of the power he now held that they knew nothing about.

Derek rationalized that The Voice must be the spirit of the Babylonian god Marduk, who the band revered. He didn't know much about all the band's references to ancient cultures or even the symbols that decorated their website, but Derek thought some of the lyrics had to do with stuff in the Bible. He wasn't sure, though. He didn't read the Bible much; his mom and dad were the Jesus freaks.

"We're glad we have been able to bring such joy into your life, Baal Boy," The Voice serenaded. *"But it's time to check your inventory. Your family is on the way home. You don't want to be late for the concert."*

Derek jumped to his feet, grabbed the remote off the bed, and shut off the disc player.

He moved over to the closet, opening it and pulling out an old trunk that used to be his father's. Derek dug into a jean pocket, producing a set of keys, fumbling with excitement. Finally, he unlocked the trunk, revealing a small arsenal.

Derek had three guns: a cheap .38, a sawed off 12 gauge, and an old 9mm Beretta. The guns weren't the worst of it.

The smoke bomb was the easiest thing to make; it was simply sugar and potassium nitrate, mixed in the right proportions, then melted together over a low fire. Once the concoction cooled, Derek embedded several matches into it for a fuse. He made enough of it to fill the house with a thick, white cloud. Derek picked up the small, plastic container and after hefting the light weight of it, he set it aside.

Cautiously, he picked up a block of a wax covered with grayish material. It was a plastic explosive made from potassium chloride. It took him several hours to make five blocks of the volatile one-gram to three-gram cubes. He broke into his high school's chemistry lab to use a hot plate, hydrometer, and a large Pyrex container.

After heating and crystallizing the potassium chloride, Derek mixed it with white gasoline and Vaseline, kneading it into small, highly explosive bricks. Finally, he dipped the bricks into melted wax to add waterproofing.

He looked over them with pride. According to the *Anarchist Cookbook,* these blocks should have a high explosive velocity; he couldn't wait to see what kind of blast he'd get once he strapped one to the gas boiler in the basement.

"And you will see soon. Gather your things. It is time."

Derek nodded obediently to The Voice, carefully gathering the guns and one of the cubes of plastic explosives. He left the room, heading for the basement.

The first thing Alan and Patricia Cole noticed when they pulled up to the house was the white smoke pouring out of the windows. Patricia was frantic, clawing at her husband. "Oh, my God, Alan! Derek's in the house. We left him in the house!"

Alan spun the wheel of the car and they turned up on the lawn, sliding to a halt on the grass. They clamored out of the car, but Alan grabbed Patricia, stopping her from running to the front door.

"NO! No! Let go of me! Derek! Derek!" she shrieked.

Alan fought to calm her. "I'll get him, I'll get him! Listen to me! Stay here! I'll get him! Don't follow me into the house! Get the phone out of the car and call 911! Do it! Now!"

Alan turned and raced to the door, calling Derek. Patricia spun on her heel, stumbling in a panic back to the car.

She watched Alan disappear into the house; he coughed and hacked on the smoke. Patricia yanked opened the passenger door and grabbed the phone. Her hands were shaking so badly she dropped it.

"Mom!"

Patricia saw her son suddenly standing in the road in the midst of the smoke.

"Derek!"

Derek "Baal Boy 2000" smiled and waved to his mother, like a child in an amusement park. "Mom! You're standing too close to the house!"

"What?!"

Baal Boy 2000 laughed and laughed at his mother's predicament, a ghoulish howl that wasn't his own.

Patricia felt something pinch her heart. With realization, she turned a frightened, tearful gaze towards the house.

"Alan!"

The explosion rocked the block. The last thing Patricia Cole saw was a wall of fire, wood, and glass bearing down on her in a wave. The concussion lifted her body off the grass and tossed her to the street.

Baal Boy 2000 felt a rush of heat and force as the blast punched him in the chest. His arms and legs flayed as he was suddenly airborne, flying backwards. When he hit the asphalt, he almost blacked out. He opened his eyes and saw a cascade of burning debris raining down all around him.

Derek ignored the searing cuts and gashes across his face and body. He lay there on the ground, laughing and laughing. He whooped at the top of his lungs with the thrill of it. Watching his house explode was the most incredible thing he'd ever seen. He couldn't wait to tell Lilia and the band. It was exactly how they said it would be. Just like they said.

"We thought you'd like it, Baal Boy. We knew you would. We always knew."

Chapter 14

The front-page headlines of the *Seattle Times* held three stories that caught Scott's attention:

City Prosecutes Vandals From WTO Protests
Kingdome Demolition Soon
North Carolina Teenager Bombs House – Two Dead

Scott read further about the house bombing. Apparently, the boy was some wacked-out kid who'd visited one too many bomb-making, do-it-yourself websites, a sick trend these days.

Scott shook his head, flipping to the full story on page A3. He learned that the boy, whose name was Derek Cole, had a history of mental illness, having stated to authorities that a voice inside his head told him to blow up his house. He even claimed that the same voice told him to go to a Web site to learn how to make the bomb.

Scott looked up from the story to the Asian clerk behind the counter at the Pike Place Market International Newsstand. The rain was falling in a monsoon behind him on First Street. "Hey, I'll take this," he said, handing the clerk a twenty-dollar bill.

The young man bumped into another clerk as he moved to his register. The two of them hustled to wait on the patrons, who moved in and out of the market, drenched with rain.

The clerk came back to Scott and pressed his change into his hand. Scott moved away from the counter, shoving the paper under his arm, flipping up the collar of his raincoat. As he reached for his wallet, the back of the dollar bill in his hand caught his eye and held it.

Scott stared at it.

The Eye.

The Eye shone above the pyramid before a desert backdrop. Underneath the base of the pyramid, he saw the banner and read the Latin, but of course, he didn't understand the words or their meaning; he didn't understand the implications or the deep significance of those three words. His gaze caught The Eye again as the wind splashed a little rain across his hand.

The image, the seal, grew in his mind, filling him with a childhood emotion, a foreboding and fearsome testament of malevolence. A power of darkness.

That same spirit moved in the tower crane cab with him and Crazy Carl, manifesting itself in something Carl had said: "They are legion, they are many." He remembered the man who warned him of it long ago. "Thass the devil, boy. Thass the devil…"

Scott's mind clouded. He rubbed his brow against the oncoming migraine. What in God's name is happening to me? he thought.

"Spare some change, sir?"

"What?" Scott's mind broke free.

Biggsby stood in the rain, unprotected by the newsstand awning; Scott could barely make out his features, hidden under a dirty, wet mat of hair.

"Ya act like you ain't never seen one of those before. If you're not gonna keep that, buddy, I could use it." The man's accent drifted in and out of a gravelly, southwestern Texas twang.

Scott hesitated for a moment, not liking the way Biggsby sneaked up on him. He gave away his share of loose change over the years, but he'd always felt like he was gratifying some need of his to help someone. He often wondered if he was really doing any good. This guy looked like your basic wino; Scott figured he'd see him again sitting in front of the liquor store, drunk off the change he'd given him. Still, he stepped into the rain, held out his hand, and Biggsby reached for the dollar.

"Ah…yeah. There you go," Scott said.

Biggsby smiled at him, but Scott only saw it in his eyes, his face covered by the beard. "Thank ya. I thank ya, sir," he replied.

Scott smiled, moving past Biggsby, heading across the cobblestoned market street. Biggsby watched him tread off into the rain. "It's amazin' the things you notice, ain't it?"

Scott stopped in the middle of the street, turning back to him. "What's that?"

Biggsby glanced at the back of the dollar, and then stuffed it in his coat pocket.

"The things you notice, you know? Things that pass by ya everyday. Things that you never really see until… until the moment you finally see 'em."

Scott frowned. "I don't think I know what you're talking about. I mean, just… get yourself a warm, dry place or something, okay?"

"Well, I don't think I'm gonna get much on a dollar, buddy."

Scott looked across the street, embarrassed, as if someone was judging his actions. After a moment, he moved back to Biggsby, digging the remaining change from his coat pocket.

"Here… take the rest of this."

Biggsby eagerly grabbed the remaining cash, grinning warmly at Scott. "Thanks."

Scott nodded, turned again, and moved away. Biggsby called after him, holding up another dollar bill. "He opened your eyes, didn't He?"

"What?"

Biggsby playfully held the bill under his eyes, peeping at Scott. "Ya know what this means, don't cha? You got sight now, don't cha? Ya didn't have it before, but now ya do."

Scott held up his hand. "Listen, man, I gotta go, okay? That's all the cash I've got, all right? Now you try and have a good day. That's the best I can do for you." Scott ran off across the street, ducking under the sidewalk awnings, to the far side of the market entrance, at the north corner of First and Pike Streets.

Biggsby watched him leave, tears brimming in his eyes. He pocketed the money.

You have a good day too, Scott, he thought. You have a good day.

—◆—

The view from the Top of the Hilton was impossibly beautiful, but nothing compared to the radiance of Denise's smile. This had been an evening of personal triumph for her; Scott was bursting with pride and love.

He could hardly take his eyes off her. They sat at a window table, which afforded a view of the Cascades; the violet light of dusk and the orange glow from the glass wall sconces cast a beautiful shade on her skin; the elegant table lamp and candles reflected in her eyes.

They sipped champagne from tall, thin glasses.

Denise finally relaxed after overseeing six months of planning and preparing this meeting for her investment banking firm, Sievering and Rahn Securities. Her first year as an analyst at the firm began on shaky ground, but she soon proved her mettle by taking on tasks normally handed out to seasoned associates.

Denise was coming into her own, learning all the nuances of a volatile, competitive, market-driven business. All the schmoozing and juggling of egos became her forte, as she mastered the art of bringing together the right people to the right table, in order to move vast amounts of monies into the hands of company clients and investors. In spite of this, Scott marveled, Denise managed to keep her small-town-girl humility.

Scott glanced around the Top of the Hilton as the hotel staff moved efficiently, serving Northwest style cuisine to the guests. The company's profitable third-quarter numbers brought rich applause and appreciation from the attendees. Scott saw smiles and gratitude all around as Sievering and Rahn money served up a lavish dinner.

Denise reached across the table, taking his hand, gazing at him. "What do you want to do after this? I feel like we should celebrate. Just us."

"Well, I don't know," Scott said. "I don't think I can top all this, sweetie."

Scott was obviously impressed with the design and layout of the marble-adorned room. Denise grinned at him, looking like a princess in her dark evening gown.

"You could've designed it. I've seen drawings in your old school portfolio that were more impressive."

"I appreciate that, baby, but I don't know what to do for the girl who seems to have everything."

"I have everything?"

"That's right." Scott drummed his fingers on his chin, looking at the ceiling with mock concentration. "Let's see… First off, everybody in this room loves you, though not as much as I do…"

"Okay…" Denise chimed, playfully. "What else?"

"The presentation was flawless, due to your logistical brilliance and usual organizational acrobatics…"

"Okay…"

"Your company CEO actually knew your name and spoke very highly of you…"

She laughed at that. "Right, right…"

"And, it looks like you've gotten over the beginner's slump. You have a lucrative future with a highly successful company. You access a top-notch clientele. If everybody in here dropped a wallet, you'd have enough money to pay off the debt of some small, third-world country. Looks to me like you've got it all."

Denise smiled, leaned back from the table, and held up the back of her left hand at Scott, waving her fingers. "I might have most of it, but I don't have *everything* I want. I still seem to be missing something…"

As she wriggled the fingers on her ringless hand, Scott jokingly feigned ignorance. He tenderly took her hand, examining it. "Let's see, you've still got…one…two…three…four…five fingers. I'm not sure I follow you, sweetie. Everything looks good to me."

Denise yanked the napkin off her lap and tossed it in a ball at Scott's head. He laughed and she joined him. "I'm gonna hurt you…" she giggled.

Scott was glad for her, glad for both of them. It seemed like months since they'd had a stress-free moment. He knew she was anticipating the question, but he didn't want to do it here, not tonight. Soon, Denise, he thought. Soon we'll both have everything…

"Am I interrupting?" someone said.

They both looked up from their moment to catch the devilish smirk on the face of Kile Tatlock.

Denise was cordial and pleasant; Scott leaned back in his chair, trying not to show his displeasure. Your timing is perfect as usual, Kile, he thought.

Tatlock took Denise's hand and kissed it, cutting a predatory eye at Scott. "You look lovely, Denise," he hissed.

Feeling the tension from Scott, Denise kept her response as dry as possible.

"Thank you, Kile."

Tatlock was a premier associate for Sievering and Rahn, specializing in corporate mergers and acquisitions. He possessed keen business savvy and a no-nonsense approach that earned him the name "The Liquidator." In one deal that made him a ruthless legend, he organized the buying, breakup and selling-off of a local aerospace company, putting over 2000 workers in the unemployment line. Sievering and Rahn made millions and then funneled the monies into redirected cash flows for company investors.

Tatlock's social breeding taught him that bright and beautiful woman like Denise didn't, and shouldn't, choose men like Scott, men who had to actually climb the corporate latter. Why climb when you could ride?

Tatlock had known and worked with Denise for two years and couldn't understand why she chose to champion the mediocre; after all, the man was only a junior architect.

Well, after he gave her his offer, Tatlock knew she would make the proper career decision; soon, she would be thanking the better man.

"Please, I apologize for barging over to your table like this, but—"

"But, you're going to do it anyway, right?" Scott said, annoyed.

"Sweetie…" Denise interjected, surprised by his tone.

It was all Scott could do to keep his poise. He knew full well Tatlock had designs on her. He was never jealous and he trusted Denise completely, but there was something deceitful about Tatlock that he couldn't quite put his finger on.

For her sake, he ingratiated himself, smiling instead of cursing. "Just kidding, Kile. Just kidding. Good to see you." He extended his hand, and Kile shook it.

The two grinned uncomfortably at each other. Denise squirmed a little between them, feeling objectified.

"Scott, seriously, I do apologize," Tatlock said. "I just… well, there's something… an offer; an opportunity for Denise—and you, of course. But I… would like to discuss it with her first, in private. The guests are moving to the ballroom for drinks. If you could join us there shortly…"

Tatlock reached for Denise's hand, but she was looking at Scott intently. "Scott?"

He threw up his hands up, but fixed his gazed steadily on Tatlock. "No, no. Go ahead, I'll be there in a minute. You two need to talk about something; go ahead and talk about it." He leaned back, sullenly.

Denise sighed. "It'll just be a few minutes. Come in soon and join us, okay?" she said.

Scott nodded and then turned his gaze to the window.

Tatlock clapped his hands. "Good," he said, reaching for Denise's hand again. "Denise?"

She took it, rose, and walked with Tatlock toward the ballroom, but not before giving Scott a worried, backward glance.

He watched them leave as a waiter approached his table with another bottle of champagne. "Would you like another glass, sir?"

Scott gestured toward his half empty glass. "Yeah," he said. "Yeah, I would."

———————•◦•———————

"New York? New York City?" Denise exclaimed.

"That's right. I'm sure you've heard of it," quipped Tatlock.

They stood in the lavish Seattle Hilton ballroom among the Sievering and Rahn clientele. The opulent room buzzed with talk and occasional bursts of laughter; a piano player's nimble fingers moved across the keys, filling the room with soft jazz.

Denise couldn't believe the career offer that Tatlock just laid before her, so she asked him to repeat it. "Vice President?"

"Yes. That's right."

"But when did this happen?"

Tatlock smiled. He knew he had her. "Well, I haven't made the announcement yet, but as you know, I've been promoted to Managing Director over acquisitions at our Wall Street offices. I'll need someone with good advisor-to-client skills, a knowledge of values transactions, and an ability to assist in creatively structuring deals and negotiating favorable terms. You have shown strong potential in all of these categories, Denise."

Denise shook her head, awestruck at the possibilities. "But, I didn't expect a move like this for at least another three years, Kile. Has management approved all this?"

"They gave me carte blanche. I can choose whomever I want, but I've chosen to tell you first." He moved closer to her; Denise was ashamed at the attraction she felt to his power. "This is your time now. Every door in the world will be opened to you. We'll make all the arrangements for your transition: a townhome, living expenses, investment program, a handsome benefits package, and a salary that I'm sure you will find... munificent."

Denise was spellbound. Her whole life had come down to this moment. *Vice President*—just like that. The work she had done over the past few years had been the most intensive in her life. The pressures were enormous; they took a toll on her, her family, and her relationship with Scott. She knew one day the payoff would come, but not this soon; not this fast. But, there it was; there was the offer right in front of her. All she had to do was reach out and take it. So why was she hesitating?

"Denise?" Tatlock grinned.

"Ah… I, uh… I'll need some time."

"Time?"

"Ah… I have to think about it. This is a… it's a gracious offer. It's just so… completely unexpected, I just… I need some time to make a decision."

He nodded. "Well, good. I wouldn't expect you to come to a decision tonight; it is a great deal to mull over. But, I'll tell you this: you *are* the first I've chosen to tell, but you are not the only one I've considered."

Denise felt herself breathe again. "Thank you."

"Relax. Just call me in a few days. Don't make me wait too long," he smiled.

Denise smiled nervously back at him, feeling like the conversation had gone on long enough. She sipped her drink and glanced around the room, looking for Scott.

"Tell me," Tatlock asked. "Most would say yes right away. What's stopping you; what's holding you back?

Scott entered the ballroom and found Denise. He smiled and headed in her direction, stopping along the way, cordially greeting and introducing himself to the clients. Some of them recognized him from his work, but most of them commented on the crane accident.

Tatlock followed Denise's gaze as she watched Scott move toward them. He frowned. "How serious is this… relationship, if you don't mind my meddling?"

Denise shot him a hard look. "Very. It's very serious."

Tatlock shook his head like a disappointed father. Somehow, he still managed a smile. "I shouldn't really say this but… well… in this business, the key to success and longevity is the ability to know when to initiate change, to know when to move on. Your career is about one thing: you and only you."

A sudden chill crossed Tatlock's eyes.

"So, you two finished?" Scott asked, suddenly upon them. "I don't know about you, baby, but all these social circles are starting to make me dizzy."

Denise was grateful for his sudden presence, throwing her arms around him and kissing him. "You ready to go?"

"Yeah, yeah. Let's get out of here. Hey, Kile listen—"

Tatlock was gone, nowhere to be found.

⬥

The CD spun and an old Al Green love song warmed Scott's townhouse. Denise and Scott held each other in a tight embrace, slow dancing in the dim light, relishing the moment. It had been so long since the two of them had been able to hold each other and cherish the time. Scott could hardly believe the power of the love he felt for her. He knew where this night was heading, like so many others. Then, somewhere in the back of his mind, the Bible quote Bryce had shared from Ephesians suddenly made sense to him. "…just as Christ loved the church and gave himself up for her to make her holy, cleansing her by the washing with water through the word, and to present her to himself as a radiant church, without stain or any other blemish, but holy and blameless."

As their feelings took over, Scott wondered if maybe they were making a mistake. Could making love with this woman he so deeply and passionately cherished be a sin? Why does God insist on marriage? How can a man resist a woman like Denise? The thing that struck him their first night together was the power of her sensuality. First, her laugh, then her smile, then her light, strategically placed touches, her kisses… and eventually the rest.

As her warm, soft lips kissed his face and neck, Scott stopped feeling obligated to a God who would allow a son's father to die before they could know each other.

Between kisses, the question came, but not the one Denise was waiting for.

"So…what…what did you and Kile talk about tonight?"

She looked up at his face, smiling with pleasure, only half hearing his question. "What?"

"Kile. What was the big deal? What did you two talk about tonight?"

"Honey, just in case you haven't noticed, I'm not interested in talking about Kile or anything else right now."

"Yeah, I know. Me neither. But this clown comes over to our table, interrupts our dinner, drags you off to the ballroom... and I mean... you don't even tell me what it's about."

"Sweetie, it was about nothing. It was just business. Now come on..."

Scott threw his hands up. "Denise. What did he need to talk to you about?"

Denise scowled, pushing away from him. "It's just work. I told you it's nothing."

"No, no. It's somethin'. You just don't want to tell me what."

"And we were having such a good night..."

"What?"

"I said we were having such a good night, and then you drink too much and start acting like this."

"Hey, I'm not the one keeping secrets."

"I don't keep things from you, Scott. I've never kept anything from you."

"Well, what was the conversation about?"

Denise was exasperated. She stormed away from him toward the stereo system, shutting off the CD. Then she moved around the room, switching on lights. In a few moments, it was bright enough to kill the romantic mood. She was angry at him for not trusting her, but feeling guilty anyway.

"It was about my job, Scott."

"What about it?"

Denise looked to the polished hardwood floor, then back to Scott. "I was offered a position in New York."

Scott was dumbfounded. "What? Where?"

"I was offered a position at our Wall Street office. Kile is looking for an acquisitions VP."

"You got promoted?"

"Yes."

"To New York?"

"Yes, Scott."

"They're gonna give you more money?"

Denise shook her head, stooping to gather their empty glasses and a wine bottle off the coffee table. She stormed for the kitchen. "Yes, Scott. More money. More everything," she said, with a touch of cynicism.

Scott followed her down the dark hallway.

"So, when were you going to tell me? This is the first you heard of it, tonight?"

Denise slammed the bottle on the counter and placed the glasses in the sink.

"I don't know when I was going to tell you!"

"I'm just not sure I follow this, Denise. Are you saying you just found out about this tonight?"

"That's right!"

"But, what I don't understand is why he couldn't tell you in front of me! Did he not think I'd be interested in your career?!"

"What I don't understand is where all this jealousy over Kile is coming from!"

"I don't like him! You *know* I don't like him! You don't think I see what's going on?"

"What are you saying?"

"I'm saying every time we go to one of your company functions and this guy shows up, he's pawin' all over you! Is giving you this job gonna be the way he finally gets what he wants?!"

"How can you say that to me? I've never done anything to make you distrust me! You're the reason I'm hesitating to accept the position!"

"Well, what are you going to do? You gonna take it?"

"I don't know yet! I might!"

"I'll tell you what! Why don't you call Kile and conference him in! I'll leave the room and then maybe he can help you make a decision! You two can work it out!"

"I don't need any help with my choices, Scott, but you're making this one a lot easier for me!"

"So, you're just gonna throw away everything we have here, throw away this relationship we've built together, and run off to the East Coast?!"

"What relationship, Scott?! How long have we been together?! Almost seven years! Doesn't that tell you something?! Because it's telling me something!"

"What are you talking about?! Telling you what?!"

Denise choked on tears. "It tells me that you don't want me as your wife! I've been nothing but your glorified girlfriend for over half a decade, and I'm starting to see less and less of a reason to consider this relationship!"

Scott felt like someone just hit him dead in the chest with a sledgehammer. He stepped back from her, stunned. Denise could hardly believe she'd said it, but she had, and the thing that frightened her the most was that she'd really meant it.

"So you're takin' the position, then?"

Denise looked at him sadly, longing to give a different answer than the one in her mind. "I might have to, Scott. I don't know if…"

Scott moved closer. "If what?"

She turned from him, leaning against the sink. "I don't know…"

They couldn't speak for a long moment. For the first time since they'd known and loved each other, something threatened to destroy them.

Scott reached for the bottle of wine, seeing that it was half full.

"Don't drink anymore tonight, Scott."

He ignored her, reaching for a glass from the sink. "Don't you think you've had enough?" she frowned.

Denise reached for the bottle and glass, but Scott jerked away from her.

"Hey," he grimaced. "Just back off, Denise."

Denise grabbed at the glass and it shattered; a jagged piece cut across the flesh of her palm. She yelped and Scott's heart raced at the sight of her blood on the counter. For a split second, his eye was enthralled as her blood ran into a pattern of a cross along the grout of the tiles. "Denise…"

Scott flipped on the sink faucet and gently held her bleeding hand under the water; Denise winced at the sting. "Baby, I'm sorry… Oh, baby… Hang on a minute… Hang on… Hold it right there under the water. Just… Just keep it right there."

"Okay."

Scott reached into an upper cabinet and found a first aid kit, fought it open, and pulled out some gauze bandages and a bottle of peroxide. He dabbed the cut with some gauze and poured on peroxide, which foamed and fizzed on the wound.

After slowing the bleeding, they took a good look at the cut.

"You're gonna need stitches."

"It'll be fine."

"No. I'm gonna take you to the emergency room."

"It's okay. It's just a little cut."

"I'm sorry…"

"It's okay. I guess we've had ourselves a night, huh?"

Her eyes filled with trust, love, and uncertainty.

Scott warmed, flushing with emotion for her. "I guess we have."

"I'm sorry. I really don't... I don't know what I'm gonna do about the promotion, Scott. I just don't know if I'm ready for New York."

"Denise, don't worry about it. I was just acting like a jealous idiot. I'm sorry."

"I love you."

"I love you, too. Very much."

As he kissed her, they clung desperately together, but it was bittersweet. The end of their time was coming.

Scott was a quarter-mile away from his finish line as he raced along Alaska Way toward the public pier. His knee was throbbing with pain from a seven-mile run. The countdown timer on his watch spun the minutes down to seconds; he felt the time and he pushed himself. He was yards away from the goal and time slipped away like water; he was spilling all of it, but kept pushing. Scott concentrated his breathing and focused his eyes on the goal, a mooring pole that marked the beginning of the pier.

Come on... push it... push it...

The timer hit zero, and started beeping, then counting backwards in the negative, adding numbers to Scott's program time of 40 minutes over seven miles. By the time he limped past the mooring pole, the timer ran two minutes 53 seconds over.

Scott walked it off, resting his hands on his hips. He held back his head, eyes closed, feeling the warmth of the sun reflecting off the bay. Pain in his knee was nothing compared to the sting of the fight last night with Denise. Her promotion had completely caught him off-guard; he knew he would have to act quickly if she was to be his bride.

Scott understood the corporate environment all too well, though he himself worked at a small firm. There would be plenty of pressure on Denise to take the position and if that happened, they would be separated. He never considered working in New York. It would take several months to plan a relocation for himself, not that he would have any trouble finding a new firm; what really worried him was what the environment in New York City might do to their relationship.

Would she change on him? Would she become the quintessential high-climber, losing her simple love for him, preferring the allure of wealth and power?

Scott shook the thought from his mind, wiping the sweat from his face with the edge of his shirt. He turned, heading across Alaska Way to the parking lot, formulating a plan in his mind.

He would get the ring.

Bryce certainly wouldn't mind extending him a long lunch to go purchase the one he'd seen at De Beers in Bellevue. Denise was right. It had taken them too long, but now he was going to make his move.

Scott stopped suddenly as he approached his car, staring in disbelief. "What the…"

Biggsby was sitting on the trunk, his filthy boots propped up on the silver bumper of Scott's Lexus. Despite the pain in his leg, Scott moved fast, waving his arms as if shooing away birds. "Hey! What are you doing on my car?! Get off of there!"

Biggsby jumped to attention. "Oh. Hey, sorry about that, buddy. Is this yours?"

Scott reached him. "Yeah, it's mine, what are you doing? You're gonna dent it! Get off of there! You're screwing up the finish!"

Biggsby pulled out a rag that was just as dirty as his coat and started to wipe at the muck where he sat. "Oh, I know, I know. U'm really sorry about dat. I'll get dat. It's just a little smudge."

"No! Just get away from it, all right? Just get off my car!"

"Hey, hey, relax, Chief. No need to get bunched in the shorts. Man's just tryin' to rest up, takin' in the view."

"Take it somewhere else. Of all the spots in the city, you have to pick my car?"

Biggsby looked at the Lexus. "I like the color. It's a nice silver color. I was jus' passin' by, is all. Saw it was a nice car, just thought I'd take a closer look at her. I saw you comin', so I put my feet up."

"What do you mean, you 'saw me coming'? How did you know it was mine?"

"Son, ya parked her here this mornin'."

"Okay, well now you've seen it. I'm tired; my knee hurts… move on."

Scott moved past Biggsby, holding his breath against the smell.

"Well, ah was really hopin' that you and me could finish that conversation from the other day."

Scott pulled his keys from his runner's pack. "What conversation? What day are you talking about?"

Biggsby dug into his coat and produced a dollar bill, holding it up to Scott. "The one about this here."

"Look, I don't have any change, all right?" Suddenly, Scott recognized him from the newsstand. "Hold up. That was you the other day in the market."

"Son, you might look like Chief, but you ain't got his brains, for sure."

Scott eyes lit up. "What did you say? What do you mean, 'Chief'? Did you say Chief, again?"

Biggsby knew he had his interest now. "Thass right. Yo' daddy. Chief Mac."

Scott's jaw dropped with astonishment. How could this homeless vagrant know his father's nickname? "That's my father's name. How do you know it?"

"Ya want me to scare ya s'more? How 'bout this? I know you, too, Scott."

Now Scott's intrigue was doubled. "How do know my name? How do you know me?"

Biggsby dug into a coat pocket and found a photograph, handing it to Scott. It was the picture of Biggsby, Karen, Kathleen, and Thomas in Waikiki, circa 1972. His parents looked so young, but Scott recognized them immediately.

"How did you get this?"

"Well, ah paid the photographer who took it, thass how I got it."

"How do you know my mother and father?"

"Heck, thass me right there next to yo' momma and my wife. And, there's Chief right there. I know 'em 'cause we was practically family. We took this at the Tiki Lounge in Waikiki. It was after we got back from the war."

"Vietnam. You mean Vietnam?"

"Look at the date on the back."

Scott flipped it and read the smeared, blue ink inscription. "Aloha from Waikiki. Mitch, Thomas, Karen and Kathy, 1972."

"You know any other war goin' on in 1972, son? 'Cause I don't."

Scott's eyes glowed with shock, disbelief, and admiration. "You served with my father in Vietnam?"

Biggsby extended his grubby hand. "My name's Mitch Biggsby. You can call me Mitch."

Scott shook his hand.

"Well, saw ya stop here this mornin', like I was sayin'. Just thought I'd wait here till you got back and give ya that. It really should be yours anyway," Biggsby said.

Scott was speechless.

"Anyway, Scott, I gotta go make my rounds. Get some cans over to the recyclin' place before it gets late. They're picky down there. Won't take no cans after twelve."

"Where are you staying? Are you in a shelter?"

Biggsby started to walk away. "I live under the freeway. If ya ever need ta talk about that picture, just stop on by. But don't try to call me 'cause I ain't in the book."

Scott dug his wallet out of the runner's pack. "Wait a second, hold on, hold on."

He pulled out twenty dollars and put it in Biggsby's hand.

"Well, thanks again, son. I'll use this ta diversify my portfolio." Biggsby laughed, revealing a decaying smile, but a smile nonetheless. Scott laughed with him, feeling a sudden lightness to the weight of all his problems.

He watched him walk away for a moment, and then climbed into his car. As he drove away, the mirth of Biggsby's laughter stayed with him.

CHAPTER 15

From his room in the Washington Dulles Airport Marriott, Baron watched the sun rise over the Potomac River; he reached for a phone to make a simple call.

"Locate Prichard, Los Cruzado, and Dr. Walters," he ordered. "Bring them the disc containing the Biggsby interrogation."

He hung up.

The sun burned in the clear morning sky as it hung mightily over the Washington Monument and the dome of the Capitol. The interview was in six hours and he had to prepare. Baron moved into the study, spending the next hour in deep, concentrated prayer.

———◆———

Rachel awoke from her sleep in one of the reclined back seats of the Blazer. Her eyes were sticky; the sunset light blinded them at first as they adjusted. She rubbed her face, wondering how long she'd been under; a glance at the bluish-green numbers of the dash clock told her it was five-forty in the afternoon.

Prichard and Los Cruzado were engaged in a heavy conversation as they sped west along Interstate 70, halfway through Sherman County, Kansas, roughly 20 miles from the Colorado border.

Rachel decided the interior of the vehicle looked exactly like three people had traveled in it for over 60 hours. Prichard and Los Cruzado's backpacks took up most of the storage space behind the back seats. Rachel's garment and overnight bags filled up the other passenger seat; her laptop and case were at her feet, under the driver seat. There were bags of food, mostly travel snacks, and a large cooler with ice bags, bread, bottled water, cheese, and cold cuts. Prichard wanted to make the trip to Seattle as quickly as possible with few stops; they only pulled in for bathroom breaks, gas, and to restock the food supply. Rarely, they would stop at a hotel when the road became too much. It took them two and a half days to reach Kansas.

Rachel turned her gaze to the rolling, sunbathed fields of wheat. The long shadow of the Blazer stretched and flew across the grain, as if in a race. The silos on the horizon stood like castle towers against a cobalt sky. It was beautiful; it was America, but what was happening to America, indeed to the world, wasn't so beautiful.

Rachel remembered the mental torture of her brother, the way his illness cast a deep murkiness over their home in Kenton, Ohio. She remembered her family's pain just before it happened; she remembered how her father, a proud man, prominent in the City Council and Superintendent of the Hardin County School District, could control everything but couldn't stop his son from taking his own life. Rachel remembered the way her mother would watch her son with an expression that Rachel could not translate until she became an adult herself. Her mother's face had twisted with sadness, regret, and guilt, but especially guilt. Rachel's mother bore a son with a disease that she couldn't comprehend.

Rachel squeezed her eyes shut, and the fields of Kansas flickered into darkness like an ancient cinema; she saw her brother's feet dangling above the floor of the garage, the cord around his neck, and his blue skin. Before she could say a word, hands gripped her and pulled her away; her mother's voice shrilled as her father raced past, reaching for the boy…

Now, she said it; his name came up in her throat… "Michael…" she cried softly, as she felt her eyes warm with tears. She let a few run down her cheeks before shutting off the flow of them, before they spilled uncontrollably. What killed her brother that day? She had to ask this question because now, more than ever, she knew he hadn't acted alone.

Sniffing and wiping her eyes, she turned to Prichard and Los Cruzado, grateful to be on this journey with them. Somewhere on the horizon was an answer; Rachel knew because of them, she would have it.

"*Si*. In fact, Prichard, demonic possession is written about in the Scriptures."

"Yeah, but is there anything about possessed people having inhuman strength and agility?" Prichard's face was recovering from his little tussle with the Ft. Mitchell Cemetery Grounds Keeper.

Los Cruzado glanced out the cracked passenger side window, formulating his thoughts with a creased brow. "*Si, si*. There is one passage in Acts 19. There were some Jews in Ephesus who were trying to exorcise demonic spirits, but they weren't true believers in Christ."

"So, what happened?"

"Well, when they tried to cleanse the evil spirit from a certain man, they became completely overpowered by him; the Bible says they were beaten and sent running out of the man's house, naked and bleeding."

"Oh."

Rachel leaned up between the two men with her hands on the back of their seats.

"So, Father," she asked, " that man in the cemetery was possessed?"

Prichard smirked. "Well, he was on somethin', I know that much."

Los Cruzado nodded grimly. "*Si. Aquello del exacto.* That's right. This is why I warned you not to chase after him, Prichard. He could have killed you. I'm surprised he did not."

"But, what clued you in? How did you know what was wrong with him?" Prichard queried.

"What he said before you went after him. He said 'they were legion, they were many'."

"So what? What's that to me?"

Los Cruzado smiled. "Lord love you. When was the last time you even *looked* at a Bible, Prichard?"

Prichard shifted uncomfortably in his seat. "Ah... I don't remember."

"The Book of Mark," Rachel answered. "Jesus spoke to a demon that was possessing a man, commanding it to leave. Jesus asked the demon if it had a name and the demon called itself legion."

"Well, here's somethin' I do remember," Prichard added. "A Roman legion was made up of about 6000 soldiers."

"*Si. Exacto.* There were *many* spirits controlling this man. Before Jesus arrived, the people tried all manner of ways to subdue him. According to the Gospel of Mark, they tried to bind him with chains, but he would break them; no one could hold him."

"There's one thing that's bothering me, though," said Prichard. "Now, I don't know much about the Bible, but from what I can understand, people who are demon-possessed don't have any control over what they're doing, right?"

"*Si.*"

"So, what are you saying?"

"What I'm saying, Rachel, is that that Grounds Keeper *had* control over himself, over his body. At one point, he was running right along side of me and I was doin' at least forty. When I hit the back of the cart he was driving, he jumped off the thing and flew through the air like an acrobat. When he hit the ground, he rolled to his feet and ran straight for those trees. He knew how to escape. He was fast, I mean inhumanly *fast*. When he attacked me, I didn't even see him. I just felt his fists. Next thing I knew, I was on the dirt."

"I have a theory," Los Cruzado posited. "The spirits of evil, over the centuries, have advanced. Humankind has shown itself willing to be manipulated by the evil, therefore evil has mastered its use of us. Just as there are those who are advanced in the holy ways of God, this Illuminati must be, how do you say, the culmination of evil integrated with humanity. These men, who are The Illuminated, ultimately are not in control of the powers they are wielding; ultimately, the great adversary of God is the one who controls them. They have simply learned to use this power with great skill."

There was a moment of silence as they absorbed Los Cruzado's words. Prichard spied an interstate sign; they were less than 15 miles from Colorado.

"When did all this begin, Father?" Rachel asked. "Historically."

Los Cruzado took a deep breath. "*Bien cuesion.* Good question. History teaches that the first man to place the blame for all evil on one entity was a sixth-century prophet from Persia named Zoroaster. The Greeks and the Jews produced the names we have today to describe the evil one: Satan is Hebrew, which means adversary, and devil is Greek, meaning slanderer.

"There are few references to the devil in the Old Testament; before Christ, there was hardly any information about him or about how he controlled us. Christ called Himself the Light of the World for a good reason, eh? Well, the church often made grave mistakes in its war against the devil, beginning when Christianity spread to Europe. The Druids and other tribal groups practiced rituals reminiscent of the Canaanite people, to whom God had sent the Israelites centuries earlier, to destroy them.

"The church grew, eh? Soon it held great political power, and this led to many un-Christ-like persecutions of non-believers. The satanists formed as a result of this, and as a backlash against the young church. There were black masses and rituals where people urinated into communion chalices and worshiped upside-down crosses. There was ritualized murder, pregnant women were convinced to give their children as sacrifices, and so forth. There was one story where eight hundred children in a medieval town in France were kidnapped and murdered sacrificially.

"Soon, with the Reformation and the Protestant Church, the Roman Catholics put into place reforms and most of the persecutions stopped, with the exception of the Salem Witch Trials in the 1600s.

"In America, satanism seems to have developed in waves, eh. In the fifties, Americans reacted strongly against the rise of atheistic communism and then in the sixties and seventies, against the creation of satanic churches. Anton LaVay began a major church in San Francisco and Michael Aquino started the Church of Set.

"Modern Christianity is being affronted by the evil one, who uses things as seemingly harmless as astrology, to new age, neo-paganism and full worship of the devil. Statistics show that black masses and other anti-God rituals are rare, but the number of people who experiment with satanism is on the increase."

"How do you categorize The Illuminated? Where do they fit into the picture?" Prichard asked.

"*Ellos hacer no ajuste en alungo categoria.* There is no category for them. As far as I can see, they are a mystery. Nothing I have studied or anything in history gives a clue. It's as if they do not exist."

"So, I guess our boy back at the cemetery was a figment of my feeble imagination," Prichard grumbled.

"How do they control us?" Rachel asked.

"A spirit gets inside a man, influencing his will. The stronger-willed can resist them, but the weaker-willed, and those who have no holy knowledge or faith, leave themselves open to attack and manipulation by dark forces, subtle and overt."

Rachel leaned back in her seat, pondering her next question. "What about voices? Do you think they influence behavior using hallucinogenic, auditory commands?"

"*Yo hacer no saber.* I do not know, Doctor. I think your experience and knowledge can answer that question."

"Well, in case after case, I've seen the same pattern of violent behavior. Almost every time. If the suspects survive, they say that something, a voice, told them to do what they did," she said.

"'The devil made me do it'," Prichard retorted. "Never thought that excuse would hold water. As far as these voices are concerned, how do you distinguish between them and say... the Voice of the Almighty?"

Los Cruzado nodded. "The more we know of Him, the better we can tell the difference."

Rachel folded her arms. "They killed my brother," she said softly, forlornly.

"What's that?" asked Prichard.

Rachel hesitated to share her thoughts, but she knew she could trust them. "I think... I think I've heard them before," she finally said.

"*Que?*"

"What are you talkin' about?"

Rachel let out a long, tired sigh. "I'm sure you heard about that case in Chicago, where eight people were killed in a downtown office building a few weeks ago."

They said nothing; both of them read the account in Baron's information.

"On the roof of the building... afterwards... when it was over. I heard it."

"What did it say?" Prichard asked.

"It just said...my name. It felt like another person was inside of me, or like something climbed inside my head. It sounded... like they were warning me."

Prichard's hands gripped the steering wheel, squeezing tensely.

"I heard something, too," he confessed. "You were right, Father. The Grounds Keeper almost did kill me. I guess I didn't tell you two this part, but he was just about to gut me when... this voice suddenly filled up my head. I know we both heard it, 'cause we reacted to it at the same time. It was a deep, raspy sound, a man's voice. It said, 'Withdraw'. That's when the Grounds Keeper pulled back and disappeared. I think the voice may have saved my life; maybe they're holding back, delaying the inevitable. I'm not sure how we're gonna stand up to them, but we'd better come up with something soon. I have a feeling that the closer we get to recovering Biggsby's information, the more of them are gonna show up."

They were silent until Prichard turned to Los Cruzado. "Okay, Father, your turn. Have you heard anything?"

Los Cruzado kept his gaze away from Prichard. "*Si. Yo tener.* I have. Twenty years ago in the jungle in Nicaragua… just after I met you, Prichard."

Rachel saw a look pass over Prichard's face as he turned to the priest; she wondered what was between them.

The profound silence accentuated the sound of the wheels against the road. The persistent ringing of Prichard's cell phone broke it; he reached for it on the dash cradle, careful not to unplug it from its power jack.

"Prichard," he answered, coarsely.

"Good to hear from you, Prich!" It was Sikes's singsong voice.

Prichard resisted the urge to toss the phone out on the interstate. "I happen to be in the middle of good conversation here, Sikes. If you need to send me a message, I've got an e-mail account." He tapped a button and Sikes was on the speakers.

Sikes laughed and the sound of it chafed Prichard's nerves. "Well, I know how disappointed you'll be," Sikes said, "but I can't talk. I apologize for the short notice, but this one just came down my line."

"Spill it."

"You've got a package to pick up at a rest-stop off the Ruleton exit."

"Rachel?" Prichard asked, but she was already on it, tapping the keys on her laptop to pull up her map. "I got it. Looks like… that exit should be right…"

She looked up just in time to see the exit lane passing by. "Right there!"

Prichard gritted his teeth and turned the wheel hard right. The Chevy rolled down a shallow embankment, up, and over again. They narrowly missed an old wood-paneled station wagon, before swerving back onto the exit lane.

Prichard ignored the shocked expressions of Rachel and Los Cruzado, jumping back on the phone. "How 'bout givin' us a heads up next time, Sikes, you idiot! Sikes!"

Sikes was gone.

They spent an hour combing the rest area, stretching their legs. They looked everywhere, including under the picnic tables, in restroom stalls, and in garbage cans, but found nothing. Prichard was starting to think Sikes was playing with them. He didn't like the spy routine, and Sikes made it even more unbearable by reducing it to a boy's game.

Prichard kicked over another trashcan, spilling nothing but the requisite fast-food refuse and empty pop cans. After kneeling to fish through the pile, he rose to find Los Cruzado and Rachel moving toward him from the rest area building. Both wore dejected expressions. Prichard frowned at them. "Nothin'?"

They shook their heads. *"Nada,"* said Los Cruzado.

"What now?" asked Rachel.

Prichard angrily pulled the phone from his belt, about to redial Sikes with a few choice words, when he noticed the blinking email icon on the screen. He highlighted the icon, and tapped the button to open the message:

> Sender Unknown: Prichard, check the vending machines.
> You're right, I think I like e-mail better.
> With you driving, it's so much safer.

Prichard shut off the phone and moved past Rachel and Los Cruzado.

"What?" Rachel asked again, throwing her hands up

Prichard turned back to them. "Sikes," he spat. "Just be glad you don't know 'im."

Prichard found the manila envelope taped behind one of the vending machines in the rest stop building. He barely squeezed his arm between the wall and the back of the machine, grabbing the envelope and ripping it from the wall. Prichard pulled out a nondescript CD. He placed it back in the envelope and pocketed it, ignoring the curious stares of some travelers.

The disc spun in Rachel's laptop, where it sat on the hood of the Blazer. The three of them gathered around it, after parking farther away from the rest area building for more privacy. The interstate traffic roared behind them as the sun made its daily, final curtain call.

They moved closer to the screen when the image came up.

The black-and-white, grainy video showed Biggsby sitting at a table in what looked some type of interrogation room; the angle came from a security camera high in a corner. A clock and counter ran in the bottom left corner of the screen; the date on the video was February 11, 1984. Biggsby looked like death just passed before him; he sat motionless, staring ahead. His face and the front of his sweatshirt were smudged with what looked like dirt, and both his hands were wrapped with gauze. Rachel deduced from his expression that he was in shock.

Apparently, a door off-camera opened, and for an instant office sounds could be heard as the shadow of two men passed over Biggsby. The door closed and they entered the room. Biggsby reared back with a look of hope on his face, but the men didn't appear to bring good news. The two men appeared to be detectives, one in a suit, the other in a cowboy hat and bolo tic.

"Let's get your story straight here. Take it from the top," Cowboy Hat said.

Biggsby glanced up at the two detectives and the stark lights made his eyes look like black sockets. His voice quivered with pain and loss. "I went into my garage ta do some paint strippin' on my boat. We'd planned a trip to South Padre this summer, and I had to get 'er fixed up."

"What time did you start working on it?" The Suit Detective asked.

"Three-fifteen, three-thirty."

"Why'd you leave?"

"Supplies... I had to pick up dinner and I had to get some tape and utility blades."

"I got another question for you," said Cowboy Hat "It's February. Normally, people don't start doing that kind of thing until spring. You're using paint thinner and solvents without proper ventilation, locked up in a small garage. It just doesn't make any sense. How did you breath in there?"

Biggsby rubbed his bandaged hands through his hair. "I had fans on. There was plenty of air. I was just tryin' to get an early start on my boat, that's all."

The Suit Detective moved away from the table, leaning against a wall. Cowboy Hat sat imposingly right in front of Biggsby, and then leaned over him.

"You wanna know what Arson Division found?" Biggsby stared ahead as if Cowboy Hat wasn't there. "Residual amounts of methylene chloride splashed on the carpet, the walls, and the burned curtain material. You know what methylene chloride is, right?"

"Paint thinner," Biggsby said, quietly.

"What's that?" Cowboy intimidated.

Biggsby looked up at him. "That's paint thinner."

"Could the kids have gotten a hold of it while you were gone, Mr. Biggsby?" asked the Suit Detective.

"No. I locked the kitchen door to the garage before I left. I never let my kids in there."

The detectives held back their questions for a moment, hoping the silence and the tension would break Biggsby. The Suit Detective moved behind him, pacing, his hands behind his back.

"Your wife was insured, wasn't she?"

Biggsby turned back to him in the chair, shocked at his question. "Yes."

Suit Detective nodded. "In fact, you just recently renewed the policy, ain't that right? On your kids, too, right? I think it's over a hundred-thousand?"

The implication hit him dead in the chest, and his anger rose like the flames he could still see in his mind. "If I was gonna kill my family, I wouldn't have gone back into the house! I tried to save them!" He held up his burned and bandaged hands.

Cowboy Hat folded his arms, skeptically. "Right, right. Maybe you just wanted it to look good."

Suit Detective moved back in front of Biggsby. "You have any enemies, anybody who'd hate you enough to want to kill you?"

Rachel, Prichard, and Los Cruzado waited for his reply, straining to hear the audio over the traffic noise. Rachel turned up the volume.

Biggsby ducked his head. After a long pause, he looked up with his face twisted in deep despair. "No. I don't know anybody like that." His eyes were lying.

The two detectives looked at each other like jungle cats over wounded prey. Cowboy Hat stood up and moved toward the door as Suite Detective summarized. "Well, I'm glad you said that, 'cause we ain't lookin' for any other suspects. You're our primary. We're gonna let you sit here and think about that for a minute. Then you can make a phone call. I suggest you talk to a lawyer. It's real simple, Mr. Biggsby. You had motive and opportunity. My gut tells me that once all the physical evidence is analyzed, everything's gonna point to you."

Cowboy Hat moved from the cameraview and out the door. Suit Detective followed, but stopped and turned to Biggsby. "By the heinous nature of the crime, I hope the D.A. pushes for the chair for you, Mr. Biggsby. I really do." He walked out the door, slamming and locking it.

Biggsby sat there a moment, then leaped to his feet, kicking the chair, flipping it off a wall, and pounding his fists on the table. He brought his hands to his face, shaking with anger and tears. "God…God…why? Karen…my family… why? Why?" He threw his hands up, pleading, then fell to the floor on his knees, moaning in deep, broken pain. A few seconds later, the screen went blank.

Rachel ejected the disc and shut down the computer.

"Looks like they got him pretty good," Prichard said. Los Cruzado and Rachel couldn't say a word. "Come on. We're about two more days from Seattle. Let's hope we can find him."

They loaded into the Blazer and drove west out of Kansas toward Burlington, Colorado.

CHAPTER 16

A jetliner cut the air over Dulles Airport; Baron watched it bank against the sky, turning sharply and heading west. He kept his eyes on it until it became a dark speck, then removed his glasses and rubbed his irritated, fatigued eyes. When he looked back to the sky, the jetliner was gone. I'm ready for the interview, he thought, and just then the knock came on his door.

Baron moved across his airy hotel room to the entrance; when he opened it, he was greeted by the disenchanted expression of Bruce Faber of the *Washington Post*.

"First thing I wanna say right off the bat: I don't think this is gonna make good copy."

Baron smiled. "You've made clear all your reservations during our initial communiqués, Bruce; however, I think you will find I have something very important to say, something that concerns all of us."

Faber entered the room and Baron closed the door, locking it behind them. Faber's confidence and swagger characterized a worldly, seasoned journalist, peppered with a good measure of caution and skepticism. He dressed more like a TV anchorman, in a suit and trenchcoat, but the clothes softened a gruff interior. Faber had long been out of his Brooklyn, New York, neighborhood, but there was still a hint of the accent.

"Is this thing important enough to move newspapers?" he asked.

"If that's what's important to you."

"Well, what do you think? I'm a senior columnist, Art. Selling newspapers is only *a little* important to me. It's just my job, that's all."

Baron gestured to the main room. Faber hesitated for a moment, but then the men moved there, sitting on couches opposite each other. Faber opcned a leather briefcase and produced a pen, a legal pad, and a tape recorder. He placed them on a table between the couches, next to a serving tray with coffee. Baron reached for a cup.

"Coffee?" Baron asked.

"Nah. You mind if I light up?"

"Not at all."

Faber pulled out a pack of cigarettes; in a few moments, a gray smoke formed a strata above him and a haze in front.

"I mean, how long have you known me, Art? Twenty, twenty-five years? You know the only reason, the real reason I'm doing this is because we're friends. But, even still, I'm not so sure about you these days. I think you're slippin'."

"'These days,' indeed. These are some interesting times, aren't they?" Baron asked.

"Right, right. What you're referring to are all your doomsday theories: the End Times, the Last Days, apocalyptic mumbo-jumbo. Look, I've been all over the world; for the past 40 years, I've covered stories in the Middle East, South America, Laos, Cambodia, Greece, Albania, Lithuania, Cuba, the Congo, the Balkans, Europe and every other placc in between. I've interviewed Eddi Ameen, Sadat, Pinochet, Castro, Ghadafi, Khomani, Thatcher, Kirkpatrick, Kennedy, Nixon, Johnson, Ford, Carter, Reagan, and Bush. I've known men and women of great prominence, influence, and power; I've seen coups, countercoups and states of government rise and fall on the world stage. But for some reason, I don't see any evidence of some omnipresent, cohesive New World Order, like you keep talkin' about."

"You're not making the proper connections."

"What connections? All I do is connect. I make a living connecting. How do you think I put together my stories? I've got awards for making connections."

"Is this the interview?"

Faber frowned. He knew he'd regret it, but he reached over and started the tape recorder. "Okay. Now, this is the interview."

"Ask me that question again."

"Hold on. You can't tell me what to ask, Art. You know that."

"I apologize."

There was a deep pause as Faber grabbed the pen and legal pad, flipping some pages. He found his first set of questions and looked up at Baron, dragging on his cigarette and blowing a thick cloud. "What is the New World Order? What is the probability of such a thing actually existing?"

"Well, to answer the latter question first, the probability of such a thing is very high. After I explain to you just what the New World Order is, you'll understand that it not only exists, but it has been expanding in power for some time."

"How did it begin?"

"I do not wish to delve too deeply into history; but this all-encompassing world system has its roots in ancient times, beginning with the Pharaohs and the kings of Babylon. In more recent history, our first American president was aware of the formation of such a power, as he read of it in a book called *Proofs of Conspiracy*. After two terrible world wars, the momentum for the creation of such an order intensified; certain men saw that in order for there to be a true world peace, there would have to come about a conglomerate of nations."

"Do we see something like this happening today?"

"Yes."

"How?"

"Technologically, over the past 15 or 20 years, we have developed the means to move information and currency instantly; political power itself is no longer limited to the few, and governments and corporations are becoming more transparent; we've broadened our communicative capabilities on a world scale. In essence, the world is shrinking, which fosters a new type of worldly-thinking individual."

"A new type of world citizen via the Internet or the Web."

"Precisely. Internet and Web technologies have made international business more accessible for both the west and the east; the private citizen has gained more of a voice on the world scene and doesn't have the same concerns of sovereignty as the state."

"But what does all this have to do with the New World Order?"

"First of all, the term itself is passé; it conjures up the thought of so many fringe element ideologies which, in turn, tend to weaken the true meaning at the center of so many theories of conspiracy."

"Everything from Adam Weishaupt, to Bigfoot, to UFOs hiding in volcanos."

"Exactly. Those kind of things. The absurd is often grafted onto the truth, rendering the truth innocuous."

"So how do you make sense of everything?"

"By paying attention to the truer meaning of certain global events, you'll find there is a word better suited to defining the formation or the shaping of the New World Order."

"And that word is…?"

The sound of another jetliner thundered along the horizon. Baron turned his gaze to a window, but couldn't see the plane; the sunlight sparkled off his glasses.

Faber coughed and then smothered his cigarette in a crystal ash tray.

"Globalism," Baron concluded.

"How does globalism shape the New World Order?"

"It is the catalyst."

"What are its elements?"

"Multinational corporations, governmental and non-governmental organizations, and world religious groups such as the World Council of Churches."

"Name some others."

"Certainly. The International Monetary Fund, the World Bank, the World Trade Organization, the United Nations, the Council of Foreign Relations, the Trilateral Commission, the European Union, the World Economic Forum, and so forth. So far, these groups have met with resistance from the public, as evidenced in the riots in Seattle and the protests in Prague. The people of the Third World and the disenfranchised have yet to play a significant role on the international scene, but their voices are being heard. The soft sell of inclusionism will eventually become a way of seducing everyone into the system. The common people are unimportant to the intellectual elitists, but they will become a useful tool for the development of a global system. As much as some would like to impede its progress, time and Biblical prophecy will side with the purveyors of the global order."

"Now, you mentioned two things here that caught my attention. First off, you said 'seducing everyone into the system', and second, you mentioned 'Biblical prophecy'. We've talked about these things at length before, but explain to our readers how Christianity ties into these events."

"In Revelation, the Bible speaks of two beasts that will bring about great evil in the world. The first beast, a man, is given great power, authority, and influence over the entire earth. Let me quote Scripture here. 'He was given power to make war against the saints and to conquer them. And he was given authority over *every* tribe, people, language and nation. All inhabitants of the earth will worship the beast—all whose names have not been written in the book of the Lamb that was slain from the creation of the world.' Notice that it reads *'all inhabitants of the earth'*. It is quite clear that the entire world will be affected; you see, the only way for anyone to have authority over the entire earth is for there to be a system in place from which to wield the power. All the organizations that I mentioned earlier are simply the sub-groups of the eventual world authority; one or more of these groups will develop into the global order. Then, one man will rise, becoming the world leader. That man will be the beast."

"And what about the second beast?"

"He will be a man whose primary task will be to head a world religious system. This system will encompass all religions under one umbrella, necessary in order to bring about world peace. Once the first beast takes full power, the second will establish a new religion for compulsory worship of the first."

"Will people really fall for all this?"

"Of course they will. Did people fall for the emperors? Did people fall for Hitler? Do people bow to dictators and ruthless tyrants everyday? Wouldn't you fall for the man who finally brings full, unified peace to the world?"

Faber paused, stunned by his own sudden sense of clarity. He'd read those passages of Scripture before, but somehow the truth of their meaning had just become strikingly real. "Shouldn't people be made aware of what's happening?"

"Yes, they should and they will be. Since I've become a Christian, I've used my influence as a former head of state to develop a network devoted to the discovery of all truths concerning the rise of the world order and the beast. Christ commanded that all believers should watch, so as not to be caught unaware at His coming. The true meaning of these events will be revealed. There will be great chaos and upheaval; many will be saved, but many will fall."

Faber pressed on. "Recently, the National Foreign Intelligence Board, under the Direction of the Central Intelligence Agency, issued a report called *Global Trends 2015,* in which they predicted four alternate global futures taking place in the year 2015. I'm going to briefly paraphrase each of them here, then I'd like you to explain which alternative is the most likely to occur.

Scenario One: Inclusive Globalism. Technology, business, shrinking government systems, economic growth, and other positive demographic factors merge to benefit the majority of the world. Scenario Two: Pernicious Globalism. The elite and highly developed countries benefit from the expanse of technology and economic growth, while underdeveloped countries suffer from economic collapse and regional conflicts. Weapons of mass destruction are used in at least one of these conflicts. Scenario Three: Regional Competition. Nationalism and regional identities strengthen in Europe, Asia, and the Americas. Countries in these regions become more concerned with their own issues, and a resentment to U.S. backed globalism persists. And, finally, Scenario Four: Post-Polarized World. Europe and U.S. alliances collapse as Europe becomes more dependent on her own resources. The U.S. has to solve problems in South America as governments there falter."

Baron nodded, taking in a deep breath. "I do not see any of those scenarios on its own reaching fruition; rather, according to Scriptural prophecy, they appear to be progressive stages in the development of the global order. Ultimately, we will experience a short-lived, unprecedented peace and prosperity on a worldwide scale, followed by deterioration into chaos and upheaval, as the beast betrays mankind and God brings His wrath upon us. I believe certain states of government will fight for their sovereignty, but eventually, they will be absorbed into the global system."

"Can we place a time frame on it?"

"No. The Lord has given us plenty to watch for, and I sense that we are close; never in history have there been such ideal conditions for the fulfillment of the Scriptures. We must use caution, however, for the Lord warned us against trying to predict the exact times of these events. After all, we must continue to live in faith."

Baron stood and moved slowly to the window, which was bathed in the setting sunlight.

Faber reached over and shut off the tape recorder, watching Baron as he turned his gaze to the sky.

"In the meantime, until our Lord returns, we will do everything we can to dispense the truth. We will save...yes, we will save as many as we can until the end comes."

Chapter 17

The sky was clear blue, azure. An automobile fell out of the fathomless blue; it spun and twisted, the sound of metal creaked as it cut the air. And it fell…and fell… and fell…

—◆—

Scott stirred and writhed in his bed, his eyes darting in REM sleep. Beads of sweat shimmered on his face. The nightmare shifted. In the dream, his father's car would never hit the earth. It would simply drop endlessly.

His muscles relaxed and his breathing eased as he felt the cool pacific waters of a beach kiss his toes. The waves crashed in the distance, the breakers churning and foaming. The sky was blue here, too, incredibly blue, mirroring the ocean, which expanded forever into the distance. The sun hovered graciously, and Scott felt the warmth embrace his bony shoulders. Suddenly, he realized he wasn't himself; he was no longer in his adult body. When he looked down at his toes, he saw a tiny boy's feet, shriveled from hours in the water and covered in wet sand.

He was a child again playing along the beach, and he wasn't alone.

Scott turned his child eyes upward to find the face of a smiling white man, grinning down on him like a father. He noticed that the man had a broad, generous grin, but the man's eyes were worried, afflicted by the things they witnessed.

Scott knew this man was a friend who had been with his daddy in a war, far away across the ocean. "I got somethin' to show you, Scotty."

"'Kay."

The man stooped in the sand, scooping away several handfuls. He reached for Scott's arm, pulling him close and pointing into the shallow hole. "Scotty, c'mere. Look, look!"

Scott's eyes lit up as a cluster of tiny, translucent sand crabs wriggled and scrambled over each other in the hole. "You see 'em, Scotty! Look at 'em!"

In seconds, they squirmed and dug themselves back under the sand. Scott looked at the man, incredulously. "Why did dey do dat?" he asked.

The man smiled again, patting him on the back. "They hide in the sand because they don't like the light too much. They need the dark, so they hide under there."

"Do dey bite?"

"No. They can't really hurt you."

Scott nodded, his eyes locked on the hole, fascinated.

"C'mon. Let's catch up with your mom and dad." The man extended his hand and Scott took it. They moved down the beach as the dream shifted.

———— ◆ ————

"There's nothing to be afraid of in the dark, son…"

Scott was standing at the edge of the bottom of the steps. The room in front of him was completely black, except for the streetlight shining through a split in the curtains. Scott stood there, on the last step, on the edge of blackness.

He was older in this dream, but not by many years; his heart raced with the dread of what could be waiting in the shadows. Scott turned with uncertainty to see his father standing at the top of the stairway, bathed in the dim hallway light.

Scott couldn't count how many times his father had spoken those words. How many times had he entered his room and shaken him from the throes of a nightmare? Nightmares where creatures crept and clawed at him, filling his heart with a fear that iced his soul.

The Chief stood at the top of the steps in olive green fatigue pants and a white t-shirt, hands on his hips, patiently looking down at his son. "All you gotta do is go into the kitchen, flip on the light, get me a beer, and come right back."

Even at that age, Scott understood what a coward was, and he didn't want his father to think he was afraid. The kitchen seemed miles away; Scott knew everything that kept his eyes wide open in his room at night was waiting to ambush him in the darkness, somewhere between the family room and the kitchen. He turned his eyes up to his father.

"Come on, Scott. You've been talkin' about bein' a Cub Scout, right? How are you gonna be a Scout if you afraid of the dark? You still want me to sign you up?"

Scott turned back to the darkness, feeling his courage rise. Before he knew it, he was racing down the steps and into the room. He couldn't see, bumping the edge of his hip against the corner of an end table. A lamp on the table wobbled on its base, but didn't fall. Scott moved quickly, assured that at any moment, the dark would suddenly become a material substance, twisting and molding itself against him, covering and smothering him alive.

Scott reached for the wall switch in the kitchen. As he got closer, the monsters reached for him with the same tenacity. Something flickered outside his vision. A flash of bluish fire graced past the dining room window, moving with the wind that rustled the trees of the foreboding woods beyond the house.

Scott's hand smacked the light switch; the kitchen and dining room filled with brightness. His racing heart began to calm, and he ducked his head in relief. Light. Wonderful light.

He glanced at the dining room window, but saw behind the glass only the windblown pines at the edge of the yard.

Scott moved to the refrigerator, yanked open the door, and grabbed a can of Budweiser. He took it to the sink, turning on the faucet. His father always liked the top of the can rinsed before he drank it; Scott never forgot that little detail.

He shut off the water and started to leave the kitchen. His father's voice boomed from the top of the steps. "Don't forget to shut off the light, Scott. Don't leave it on."

The dread swelled up in Scott as he shuffled, slowly, back to the wall switch. He found the light spilling down the steps, stopping right at the bottom. Scott decided to keep his eye on it; he had a beacon to guide him. Then, something came over him, and the feeling of fear dissipated like a mist sprayed before the spinning blades of a fan. His pulse became calm again, and steady, his mind lucid. What was this new feeling?

Courage.

Scott flipped off the light and walked through the darkness, but not before taking another glance back at the dining room window. What had been out there?

At the top of the steps, he handed the beer to his father, who patted him on the head.

"I didn't run this time," Scott proclaimed, proudly.

"That's good, Scott. That's how you do it. You might be an Eagle Scout someday."

Neither of them noticed the movement of the shadow at the bottom of the steps, The dream shifted.

———◆———

The hamlet huts were on fire. The mortar shell fragments cut and whistled hotly through the damp jungle air. His eyes stung with sweat and ached from particles of dirt. This time, his feet didn't feel the cool of an ocean. Instead, they throbbed and burned, heavy with boots and mud.

The uniform didn't fit and the helmet rolled on his head; the heat under it cooked his scalp. The weight of the pack on his back dug its straps into his shoulders. He was running with something heavy in his right hand, an M-16 assault rifle.

Mortar shells riddled the earth in deadly variegated patterns. Scott dodged them, but not without tasting the steely hot of the explosions.

At his right side ran another soldier. This man was taller, stronger, and more cunning. He carried his rifle with both hands, dodging the explosions like a star running back through a defensive line.

The man was a consummate warrior, his face blackened with earth. He gritted his teeth and raced through the onslaught as if it was his reason for living. Blood and sweat stained his uniform. The sun silhouetted him like a bronze war memorial.

When the man turned to him, Scott saw his father's face.

"SCOOOTTT!" the man cried.

Scott felt a wall of heat and an invisible force as the mortar exploded right in front of him; his body was flung backward into the air, his ears burst, and suddenly there was no sound. Blackness engulfed him as the dream came to an end.

———◆———

He shot straight up in bed, catching his breath like a man coming up from water. A line of sweat ran cold down his back and the sheets were cool and damp with it. He brought his hand to his face, exhausted from the dreams and nightmares that seemed so real, but already were fading. Already, the details were lost.

A knot of pain for his father throbbed in Scott's chest; he thought of his mother and brother and sister, wondering how they were coping with the loss. It had only been a few months since they'd buried him, but Scott was losing him all over again, everyday.

He turned to find Denise lying in peaceful oblivion next to him. She slept on her side and he watched the lovely curve of her waist as it rose and fell. Her hair cascaded over her shoulder, revealing the beautiful skin of her neck. Scott allowed his eyes the pleasure of watching her sleep, grateful for the way her presence eased the troubles that plagued him.

He leaned over her and kissed her gently on the neck, remembering their first date. She had made the mistake of telling him that one of her erogenous zones was the right side of her neck. It never failed to stir her when he kissed her there; when he did, she'd often writhe her body against his, cooing like a kitten. He would smile as Denise melted against him, pressing her lips to his, and the evening pleasures would come with the suddenness of rain over the city.

She stirred, turning toward him, and Scott marveled at the youthful beauty of her face. Her natural radiance came through without makeup; she was sheer loveliness. Without waking, she threw her arm around his waist, curling up next to him. He almost laughed as her jaw dropped drunkenly, and in a few moments she was still and snoring.

Denise had become the bright center of his life; she energized him. He always knew he had talents, but he'd never fully believed in himself until he met her. She never ceased praising his work, tireless in her generosity, support, love, and affection.

But what future did they have? Scott knew she was considering the promotion and the move to New York. He asked himself over and over again if he really wanted to make the move. Seattle had been his home for over a decade. Still, contemplating the thought of her leaving without him terrified him like a man waiting for a flood to take his home.

He watched her sleep a little while longer, then slowly left the bed.

Scott went to their walk-in closet and dug out a pair of jeans, a light sweater, leather jacket, and boots. He found a pair of socks on his side of the shelf and a Mariners ball cap. Scott threw it all on; after taking one last glance at her, he went downstairs. He picked up the photo album on the coffee table and flipped through pages of pictures of himself, Denise, their families, and friends. He found the newest additions to the album, the pictures of his father, and the photo of his parents with Biggsby and Karen.

The photograph of his parents gnawed at his mind and he thought about the man who gave it to him. Who was Biggsby, and how did he know Scott's family? How can a man just show up in your life, a complete unknown from the streets, and have connections to you?

Scott felt his life slipping out of control. He'd lost his father and now he was losing Denise. Bryce had reluctantly granted him additional time off to recover from the crane accident, but he was starting to wonder if he really *wanted* to get back to the office. Was his career, the thing he'd worked so hard for, losing its appeal? Nothing was making sense anymore. Where did he really belong? Was his view from this lofty perspective even real, or was it somehow skewed?

Scott closed the album and dropped it on the table. He could feel it again, the thing he'd run from since he was a child, the thing in the dark his father told him not to be afraid of. The thing isn't real, his father had said, but something *was* there in the dark, and it was catching up with Scott Macklin.

He brought his hands to his face in frustration, feeling the tension prickling his mind. Scott was exhausted from lack of sleep, but he didn't want to go back to bed. He was dressed for a reason, but now he couldn't remember why. "God, I think I'm losing my mind," he said. "What's goin' on? C'mon, man, think. Think straight."

Maybe a walk in the night air would help him sleep, help him clear his mind of the laughter of the man who lived under the freeway. He grabbed his keys and headed for the door.

The streets of downtown Seattle were, for the most part, deserted at three o'clock in the morning. Scott wandered west on Wall Street toward the waterfront. The night was cool and still, contrasting with the heated turmoil within him.

Scott glanced up at the condo high-rises of his section of the city, Belltown. This had been a nondescript area of town until a decade ago when the wealthy chic moved in with their art galleries, restaurants, and boutiques. Belltown was now almost exclusively young and upscale. Scott easily fit in.

Now, as he shuffled downhill towards the shimmering black waters of Elliot Bay, Scott's eye caught the minute details of the street that he hadn't noticed before, when he'd flown by in his silver Lexus. The graffiti, bits of windblown garbage, the smell of urine wafting from the alleys, the shifting shadows of creatures that may have been human once. Time on the street and the seduction of crack transformed them into something less.

Cocaine slithered through these streets like an illicit lover. Scott felt the guilt many of the well-off feel observing the poor and the decay of society. He lived above this, high above with a soft bed and a soft, warm woman. Not that he hadn't earned those things. He'd worked hard to gain what he had, but what brought him down from his world to this tragic underbelly? Why was he drawn to the poor and destitute? What were they to him?

He remembered the time he'd run into this woman at the market, the Lady with Half a Foot. She was bedraggled from head to toe, her body covered in layers of old, rotting clothing. She held out her hand to him with a smile and a sparkle in her eyes; Scott reached into his pocket. He was shocked when he saw part of her left foot was gone, rotted away by some disease of the flesh. Why on earth was she smiling? He remembered the crucifix that dangled from her neck.

Once, he'd stepped over a man who lay half-naked on the sidewalk on First and Union. The man was asleep, no doubt unconscious from the previous night's indulgence of cheap liquor. But, in his sleep, he was whimpering and crying to himself, begging for some relief from his physical and mental tortures. Scott remembered walking over him, and bringing his hand up to his own throat to smooth his 60 dollar tie as he stepped. He'd barely even seen the man, but what scared him now was that he could see himself lying there in the gutter, crying like a lost child. He knew that man was everyman, and he almost broke into a run to avoid meeting him again.

He walked over the railroad tracks, across the street, west of Alaska Way. The I-99 Viaduct overhead was silent except for the hum of a passenger car.

Scott found himself alone, with only the glistening lights of the downtown skyline for companionship. A few moments later, he ventured onto the huge, open public pier. He walked until he stood on its edge and placed his hands on the railing. The Bay was calm and starless; high, dark gray clouds clotted the sky. Beyond, the mountains of the Cascades stood like guardians to the waters, watching for intruders.

The wind picked up, and Scott shuddered. It wasn't cold at all; he shouldn't have been shivering but he was. Something lived in the wind; something Scott had known before. Dread tingled and washed over his nerves, exposing him like a raw wound. All sense of logic and security evaporated as the wind came in stronger. Chimes whispered in the distance, somewhere on the horizon. The wind brought it even closer now, and his mind grew more disturbed. Still, he came here to meet it, hadn't he? To have a rendezvous with darkness.

Suddenly, The Voice spoke like a master who just entered his home after a long journey; it spoke with a lofty assuredness.

"Scott Macklin..."

The air rushed from Scott's body and he gasped, turning quickly, expecting to find someone standing there. No one. The wind buffeted him.

"What...?"

"Scott Macklin..."

Scott felt a physical shock as The Voice filled him with his own name. Scott knew it wasn't his own thought, though; it felt like a spider had crawled inside his head and birthed a writhing turmoil.

"Who... what... Who are you?"

"I am someone who has wanted to meet you for a long time. I've finally been given... permission to contact you. Your benefactors are quite possessive, but my arguments are known historically to be very...persuasive."

Scott reeled at the familiar presence, with all its accompanying fear and terror.

"Oh, my God. What... what are you?"

"You have known me all your life, Scott Macklin. We are Legion and now it is time for you to know more. Turn and look. Look at what we have wrought upon man."

Scott turned, facing the east and the Seattle skyline.

"Yes... Turn up your eyes and see that with which you are acquainted, that which is hidden, yet not hidden."

Scott felt both the power of The Voice and the compulsion that came over him to obey it. His eyes scanned the gleaming towers, searching.

"Yes... seek and ye shall find... Seek, Scott... Seek..."

Finally, his eyes locked on the fifty-story Washington Mutual Tower as it rose into the mist. Mesmerized, his eyes found the top of the tower, a shining pyramidal apex. His heart thrashed with a realization. How could he have missed it? There it was, right there in the open, in the heart of the city.

"The world has known of us, though man lives in denial. And, now your eyes are opened to our subtleties. Now you will not need to seek us; rather, we will seek you."

Scott ran down the pier, turning south on Alaska Way.

Racing past the Seattle Aquarium and Waterfront Park, Scott turned east and headed up the steep steps leading to the Pike Place Market causeways. Soon, he was on First and Pike, continuing east.

Scott hit Fourth and Pike and turned south. The pain in his knee flared and throbbed but he raced on. His lungs burned with the cold air. He understood. He'd always known there was something greater than the feelings of dread in his heart since childhood, something bigger than just his own simple fears. Finally, the abyss into which he gazed, the pit into which he screamed his questions and received only echoes in return, had responded. Finally, the darkness gave an answer.

He limped to the corner of Fourth and Madison; The Washington Mutual Tower was a block south of him. He panted for breath as his knee threatened to give out. He leaned against a streetlamp and gazed at the top of the tower. There it was... At the very top of the building was a pyramid and a box fashioned into a starburst. The structure, lit from within, glowed with an eerie, greenish brightness, enshrouded with the mist and rain. The Pyramid and the Eye.

Spellbound, he glanced around the street to see if anyone else saw what he saw, but the streets were empty, the world still with his dread and discovery. He dug into a pocket and pulled out a dollar bill, flipping it over. The green pyramid and eye held more significance now and Scott shoved it back into his pocket as if to hide it. But, how could he hide a hidden thing? How could he push away something which could not be contained?

The rain pounded him but he turned his gaze upward. The low clouds drifted past the top of the tower, which stood as an ominous testament. The Voice. The shock of his realization numbed him. Something was out there, speaking to him from nothingness, and it was connected to the Pyramid and the Eye.

Scott wanted to go home. He knew Denise was probably awake and wondering where he'd gone. He also knew he wouldn't leave the streets tonight until he found him. Biggsby.

Biggsby had smiled at him, winking from behind the Seal on the dollar. He knew something. The Man Under The Freeway. Scott knew exactly where to find him.

CHAPTER 18

A George Washington weather vane turned in the wind as Scott climbed the steps into Freeway Park. He glanced around the open plaza next to the green, cubic glass structure of the Washington State Convention Center. Scott moved through the park, which was deserted, the only light coming from the tungsten glow of the occasional street light.

Scott always admired the design and layout of the park, with its five acres of lush greenery and walls of abstract concrete. In the spring and summer, the city ran thousands of gallons of water down man-made sluices and waterfalls. The park was a bit of nature, straddling Interstate 5 in the middle of the city, designed back in the mid-seventies by Lawrence Halprine. Scott couldn't fully appreciate it in the dim of the night, but he was glad for the many hours of solitude he'd spent here.

Biggsby said he lived under the freeway. What he must have meant was underneath this park.

In a few moments, Scott turned the corner of Seneca and Eighth. There was a wooded area underneath the park where Seneca crossed Sixth and Eighth Avenues, a perfect hiding place for a homeless man. It didn't take Scott long to find Biggsby. A fire burned in a steel drum and Biggsby slept, soundly protected from the rain underneath the park. He didn't sleep as deeply as Scott imagined, though, and turned over suddenly to stare up at him.

The rain continued to fall behind them as Scott looked down on the man. Biggsby sat up and Scott winced at his stench.

"Well…you got to me a lot sooner than I thought you would, Scotty. What, you couldn't sleep? What drags a man outta bed at three-thirty in the morning to come down here lookin' for me?"

Scott moved closer to him. "Who are you?"

Biggsby stood on his feet and moved closer to the fire. "If… if you wanna talk about me, I think we should start with your father. That's what you really wanna know, ain't it? About your daddy?"

Scott nodded. "What do you know about him?"

"Well, we'll have to go back. We'll have to go back to the war. So, listen up if you gonna learn a new song, son. Listen to the words…especially the words…"

The deuce-and-a-half bounced on the trail on its way back to Phou Vien. The war orphans ran behind the truck screaming and begging in Vietnamese. *"Toy doy! Toy caht!"* I am thirsty! I am hungry! The dust from the road swallowed them with the same hunger that nestled in their bellies.

Sergeant Thomas Macklin watched the children, thinking about his own son back home, Scott. He and four other men from the 2nd of the 8th Field Artillery Company, Battalion, B Battery, were on their way back to base with supplies from the 2nd of the 7th.

It was Vietnam on a sweltering day in August, 1970.

Private First Class Alex Ketchum, the 2nd of the 8th parts clerk, sat among crates of vehicle parts and c-rations. He watched the begging children with a special hatred, one Thomas couldn't understand. They were children of the enemy, but they were still children. PFC Ketchum was what they called a *Crazy Jake,* the type of American soldier who brutally hated the Vietnamese. If he wasn't field artillery, Thomas suspected that Ketchum would love to be in-country someplace, killing. Ketchum loved the word gook, and he'd say nigger a lot more if he could get away with it. Thomas didn't expect much from a man raised in ignorance.

"Why don't we feed them little gooks?" Ketchum asked.

No one said a word, not wanting to get him started on some racist tirade.

"Well, they look hungry. Don't they look hungry to you, Sarge?"

Thomas turned to him, the sweat soaking his fatigues as if he were in a sauna. "Shut up, Ketchum. You ain't got a compassionate bone in your body. Leave them children alone. It's bad enough on 'em as it is."

"Well, that's what I'm sayin'. I mean, shoot, I care. They ain't got no mommies and daddies no more. Who's gonna take care of 'em?"

"What are you, the Pope? Sit down, Ketchum, and shut up."

Ketchum didn't sit down. He got up and wrapped his hands around a green, five-gallon drum of peaches. Grunting, he tossed it up over his shoulders, balancing himself against the movement of the truck. He managed to shuffle to the back of the deuce, the other soldiers moving out of his way. "I mean…why not… show a little…. generosity?"

Macklin was on his feet. "Ketchum, drop them rations and sit down!"

Ketchum turned back to the others with a sadistic grin. He then looked down on the running children with a monstrous glee in his eyes.

"Well, here you are you, little gooks! COME AND GET IT!"

Ketchum tossed the can off his meaty shoulders like a lumberjack. It sailed through the dusty air and cracked one of the children, a small, half-naked girl, in the face. There was a loud bang, then the splatter of blood, as the child hit the dirt, unconscious. She couldn't have been more than 10 or 12.

Ketchum let out good-ole-boy holler, then turned his face into the fist of Thomas Macklin. Ketchum was slower, but managed to land a few to Thomas's mid-section. Thomas roared and charged him; the two men flew out the back of the deuce, landing hard on the dirt. They caught their breaths and then tackled each other, rolling, cursing and exchanging punches.

The truck stopped and the other men jumped off, circling them and cheering.

—•—

"Chief, this isn't the kind of behavior I'd expect from an E5 Motor Sergeant. I mean, just what were you thinking? What kind of leadership example are you trying to set with *my* men?"

Thomas and Ketchum stood at full attention in front of the desk of the Battery Commander, Captain Griggs. "Ketchum, I'd expect this kind of behavior from an idiot like you, but Chief, I've worked with you for almost two tours, and you haven't disappointed me yet, up until today."

A ceiling fan spun over the Captain's head in an office decorated with plaques and a huge mounted bass he'd managed to pull out of the Colorado river.

"You know that girl almost died, Ketchum? You shattered her cheek bone and busted out five of her teeth."

"No disrespect, Captain, but she was just a goo—"

"I know what she was, you inbreed hilljack! Now, I'm gonna say this one time and one time only! We are here on a mission to liberate these people from the communists and we will conduct ourselves in the appropriate manner at all times! As professionals! You will not embarrass me or this Battalion or this man's Army! I'll let you off this time on a warning, but if I hear of you two so much as side-looking each other, I'll Article Fifteen both of you out of my motor pool! Ketchum, if you even spit in the wind and it lands on an unarmed civilian, I'll frag your butt and send you home in a cigar box! Chief, from now on bring any problems concerning Ketchum directly to me. Gentlemen, is this understood?"

"Yes, sir!" they both said.

"Good. Ketchum, get out of my office! Chief, you hold on a minute."

Ketchum vanished. Griggs waited until he was gone before he spoke. "All right. At ease, Sergeant. I kept you because we got ourselves a situation. Five years ago, several Marine Battalions fought and secured Hill 43, south of An Cuong. Yesterday, 1st Platoon Company D, of the 1st Battalion 6th Infantry, lost 20 soldiers in combat with the VC 48th Local Force Battalion. The Marines cleared out most of the Force Battalion back in '67, but there are remnants, pockets of resistance, trying to regain a foothold on Hill 43. The 6th Infantry and the 59th Engineering Company have control of the hill for now. The engineers are clearing the land to locate any VC tunnels, weapons, and supplies, and to deny the enemy any cover.

"We're gonna provide them with artillery protection, Chief. I need you to ready six M101 A1 guns and deliver them to a firing position two klicks south of An Cuong. Here are your orders, coordinates, and mission objectives."

"Yes, sir. What about Ketchum?"

"Leave him here."

"Thank you, sir."

"You'll have a security escort but it won't be the MPs as usual. Two heavy Ranger teams, who've trained with the 5th Special Forces in Nha

Trang, will be joining you. I don't know that much about them… Let's just say they're really good at the job."

Thomas thought he saw an anxious look cross the Commander's face.

He stepped out of the CO's office just in time to see the double blades of a jolly green giant, a Chinook helicopter, drop in out of the sky and touch down on the Company LZ. The soldiers who dispensed from the chopper moved in robotic fashion, with crisp purposeful steps and no wasted body movements. They were the two Ranger teams, made up of 12 men each. They moved past Thomas so quickly, he could barely see their faces. Their eyes were sunken and as black as the jungle camos they wore.

Scott leaned up, closer to the fire. "So, where do you come in the story?"

The fire glowed on Biggsby's bearded face. "Right about here…"

"Hey, Mac. You ready to roll?" asked Biggsby.

It was 0430 hours and the trucks and guns were ready. Biggsby was the Motor Sergeant for the 2nd of the 7th . Thomas requested him to help with the transport. He and Thomas often traded supplies and swapped parts; over time, they'd grown close.

"Looks like we got everything we need. You got the trip laid out?"

Thomas pulled out a map and spread it on the hood of the lead truck. Biggsby moved up next to him. The Rangers stood outside in the rain. Thomas pointed at the map. "On the way to the firing position, we're gonna have to cross through the Ruong Ruong Valley. This is where we might run into the enemy. I hope this escort is as good as they say. We're early. Unless anybody's got any questions…let's move."

Biggsby dispersed his team, two men to each of six trucks, the trucks towing the Howitzers on two-wheeled a-frames. The guns, mounted on the a-frames, were secured with lunettes locked around a towing pintle, held fast by a cotter pin. The Ranger escorts loaded into two deuces, one taking up the rear and the other on point.

Thomas climbed aboard a gun-towing truck just behind the lead escort. At 0445, the trucks rolled out of the maintenance bay and moved toward the main gate. Thomas checked his watch, logging the departure time. The sun was rising, and the heat of the early morning with it, as they departed on the 80 kilometer trip through the Ruong Ruong Valley. The rain didn't do a thing to cool them.

The attack came just after the convoy rolled into the mouth of the valley. The trucks and guns moved through a mist thick enough to taste. Thomas Macklin peered through the heavy fog, turning on the truck's wiper blades to clear the condensation from the windshield. Biggsby rode with him.

"I ain't seen it this bad before, Chief. I'm not likin' this one bit."

The fog covered them; Thomas could barely see the truck just ahead of them. "Naw, I don't like it either. I got a bad vibe, too, Mitch. We shouldn't be here. This is way too much cover. If Victor Chuck is out there, there's no way we can see him. Recon reported that this area was cleared a couple of weeks ago, but that don't mean squat."

"Since when does Recon give a flip? They ain't the ones gonna get their heads shot off. We're two hours out from the drop point and this fog looks like it ain't liftin'. Man, I got 133 days 'til I'm short—and buddy, I'm countin' 'em down."

Thomas looked around, overcome by a feeling of apprehension. Vietnam was its own special nightmare. The jungle, thick with heat, insects, fear, and death. He'd heard of the many NVA/VC booby traps. Between January 1965, and June 1969, 17 percent of the injuries sustained by troops were caused by traps. Charlie Company of the First Battalion 20th Infantry took in 40 percent of their injuries from traps. Thomas imagined man-sized punji traps with poisoned spikes, bear traps, crossbow traps, double-spiked caltrops, and scorpion-filled boot boxes.

He'd heard of one company that entered the jungle in fierce fighting near Long Binh. A whole company was cut to pieces, down to only a squadron.

Of all the stories of death he'd heard, nothing compared to the feeling overwhelming him now; he sensed eyes in the fog, watching them. "This is a blind run, Mitch. We need to *dee dee* out of here," Thomas sneered, just as the jungle lit up.

The tracer bullets shot laterally into the convoy from both sides of the valley, lighting up the trail like a madman's Independence Day. The bullets cut through the trucks, instantly killing some of the drivers and troops. Thomas punched the gas and the deuce-and-a-half swerved and spun on the dirt, its Howitzer in tow. The Ranger teams fired randomly into the fog from their lead and rear trucks.

One of the deuces was pummeled with tracers. The bullets cut the a-frame brake lines. The deuce driver slammed on his brakes and the Howitzer it pulled crushed into the back of the truck, fishtailing and tearing off its mount with a shriek. The gun rolled, tilted, and crashed on its side, the a-frame wheel spinning. The lead truck, carrying the Rangers, pulled over to the side and stopped. The Ranger Teams Leader jumped from the truck and screamed at Thomas to push through; he did, followed by what was left of the convoy.

The Ranger Teams split up, and charged off both sides of the road, racing into the fire, blasting their weapons. The men seemed transfixed as they ran with machine-like precision into the dense fog. They somehow *dodged* the tracer fire, moving through the jungle with quick, hyper-athletic dexterity.

The deuces roared along the trail, rumbling through like old buses; in a few miles, they were clear of the attack. Thomas pulled to a halt and the convoy stopped behind him. "You hit?" he asked Biggsby. Biggsby shook his head, stepping out of the truck.

The men stepped down from the vehicles, checking their various cuts, scrapes, and bruises. The tracers had cut through the trucks' canvas coverings like knives, one of the them had a tire that was torn, but somehow the driver managed to roll it through the fire. In the background, they could still hear the sound of gun blasts. The fog rolled over the shaken men like a protective covering.

Thomas moved methodically; checking the five remaining guns, he found some had taken tracer hits, but they looked operational. "Well, I guess five out of six ain't bad." he muttered.

The gunfire beyond the fog suddenly stopped.

The men all turned to the horizon. "Looks like we lost our escort," Biggsby said. "We better move."

They all started for their trucks when they heard the movement in the jungle. Quickly, they drew their weapons and took up defensive positions around the vehicles. Thomas held his breath, turning his eyes skyward. So this is it, he thought. I'm gonna die on this dirt road in a valley in the middle of nowhere. This isn't how I saw it, Lord, this isn't it, he prayed.

They heard the trucks before they saw them. After what seemed like an eternity, the trucks appeared through the mist, stopping a few feet from them. Their escorts, the Rangers. The men climbed down from the vehicles and stood there, triumphantly. The Teams Leader spoke up in a brusque, gravelly voice. "We shut 'em up for a while, but they'll have reinforcements. Let's get those guns deployed, Chief."

Thomas and the other men moved from their positions. "How?" Thomas asked. "How did you get outta there? You're only two teams."

He noticed all the Rangers were accounted for and not one of them had a scratch. The Teams Leader didn't answer; silently, they climbed back on the trucks. The lead deuce pulled in front of Thomas's truck and stopped, waiting.

Thomas ordered the men back into their vehicles and in minutes they were on the trail again.

"What in God's name?" Biggsby asked. "How'd they do it?"

"I don't know… I don't think I wanna know."

———•◦•———

They had been driving in the dank heat for an hour when the boy appeared in the road. He was another war orphan, thin, starving, and frail. He grinned impishly as first the lead deuce and then the convoy halted. The Ranger Teams Leader jumped from the truck and moved closer to the child. Thomas and Biggsby stepped up next to them.

"Sin my dee dee. Sin my dee dee," the boy said through a rotted grin.

Thomas frowned. "Hey, Mitch, what's he sayin'?"

Biggsby, who spoke decent Vietnamese, stepped up to the boy.

"He's tellin' us to go away."

Biggsby knelt in front of the boy, who couldn't have been more than seven years old. *"Sin chow. Ang ten zee?* What's your name?" The boy grinned up at Biggsby, moving his small hands over the man's pockets, finding a pack of gum. Biggsby let him have it.

"Sin my dee dee! Beaucoup Vee cee!"

"What's he sayin'?" Thomas pressed. "Where's Victor Charlie at?"

The boy pointed into the fog, gesturing for the men to follow. "He wants us to follow him. He says Victor Charlie is down that way. We're close to the gun drop. Gotta be pockets of that VC battalion close by."

The Ranger Teams Leader spoke up from behind them. "There's a hamlet near here at Dong Phuroc. That's probably his home. I say we should follow him."

"That's the 6th Infantry's job! It's not part of our mission! We're droppin' these guns and we're *dee deein'* back to base, as ordered!" Thomas roared. He caught a glimpse of the Ranger Team Leaders eyes and saw nothing but a void.

"Look. We're your protection," the Ranger Team Leader said. "You can take a chance and stay here with the 48th VCs runnin' around, or you help us recon this village, and then we drop the guns. Or have you already forgotten how many people you just lost back there?"

The hamlet emerged from the dense air like a fairy tale. The men walked through the soupy marsh fields, hacking away at bugs and brush, feeling the weight of the mud on their boots, and the heavy packs on their sore backs. This day was growing weary on them. A simple artillery drop had turned into a seek and destroy for soldiers who weren't trained for deep, in-country missions. The village at Dong Phuroc was more likely a cover for the VC; if evidence was found, it would soon be burning to the ground. Thomas had heard of many such razings, but had never been involved with one. God help the people in this village, he thought. Judging by the mindset of the Ranger Teams Leader, they would soon be a memory.

The Teams Leader dispersed his men to look for evidence of the Vietcong. In a few minutes, one of them reported back, holding an ammo box with maps and grid coordinates. Still another came back with a report that he'd found several 7.62 millimeter shell casings and empty AK-47 clips. They also found grenades and a .30 M-1 rifle in the rice stores. Something bleak crossed the eyes of the Teams Leader, and his men knew what to do now. They moved among the hamlets, lighting the thatched roofs with silver Zippo lighters. Soon the village was ablaze.

Thomas, Biggsby, and their men could only watch in terror as the screaming and crying women and children were forced out of the huts and clustered together to be shot.

Thomas stepped up to the Teams Leader. "There's a processing center in the Binh Son district! We can take these people there! We don't have to do this! We can take —"

The Teams Leader ignored him and moved among the villagers who were now kneeling, holding each other, and crying. He pulled out his CAR-15 and fired one shot into the back of an old woman's head. She fell dead instantly.

Thomas didn't even know he was in motion until he was tackling the Teams Leader, and both men hit the ground. Thomas tried to land a few punches, but the Teams Leader was impossibly fast, his movements blurs of gloved knuckles, pounding Thomas's mid-section and face. He jumped off Thomas, leaving him rolling in pain on the dirt, and the Rangers quickly brought their guns to firing positions. The men stood there in the midst of the burning village, aiming their weapons at the artillery teams in a standoff.

Thomas heard The Voice for the first time in his life. It roared inside his mind, emerging from the deep recesses of hell. The heat from the burning hamlets seared on his consciousness in a place that was merely a counterfeit for the true darkness. The Voice shattered the surface of this world, bearing its evil toward mankind, offering the poisoned, bitter fruit of war.

"Kill them. All of them. Destroy this village."

Thomas, Biggsby, and their men reacted with shocked movements at the sound of The Voice. The artillery team dropped their guard when they heard it; the Rangers opened up on them with a barrage of fire. The men were cut down in seconds.

Thomas moved on one knee, wildly firing his M-16, and then he was up, cutting a retreat path across the rice field. Along the way, he saw the boy from the road standing there, shocked and frozen with fear. Thomas scooped him up with one arm and ran on.

Biggsby let off a few rounds and then hit the ground rolling, evading the weapon fire. He leaped to his feet again, racing off after Thomas and the crying boy.

As the men churned across the field through the heavy mud, The Voice echoed in their minds.

"Regroup..."

Thomas turned to see the flames off the hamlets. The men of the Ranger Teams all moved together in perfect sync, reloading their weapons. Every one of Thomas's men was dead and the Rangers were completely unscathed.

Thomas's leaden legs shuffled through the field. Sixty yards away was a treeline and relative safety, but he didn't think they would make it. He looked and saw the Rangers bringing their weapons to bear.

The Voice broke into the minds of the Rangers as Thomas and Biggsby retreated.

"Attack..."

The Rangers chased after the escaping men, firing their weapons; the bullets exploded around them, shooting up streams of water and mud. Thomas heard the hot rounds zipping past them as they ran for the tree line. One bullet grazed his right shoulder and they stumbled, nearly falling into the bush.

The heavy morning fog still shrouded the jungle as they raced through it headlong. Blindly, they searched for some kind of path. If only they could get back to the trucks...

Seconds later, the Rangers moved in behind them, appearing in the foggy shroud like death phantoms. They moved inhumanly fast, passing like fleeting shadows. The Shadows of Men.

Then there was the light. Thomas saw it first, then Biggsby—a bluish-green sphere of power soaring in over them through the trees. They stopped, spellbound as it hovered in front of them for a moment. Abruptly, the light moved closer to the ground, altering its shape. The power undulated and churned, forming the shape of a man. Soon, a figure stood before them, radiating a light as bright as sunfire. Thomas could just make out the face. The man had a thick beard and his hair touched his shoulders. He was majestic and powerful. He stood in the middle of the fog, in a robe with a hood, colored on its edges with a thick line of blue. Thomas, Biggsby, and the boy knew who it was standing there, but they couldn't say a word.

The Christ turned and pointed His right hand toward another light in the sky. It was the search lamp under the belly of a UH-1C Huey as it spun over an LZ in a clearing some 40 yards away.

The eyes of the three followed the bird and when they looked back, the Christ was gone.

"Come on!" Thomas shouted, in pain from the shoulder wound. They took off after the chopper.

As they ran, The Voice entered Thomas's mind, but he didn't let it stop his feet.

"You will now see how we have enraptured man, Sergeant Macklin. Now you will learn true knowledge and wisdom. And before it is all over, you will belong to us…"

Thomas was horror-struck but he kept moving; the questions played in his mind. What had they just seen? Was that Him—here, in the middle of a war?

The helicopter landed, fanning waves of tall elephant grass. Thomas, Biggsby, and the boy entered the LZ and ran low for the bird. A door opened and a copilot stretched his hand; the three climbed on board. The chopper gunner manned an M-60 mounted on the side, firing it into the jungle. The Rangers arrived at the clearing just in time to see the Huey pull away into the deep mist.

Thomas held the boy as they rose. He was no longer crying, but gazing up into the sky. Thomas followed the boy's look.

"Jesus…" the child whispered.

———◆◆◆———

Scott sat mesmerized by Biggsby's tale. He watched the veteran's eyes glow with fire and awareness.

"That was who I think it was? You saw Him? You saw Christ?"

Biggsby smiled, looking up at the night sky. "Our Lord lives, my friend. He lives. And, there's more, much more." Biggsby stood and paced in front of the glowing can of fire. "Shortly after that, we were brought up on charges of desertion durin' combat. They court-martialed us, but they couldn't make it stick. A little while later, your father and I were on leave in Hawaii when we ran into our old pal, Captain Griggs. Well, he wasn't no Captain anymore, but a Major, switched over to the Navy and assigned to CINPACFLT Command in Pearl Harbor. We mentioned the incident at Dong Phuroc and he laid it out for us.

"He said that the NSA had been conducting experiments in mind control through psyops in a project called MKULTRA. They wanted a soldier who would be able to receive commands telepathically and be compelled to obey them. It turns out those Ranger escorts were part of the MKULTRA experiment. CINPACFLT gave Griggs Q-Clearance to a huge intelligence community network through a system called the Global Reconnaissance

Information System, or GRIS for short. It's a database containing minute details of the very mission me and your dad were on. GRIS monitors every aspect of all U.S. recon missions. We learned that those Ranger troops had in fact intended to kill us, just to prove they'd obey telepathic commands.

"Griggs gave me a copy of some information that he ran off GRIS, and some discs with access codes." Biggsby shuffled over to his duffel and pulled out the green Army portfolio. Scott took it and stared at it as if it were the Holy Grail. "Your father made me promise that if anything happened to him, you'd learn everything. Now you know."

Biggsby looked as if a huge debt lifted from him. He sat down on the ground, relieved of his burden. "Now, all I've gotta do is wait for them to find me. Wait to die."

Scott pleaded with him. "You're not gonna die, man. You're coming with me. I'll put you up, keep you in a safe place until I can sort all this out."

"No. You don't understand. There *ain't* no safety from them. You're in the game now. I wouldn't worry about me. I'd start worryin' about yourself. Start worryin' about them."

"Them? Them who?"

Biggsby looked off into the darkness. "The Shadows of Men. The Illuminated. Now that you are aware of them, they'll be after you. One of two things will happen. You'll either join them, or be driven homicidal or suicidal, or maybe both. My time has come. I've done what I promised and now I'll get to go home, to our Lord."

Scott looked at Biggsby with overwhelming respect and admiration. This simple-looking man had been through more than Scott could possibly imagine. His father had also, and he was—a glorified building designer. Maybe now he'd have a chance to really understand what his father and men like him had gone through. All the horrors of war, and of coming home.

"I wish I could've gone," Scott said. "I should have been a soldier like my father."

Biggsby moved close to Scott, putting a hand on his shoulder. "So you think a war makes a man? Let me tell you what one warrior said about the ultimate man, Jesus Christ. This warrior was in exile on the island of St. Helena. He was looking back on all the conquering he had done in his life, but still he felt powerless. Count Montholon was with him. The warrior asked the Count, 'Can you tell me who Jesus Christ was?' The count didn't have the answer, so the warrior said, 'Well, then, I'll tell you. Alexander, Caesar, Charlemagne, and I have founded great empires, but all of our conquests depended upon force. Jesus alone founded His empire on love, and to this day millions will die for Him... I think I understand something of human nature; and I tell you that all these were men, and I am a man; none else was like Him; Jesus Christ was more than man... I have inspired multitudes with such an enthusiastic devotion they would have died for me...but to do this, it was necessary that I influence them with my looks, my words, my voice. When I saw men and spoke to them, I lit a flame of devotion in their hearts...Christ alone has succeeded in raising the mind of man toward the unseen, so that it becomes insensible to the barriers of time and space. Across a chasm of 1800 years, Jesus Christ makes a demand which is, beyond all others, difficult to satisfy; He asks for that which the philosopher may seek from his friends, or a father from his children, or a bride from her spouse, or a man from his brother. He asks for the human heart; He wants it entirely to Himself. He demands it unconditionally; and forthwith, His demand is granted. Wonderful! In defiance of time and space, the soul of man, with all its powers and faculties, becomes an annexation to the Empire of Christ. All who sincerely believe in Him experience a remarkable, supernatural love for Him. One cannot account for this phenomenon; to do so is beyond the scope of man's creative powers. Time, the great destroyer, is powerless to extinguish its sacred flame; time can neither exhaust its strength nor put a limit to its range. This is it, which strikes me most; I have often thought of it. This is what proves to me quite convincingly the Divinity of Jesus Christ.'"

Scott was dumbfounded at the power of the words.

Biggsby smiled like a teacher at an awakening pupil. "Do you know who the Warrior was?"

Scott shook his head.

"Napoleon."

Scott could only stare at him blankly. "Napoleon said that?"

"That's right. War don't make a man, Scott. Your father wouldn't have wanted you to go through what he went through. Soon, all men will know the true warrior, as Napoleon knew. Christ will rule and there ain't gonna be no more war."

The freeway was getting louder, the early morning traffic picking up. Scott watched the morning light paint the sky over Seattle.

"That's it for now. I'll teach you as much as I can while we still got time. But, for now... go home..."

Scott wavered for a moment before walking away into the morning.

Minutes later, he found himself standing on the corner of Fourth and Union, waiting for a northbound bus into Belltown. He clutched the portfolio, cautiously waiting until he was home before peering at the contents. His heart raced at the feeling in his chest, a foreboding like his father must've felt in the jungle that day, just before the enemy pounced from the fog.

CHAPTER 19

Scott typed the name in the search window of his Internet service provider, and came up with over 400 hits.

The Illuminati.

He stared at the word for a moment, absorbing it, feeling the sense of iniquity that came with it. He scanned through the hits, looking for a relevant entry, something that would explain the Pyramid and Eye. In a few moments, he ran across a listing titled, *The George Washington Papers.* He clicked on the Library of Congress database, which contained over 65,000 documents from the first American president including notes, military records, diaries, journals, and financial accounts. The documentation spanned the time period from 1741 to 1799. A narrower search pulled up two documents referring to the Illuminati. They were pieces of correspondence between George Washington and two men named George Washington Snyder and William Russell. One was dated September 25, 1798 and the other October 24, 1798. The database gave the user two ways to view the letters; it contained scanned copies of the original letters, and also transcriptions into text.

He clicked on the first scanned original letter. Scott found it impossible to decipher the nearly 300-year-old ink, and the feather quill script didn't help.

He clicked on a text transcription link and the screen blinked to the same letter in normal text. He read:

I have heard much of the nefarious, and dangerous plan, and doctrines of the Illuminati, but never saw the Book until you were pleased to send it to me. The same causes which have prevented my acknowledging the receipt of your letter have prevented my reading the Book, hitherto; namely, the multiplicity of matters which pressed upon me before, and the debilitated state in which I was left after, a severe fever had been removed. And which allows me to add little more now, than thanks for your kind wishes and favorable sentiments, except to correct an error you have run into, of my presiding over the English lodges in this Country. The fact is, I preside over none, nor have I been in one more than once or twice, within the last thirty years. I believe notwithstanding, that none of the Lodges in this Country are contaminated with the principles ascribed to the Society of the Illuminati. With respect.
George Washington

Scott sat back, rubbing the three-day stubble on his face. There it was, the first president of our country speaking of the Illuminati as if they actually existed. So, George Washington didn't consider the Illuminati to be the imaginative invention of conspiracy theorists? Clearly, he stated that he'd heard of them and their plans. Scott eagerly clicked on the next letter, to Washington from William Russell. Two paragraphs read:

Our present time is pregnant with the most shocking…calamities threatening to ruin our Liberty and Government. The most secret plans are in agitation: plans calculated to ensnare the unwary; to attract the irreligious and to entice the predisposed; to combine in the general machine for overthrowing all governments and all religion. …a book fell into my hands entitled, "Proofs of Conspiracies" by John Robinson, which gives a full account of the Society of Freemasons that distinguishes itself by the name of Illuminati whose idea is to overturn all government and all religion, even natural; and who endeavors to eradicate every idea of a Supreme Being, and distinguish man from beast by his shape only.

Scott downloaded the letters into a file on his hard drive, and sat back from the computer. The rain ran down the windowpane in front of him, and he gazed through the glass, mulling over his newfound knowledge. The implications were enormous. As early as the beginning of our country, we were deep in it. An organization secretly planned to take over all governments and abolish all religions, even the very idea of God.

Now that he thought about it, society was becoming more and more godless everyday. Decay, violence, drug addiction, poverty, disease, and war were rotting the fabric of society at its moral center. Families were divided, and the love of people for each other was eroding steadily. Was this the cause, the Illuminati? How could something this devastating to mankind be kept secret? Was anything being done about it? Was the only hope the conspiracy nuts and homeless madmen?

"What's the answer?" Scott asked himself aloud. Would Biggsby know? "Well, I guess there's only one way to find out."

Scott shut off the computer. It was well into the afternoon and he hadn't slept. It occurred to him that he hadn't looked at the documents inside the portfolio yet. He moved to where he had hidden it just as Denise walked into the room.

Her eyes shimmered with pain, as if she had been burdening herself with something she could no longer contain. "Hi…"

Scott didn't expect her until later in the day. He saw the look on her face and felt a wave of love wash over him. "Hi."

"Did you get any sleep?"

"No. No, I've been working. Doing some research."

"A new building project?"

"No. It's kinda hard to explain. Something's happened, something I didn't expect. I've met a man who knew my father; they served together in Vietnam. They were best friends. This guy's life is pretty messed up. The man's a homeless vet sleeping under Freeway Park, Denise. I gotta do something for him, try to help him."

She looked away. Brimming tears made her eyes sparkle beautifully. Scott longed for her.

"I understand," she said. "I guess I don't know how to tell you this… I'm going to take the offer. I'm going, Scott."

There was a deep pause between them. It finally happened. The end had come.

"When are you leaving?"

She moved closer to him. He reached to touch a curl that rested on her bare shoulder. "In a week. They're setting me up in a condo or something…"

"Oh… Okay."

"When do you think you'll be able to come?"

"I don't know. This man… he's enlightened me on some things… He knew my father. I've got to learn as much from him as I can. I'm not saying that I'm not going to come. God knows I love you. I need you, Denise."

She caressed his face. "I love you, too, Scott, so much. You're my life. I know your father was important to you, and I want you to do whatever you have to do to find some closure over his death. I'll be in New York. You know I'll be waiting for you, whenever you're ready."

Scott could hardly believe what he was hearing. This was vintage Denise, as loving and supportive as she'd always been. She was right. He did need closure, and despite this test of their relationship, she loved him enough to grant it to him.

He reached for her and kissed her with everything he had. When they parted, she cried softly.

"It's all right," he said. "We'll be fine. Everything'll be okay." They embraced, and this time she broke into full-blown tears. Scott held on to her for dear life.

—◆—

Biggsby knew it would happen tonight. Something lurked in his bones; something lingered in the rain, shifting in it like the wind. Death. The name of the rider on the pale horse. Biggsby knew they were coming for him.

He watched his last sunset with fascination. The sky over the park was brilliant with its end-of-day colors. Biggsby thought about the One who created it, and he wondered about heaven's sunsets. This evening's beautiful light was only a candle compared to the celestial wonders he would soon encounter. One thing Biggsby longed for and missed was the beach. He imagined heaven's glorious beaches, with infinite blue waters and thousands of miles of crashing waves. The only thing he'd ask for would be a spot of his own on one of God's beaches. He was sure it could be arranged.

Biggsby would soon encounter Jesus; he wondered what Christ would say to him, wondered if he was ready.

"One never knows if he is ready for Him or not, Biggsby. That's the biggest problems I have with Him. He keeps everything mysterious, reserving the greater secrets only for Himself, while we remain woefully ignorant. How can you stand it?"

The Voice spoke unexpectedly from out of the coming darkness.

Biggsby shrugged, knowing the truth about his Savior, knowing The Voice was completely wrong. "That's God's prerogative. He gives or holds back His knowledge as He sees fit. Most of the time, He's just protectin' us from you."

"He is keeping you from being like Him. He knows that His knowledge cannot harm you."

"Oh no? Then explain death. Why do things decay? Ever since you misled us in the garden, man and all of creation has been slowly dyin'. Not until His Son have we even had a hope of life. You devils are simply tryin' to destroy us; you have been all along. Now if you don't mind, I don't wanna have any conversations with you. I know you plan to kill me tonight, and I'd just as soon you get on with it."

"Very well. Never let it be said that I was negligent in my service to mankind. Behold, here are your executioners."

Biggsby turned and they were there, a group of 10 to 12 men who simply emerged from the dimness. Biggsby didn't see a vehicle or hear a sound, except for the whisper of the wind. They hide themselves from mankind; they exist and operate under veils, in obscurity where good souls never tread.

The Illuminated. The Shadows of Men.

"Two dinners. One teriyaki beef, and the other chicken with extra rice, and two Cokes," Scott ordered. He was in Yasukos, his favorite fast-food place since college. He couldn't count the number of times he and his roommates had managed to scrape together sofa change to share a meal here. Strangely, he longed for the lean years of his college days. The world made much more sense back then.

The Asian man, in an apron behind the counter, grinned at him as he delivered the order. Scott paid for it and hit the door, heading for Freeway Park. Scott hoped that after he got a hot meal into the man, Biggsby would reconsider staying on the street. Maybe, eventually, Scott could convince him to come to New York. The rain started falling with its usual abruptness.

◆◆◆◆

Biggsby was surrounded by The Illuminated, and he watched as one of them, who seemed to be a leader, knelt and rummaged through his belongings. The Illuminated One upended his duffel bag, spilling everything Biggsby owned, including his Bible and a .38 caliber pistol. The Illuminated One reached for the gun, ignoring the Bible. He looked at Biggsby, but the only facial feature Biggsby saw was his eyes. Biggsby stared into them, frozen in fear. The thing's eyes glowed like burning embers of coal.

Biggsby knelt on the ground and began to pray silently, turning his face heavenward. Doubt crept around his heart like a thief seeking for a weakness to exploit, but Biggsby had long ago learned to stave off unbelief. He didn't want Jesus to detect any lack of faith in him; he knew a beach was waiting for him in heaven.

The Illuminated One pointed the .38 at Biggsby's head and Biggsby looked up to see a break in the rain clouds. The full moon hung heavily in the sky. The clouds covered the moon again and when the next break came, Biggsby saw the shape of a man with a powerful face, dark beard, and hair touching his shoulders. Biggsby's eyes lit up with grateful tears. At long last, his journey here was over and the new one was about to begin. The man in the clouds smiled at him.

"Look, I see heaven open, and the Son of Man standin' at the right hand of God," Biggsby said.

The Illuminated One fired three shots into his chest; the gun blasts echoing under Freeway Park.

———•◦•———

Scott paused, shocked at the sound of the shots. Suddenly, he knew.

"Biggsby…" Dropping the food, he sprinted off into the rain.

When Scott found him, The Illuminated were gone and Biggsby lay in a bloody heap. Scott dropped to his knees next to the man, who was barely alive, his breath coming in short, rattled gasps.

"Biggsby! Biggsby! No! Come on, man, stay with me! You can't go yet; you can't!"

Biggsby opened his eyes, choking and spitting blood. He looked at Scott with a warmth in his eyes.

"L-L-Listen….to…me, S-S-Scott. T-T-They will come after…after you now. Find others…. F-F-Find others who believe… Spread the t-t-truth…"

His own sudden tears surprised, Scott. Had he really just met this man a few days ago?

"I will. I will, Biggsby. I promise, I will…"

Biggsby reached desperately with his right hand, groping in the darkness. "What?" Scott asked. "What is it?"

Scott realized Biggsby was reaching for the Bible, almost buried under his spilled belongings. Scott grabbed it and put it in Biggsby's groping, bloodied hands. Biggsby pushed the Bible hard into Scott's chest. He looked down on the dying man, confused.

Biggsby spoke through bubbles of blood. "T-T-Take this book, Scott… L-L-Learn everything you can. F-F-Faith…Faith is the only thing that can save you. The only thing. R-R-Remember… Faith…"

Scott comprehended and took the Bible. Seconds later, Mitchell Biggsby was dead, the rain mingling with the tears of joy that coursed down his still face.

"Biggsby? Biggsby?" He was gone, and Scott bowed his head and cried. If only he had been there sooner, just a few minutes sooner. The only man who had the answers was gone. What could Scott do now? Where was he going to find others who knew what Biggsby knew? Scott couldn't let Biggsby's death be in vain; somehow, he'd find a way to spread the truth.

He stood on his weary legs and looked around at what had been Biggsby's home; he hefted the Bible in his hand. There on the ground was the .38, the gun that killed him. Why had they left it? He reached over and picked it up just as a Seattle police cruiser skidded to a halt. A voice boomed over the cruisers P.A., and the passenger side cop jumped out of the car, taking a defensive position behind the door.

"FREEZE! DROP THE WEAPON NOW OR WE'LL BE FORCED TO SHOOT!"

Scott felt the weight of the gun in his hand as he ran for a fence separating the wooded area from the street. The bullets whirred hotly over his head as he hit the fence, banging against it painfully with his injured knee, but still managing to swing over. He ran through a wooded section, heading uphill to the park.

The police cruiser pulled back, spun, and headed east on Seneca. The driving officer reported in. "Suspect is a black male, six-feet, one-hundred-ninety pounds, in a black jacket, ball cap, jeans, and boots. He's heading west into Freeway Park. Suspect is armed and dangerous. Officer in foot pursuit..."

Scott raced full-blown through Freeway Park, feeling every painful step in his right knee. He shot past the George Washington weather vane and the green glass of the convention center. Several yards behind him, the chasing officer barked his position into a radio receiver mounted on his shoulder. He was big and slow, wheezing as he ran, but managing to keep Scott within a close distance.

Scott hit a set of steep steps leading to University Avenue and raced down them, almost tripping near the bottom. He sprinted until he crossed first Fifth and then Fourth Avenue, where he turned right and headed north.

The police cruiser skidded the corner of Eighth and Union, speeding west on an intercept.

Scott pushed along, holding the bloodied Bible tightly in his right hand. He dodged and weaved through the early evening umbrella crowds that perused the coffee shops, movie theaters, and upscale boutiques of Fourth Avenue. The throb of his knee felt like daggers cutting through sinew and bone. Not knowing how he might escape, Scott kept running, the wind ripping through his lungs. He suddenly remembered the gun in his jacket; they believed he had killed Biggsby! Now he ran for his life.

He almost couldn't believe the sound of his own voice as he ran, calling out to God. It was the first time he'd prayed since his near-fall from the crane.

Scott summoned all his experience as a runner and modified his breathing. Checking behind him, he saw that the chasing officer wasn't closing in, so he paced himself, settling into the run. Despite his knee, he kept a good stride; he'd be near Westlake Mall soon. His best chance would be the underground bus tunnel on the lower mall level.

At the corner of Union and Fourth, he nearly ran over a group of Japanese shoppers. Scott twisted his body, deftly avoiding them, just as the police cruiser skidded to a halt in front of him. Scott didn't have time to think. The driving officer was halfway out of the cruiser, reaching for his weapon, when Scott leaped onto the hood of the vehicle like a hurdler. He took two steps across the hood, landed hard on the street, and wrenched his knee. Scott yelped in pain. Dropping the Bible, Scott fell to the wet street. A city bus screeched to a dead halt, blocking the aim of the driving officer. The Bible was just out of reach as Scott jumped to his feet, and he almost left it behind. He reached back and snatched it up, pushing on to the mall.

The driving officer climbed back into the cruiser and the chasing officer ran, heaving, past the vehicle. "Suspect heading north on Fourth toward Westlake Center. Continuing pursuit. Requesting backup at this time." The bus slowly cleared and the cruiser spun around the corner onto Fourth, heading north.

Scott hobbled through the intersection of Fourth and Pike into Westlake Park, a block from the mall, scattering a flock of pigeons feeding on wet breadcrumbs and popcorn. He moved past the throngs of tourists and ragged, skateboarding runaways gathered on the open plaza.

The police cruiser's lights flashed, catching his peripheral vision, and he turned left to see the car barreling through the intersection. The cruiser shot ahead of him, skidding to a halt at Pike and Fourth.

Pike Street, in front of the Westlake Mall, was blocked to normal street traffic on both its east and west ends, making it part of the park. Scott thanked God for that. The cruiser stopped at the west end of the street, blocked by concrete planters.

The driving officer would easily catch him if Scott headed for the front, south entrance; Scott angled away from him toward Fifth and Pike, to the east entrance below the monorail terminal.

He glanced to his left and saw the driving officer scrambling out of the cruiser; Scott kicked up his speed to beat him.

He focused his eyes on the corner of the building; he'd cut around, leading to the entrance only a few feet away. Scott stretched his stride, increasing the speed with each step, pushing himself...faster...faster... The fire in his knee flared with renewed intensity, but he drove the pain from his mind. The rain and his own breath blinded him, but he could see just enough, and he listened for the sound of closing footsteps. He heard them, farther behind him now, as he sped around the corner.

Scott burst through the east doors of the mall, bumping past a pack of frightened shoppers. He nearly slipped on the waxed floor in his wet boots, but managed to keep his balance, running past the bus tunnel signs.

Scott ran down the steps leading to the underground bus concourses, grateful for the crowds waiting for the north and southbound electric buses. He blended in with them. The bus tunnel was fairly new, not yet given over to graffiti, the walls of the concourse adorned instead with the artwork of city children.

Scott hid close to a wall, peering through the crowd, watching the police, METRO, and mall security descending into the terminal. He looked across the concourse; METRO transit officers moved onto the platform. There wasn't much time.

The first bus came and Scott shifted with the crowd, funneling himself through them. He climbed onto the bus, dropped some change in the meter, and moved to the back, lying on the floor in front an empty seat.

An old Native American Indian woman sat across from him as the aisle crowded with standing people, blocking Scott in a tight hiding place. The old Indian woman frowned at him, noticing the blood on his shirt, his hands, and the Bible. Her eyes fixated on the Holy Book, then on Scott. He looked back at her pleadingly, hoping she would avert her convicting gaze.

The old Indian woman turned and found several security and police officers standing outside her window. She tapped on the glass. Scott rose from the floor, ready to run; if he had to, he'd climb out the window. He couldn't let them catch him now; they'd never believe he was innocent.

A police officer turned to the woman. Her eyes almost gave him away, but she turned back to Scott. The Bible shook in his hand and her heart melted. She looked back at the officer, shaking her head. Irritated, he joined the rest of the security team.

Scott sank back under the seat in a cloud of relief, which doubled as the bus began moving, traveling south through the tunnels under Third Avenue, emerging to the streets in the International District.

Scott climbed off the bus, greeted by Asian faces and the smells of cooking meats and steaming foods, along with the omnipresent script of Vietnamese, Japanese, Chinese, and Korean cuneiform. Scott was not a stranger to this part of town; he and Denise had eaten dinner here many times. But he was unfamiliar with this street.

He was unfamiliar, too, with an English word trying hard now to make his acquaintance:

Murder.

"No..." Scott whispered. "No..."

He would know what it was like to run, to live like Biggsby and who knows how many others.

"Oh, there are many of you, Scott Macklin," The Voice said. *"Shiftless fools who think they can prevent the inevitable. Fools who think they can resist. Now your education begins."*

Scott didn't react to The Voice; he simply stopped and listened until it was gone. It didn't frighten or surprise him anymore. In fact, he half-expected it. He felt his mind slipping away.

"God help me. Please help me," he pleaded softly to the dark sky.

He started to move, but hesitated. He couldn't go home. The police would be waiting for him. When they chased him, had they clearly seen his face? Could he even take the chance?

He crept into the darkness, seeing in the shadows the faces of everyone he loved, wondering if he'd ever get back to them. For the first time in his life, he wondered where he'd sleep.

Chapter 20

The police-issue Chrysler Sebring was parked in front of a diner called the Night Owl Café, near the corner of Second and Stewart.

Detective David Fumiko, of the Seattle Police Department's West District Homicide Unit, cradled the receiver back in the radio after answering the call. He glanced at his partner, Nelson Blanchard, who was deep into the pages of the latest J.A. Jance mystery novel.

"You ready for an all-nighter?" Fumiko asked, his English not even hinting that he was Japanese.

Nelson, the senior partner, glanced at Fumiko from bespectacled eyes. "Can I finish my chapter?"

"I don't think this one's gonna wait, Nelson. The rain's washin' away the evidence right now."

Detective Nelson patiently inserted a bookmark and tucked the paperback inside the pocket of his coat. "Well, what've we got?"

"Didn't you hear the dispatch?"

"I block out the world when I'm reading. You know that by now."

Fumiko started the car and pulled away from the curb, heading south on Second. Nelson flipped on the dash flasher, and the interior of the Sebring glowed a blood red.

"What we got is a vagrant, shot to death in Freeway Park, less than an hour ago."

Scott's legs were dead with fatigue as he entered Pioneer Square. The cobblestone shone with the rain. He stayed close to the opening of an alley, between a bar and an antique shop. The oldest neighborhood in the city was lit up like a miniature Mardi Gras. The tourists and night crowds had just begun to gather, and Scott was glad of it. The more people, the easier he could hide. He moved into the blackness of the alley, taking a minute to look himself over. Most of Biggsby's blood washed away during Scott's run through the rain, but there were faint tints of it on his sweatshirt. The Bible had splotches of it, too, somehow drying on the edges of the pages.

Scott turned his eyes upward to see the breaking clouds, and the stars beyond them. The rain had stopped, but he was completely soaked. The cold worked its way into his bones. He guessed it must've been in the mid-forties; the temperature would steadily drop, and within an hour he'd be shaking with the icy air of the late fall. He clasped the Bible between his knees and leaned back against the alley wall. Scott removed his gloves, squeezing the water from them, and then put them right back on his hands. Cupping his hands together, he blew into them; the tips of his fingers were numb with dampness.

Scott hazarded a look at his knee. He winced at the flare of pain when he tried to move his leg and leaned off of it, favoring his left leg. He rested against the wall, knowing he couldn't stay there for long. Going home was out of the question, at least for now. He didn't know how long it would take the police to find out where he lived. For all he knew, they were already there. Scott nearly cursed himself for running, and especially for picking up the gun. Why had he run in the first place? He hadn't killed Biggsby, but how was he going to convince anyone of that now? So, who *had* killed him? Biggsby said that *they'd* come after Scott, too, and now here he was— running, wounded, and exposed. Somehow, he didn't think it would take long for The Illuminated to find him. He was in their territory now—the streets and the shadows.

Scott mulled it over, and decided he had two options. He could turn himself in, and explain to the police that he really hadn't killed Biggsby, that the murderers were members of an ancient, invisible, secret group bent on creating a one-world government in order to establish a satanic order. Or, he could find a room for the night, sneak back to his apartment in the morning, pack, clean out his bank account, and take a two-hour drive to Vancouver, Canada. Option one sounded downright insane; option two was looking good.

Scott reached for his wallet and it was missing. He panicked, frantically checking every pocket. Nothing. No driver's license, no cards, and no money. He inventoried his keys, cell phone, and 38 cents. He could still get to his bank and drive illegally to Vancouver, but for now, he had nothing to pay for a room. The wallet must've been lost during the run, probably when he jumped over that fence or fell onto the street. So this was it then—a night on the street and a trip out of town. How would he explain his sudden disappearance to Denise? Surely, she'd understand that all the evidence would point to him, and that going to prison for something he hadn't done was out of the question. Doom clouded his mind, jolting his faculties of reason. Who would believe him? No one.

He glanced down at the Bible and remembered what Biggsby said. Scott would have to find others who knew. Did the Bible contain the answers he needed? He opened it slowly, as if afraid he'd set off a bomb. Scott flipped through the pages, unable to even pronounce some of the titles of the many books. Near the middle of the volume, he found a book called *Psalms*.

The Psalms read like poems, and Scott saw that most of them were written by a man named David. Of course, he knew David had killed a giant with a sling and a small stone. He remembered the story from a children's illustrated Bible he'd had as a boy. But, the words he read at the beginning of Psalm 22 didn't have the same warmth and comfort as the colorful illustrations of the children's Bible. He read it aloud, the mist rising from his mouth like a prayer. "My God, my God, why hast thou forsaken me? Why art thou so far from helping me, so far from the words of my roaring?"

Looking around the alley and toward the drunken crowds, Scott was hit hard by David's words. The words came alive in his life at that very moment, and Scott suddenly understood the awful meaning of them. God wasn't there. Not in that alley, not among these people, and definitely not in his life. When David wrote this, he must have been in a lot of trouble, like Scott was now. Scott closed the book, and fear rose in his chest; a queasy dread thrashed his heart. The need to run again overtook him; he had to get out of this alley.

Scott tucked himself into his coat, braced against the cold, looked, and then limped out of the alley. He paused, letting the oblivious crowds shuffle past him; he avoided eye contact with a pair of SPD patrol officers as they spun by on mountain bikes. Once they passed, he disappeared into the crowd.

———•◦•———

The Sebring pulled up to the scene of the murder, a few feet from the perimeter tape. Fumiko and Blanchard both caught the pop of an on-camera flash as an evidence technician took a photo of Biggsby's body. They climbed out of the car and walked to the tape. Fumiko, a foot shorter than Blanchard, moved energetically, while the older partner casually fumbled in his coat pocket for the Jance novel. Blanchard had relaxed features, while Fumiko's youthful face pinched with concentration, like a college student wrestling with some complex philosophical question.

The coroner, Tony Lupo, a stout, balding man with a layer of wispy, dark hair languishing across his forehead, was a Los Angeles transplant. He still hadn't gotten used to the slower pace of Seattle, but didn't mind it as long as he could breathe the clean air. He glanced up at the two detectives who stopped at the tape. He handed them each a pair of latex gloves. "You guys took long enough gettin' here. We're just about ready to bag 'im."

Fumiko threw on his gloves, ignoring the comment.

"What's your time of death?"

Lupo pulled up the tape, inviting the two detectives into the scene, lit by several portable fixtures. They moved toward Biggsby, but stopped just a few feet short of him, careful not to damage any potential evidence. Fumiko noticed several muddy footprints around the body.

"Yeah, well, he's got no pupil discoloration or liver mortis. No significant rigor as of yet, either. Couldn't be more than 35, 40 minutes, tops. Once evidence is done, we'll get him to the lab. I can get you a more accurate time by morning."

Lupo reached for the evidence technician's camera. He brought it to his eye and popped a quick shot.

"Cause of death?" Blanchard asked, with his face behind the paperback.

"Three taps to the chest. Looks like a .38. You'll have to check with ballistics, but I'm 100 percent on that. This guy looks like he was executed. He must've been on his knees when they did it."

"There's mud on his pants, right on the knees," offered Fumiko, moving closer, then squatting for a better look.

"Yeah, and look, we got a near perfect indentation in the mud for that, but notice all the footprints around it? Some of 'em are overlapping, but I count at least eight to ten pair. We'll be making casts of those in a minute."

"There appears to be another set leading into the scene, from back here," Blanchard said, with his face still glued to the novel.

"Somebody walked up on him," Fumiko concluded. "This is really preliminary, but it looks like whoever it was came up *after* he was shot."

"Or, maybe he wasn't dead yet, and they came back to finish him," said Blanchard.

"Right... Something's out of place, though," Fumiko observed.

"What's that?"

"Well, if he was shot here, judging by these indentations, then why is his body so far back this way?" Fumiko asked. "Some of these marks in the mud look to me like he crawled or was dragged back here."

Lupo threw his hands up at Fumiko's perplexed look. "Well, I don't know, you're the detective. Maybe he moved during the death throes."

"We got a name on him?"

"Yeah, on his bag. Looks like ex-military. Mitchell Biggsby, U.S. Army."

Fumiko wrote down the name.

"Another homeless vet, huh?" asked Blanchard.

"I guess so."

"Where are the first officers on the scene?" Fumiko asked.

"Well, I think that's them right now," Lupo said.

Fumiko turned to catch a glimpse of Blanchard flipping a page in his book, while an SPD squad car pulled up next to the evidence technician's van. A small crowd of onlookers gathered several feet behind the vehicles. The two officers who chased Scott emerged from the squad car. Fumiko knew immediately which one of them must have run on foot; he got out of the car limping.

The two officers made their way to the tape and Lupo gestured for them to cross the threshold. "Watch your step, gentlemen, and keep those hands in your pockets..." Lupo said. "Don't touch anything. Pretend you're goin' on your first date."

"Well, in that case," the slower officer quipped, "you'd better keep me *outside* the tape."

The first officer, Ray Dilliard, had an athletic build and all the confidence and poise that went with it. His stouter, heavier partner, Leon Leifeld, looked worn-out as he approached the tape, like he wished he could get off his blistered feet.

"We just finished up briefing with METRO, and figured you guys would need us over here," Dilliard said.

Fumiko nodded, offering his hand to the two officers. "Good. We were just about to come lookin' for you. I'm Detective Fumiko, West Division, and this is my partner, Detective Blanchard."

Blanchard absently waved at them. Fumiko knew Blanchard would somehow commit every detail of the scene to memory, even though he looked completely occupied with the paperback.

"You two chased the suspect?"

"That's right. At approximately 1930 hours we were doing a routine patrol of this area and sections of First Hill, when we heard the shots. Arriving on the scene, we found the suspect, a black male, five-foot-eleven, one hundred-ninety pounds, wearing a black leather coat, jeans, boots and a ball cap. I'm pretty sure it was a Mariners cap. The suspect was rising up over the victim, as if he'd crouched next to him. I was clearly able to see that he had a weapon in his right hand, looked to me like a stub-nosed revolver. I couldn't tell you the caliber, but definitely a handgun. It looked like he was carrying some kinda book in his other hand. Me and Leifeld took up defensive positions and ordered the suspect to drop his weapon, but he stood there for a second and then turned and went over the fence. I called it in and Leifeld went after him."

"How far did you chase him?"

"In the patrol car, I cut onto Eighth out of the park, then I hit Union going west 'til I caught up with him at Union and Fourth."

"I foot-chased him through the park, past the Convention Center, then west on University, where he turned north on Fourth. We ran into Dilliard, like he said, at Fourth and Union."

Blanchard piped up from the final page of a chapter. "Either of you get a good look at him?"

"Well, I don't know about Leifeld. Most of the time, all he saw was the guy's back. Nothin' against you, partner, I mean... the guy was pretty quick. Anyway, I got a good look at him when he jumped over the hood of my car at Fourth and Union. We may even have something off the dash camera from when we first pulled up on him. He looked like he was injured, too. He was runnin', but his gait was kinda funny."

Fumiko barely looked up from the notepad, scribbling and nodding. "What did METRO tell you?"

"Nothing much except that they've got a tunnel bus driver who may have picked up the suspect in the Westlake Station, and dropped him off south in the International District. Also, they're checkin' the cameras at the monorail entrance and in the Westlake tunnel, to verify the driver's story."

Fumiko flipped the pages of the pad. "Okay, it looks like we got enough. We're gonna need you down at West Division to help us generate a sketch, so we can get it circulated. How's that book comin', Blanchard? You think you got time to run him over to the sketch tech before he leaves tonight?"

Blanchard nodded. "Get in touch with METRO's Watch Commander. See if we can get a hold of those tapes. Talk to that driver, too. I'm finding it hard to believe that he was able to get in and out of Westlake without a METRO officer catching him, or at least getting an ID."

"Right. I'll ride with you, Leifeld."

"Well, whatever you do," said Dilliard, "I hope you find the dirtbag. Killing homeless people is about as low as you can get. Reminds me of a couple cases back in '97, when some street kids set a homeless guy on fire in front of a shelter, right across the street from the King County Courthouse. Luckily, that guy didn't die. More recently, we've got the case where a 14-year-old kid stabbed a 50-year-old man to death in Kinnear Park. The kid beat him with his skateboard, robbed him, and stabbed him 18 times with a pocket knife. In another recent case, an 18-year-old and a 19-year-old stabbed a 46-year-old man to death under an overpass north of here. I've read reports from all over: New York, D.C., Chicago, L.A., San Diego, and ad nauseam. It's an epidemic."

Fumiko nodded gravely. "Yeah, what's the world comin' to?"

Dilliard look at him, dubiously. "You just *now* askin' that question?"

He walked off toward Blanchard. Fumiko noticed, for the first time, a gold crucifix that Dilliard wore openly on his chest. As he and Leifeld moved outside the tape to the squad car, Fumiko remembered it was against regulations to wear religious jewelry with the uniform. Somehow, he figured Dilliard knew that.

Scott rested on a bench at the Convention Place tunnel station, at Ninth and Pine. The three-mile-walk from Pioneer Square had his aggravated knee throbbing with new intensity. He sat down, grunting and wincing with the pain. The temperature was dropping but the walk had warmed him. Now that he stopped, it would only be a few minutes before the cold would overcome him. He gently massaged the knee, shocked at how swollen it felt under his jeans. Scott leaned back on the bench to take in his surroundings.

The tunnel station, an elaborate glass and steel open-air structure with a neon-lit marquee, was running staggered buses now, and there were no crowds or patrolling police in the area. Scott was only a mile-and-a-half from Belltown; all he needed was a quick rest and he'd hobble on to his building. He thought better of sleeping on the street all night; he would sneak back into his townhome, grab some cash and then head out of town.

He leaned back on the cold metal of the bench, his eyes just making out the stars under a patchy sky. The stars were faint and distant, the heavens far above him, blotted by the clouds and washed over by the orange glow of the city's reflected light. Scott felt his own insignificance under the weight of the evening sky; fear shook him worse than the cold did. How had he fallen so fast? He knew that even if he escaped the city, they would find him eventually. Biggsby called them shadows, and the darkness held an infinite, incalculable number of deadly possibilities.

Scott wished he could curl up on the bench and disappear. Tears glistened in his eyes like stars, but the sky stared down at him from its empty expanse. Was He really there? The One they called God and Christ? Did He really watch over the pitiful efforts of his creatures? How could He allow such endless suffering? Why did Biggsby have to die and how soon would Scott be joining him? He knew there were worse things in the world than what was happening to him. Had God given up, too? Had He left the world to feebly fend for itself? The questions poured through his mind but no answers came. Scott resigned himself to whatever fate would fall on him.

The buses in the tunnel were electric, and nearly silent. Scott barely heard as one pulled up into the tunnel station below him. The interior of the bus was brightly lit, and it looked empty to Scott at first, but when the door opened, he saw a lone passenger step down onto the platform. The air around Scott moved and whispered. The wind lived; an alien presence blew into this realm, along with the almost imperceptible sound of a door opening, and then closing.

The Man moved over to the escalator and rode it to the top of the tunnel plaza, where Scott rested on the bench. He looked like the quintessential gentleman in a black tuxedo with a bright, red rose on the lapel, touched off with white gloves and an umbrella long enough to use as a cane. His hair was shockingly white, framing a dark face which glowed with a deep intellect and knowledge. It was almost down to the freezing mark, but Scott noticed that The Man didn't wear a coat.

The Man stepped off the escalator and smiled at Scott, as if he had found an old friend. He approached and Scott felt the impulse to run, but something froze him to the bench. Suddenly, The Man stood in front of him.

"Good evening. This is certainly a pleasant night," The Man said in an aristocratic tone. "Though a bit chilly, don't you think?"

Scott heard something familiar in the character and inflection of his voice.

"Yeah," Scott said shivering. "It's a little cold."

"That's one thing I've always hated about this city: The cold and the rain. Or, maybe that's two things, actually. Also, the winters. They seem to drag on and on, well into the spring. Now, the summers... the summers here are lovely. Do you know what my favorite kind of climate is?"

Scott shook his head, awkwardly.

"The tropics. Of all the places I've traveled, you simply can't beat the tropics. The warmer air is marvelous for the bones. I've covered just about every inch of the globe, but I always prefer places south of the equator."

"Uh-huh," Scott mumbled.

"Wouldn't it be nice if it was just a tad warmer? Just enough to take the edge off?"

Scott felt a rush of warm air whisper across his body, enveloping him. He gasped as the temperature rose 20 degrees, covering him with a blanket of heat. His shivering subsided and an odd easing of the mind settled over him. The Man smiled.

"That's better. Much better. That should make things more conducive to conversation. So, here we are at last. It looks like you've gotten yourself into a little spot of ...trouble."

"What are you talkin' about?"

"Why, the man you've murdered, of course."

Scott's heart hammered away behind his ribs. Was this man a cop? Every instinct told him to run, but he couldn't move.

"I-I-I... I don't know what you're talkin' about. I haven't killed anybody."

"Oh, come, come now. Yes, of course you have. That homeless man in the park. You shot him. You have the gun in your coat pocket right now. But, please, don't be alarmed. I'm not trying to upset you. After all, these things do happen."

"Who are you? Are you the police?"

"No. Most definitely not."

Scott was terrified now, his hands shaking. " But, I didn't do it! I didn't kill him!"

"Well, now... Then who did?"

Scott opened his mouth to speak, but the truth couldn't find words. "I... I... I don't know."

The Man placed a hand on Scott's shoulder. His voice soothed like a friend's, but his eyes hid something hungry and eager to devour.

"It's all right, it's all right, Scott. We live in a very complicated and violent world. Who can fault you for that? There are those who would blame you for the crime but what you have done is simply a social accident, a by-product of a very complex, arbitrary, and chaotic universe. We do not have a perfect system, so should we punish someone simply because of his capricious impulses? Rage... anger... lust... These things are normal and every man feels them. Why struggle to control or contain that which is grafted onto your very nature? I have always believed these impulses can and should be utilized for the advancement of mankind. It is obvious they are woven into the very fabric of your being; one cannot separate himself from *himself.*"

Scott's senses began to unravel. In the presence of this man, the needle of his ethical compass was spinning in a mad circle. Could what he said be true?

"But, murder... I... murder is evil..."

"Yes! It is! Yet, evil is part of one's nature. It is a prerequisite to achieving balance; evil separates the strong from the weak of a species, ensuring the overall survival of the race. The man you murdered was a weak man, a vagrant parasite on society. Should a man like him even be allowed to live?"

"Yes..."

"Why?"

"Because… God made him. He made all of us. We aren't supposed to kill each other."

"Did you say God? I assume you mean the Creator, the Lord. Christ! Is this the One you are referring to?"

"Yes."

"Do you believe He exists?"

"I…I… yes."

"Your vacillation tells me differently. Tell me, where is He? If He exists, show Him to me, introduce me to Him."

Scott remembered his questions. "I don't know."

"You don't know? You don't sound very confident in your faith. Why do you insist on clinging to something that will bear you either no fruit, or a rotten, disappointing, pitted fruit? There is no hope in God. Do you honestly believe that a man will one day come from the sky and right every wrong, wipe away every tear? Why does man, with all his advancements and accomplishments, all his knowledge and intelligence, hold on to such an empty-headed concept?"

Clarity rushed over Scott. Something in the center of his heart moved, and the word came to him. He couldn't take credit for it. It was there in his mind as if a gentle voice had whispered it.

"Love," Scott said.

The man grimaced with pain, with an ancient torment like a slowly re-opening wound. He stifled a curse and glanced up at the sky as if expecting something to fall on his head. His voice vibrated with agitation.

"What of it?"

"Love is what God offers us. What everyone wants is to be loved."

The man reared back his head and laughed, his bellowing like a thousand mocking voices all jeering at once.

"You simpleton! Love? That is the deepest, most desolate lie of all! It is the very thing that motivates you all to such hapless folly! The world is so full of the bleakness of humanity, it is impossible for you to truly know it! You have only succeeded in making a mockery of it; you've done just enough to prove how really unworthy you are of it!"

Scott looked off into the distance and his thoughts warmed him.

"I know what it feels like to give love, and to receive it."

"Do you? Well, I know the one who you are thinking of. Your fiancée? Denise?"

"Yes."

"Quite the charming young woman. But, do you think love will be able to sustain the two of you now? Already she is leaving you in her heart. Once she tastes what the world can offer, she will very soon forget you."

Scott fumed, ready to pound the man into the concrete. "You're a liar!"

"Am I? Well, perhaps human history has painted me as such. Come. Let me prove it to you, a short lesson regarding love, and a few other things I would like to teach you."

He grabbed Scott by the arm. Scott felt a sensation like flying and drowning in unfathomable, icy waters.

◆

Detective Fumiko sat with the METRO Watch Commander in a room lit by the bluish-gray glow of an array of video monitors. A technician manipulated the switches on a video editor/controller. Fumiko's eye caught an angle on the suspect as he quickly entered the east side of the Westlake tunnel station. They were in the process of reviewing several other tapes from various angles, but so far had no useful images. He leaned back in his chair, trying not to let out a yawn. His cell phone chirped.

"Detective Fumiko."

"Find anything?" It was Blanchard.

"Well, we've got a bunch a shots of the suspect; he fits the physical description Dilliard came up with. We just can't seem to get a good angle on him. Once he entered the tunnel, he ran straight into the crowd ducking low. It's hard to even see which bus he climbed on. Most of the cameras are set high on pretty wide shots. I think we can narrow it down to five or six usable images. We'll have to run the shots by the video tech lab. Maybe they'll be able to pull up something. How 'bout you?"

"The sketch tech has worked up an image with Dilliard. It looks pretty good. Once they're done we'll crosscheck it through the Department of Vehicle Licensing and see what we get. I think we're getting close on this one."

"Ditto. How's the book?"

"Finished it an hour ago. Not too bad. It wasn't Jance's best, but a good one."

"Don't tell me the ending. I might pick it up."

"Got it. Get back with me in an hour. I'll call you before then if we find anything from the DVL. Captain's looking for an update, so I gotta go."

"We'll have something soon."

"Okay."

———◦•◦———

Scott looked over the Puget Sound nearly 55 floors above the street, affording a spectacular view of the city of Seattle. To the north he saw Belltown, the towering Space Needle with its revolving restaurant, and the hills of Queen Ann. To the south were the towers of the financial district, the soon-to-be demolished Kingdome, and the giant orange shipping cranes that hung silently over the commercial piers.

Scott's breath left him as he realized he was standing precariously on the edge of a building. Somehow, though, he knew he wouldn't fall. A sur-realistic warmth came over him, a feeling of being in the world, but no longer part of the world. Was this real? Tendrils of wind coursed and weaved around him; he smelled the rich, almost pungent sharpness of the bay waters. An eerie silence prevailed. Seagulls made no sound, nor even the traffic speeding along the I-99 viaduct or Alaska Way, down by the water's edge. It was like seeing the world from inside a glass container. The city's business went on all around him, without him.

Scott looked behind himself and upward; his blood chilled. He was on the Washington Mutual Tower; before him stood the glass pyramid, with the stylistic starburst for the Eye. The massive pyramid glowed from a power-ful light source within it. The Man in the Tuxedo appeared and spoke, his voice echoing as if from a tomb.

"I must say again, quite the lovely evening, isn't it?"

Scott looked at him with a childlike fear. "W-who are you? What do you want with me?"

"To enlighten you, to free you… Don't you know who I am?"

Scott shook his head.

"I am the Lightbearer, the Giver of Knowledge, the Great Emancipator of the Soul, the Philanthropist of Human Dreams. Throughout history, men have painted many a picture of me, but most have simply denied my existence and my power. This is hurtful, because I have come to free you to your own wills, to give you the ability to govern yourselves without a despotic overseer. Why should man put up with a god who dictates laws and postulates morality? Man needs a god who will allow him to unleash his own resolve, and live the way he chooses."

Something besides fear resonated from Scott's childhood. He remembered the day he ran into the dark full of apprehension and doubt, and returned full of the radiance of hope and confidence. Scott spoke boldly. The words came from his mind, but they were not his alone.

"And what if man chooses war? What if he chooses death?"

"Then let that be his choice! Let the world resonate with the vibrant choices of the truly freed man! Let his will take us where it chooses!"

"If freedom of choice is the answer, then why is there still so much decay and despair in the world?" Scott asked.

"An end to a thing is beautiful! Let there be decay and destruction! Eternity is a delusion in the mind of the wishful. All things should end, so that the new may begin, just as it is with the seasons."

"But love never ends. It never decays, it doesn't destroy, and it doesn't die!"

"Oh, no, my deluded friend? I have the power to reveal hidden things. See if this supports your blind devotion!" The man moved a hand across Scott's face like a dark magician, and the vision began.

There was his love, Denise. The fire cast a glow across her skin, which shimmered with a sheen of sweat. She wore something thin, short, and clingy. She looked at him with an almost hopeless love, completely abandoning herself and her will to him. Her eyes begged him to come to her, to not prolong the moment. Scott remembered countless nights like these, how they'd loved each other with sweet desperation.

"Denise…"

Someone else entered the room, and her eyes turned away from Scott, toward him. He moved like a predator, his hands not caressing her as much as groping greedily. Who was this man?

"Denise?"

The two of them fell out of view, but just before they did, the man turned with a conqueror's smile on his lips. When Scott saw his face, he nearly raved like a lunatic.

Kile Tatlock.

"Denise! No! Why?! Why?!"

The vision was gone and The Man in the Tuxedo stood over Scott.

"Is this the power of love you speak about? Is love enough to keep her in your life? Was it enough to keep your grandmother from becoming a prostitute at the tender age of seventeen? Was it enough to keep your uncles from becoming alcoholics and drug addicts? Was it enough to keep your grandfather from dying of polio and another grandfather from dying on a minefield in France? Was it enough to keep you from becoming a murderer, and enough to keep your father from driving his car over a cliff?!"

"NOOOO!" Scott lunged at The Man, throwing a wild punch. Impossibly, The Man eluded it. Scott lost his balance, and landed in a heap against a wall that formed the base for the Pyramid. He lay there, his mind reeling, his life crushing and suffocating him.

"Denise... How could you?" He mumbled. "Why?" Scott cried in bitter silence.

The Man in the Tuxedo knelt beside him with an almost fatherly compassion, but his eyes glowed with an insatiable hunger. He anticipated the fall of Scott Macklin, and his heart leaped with the joy of it. "My friend, my friend, please. I'm sorry, I go much too far sometimes." He placed his hand on Scott's shoulders and with an unnatural strength, lifted him to his feet. "Let me show you something you can be a part of, something greater than the false promises and lies. Let me show you a power so strong that once you partake of it, you will never be hurt or disappointed again. On the contrary, others who would have hurt you will grovel at your feet. They will fear you because I will make you one of my own. Look!"

Through blurry tears, Scott saw the city laid out in front of him. The city lights burned and beckoned. Time shifted before him, moving with an impossible speed. Countless sunsets rose and set; multiple moon phases morphed and danced across the sky. The city shimmered as it awakened from a deep slumber; it became a living, growing, glowing entity. Scott saw the towers rise higher and higher until the tops of them disappeared into the clouded sky. Great ships emerged from the bay and the sea beyond, cutting majestically across the city airspace. Technology conquered the city, spreading like a voracious disease, manifesting itself in everything, even manipulating the make-up of mankind itself, altering it. The city became populated with creatures who were no longer people, but beings with powerful, cyber-enhanced minds. Even God no longer recognized them as creatures made by Him; their souls were diminished until they became less than human.

Finally, time slowed to normal. The city now extended past the far mountains to the west, and in every direction. The Man in the Tuxedo reigned in his power and turned to Scott with a smile. "You have seen the near future. This vision will extend to the entire world. Man will no longer be inhibited, but free. The god of the past will give way to the god of the future, and you will be part of it. I have the power to give you this future. I only need you to do one simple thing…"

Scott saw the hunger in The Man's eyes flare and then recede. He felt the presence of the deepest evil he had ever known.

"Bow down and worship me, and all these things I will give to you."

Scott felt the most powerful urge to believe him; it permeated the essence of his being. He trembled… Scott held his shaking fists in front of his face, resisting with all his strength. A small ember grew until it consumed him. The words came from Scott's mouth almost before he could think them. "No… No… I know who you are. I don't know how I know, but I do."

The Man in the Tuxedo was astonished. "What?"

"No. I won't worship you. I'm going to worship Christ and God. One day I'll have the answers to my questions. Maybe not as soon as I'd like, but one day."

The air and the sky shifted. Scott felt as if he was being baptized in frigid waters. In seconds, they were back at the Convention Place Station, and Scott found himself resting once again on the bench. The Man in the Tuxedo stood over him, his face flared with anger. Scott was not afraid. He felt the cold air again and soon he quivered with it, but he also felt a deep warmth soothing him from within.

The Man in the Tuxedo stomped away from Scott Macklin in disgust and contempt. He spat on the ground and cursed a litany of foul words. He turned his eyes skyward and directed a scream at the expanse, but the stars yawned at his tirade. A peel of thunder clapped somewhere in the distance in response.

"You will not win this! You will not!" The Man bellowed helplessly.

He leaned over Scott with a few final words. "It seems you have made your choice. Very well. Live with it, then! I suggest you read that book you are clinging to, and be prepared to die for what you learn in it!" The Man in the Tuxedo turned and walked away. Scott watched him hurry down the steps adjacent to the escalator, and jump on a bus which seemed to appear on cue. The bus ran its course on the track yard before disappearing into the tunnel.

Scott had forgotten he still held Biggsby's Bible in his hand. After all he'd gone through, it hadn't been lost. For a moment, he felt his troubles might be over.

He rose from the bench and his knee burned with a jarring stiffness and pain. As he limped away from the tunnel station, The Voice broke into his mind.

"You had better learn as much as you can. He will not take an unprepared mind into His precious Kingdom. And, be warned of this: We do not plan on allowing you to live long, Scott Macklin. Not long at all."

It was the voice of the Man in the Tuxedo, with the rose on his lapel. Fear seized Scott's heart as he hurried toward Belltown.

Detective Blanchard watched the computer monitors, their systems feverishly at work. One monitor showed a computer-generated image of Scott Macklin. The other monitor displayed a graphic with the logo of the Department of Vehicle Licensing in the corner of the screen. The text on the graphic read: "SEARCHING DVL DATABASE FOR MATCHING IMAGES – PLEASE WAIT…"

Blanchard took a sip of coffee, leaning his chin on a propped-up fist. He wondered why the face seemed familiar. Blanchard gazed once more into the eyes of the computer image of the suspect. Were those the eyes of a killer?

CHAPTER 21

Thomas Macklin had been sitting for an hour in the family car, parked in the garage. He leaned his head against the wheel, somnolent and dejected. His mind was fatigued from 72 hours of sleep deprivation, brought on by the crippling, malicious, cerebral assaults of the voices. It was quiet now, but they had crowded his mind with words and visual horrors, extrapolating on the vivid and violent memories of a war that ended over 30 years ago.

The voices had taken over every synapse in his brain, making it impossible for him to distinguish between his own thoughts and their intrusions. They cursed and insulted him; they threatened to murder him and his family, laying out their plans in the most brutal, colorful detail. The minute he closed his eyes to sleep, they crowded into his thoughts. Thomas could almost see them: twisted, grotesque things with bulbous, probing, darting eyes. They were depraved creatures, smutty and gleefully violent. They were monsters, pricking his brain with bony tendrils, scratching and clawing at his soul with prying nails. They laughed and spoke in quick succession, one after the other, hundreds of them. The visions and nightmares they induced were a cacophony of death from the jungle: the smell of death, the searing of flesh, the burning of metal cutting through bone, the spray of blood, and the cry of the young. And the sounds, the noises! The thunderous roar of an exploding artillery shell and automatic gunfire, the chopper blades whipping the air, and the animal curses of men.

Then there was one voice, *The* Voice. It spoke above the others, but was a part of them. It spoke clearly and intelligently; it was quick to rage and seethe one moment, soothe and console the next. Thomas had longed to talk to this one, until he learned what it was. He'd seen how it was allied to the evil he'd witnessed in the jungle that day, the same day he'd seen The One, and soon after became a praying man. Lately, though, it seemed like Christ had left him. He held to his faith desperately, but malevolence bore down on him and on his family with an assault even the most brilliant military tactician couldn't assuage. The Shadows of Men were too close now. How could he protect his family from them?

He lifted his head from the steering wheel and watched the deep, tawny fire of the morning sun greet him through a garage window. The beautiful sunlight made a shadow pattern through the windowpane; an elongated cross stretched across the wall. Thomas fixed his eyes on it and his senses were eased, but only for an instant. He realized then that they'd been after him and his family ever since his discovery of the truth, all those years ago.

But, it was not really his family they wanted. It was him. Thomas couldn't let anything happen to Kathy and the children. Not like what had happened to Mitch's family.

With Thomas out of the way, they would leave her and the children alone, wouldn't they? He found the garage door opener in the glove box, and tapped the button. The door opened slowly and Thomas blinked at the flood of light. Before he could stop it, The Voice filled his ear with the clarity of a phone call.

"That's right, Thomas. Go on, then. You know it's you we've wanted all along. You learned some incriminating things about us, but you were a fool to think you could win. Men have been fighting to resist us for centuries, since the beginning. The failure of mankind throughout history serves to further accentuate your failure. We do not desire your family; therefore, you know what is required."

Thomas didn't say a word; he started the car and drove away from his home.

————◆————

Scott finally entered his townhome around about midnight. The minute his key touched the lock, Denise appeared in the entryway, her look one of shock and worry. The sight of Scott didn't do much to calm her fears.

"Scott, where have… Oh, my God."

She looked him over from head to toe. Scott was dirty, disheveled, and ragged from his hours on the street. Denise could see the exhaustion on his face, but her eyes widened at the sight of the blood on the front of his sweatshirt. She moved toward him, her hands touching him gingerly.

"Scott! Oh, my God! What happened? Is that your blood? Are you hurt?"

Scott scarcely looked at her; the image of Denise with Kile Tatlock loomed in his mind.

"I'm fine," he grumbled.

Denise threw her arms around him. "I got here this evening and you weren't home. I called Bryce, but he said you hadn't been at the office. I've been here waiting for you all night. Where were you?" Denise felt something heavy in Scott's jacket pocket. "What is that? What's that in your jacket, Scott?"

He ignored her, removed her arms from around his neck, and gave her a suspect look. Scott stepped from the entryway into the living room. "It's nothing." He dropped onto the couch, a dead weight. His knee seared with pain, but the ache in his heart was worse. "You say you were here all night?"

"Yes."

"Were you alone?"

"What?"

"I asked if you were alone, Denise." Scott surveyed the room for any telltale signs of a visitor, but there were none.

Denise wrinkled her face at him with a frown. "Yes, Scott, I was here alone. Why do you keep asking me like that? And why won't you tell me what happened to you tonight?"

"Nothing happened to me, Denise. Except I came to the realization that I've loved you for all these years… and you're nothing more than a liar."

"What? A liar? About what? What are you saying to me?"

Scott jumped painfully to his feet, jabbing his finger at her.

"I'm talking about you and Kile!"

"What?!"

"Tatlock! You know what! You've been with him! You been with him all this time, behind my back!"

"Are you insane? I've never been with anyone except you the whole time we've been together!"

"Liar!"

"How am I lying?!"

"I saw the two of you! Together!"

"Scott, that is not true and it is not possible! I don't know what you saw or what you think you saw, but you did not see me with Kile! The last time I talked to him was at the shareholders' dinner and I haven't spoken with him since! He's not even here; he's in New York!"

"Denise, just tell me! How long has it been going on?"

"I just told you! There is nothing going on! I don't know what you're talking about, Scott!"

Scott lunged madly at her, grabbing her by both arms and squeezing. "You're lying to me! You're lying to me right now! I know you've been with him!"

"Let go of me! You've been acting crazy ever since I accepted this promotion! You're just using Kile as an excuse! You know I'd never cheat on you, Scott! I'd never do anything like that to you!"

She broke free of his grip and broke into tears.

Scott never behaved abusively toward her, and Denise had never been afraid of him until now.

"Why are you acting like this? You're crazy! Why are you pushing me? Don't you know I love you?"

Her words barely penetrated him. "I don't know anything about you anymore."

Denise was frightened, but moved closer to him.

"Scott, tell me what you want. Tell me what's wrong. Do you want me to turn down the job? Tell me. Do you want me to stay? Tell me what you want me to do."

Scott pushed her away. "No, Denise. No. I don't want you to do anything for me. There isn't anything else you can do. You don't want me; you want money and power. That's what you've always wanted. So go get it."

"Scott, I've never wanted any of those things. Even if I have them, it's no good without you. I need you. Don't do this. We've been through too much for too long. You can't...you can't just end us like this. You don't have the only say in this..."

Denise searched in his eyes for a trace of the feelings he had for her, but there was nothing. The warmth was gone, iced over by a cold, dead visage. "It's already ended. Pack your things and leave, Denise. I don't ever want to see you again. Go to New York and have your life."

Her shocked heart elicited a flood of tears, and she let them course down her cheeks. The man standing in front of her was not the one she knew. This man was emotionless and empty, and she had no way of knowing what had caused it. Something had killed them. Denise felt a crushing despair and hopelessness.

"Scott, please…"

"I said go."

There was no mistaking the look of finality on his face. Stooped with pain and tears, Denise moved into the bedroom. Soon, Scott heard only the sound of her sobbing.

—•◦•—

When Detective Blanchard opened his eyes, he almost lost his balance in the chair. He had fallen asleep, but now the ID confirmation from the DVL jolted him awake like a cup of Fumiko's bad coffee. The screen read: DVL MATCH FOUND – MATCH INTEGRITY 96%.

He looked around for the sketch tech, but decided not to wait for him. Blanchard tapped the keys, and the printer across the lab hummed to life. He entered a command, sending the DVL image to the printers and fax machines of all Seattle and Tacoma police divisions. The screen blinked back a graphic that confirmed his command. He took a hard look at the name and face on the driver's license, and realized why it was familiar.

"No, that can't be right."

Blanchard linked to the police database, running Scott's name through the system. The information came back quickly; the suspect had no priors or convictions. Blanchard printed the sheet and grabbed his coat, fishing in its pockets for his cell phone.

"Detective Fumiko."

"We got him, and you're not gonna believe who it is!"

"Thank God. If I have to look at one more tape…"

"Macklin. Scott Macklin."

"You're kiddin' me. That architect?"

"I tell you no lie. One and the same."

"Let me guess. He's got a clean sheet? No priors?"

"He had a speeding ticket four years ago."

"Well, hey, let's lock him up. What's this guy gotten mixed up in?"

"I don't know, but we're gonna need a warrant. I just woke up the Assistant D.A. We'll be chatting about the summons in a minute."

"Can we put him on the scene?"

"Forensics came back with some microscopic fibers from the fence, where Macklin allegedly went over it. They were able to trace it back to the manufacturer, and we nailed it down to a specific brand. There are three Gap stores in the Seattle area that sell them. I took the liberty to stop by all three of them this morning, and had them check their credit card records, going back two years."

"Outstanding, Detective."

"Yeah. Scott Macklin American-Expressed a gray sweatshirt at the Gap on Fourth and Pike just over a month ago."

"We find the sweatshirt…"

"He's at the scene."

"What about weapons registration?"

"That's a tough one. He ain't got any."

"I wonder where he found the piece, then."

"Yeah. Well, we've got enough to run him in. A guy like this with no record probably won't be your average, hardened-criminal type. I'm betting we won't have any trouble with him in the interview. I don't know what happened to this guy, but that crane accident must have shaken his brain loose."

"Right. The suspect is never who you suspect. ETA on the warrant?"

"As soon as I get the Assistant D.A. in front of a judge. They've got a backlog on search warrant requests."

"Imagine that."

"About an hour and a half. Meet me at Macklin's address in two hours. His DVL info should be sitting on the METRO fax machine."

"Got it."

"One thing that bothers me about this one, Fumiko."

"What's that?"

"This guy just ain't the type. He doesn't have the looks of a killer to me. They usually have this thing in the eyes, you know?"

"Well, sometimes they don't."

"Yeah, I guess. I'll see you in two hours."

———◆•◆———

Thomas had driven on Alabama State Route 280 north for almost two hours, until he found himself 15 minutes south of Birmingham. He took the Homewood exit, heading southwest past the industrial town of Bessemer, on Interstate 459. With nearly thirty years as a soldier, Thomas knew how to give and take orders; he drove on with an unwavering, hypnotic obedience to the commands and instructions he was given by The Voice. A limestone quarry just west of Bessemer was to be his final stop.

"Good soldier…"

———◆•◆———

Scott Macklin fixed his weary eyes on the framed John Coltrane poster that dominated the south wall of his living room. He read the caption, the title of the landmark jazz album, but the words meant nothing: *A Love Supreme*. A saxophonist, Coltrane wrote the album as a tribute to God, reaffirming his belief after a tumultuous time in his career. Scott felt the chasm widening between himself and God, as his faith and hope eroded away.

His confusion mounted without a clear, discernable explanation. Nothing made sense. The world held nothing for him. He felt that he stood on the edge of a great precipice, with nothing below but a deep, endless blackness. Beneath him, *they* beckoned with whispers that grew in volume until the noise finally drove him to cover his ears. To Scott Macklin's horror, he found he couldn't stop the voices, for they were somehow in him, a multitude beckoning from a devious void. It was the void itself that called him, and he felt its pull like gravity, dragging him down… The strength to fight it was gone.

Scott stumbled backward, tripping over the edge of the coffee table. He landed in a nerve-jarring heap on the floor, his hands over his ears, rocking back and forth.

"Wearelegionwearelegionwearelegionwearelegionwearelegionwearele-gionweare wearelegionwearelegionwearelegionwearelegionwearelegion-wearelegion..."

What did they want with him? How could he stop it? A sliver of hope came to his mind, making its way through the quagmire of his thoughts. He could barely form his own notions because of the voices, chattering away incessantly. Should he answer them? Could he reason with them?

"What do you want?"

"Wewantyouwewantyouwewantyou...Doaswesaydoaswesaydoaswesay doaswesaydoaswesay...Youwillfeelnopainyouwillfeelnopain youwillfeelnopain..."

Scott stood shaking, the morning sunlight cutting through the slats of the window blinds. His body vibrated and twitched with frayed nerves, and resonated with waves of childhood fear. If not for the horror of realizing he'd been communicating with something unnatural and inhuman, he would have been fascinated.

"W-w-what are you?"

"Wearethosewhodothewillofourfatherwearethosewhodothewillofourfa-therwe arethosewhodothewillofourfatherwearethosewhodothewillofourfa-ther..."

"Who is your father?"

"Theprinceoftheairtheprinceoftheairtheprinceotheairtheprince-oftheairtheprinceoftheairtheprinceoftheairtheprinceoftheair... Hiswillisstronganditdesiresyouhiswillis stronganditdesiresyouhiswillis-stronganditdesiresyouhiswillisstronganditdesiresyou..."

Scott revolted against them. "NO! No! No!... Leave me alone! Get away from me! Get out of my head!"

"Wewillneverleaveyouwewillneverleaveyouwewillneverleaveyouwewill neverleaveyouwewillneverleaveyou...Hereheishereheishereheishereheisher eheis... Our masterourmasterourmasterourmasterourmasterourmasterour-masterourmaster..."

Scott felt a shift in the air around him and they were silent. The Voice entered and cleared his mind with its presence. Scott's breath rushed from his lungs as The Voice invaded him. It was the exact voice of the man he'd met at the Convention Place Station, calm and assured.

"My children have informed me you have some reservations con-cerning your newfound destiny with us?"

"I don't have anything to do with you. I don't want any part of you."

"Well, I see you at least have the integrity to stand by your decisions, Scott. That is a sign of a mature man. Mature, yet woefully lacking in other areas."

"You're a liar. Why should I believe anything you say?"

"You believed what I showed you concerning your beloved, did you not?"

"I lost her because of you!"

"You've lost nothing. Who's to say that what I showed you was something that had not happened yet? She has been faithful to you up until this point, but how long do you think that will last? There, you see? I can sense your doubt in her. Women. They are only good for a few things, Scott. Eventually, you have to get rid of them. I'm not sure why He made them. Worrisome creatures if you ask me."

Scott felt his life drain away at the realization of what he had done. "Oh, God no... Denise..."

"If only you could know the sheer joy and contentment I feel at beguiling you, how a soul weakens at the moment of deception and betrayal, how it softens and ripens, perfect for the harvest. But I'm not done with you. I will pluck you out of this world yet, but first, one more thing to crush you, just one more bit of a stab. Turn on your television."

Scott hesitated, but his resolve was weak.

"Turn it on now, Scott."

His limbs moved discordantly and in the next moment Scott held the TV remote in his hand. The television lit up and Scott's eyes bulged at the image of his own face on the screen. It was the early morning edition of King 5 News. Scott Macklin was the top story. He listened to the excited voice of the female anchor.

"...the local architect who, just a few weeks ago, was involved in a crane accident at the site of the now-on-hold Washington Lake Office and Retail complex. Again, a King County judge has issued a search warrant for the home of Scott Macklin, in connection with the death of a 50 year-old homeless man, whose identification is being withheld until next of kin have been notified. We will bring you further developments as this story..."

Scott tapped the off button on the remote, dropping it absently on the hardwood floor.

"You see... Now it is over. The police are on their way..."

285

———•—•—•———

Blanchard was on the Sebring's police radio as Fumiko darted in and out of early morning traffic. They headed north on Fifth toward Belltown.

"No," Blanchard said dismissively, into the receiver. "Two squads will be plenty; this guy ain't goin' anywhere. His building's got a parking garage; I'll need two officers to cover the entrance and exit. Then we'll need two guys to cover the front and rear of the building... Okay, great... Yeah, we're on our way now, ETA in fifteen minutes... Right... Okay... I copy... Blanchard out."

Fumiko shot the Sebring through the intersection of Seneca and Fifth, sparing no pressure on the gas pedal.

———•—•—•———

Thomas Macklin's sedan left a plume of dust in the air as he turned onto a dirt road that lead down to the Oakforest Boulevard Limestone Quarry. His pulse heightened as he rumbled along the stony downgrade. The massive quarry excavation was at least a mile in diameter and over two-hundred-feet deep. Thomas drove past several excavation company trailers; his daze broke just long enough to notice the mammoth earth-moving equipment dotting the quarry. The edge of a sheer drop was just 300 yards away, but Thomas showed no sign of slowing.

Through tears, he glanced into the sky, as if his persecutors came from there.

"I'm doing this for my family... Do you hear me? If you want me, here I come. But you can't touch them after this; you understand me? You leave them alone after this. You leave them alone!... I know you're there! Speak up!"

"Yes, Thomas... I'm here and I understand. I will honor your request. Now, keep driving... Just a little farther..."

———◆◆◆◆———

Scott entered his bedroom, feeling the metal of the .38 in his right hand; it was death wrapped in a fist. His mind had gone numb, clouded and choked by madness. Fear paralyzed his reason, crippling all logic and judgment. He was going to prison for a murder he did not commit. His new, twisted discernment convinced him he would die in prison, but left him one way out of the problem. He hefted the gun in his hand and came to a clear and rational decision: It would be better to die here, now.

Again, like last night on the street, he saw the faces of all the people he loved. How would they take this; would they understand why this was his only choice? And Denise? He had driven her away, but he'd had no choice there, either. She would never be able to accept the truth he had discovered. It would shatter her world, perhaps disturbing her even more than it had him. He couldn't do that to her, or to anyone he loved. Maybe it was better that the majority of people lived in ignorance of the truth, better for people to go about their lives without ever confronting the evil that was apparently in control. Once it has been revealed, how can anyone fight against it?

He stood in front of his open bedroom window, and gazed upon the most beautiful morning sky he had ever seen. What would he like to see before he died? Denise's face entered his mind, but it also brought pain, so he pushed the image away. He focused instead on the sky and the glow of light from the Cascades.

Scott looked at the gun, a simple mechanism, really. He pressed the barrel release and it flopped open. Turning it upward, he spilled six bullets, oily from their individual chambers, onto the carpet. He stooped, picking up one of them and loading it into a cavity. He turned the barrel to align the bullet next to the firing chamber. Slowly, he pulled back on the hammer until it locked, and the bullet revolved into firing position. The trigger was cocked back, millimeters from firing.

Scott felt the rush of tears as he prepared to die. What was waiting to greet him on the other side? Would there be nothing, a cold blankness?

"There is no more time for questions, Scott. Just simply do it. Why else would you have taken the gun in the first place? Your entire life has been

leading up to this moment. You've always known it. All this time it was not us seeking you, but you who were seeking us. Now come..."

Scott brought the gun to his right temple with a shaking hand...

———◆———

Blanchard and Fumiko entered the lobby of Scott's building. Blanchard pulled out his badge and flashed it at the boyish, acne-spotted face of a man behind the counter. His name tag said SAM, Assistant Building Manager.

"Seattle P.D.," Blanchard said, as they reached the counter.

"We're here to check Scott Macklin's townhome. Do you know if he's in?" Fumiko asked.

"He came in around midnight, right after I did."

"We need you to take us up," Blanchard scowled.

"Well, I'm sorry, gentlemen. I can't do that without a warrant or the proper authorization."

———◆———

Blanchard reached into his coat, irritated. The 24 hours without sleep were starting to take their toll. He pulled out the warrant, held it up in Sam's face, and stopped himself before rapping the guy on the forehead with it.

"Sure, you can. Get the key, now!"

———◆———

Thomas's eyes were blotted with tears, blurring his view of the quarry's edge. He was almost a hundred yards away from the drop. The sedan bumped and jostled over the rocks and dirt; the sticky, cloying Alabama heat drenched him in a heavy sweat that rolled into his eyes, burning them. The heat reminded him of the jungle. He had managed to cheat death there, but couldn't manage it back here in Alabama. He never imagined that the enemy, the *real* enemy, would take him. He uncovered just enough of their evil to fall into their trap.

Thomas felt death rise in his chest. A sickly, queasy fear. His mind brought up vivid images of the coming crash. He agonized at the thought of dying, crushed and burned in a tomb of twisted metal. He pressed his boot harder against the pedal, and the car roared madly down the hill.

He closed his eyes. A prayer move from his heart to his mind, and then to his lips, though he only half-believed God could save him now.

"Lord, please… Lord please, help me… Is there another way…? Is there another way…? I don't want to leave my family…"

When Thomas opened his eyes, what looked like a tear or a rip appeared across the surface of the blue sky. The tear widened and opened, and he heard a sound like roaring oceans and blustering winds. The tear stretched and undulated, becoming a glowing sphere, hanging like a second sun. It was even brighter than the sun, but not hot. Thomas felt awe and comfort, along with a disconnectedness from time. The shape of a man approached him boldly from beyond a corridor of light in the sky…

"Do it…"

Scott's hand trembled with the gun; the compulsion of The Voice weakened him. The muscles of his finger pressed gently against the trigger. Scott's eyes opened wide against the sky, aching because he wouldn't closed them. He gazed at the sky and the mountains beneath it. His prayer was despondent, his words spoken with the automatic reflex of a wounded soul.

"God… Help me… Help me…"

Scott gawked into the sun, but how could it be the sun? He was facing the west at sunrise; the light of the sun was against the mountains. This light was not the sun! He heard voices, millions of them, but they didn't sound like the others he'd heard. He focused, but was unable to decipher their words; still, the sound soothed him, and the ache of his mind and soul dissipated. The wind surged against his window, waving the curtains and blinds; it sounded like singing.

Scott saw a man step through the shape of light as if he entered through a curtain onto a stage. An electric shock moved through his hand and the gun dropped. When it hit the carpet, the hammer tripped and fired, the bullet smashing harmlessly into the wall just right of the window.

Scott's fear mingled with comfort as the man stood there, haloed by fire, in front of his window.

In the elevator, Blanchard and Fumiko heard the shot and drew their weapons. When the doors opened, they darted into the hallway. Fumiko reached back and grabbed the apartment keys out of Sam's hand, holding up a finger at him. "Stay here." Sam nodded, and Fumiko chased off after Blanchard, who yelled at him from down the hall.

"What's the number again?!"

"1507! It should be down on the right!"

"Call it in!"

Fumiko pulled out his phone from a coat pocket. "This is Fumiko. We've got a shot fired on the fifteenth floor of the Cedar Townhomes Building at 2236 Cedar Avenue. Hold backup on standby; we've already got two units on sight. We will advise on further assistance."

Fumiko ran down the hallway, watching Blanchard turn a corner.

The Man in the Light opened His arms and spoke. Thomas felt his voice like a crack of thunder, yet it was kind and temperate.

"STOP. DO NOT DO THIS. YOU MUST LIVE. I WILL USE YOU…"

Then He was gone. The sky was instantly whole again.

The voices of the shadows rose in his head again, in a massive, blistering protest. They cursed and howled in his ears, but Thomas felt the presence of something else, the presence of the Man From the Sky. The voices subsided until they were gone. Thomas's mind filled with comfort like lungs filling with fresh air. His thoughts became lucid and alert.

Suddenly awake, his eyes blinked at the immediate problem. The sedan was only 50 yards from the edge. He stomped on the brake, but the momentum and weight of the car against the downward slope was enough to propel it forward. He couldn't stop.

Thomas unbuckled his seat belt, pulled on the door latch, and flew from behind the wheel.

———•◦•———

Blanchard fumbled with the keys while Fumiko pounded on the door.

"Scott Macklin, this is the police! We've got a warrant! Open up!"

Blanchard cursed. "These aren't the right keys! He gave us the wrong keys!"

"Are you sure?"

"I'm sure!"

"Well, move! Move out of the way!"

Blanchard jumped clear as Fumiko took three steps back from the door, then charged it, kicking hard. The door flew open, slamming against a wall and knocking down a picture frame. Blanchard and Fumiko burst into the entranceway, defensively brandishing their weapons.

Scott's fear was tinged with peace. He dropped to his knees and fell forward on the carpet. He knew Who stood in front of him. The Man said only one word, but His voice shook the building.

"LIVE..."

When Scott dared to open his eyes and look upward, he saw the Man looking down on him. The light enshrouding the Man made it almost impossible to make out his features. Without a doubt, though, Scott could see that the Man was smiling at him. He rose to his knees with his hands folded prayerfully. He smiled, too, and the room began to fill with the light. It filled until Scott could no longer make out his surroundings. The apartment was gone, the city was gone, the world and time no longer existed. Scott felt his body lift from the ground, and his soul touched a place that was not of the earth.

———◆•◆———

Thomas hit the ground hard, and heard a loud snap. The nauseating pain shot in a wave from his broken left arm across his body. He yelled out, then grunted and grimaced as he rolled and slid on the rocky dirt. He could see the sedan next to him, the open driver side door flapping and the steering wheel spinning wildly left and right. The dust and dirt from underneath the speeding tires flew into his eyes and choked him. The broken arm sent waves of fresh pain through his body as he banged it against the rocks. The edge of the quarry was just a few feet away, and he still rolled toward it. He slowed, however, and the sedan passed him just before he watched it disappear over the edge. Seconds later, he skidded to a stop, knocking some rocks and dirt over the cliff. Through eyes squinted with pain, he saw the car spinning downward into the quarry.

The sky was clear blue, azure. The sedan fell out of the fathomless blue; it spun and twisted; the sound of metal creaked as it cut the air. And it fell…and fell… and fell…

———◆•◆———

Scott's bedroom door was open, and Blanchard poked his head in and back out to avoid a bullet. Then he jumped into the room, holding his gun in front, but relaxed his posture when he saw the room was empty. He moved to the closet, pulled it open, and pointed the gun in, but no one was there. He brought the weapon to his side, but didn't holster it yet.

"Fumiko!"

Blanchard looked around the bedroom and saw the .38 on the carpet in front of the window, and a fresh bullet hole in the wall. The window was open and a soft breeze coursed through the room. Had this guy jumped? Blanchard raced to the window and poked his head into the morning air. No body littered the sidewalk 15 floors below. There was only the usual sporadic flow of pedestrians and morning traffic.

Blanched pulled his head back in and reached for his radio.

"Unit Two, Unit Two. This is Unit One, come in." He moved out of the bedroom, careful not to step on the .38.

"This is Unit Two. You guys all right? You got 'em?"

"We got nothin'. He must've have gotten past you."

"Negative. Nobody even close to the description came out back. You might wanna check with Unit Three in the garage."

"You're positive nobody came by you?"

"Affirmative."

Blanchard moved into the living room, switching the channel on the walkie-talkie.

"Unit Three, this is Blanchard. You copy?"

"Copy, Detective."

"Did you see anything?"

"Sir?"

"Did anybody fitting the suspect's description get past you?!"

"No, sir. We checked people driving out this morning, but nobody fitting the suspect's profile."

"All right, all right. Shut up. Get out of there. I want you to circle a four-block perimeter and give me a block-by-block report."

"But how could he have gotten past you? Who is this guy, Houdini?"

"Don't ask me that right now; just do it!"

"Yes, sir."

Blanchard ran a hand through his hair in frustration. "Fumiko!"

"Yeah…" Fumiko was standing right behind him.

Blanchard almost jumped out his coat. "Ah! Don't do that!"

"Don't do what?"

"Never mind. You didn't find him?"

"I checked every room. He's not here. He's gone."

"I don't accept that. How could he have gotten past us?"

"He had plenty of time."

"No, he didn't. At the most he had 10, maybe 12 seconds, and I'm sayin' maybe twelve seconds, from the time we heard the shot and moved on the door. We would've seen him running down the hall. I didn't hear any footsteps. Did you?"

"All right, all right. You made your point. So... how did he get out of the building?"

Blanchard stared at Fumiko, dumbfounded. He shook his head, holstered his gun, and proceeded to pace the room...

• • ● • •

The sedan hit the bottom of the quarry; the gas tank ruptured and exploded. Metal and shards of glass shot in all directions, but Thomas watched safely from above.

The car burned and as the black smoke rose against the sky, he stood on his feet. He felt the sharp stab of pain from his broken arm, and the cuts and scrapes everywhere. But he was alive. Alive! This was the second time in his life he had been in the presence of something inexplicable, something otherworldly and holy. The name rolled over in his mind, a salve for all his pains.

Jesus...

Even though the voices were gone, he knew they would be back. But his fear subsided. He knew now that he had an ally, a powerful one.

He did have the right idea, though. Getting away from his family would be the best he could do to protect them. Now they would believe he was gone, and he could carry on his work against the shadows. He would see his wife and children again, God willing. Turning his gaze to the sky, he smiled and then laughed, knowing one day they would all be together; knowing that when the time came, the world would be a different and wonderful place.

Thomas carefully tucked his arm, looking around. He found a line of trees edging the quarry several yards away. He raced toward it, disappearing.

• • ● • •

Scott ducked back into the alley as Unit Three shot by on Second and Bell. His eyes watched the traffic and people as they moved about Belltown. He was different from most of them; he had been chosen.

Scott reached down to check the swelling of his knee, but the soreness and inflammation was gone. He couldn't explain how it had healed. A name flooded his thoughts, the only name that could explain what had just happened.

Scott opened Biggsby's Bible, now his, and flipped through it. His eye found Matthew 19:26. When he read it, he felt the truth warm him with strength and solace.

"But Jesus beheld them and said unto them, 'With men this is impossible, but with God all things are possible'."

He closed the book and looked around the alley, nodding with confidence. Now it was time to take up Biggsby's work and find others who believed; Scott, too, would be a soldier, a soldier in the war that would truly end all wars. He walked stealthily out of the alley, into the street.

CHAPTER 22

The keys of the computer stared back up at Raymond Foster in a muddled, hieroglyphic jumble, mimicking the drug-induced chaos that ran through his mind. When he sat to write, he usually beamed with all the joy and promise associated with a new project. But it had been weeks since he'd been able to type a sentence or even a word, and the deadline had long passed. All the flowing streams of his creative consciousness had become dried-up, stagnant riverbeds; they once were vibrant with life, but now the rivers ran dead.

He leaned back from his desk, rubbing tired, red, sticky eyes. His hands shook from the crystal-methamphetamine binge of two days ago. It was the "good" stuff, on the pharmaceutical level, stolen from a hospital lab. It had him so wired, he hadn't slept in over 48 hours, which was okay by him because he needed to write. The drug sped up his metabolism so much he felt like he could run a marathon. His thoughts raced along the edges of schizophrenia, where he had no control of them. Even when he could write, his words and ideas were vague and hollow, almost childishly incomplete. The night before, his fingers had typed with blistering speed, but when he read the words through now, he found them stale. It had gotten to the point where he couldn't think of a single word to write. He had been sitting there since two in the morning, staring.

At first, Raymond thought he just needed to come down off the speed. He was too amped to write. Yeah, that was it. If he could just come down off the crystal, he'd be able to slow his thoughts and something would come to him. He'd compounded his problems when he bought a twenty sack of marijuana from a friend of his with a Cajun accent who lived across the street. The bag sat half-smoked on his desk, the residue of the smell hanging in his apartment. Once again, his bad judgment—in this case, combining the hallucinogenic effects of marijuana and its acting ingredient, cannabis, with a powerful amphetamine—wreaked havoc on his mental state.

He'd spent two nights in a sleepless terror as violent, maddening delusions crowded his mind. It seemed as if all the evil he had fed himself over the years came to vivid life right in front of his eyes. The drug wouldn't let him sleep, even if he dared to close his eyes.

He'd spent five years in Hollywood, and the things he'd witnessed on the streets now made themselves evident and tangible in the recesses of his mind. The evil within him took the shape of shadowy monsters, shimmering and wiggling their ugly heads on the edges of his vision. They swayed and danced in the apartment, darting and avoiding his direct stares, but he knew they were there as he curled on his bed, quivering.

He saw vast fields of human violence, death, and sexual malfeasance, and the many grisly tales his hand had penned returned to him, dominating his nightmarish visions. Raymond became convinced he was the worst sort of man, a man who had wasted all his creative power writing filth and pulp. He knew there was a growing audience for that type of work, but what did that say about the state of the world? And, more to the point, what did it say about him and his place in a world that relished and embraced madness? What kind of hell was he headed for? Raymond had written desperately for five years, hoping to become a part of an industry that for decades seared the conscience of audiences with its blinding, seductive imagery. What made him want to be a part of it?

Hollywood.

Raymond had read once that Hollywood was founded by priests, who named it *Holy Wood*. The irony was as stifling as the smog hanging over the L.A. basin. There was nothing holy about it now.

The apartment building he lived in was a gunshot away from Hollywood Boulevard on the corner of Orchid and Franklin, a half-block east of Highland. Eighty years ago, it had been a youth hostel; the art deco accents on the building and the vintage movie posters adorning the halls attested to its age. The graffiti of the East L.A., Eighteenth Street Gang, heavily decorating the exterior, attested to the current times.

Raymond kept a day job, working as the maintenance man at Mann's Chinese Theater just a few blocks away. He spent most of his time there buffing the floors, changing light bulbs, and lifting heavy canisters of film into the projection booths.

The boulevard was a mecca for tourists from all over the world, especially the Japanese, for some reason. Represented in Raymond's neighborhood was every type of lost and low character you could think of: runaway teenagers, prostitutes, drug addicts, and an endless stream of beggars and homeless. They lined the street in a gauntlet of pain, depravity, and suffering, almost overshadowing the beckoning glitter of Hollywood.

On the boulevard, there was the headquarters of the Church of Scientology, the famous Wax Museum, a McDonald's with a menacing tyrannosaurus rex atop it—eating a neon clock—and the names of the stars embedded on the sidewalks along with an assortment of other oddities and human strangeness.

Just across the street, on the corner of Franklin and La Cienega, stood a Christian church whose door Raymond had never darkened. He'd passed by it often on his way to grab Chinese take-out, or to pick up a bottle of bourbon from a Korean liquor store. He had a good view of the church from his balcony... In fact, it was the last thing he saw just before he died.

The Voice had come to him on the previous night, a welcome audio interlude to the deranged visual menagerie. Raymond hungered for it, longed for a salve of reason in the middle of his inner turmoil. He had finally come to his end, questioning his own purpose. Looking over his past work, all he had to show for his writing ability was a stack of rejected screenplays and a file cabinet full of unpublished short stories.

Glancing around his sparsely decorated apartment, his eyes fell on the walls in front of his desk, papered with rejection letters from over a dozen studios. They all read the same, basically; they'd politely thanked him for his submissions, but they really couldn't use the type of work he was producing. Most of the time, the scripts had been returned unread, the cover pages still flat and uncurled. Sometimes, he hadn't gotten a reply at all. Raymond tacked the rejection letters to the wall only because he believed that he would one day look back, swollen with the pride of how far he'd come. But now the letters reminded him of his ineffectiveness as a writer, of his lack of talent. For a man who had spent his life focused on this career, the realization of his empty ability felt like an executioner calling him to the gallows.

What was he supposed to do now?

The Voice offered him a way out that seemed easy at first, but he should have known the offer from beyond was too good to be true. The Voice made it all seem so logical and prudent. The Voice knew what he was planning, and it questioned why he would want to take such drastic measures. Why end his life before he'd really given himself a chance to prove his worth? All he had to do was write one sentence, one original sentence showcasing the power of his talents, and he could be spared a lifetime of regret and eventual suicide. By morning, The Voice had reasoned, if he could not come up with a single sentence, he would have to do the merciful thing, the only sane thing. Why spend the rest of his life living down his failure? Why live in a prison of self-pity?

The Voice had given him a chance to redeem his work and justify his existence. He'd been given the gift of the night, but already the sun had been up for an hour. The computer screen stared at Raymond, not a word on its blank face, the cursor blinking stupidly.

Raymond reconsidered the terms of the agreement. Was killing himself the solution to his problem? So he'd failed. Maybe he had no talent, but so what? Should his life have to end? What if The Voice had been just a figment, some physiological effect of the chemical poisons coursing through his mind? Maybe there was another answer. What about God?

No sooner had he contemplated God than The Voice rose and snatched the idea from him. It was instantly as if he'd never thought of Him at all.

"Well, now. What have we come up with, Raymond?"

Raymond startled at the presence, jumping up from the keyboard like a child caught without his homework.

"Ah…I…I don't… I…I … I couldn't…"

"You couldn't come up with anything?"

"I…I… couldn't…"

"Nothing?"

"I…I…I… don't know… I…couldn't…"

"Surely a writer with as much brilliance and craft as you have could come up with a sentence, Raymond. Just one sentence?"

"I…I…I can't… I couldn't think of anything…"

"Was there something about my proposal that made you uncomfortable? It's not like I held a sword over your head and forced you to write. It's very difficult to create under duress, I know."

"Y…yes…"

"I don't understand why it was hard for you. I was hoping your career would blossom. We couldn't wait to see some of the works you would produce. But not everyone can be successful. Sometimes, our ambitions are greater than our abilities. How sad."

Raymond ducked his head and dropped onto a Futon that took up most of the space in his flat. He knew how very sad it was. Raymond's life had been spent pursuing nothing more than a fantasy, a haunting, beautiful but fleeting dream, dancing just outside his reach. What would be the purpose of living now, without longings and aspirations?

"Indeed," The Voice affirmed. *"What exactly would be the point, Raymond?"*

Raymond nodded, and got up from the Futon. Slowly, he moved over to his television and yanked the cable out of the back. Coiling it, he ripped the other end out of the wall. He looked around his apartment for the last time. The entire wall behind his desk was suddenly covered with rejection letters. Raymond knew it was a trick, but there was truth in it, too. The sum of his works was a wall of rejection.

The morning traffic on Franklin hummed as he tightly tied one end of the cable around the railing on the balcony. He then looped the other end several times around his neck, tying it off with another tight knot.

"That's right, Raymond. This is the best thing you can do for all concerned. In a moment, you won't feel anything."

Just before he jumped, a sentence finally came to him, but he knew it wasn't his own: With mercy God made the walls of Hell. Evil is incarcerated. God locked the gates…

The last thing he saw was the steeple on top of the church off Highland.

CHAPTER 23

Denise watched the 737 of Flight 120 slowly pull up to Departure Gate B14, in the Seattle-Tacoma Airport. The gray overcast and rain added misery to her already broken and sorrowful spirit. The thick glass of the tall windows insulated her and the other passengers from the high-pitched whine of the 737's engines. Denise wished she had the same sort of protection from the ache in her heart that debilitated her every step. That was her plane; soon she would take a five-hour flight to the East Coast, where she knew she'd never see Scott again. The reality sank in, and it was all she could do just to stay on her feet.

The hardest part for her was trying to understand how and why it had happened, why they were splitting. She had been willing to give all this up for Scott, but he turned her away with eyes she didn't even recognize. Was it her fault? Was she being too ambitious, maybe even selfish? She could understand his apprehension with packing up their lives so suddenly, and moving from a modest city to a vast, unyielding megalopolis. Scott was hitting his stride career-wise; changing locations could cause him to loose his rhythm or even backslide. But in spite of the negatives, she still couldn't understand how, after a seven-year relationship, he could throw it all away, based on a lie.

Sure, Tatlock and other men in her company had eyes for her. They were predators, just like the men she had known in college, the kind who go from woman to woman, taking what they want. How could Scott think she would betray his love for a callous, avaricious man like Kile Tatlock? The thought of cheating on Scott with any man had never crossed her mind. As much as it hurt for him to push her out of his life, the worst of it was that he had lost trust in her. He truly believed she was lying. His distrust was even more painful than the miles that would soon separate them.

Denise let out a deep sigh, leaning her head against the window in the departure lounge. Her tears came in a sudden flow and she cried for a few minutes until a booming voice, announcing the boarding call, startled her.

She gathered her bags, jostling through the crowds that hurried to line up at the gate. Denise caught strange looks from people as she lifted a garment and overnight bag. She must have looked a mess, her face red and swollen with tears.

Denise gave the departure clerk her boarding pass and moved into gate B14. Just as she disappeared, a local news brief flashed the face of Scott Macklin across a bank of television screens along a wall in the lounge.

Los Cruzado watched from the front passenger side of the Chevy Blazer as the night skyline of Seattle sped past. He noticed the hilly streets of Columbia, James, and Cherry as he, Rachel, and Prichard raced along the I-99 Viaduct.

Prichard let out a deep yawn, tired from the long cross-country trek. "I gotta get some sleep," he mumbled.

"*Si. Mi tambien.* Me too," agreed Los Cruzado.

Rachel sat in the back of the Blazer, feverishly tapping on the keys of her laptop. She surfed the Web via a wireless Internet service, looking for local news stories. The *Seattle Post-Intelligencer* had a front-page story that froze her busy fingers.

"Oh, no… Oh, no. Prichard, Father… We've got a problem. We've got a really big problem."

"*Que?*"

"What is it?"

Rachel looked back at the screen hoping what she'd just read was a fabrication of her travel-wearied mind, but the headline shouted again from the Web page.

"Scott Macklin."

"What about him?" demanded Prichard.

"It says he killed Biggsby."

Los Cruzado and Prichard exchanged looks of shock.

"It says the police are looking for him. He's wanted for murder."

They all sat in silence, absorbing the blow.

Prichard drove the Blazer into a tunnel, coming out on I-99 heading north. He wiped a hand across his face, trying to think of the next move.

"If Macklin was in contact with Biggsby, then he may have gotten a hold of the information we're looking for."

"But would he kill for it?" Los Cruzado asked.

"And why?" Rachel added. "I thought Scott Macklin's father and Biggsby were friends. Why would Scott kill his father's friend?"

"Well, Rachel, maybe they were friends once, but in this game, friendship dies hard. Who knows what happened? The thing that's buggin' me is that the police might already have the documents. If this stuff is as sensitive as Baron made it out to be, it won't be long before it vanishes."

"*Si. Yo acuerdo.* I agree."

Rachel leaned back in her seat, frustrated. "So what do we do now? Don't tell me we've come all this way for nothing?"

"Hang on a second. The article says they're still looking for Macklin. He's wanted for murder. They haven't caught him yet though, right?" Prichard asked.

Rachel scanned the article. "Right. It says that the Seattle police detectives went to arrest him this morning in an area called Belltown, but didn't find him in his townhome."

"*Asi, nostros hallazgo el.* We will find him. We will find Macklin and he may still have the documents."

"Right. But I wanna be sure. We've got to check out that townhome and I need to talk to those detectives. Are their names in there, Rachel?"

"Yes. But what makes you think they'll tell you anything about the investigation?"

"I know that won't talk to me; I'm just an average citizen. But they will talk to someone who has a need to know. Someone who was checking on Scott Macklin for, say… tax evasion?"

"You're going to pretend you work for the IRS?"

"Why not? That's what people at the IRS do. I'll need a partner. You wanna come along with me?"

"Okay, but how are we going to do this, Prichard? I'm not very good at lying."

"Lying? Who said anything about lying? It's just... acting. Haven't you ever been in a school play or somethin'? It's easy. How hard could it be to imitate a fed? Just remember to speak in choppy, cryptic, monotone sentences, and you'll be fine."

"You mean sound like you?"

Los Cruzado chuckled.

"Very funny. Don't worry, though. I'll do most of the talking."

"You've done this kind of thing before?"

"Many times. I'll get a hold of Sikes tonight and have him draw up some dummy credentials for us and some paperwork on Macklin. We should have it by tomorrow afternoon. Father, while Rachel and I are talking with the police, you can check the homeless shelters and parks."

Los Cruzado nodded.

"Good. Thanks. I hope we find this guy soon. Something tells me he's gonna run out of time out there."

"*Si*. And so are we."

"Okay, just answer one question for me. How did he get out of the building?"

The West Division Police Captain loomed over his desk like a frozen tidal wave, ready to pound Blanchard and Fumiko any second. The two detectives looked at each other with blank, dead expressions.

Blanchard and Fumiko moved from the captain's office to their desks. The caustic reprimand they had just received was punctuated by the captain's office door slamming on their heels. Fumiko wasn't quite out of the office yet, and the door nearly clipped him in the back.

"That went well," he quipped.

Blanchard looked back at him, incredulously. "Compared to what?"

"Well, you know," Fumiko concluded. "Considering we did lose the suspect."

Blanchard gritted his teeth with wounded pride. "Stop saying that. We didn't lose him. I don't know what happened, all right? But we didn't lose him. We need to get on the same page, Fumiko. If we don't catch this guy soon, and if he kills again, it ain't exactly gonna come down on the captain. You know what I mean?"

"I know, I know. So what's the next move?"

Blanchard noticed an official-looking man and woman waiting in the reception area. He wondered if it was Internal Affairs Division, but so far their blunder hadn't warranted an in-house investigation. Beside, IAD cops couldn't afford to dress as sharp as these two. The man looked like he was getting impatient with the wait and the woman looked around the station with an outsider's fascination.

"I don't know. We'll have to hit the streets, probably the shelters."

The two detectives' desks aligned each other. Fumiko went to grab his fourth cup of coffee and Blanchard picked up his phone to call the receptionist.

"Hey, Carol. Got anything for me?" Blanchard stood at his desk peeping though a window into the reception area. Carol, a red-haired grandmother, answered him while efficiently juggling four other lines.

"Your wife called to say she has to cancel dinner. Something came up at work."

"Yeah, we both got that problem."

"You have some guests here."

"What, those two?"

"Yes."

"Related to the Biggsby case?"

"That's what they say. They're criminal investigators from the IRS."

"The IRS?"

"They say it's imperative they speak with you and Fumiko regarding the case. Shall I send them back?"

Blanchard saw Fumiko talking with one of the uniformed officers from the backup unit that had been at Scott's townhome. He gestured for him to come by the desk and Fumiko nodded.

"Yeah, yeah, send them on, Carol. Thanks." Blanchard watched the man and woman jump to their feet and head toward him.

Fumiko appeared by his side. "What's up?"

"I don't know, but this oughta be good."

The man called himself IRS CI Special Agent Douglas; the woman was his partner, Special Agent Green. Blanchard figured the man to be the senior, and she the junior. The man was overconfident while the woman had the poise of a disciple. Fumiko took advantage of his single status to gaze into her beautiful face; her eyes pierced him even from behind her glasses. The two agents and Blanchard stood at the detective's desk while Fumiko reclined in his seat.

"So what can we do for you today?" Blanchard asked.

The two of them flashed U.S. Department of Treasury badges that looked real enough. When the man spoke, Blanchard felt he was authentic, but something bothered him that he couldn't exactly describe. His investigator's instinct scratched at his mind's edge.

"Well, first off we'd like to thank you for your cooperation in this manner. Any information you divulge will be held in strictest confidence, and used for investigative purposes only."

"Oh, yeah?" Blanchard eyed them, suspiciously. "I take it you guys are from a local field office?"

"That's right," the man affirmed.

"Where? Which one?"

Fumiko thought the woman almost flinched at the question, but the man didn't blink.

"Queen Ann Hill," he stated.

"Queen Ann? I would think you'd have an office in the Federal Building downtown," said Blanchard.

"We do, but we are part of a special investigative arm of the U.S. Treasury. We don't answer to the local jurisdiction."

"*That's* pretty funny. You got someone we can contact who'll vouch for you? Better yet, an address?"

The woman spoke up, surprising the man.

"We do, Detective, but we are under no obligation to give you that information. We have shown you our credentials, sufficiently identifying who we are. Any further questions can be answered via our Queen Ann office; however, further questions will be considered interfering in an official U.S. Treasury investigation. We ask that you answer our inquiries, so as to not impede governmental investigative processes in this matter."

"Are you threatening us, Agent?"

"Not at all. I'm simply making statements of fact. Your murder suspect, Scott Macklin, is also wanted on several counts of flagrant frivolous nonfilement. We have documentation supporting a five-year history. In the past three years, the IRS has prosecuted nearly one thousand frivolous non-filer cases; the average prison sentence comes to right around forty years. The Treasury is serious about this, Detectives."

Blanchard felt himself backing down. "Fine, but how is this connected to our murder case?"

"Well," the man said, "Mitchell Biggsby, the victim, is a member of the Freemen Society. They are part of a network of militia and patriot groups who don't believe they should pay taxes. Biggsby served with Scott Macklin's father in the Army, and we believe the man influenced Mr. Macklin to join the Freemen."

"So, how much is he in for?" Fumiko asked.

"We estimate the taxable amounts run into the hundreds of thousands," the woman said.

"You detectives have entered Mr. Macklin's townhome?" The man asked.

"Yeah. How did you know he had a townhome?" suspected Blanchard.

"We know everything, Detective," the woman said.

"Okay, yes. We entered his townhome on a warrant. We found what we believe is the murder weapon. Ballistics matched up a slug found in a wall in the bedroom to bullets we found in the body of the victim," Fumiko finished.

The woman searched Fumiko's face.

"When you were in the apartment, did you find anything out of the ordinary?"

"Such as?"

"Any very expensive items, for instance? Jewelry, cash…"

"Agent, this guy worked at one of the top architect firms in the country. I think he could afford just about whatever he wanted."

"I see. It looks like we may have to look over the townhome ourselves. Have you completed your investigation there? We wouldn't want to upset the evidence chain."

"Actually, we have. Our people didn't give the townhome as thorough a check as the actual crime scene," Fumiko said.

"Yeah, be our guests," Blanchard said. "You won't hurt anything. Look it over all you want, but one thing: Will you let us in on anything that may give us a motive?"

"That we will, Detective. The Treasury has no desire to impede your local murder investigation," the man said.

Blanchard dropped in his seat, grabbing the phone. "Well, that's good to know. If only you guys were as cooperative in April."

The woman raised an eyebrow. "Is there something you'd like to discuss with us, Detective Blanchard? We're very good listeners."

Blanchard threw his hands up. "Hey, don't give me that, Agent. I'm a legitimate filer. You people already got my stuff, and then some."

"That's fine, Detective. We're not here investigating you...yet."

Blanchard shot her a look, but the two agents stared back at him with all the personality of a concrete wall. "Yeah, well... anyway. We've got a key to the townhome in the property room. I'll call down and have them pull it for you."

The two agents stood. "Good. Thank you for your help today, Detectives. We will apprise you of anything that might facilitate your investigation," the man said.

"Don't mention it," Blanchard grumbled, dryly. "Check with Carol. She'll tell you how to get to the property room."

The two agents nodded, turned, and headed back to the reception area. Blanchard looked at Fumiko. "Tell me you're thinking what I'm thinking."

"That those two are about as much Treasury agents as we are?"

"Whoever heard of a fed field office in Queen Ann of all places?"

"As least not that we know of."

"Naw. Don't give me that government conspiracy stuff. Those two were as fake as a three-dollar bill."

"You want me to check on 'em?"

"No. Let's tail 'em. Let them conduct their little investigation."

"You're thinking they'll lead us to Macklin?"

"I'm thinking, what else do we got?"

Prichard and Rachel moved down the steps of the West Division Building and headed for the Blazer. Prichard looked with amazement at Rachel.

"I thought you said you weren't any good at this? Blanchard thought he was about to get audited."

Rachel laughed. "Right. So, I learn fast. All I did was follow your lead."

"Well, I'll dance with you anytime, lady."

Rachel smiled, surprised at how much his comment pleased her. Prichard grinned at her like a teenager escorting his prom date.

"Your think the clothes were a bit too much?" she asked.

"Maybe. That suit looks good on you, though."

"Thanks. You don't look too bad yourself."

"Well, yeah, honey. That's just natural."

Rachel smiled. "You think they believed us?"

"As good as we were, I'm still not sure they bought it. We'd better get over to the townhome. We're not gonna have a whole lot of time to look it over."

"What if we don't find anything?"

"Then Scott Macklin's gotta turn up somewhere, and soon. We're gonna have to get the heck outta Dodge in a couple more hours. The last time I checked, impersonating a Federal agent comes with some long prison time."

"Well, we better move, then."

"See if you can pull up the townhouse address."

"Got it."

———◆———

Los Cruzado stood at the entrance to Saint James Cathedral on Fourteenth Avenue, not far from Freeway Park. He gazed up at the twin mammoth spires dominating the massive church, his eye catching the white crosses that sat on the pinnacles of each tower.

The mid-week morning mass was letting out, and he felt his usual sense of renewal after the service. The cross-country trip hadn't afforded him the luxury of going to church, and he felt grateful that he could attend. At best, he'd been reading the Scriptures and having some good discussions with Prichard and Rachel about Christ and God, which had been its own reward.

It had been a long time since he had worshipped on this side of the pulpit, since he was a teenager, in fact. Which was better, to be the receiver of the Word, or the giver of it? The thing he loved most about God was the incredible, multifaceted nature of His Word. How engaging for the reader that mere words can evoke the power of a universal, sovereign God and his loving influence on human beings.

He had first fallen in love with the Scriptures in his early years with the Church, back when little emphasis was put on studying them.

The early Church of the Middle Ages had declared that the authority of God did not rest in the Bible. The Reformers forced the Church to look at this grievous error and correct itself but, even today, a widespread lack of emphasis on Bible study existed in the Catholic Church. This had bothered Los Cruzado early on, as a young priest in Nicaragua. Watching the faces of the departing congregation, he wondered how many of them had given God's authority over to the powers of the Bishops, Cardinals, and yes, even the Pope, rather than to Christ. He wondered how many of them considered the Vatican to be God's holy city, rather than Jerusalem.

As he admired the stained glass, wrought steel, and meticulously cut stone of the cathedral, Los Cruzado pondered the future of the Church and the coming world system. He knew the Church was in the position to be influential during the time of the beast. Would she become part of that system, or would she fight against it? The Church had a history of dereliction to its duty of fostering a healthy, holy relationship between mankind and God. Unless it strengthens its faith, he thought, how can the Church be expected to do anything but give in to evil? Isn't that what happened when the German church gave itself over to Hitler and the Nazis?

He knew of only one way to combat the evils of the coming order, the same way the underground church had done it in Germany, lead by believers like Lutheran pastor Deitrich Bonheoffer. By the Book. *Sola Scriptura,* he thought, remembering the passage carved on the entranceway of his beloved mission. By the Scriptures alone.

Los Cruzado crossed himself and moved down the stone steps of the cathedral, heading toward downtown Seattle. He was told there were many shelters and hotels in an old area of town called Pioneer Square. He hoped to run into Scott Macklin.

———•◦•———

Prichard looked up at the poster dominating a living room wall of Scott Macklin's townhome. The giant black-and-white image depicted a black man blowing into a sparkling saxophone. The caption read *A Love Supreme*. The name listed under the image was John Coltrane. Prichard had heard of this album, but he wasn't a huge jazz fan.

"Hey, Rachel. Come here for a second."

Rachel entered the room, watching Prichard curiously. She could no longer deny she had growing feelings for him. But while her heart became fond of him, her head told her the man had a past she might not be able to live with.

"Yes?"

Prichard gestured at the poster. "What's the deal with this?"

"That's John Coltrane."

"You know his music?"

"A lot of it. I couldn't call myself a true Chicago native if I didn't know anything about one of the greatest jazz musicians of all time. This album was a landmark."

"Yeah, well, I've barely heard of the guy. But I'm partial to Clint Black and Faith Hill, myself."

"What's bothering you about the poster?"

"I'm not sure. There somethin' to it, though. Did you see anything in the other rooms?"

"Nothing. The police gave it a better search than they let on. It's clean."

Prichard rubbed the stubble on his chin, thoughtfully. The back of his neck prickled as something told him to look closer at the poster. "What's going on with this thing?"

Rachel shook her head, staring at the powerful image of Coltrane wrestling with the sax.

Prichard pulled the framed poster off its wall hooks. It was heavier than it looked. As he brought it down off the wall, Rachel's eyes lit up.

"Prichard!"

"What is it?"

"There's something taped to the back."

"What? Can you grab it?"

"Yeah." Rachel peeled a manila envelope from the back of the frame. She ripped it open and pulled out several official-looking documents, some of them dating back to the fifties. "I think this might be it."

Prichard took the papers from her after carefully placing the poster frame against the fireplace. He took a moment to scan the papers, then glanced at Rachel with a dark look. His eyes darted around the room as if he'd just been told he had the plague.

"Oh, my God... Oh, my God... Lord help us."

"What?"

"Baron. I should've known. I should've known not to trust him."

Prichard moved toward the door, tucking the documents back into the envelope, and shoving it into his coat. He grabbed for his phone as Rachel raced behind him.

"Prichard, what? What is it?"

"These documents don't say anything about psyops or mind-control experiments. Baron lied to us. He knew I wouldn't go after something this sensitive, or this dangerous."

"Stop being so evasive. What is it?"

Prichard stopped and turned so suddenly Rachel almost ran into him.

"If the plans in these documents are carried out, the United States government will cease to exist. They're chipping away at our sovereignty, eradicating it. According to this, there are operatives within our government who are working to carry this through. He was right about one thing, though. Our country is in big trouble. We're all in very big trouble."

Rachel stood in shock.

Prichard dialed Los Cruzado. "Father. We've got what we came for. Tell us where you are. Macklin or no Macklin, we're coming to pick you up, now. We've got to get out of Seattle."

As Prichard and Rachel climbed into the Blazer and drove off, Blanchard and Fumiko followed in the Sebring.

The alley was dark and smelled of rotting garbage. Scott Macklin looked around for a dark corner and some dry cardboard. It was time to find a place to sleep for the night. The alley was empty, which pleased Scott. Others had recently used it as a temporary home, though. Cardboard, fast food wrappings, and human excrement littered the cobblestoned alley. Scott found what he needed for a makeshift shelter and proceeded to build a small lean-to against the brick wall. He lined the floor with several layers of newspaper. Soon, he had a small, fragile shelter. He would read some Scripture, and then try to get some sleep, if that was possible. For Scott, sound sleep would be a luxury. He would spend most of the night with his eyes wide open, hoping to fend off would-be predators.

He leaned back against the wall, pulled out his Bible, and searched for a passage that might ease his present misery. He found it in Psalm 59.

"Deliver me from mine enemies O my God: defend me from them that rise up against me. Deliver me from the workers of iniquity, and save me from bloody men. For, lo, they lie and wait for my soul: the mighty are gathered against me; not for my transgression, nor for my sin, oh Lord."

Scott pressed the book against his chest, absorbing the words. He wondered if David had encountered the same enemy he was facing tonight.

Apparently, the Lord had delivered this great King of Israel, the predecessor of the King of all kings. Scott prayed the Lord would deliver him, too.

He thought of what Biggsby had said, about finding others who believe and joining them. Tomorrow he would start an active search. He had so much to learn. Going it alone was probably far more dangerous than he realized. Scott climbed out from underneath his shelter and turned his eyes skyward. The stars were faint, but the Lord was there. He prayed that God would help him find others.

"Lord, please grant the prayers of a foolish man. I know I've denied You so many times in the past, yet You've clearly shown Yourself to me. Please send others to help fortify my infantile faith. I need You. Thank You, Lord."

Los Cruzado startled him, and Scott's first instinct was to bolt.

"He will grant you everything you ask, as long as you simply believe."

Scott looked at the man with dark, shoulder-length hair and glasses. He wore a coat and jeans. The dark shirt with the white collar revealed what he was.

"Don't be afraid. *Yo vuestro amigo.* I'm your friend. I have others with me who want to help you."

Scott turned and shot down the alley, only to skid to a halt. The Blazer pulled up to a stop. Prichard and Rachel climbed out.

"Scott Macklin!" Prichard bellowed.

Scott turned back and ran straight for Los Cruzado, who hadn't trained for this kind of confrontation. Scott plowed into him, both men falling to the ground. Scott was up and running instantly, but Los Cruzado languished there for a moment, holding his mid-section. Scott had knocked the wind out of him.

"Scott, wait!" Prichard ordered, pulling out his gun.

"No! Prichard, don't shoot!" pleaded Los Cruzado.

Prichard didn't intend to fire; instead, he chased after Scott, after making sure Los Cruzado was okay.

"I'm fine, I'm fine. Go after him. Don't hurt him."

"I'll try."

Prichard raced off after Scott, who was near the north end of the alley. Scott almost hit the street when the warble of a police siren and the flash of crimson bore down on him. The Sebring entered the alley, effectively blocking any escape route. The driver and passenger side doors opened; Blanchard and Fumiko took up defensive positions, aiming their weapons at Scott.

"Freeze!" Blanchard ordered. "Don't move or I'll shoot!"

Scott felt his nerves seize and he couldn't move. He shot his hands instantly into the air.

Prichard opened fired on the two detectives, peppering the Sebring with bullets. The detectives were surprised by the gunfire and ducked behind the car doors. Prichard slammed into Scott, landing on top of him on the wet cobblestone. Scott struggled against Prichard, who gritted his teeth.

"Scott…Scott, stop fighting… Listen to me! We're your friends. We've got to get you out of here! Do you understand?! We know you didn't kill Biggsby!"

Scott stopped wrestling long enough for Prichard to pull the two of them off the ground. Prichard knew the detectives were about to return fire, so he beat them to the punch with a few quick volleys.

"Get to the Blazer!"

Scott raced back down the other side of the alley, toward Rachel and Los Cruzado.

Blanchard and Fumiko came back to their feet, and then it happened.

Vernon Buford

Fumiko didn't realize both his hands had been cleanly severed from the wrists until he saw them in a puddle of blood, next to his gun on the alley floor. He screamed.

Prichard turned just in time to see an Illuminated One spin precisely on his heel. The sound of metal sang in the air, and Fumiko's scream was cut short with his decapitation. His body fell like a mannequin. Blanchard was already down; it looked to Prichard like he'd been disemboweled. When Prichard looked to the rooftops and fire escapes of the alley; they were crowded with the living shadows of The Illuminated. Their eyes glowed with the fires of perdition, and that fire pierced the soul of the beholder. Prichard stifled his own scream as he turned and ran, firing uncontrollably at them.

Rachel and Los Cruzado were already in the Blazer when Scott and Prichard clamored on board. Prichard took the driver's seat from Rachel, nearly sitting on her. He threw the SUV into reverse and punched the gas. They flew out of the alley at a reckless speed. Prichard geared the Blazer into drive and nearly smashed the gas pedal into the floorboard. They shot away from the alley, screeching from the scene, but Prichard's mind couldn't leave behind the glow of the eyes of the Illuminated Ones.

"Now, I'm really sure... That was them," he muttered.

They had all seen them this time. No one said another word.

Prichard didn't slow down as they sped out of the city, heading east on Interstate 90.

CHAPTER 24

Baron stood in the press hall of the building that housed the U.S. Commission on International Religious Freedom on North Capitol Street in Washington. He watched with increasing anticipation as Elliot Abrams moved to a podium laden with microphones. He was about to give the commission's annual report on worldwide religious persecution. The room was crowded with press and government officials. Baron hoped the report would shed some light on the need for U.S. involvement. The crowd settled. Abrams stood with eight other members of the Commission at his side as he gave the address.

"Good morning, ladies and gentlemen. I'm Elliott Abrams, Chairman of the U.S. Commission on International Religious Freedom. Today the commission releases its Second Annual Report, as required by the International Religious Freedom Act of 1998. This report fulfills an important part of the Commission's mandate to provide independent policy advice to the President, the Secretary of State, and Congress, on ways to promote international religious freedom.

"The report is a culmination of hours of work by the nine commissioners, all of whom have day jobs and serve without compensation. Let me just introduce them to you now: Professor Firuz Kazemzadeh, Dr. Laila Al-Marayati, John Bolton, Cardinal Theodore McCarrick, Rabbi David Saperstein, Nina Shea, Justice Charles Smith, and Dean Michael Young.

"As I noted a moment ago, this report consists of policy recommendations to the Executive Branch and Congress.

"Last year, we focused on three countries: China, Russia and Sudan. This year, with the experience of our first report behind us, we were able to greatly expand our activities to cover more countries and some additional issues. This year's Annual Report touches on religious freedom issues in almost two dozen countries. Besides updating China, Russia, and Sudan, we have made specific recommendations on India, Indonesia, Iran, North Korea, Nigeria, Pakistan, and Vietnam.

"The situation in China has grown worse over the past year, as the government has intensified its crackdown on the Falun Gong spiritual movement, on unregistered Protestant and Catholic Christians, on Tibetan Buddhists, and on Uighur Muslims. The Commission believes the U.S. government must make religious freedom a higher priority in bilateral relations. We reiterate last year's recommendations, including that the U.S. government do all it can to ensure that Beijing is not selected as a site for the Olympic games.

"In India, a disturbing increase in violence against minority Christians and Muslims, committed mostly by Hindu nationalists, has coincided with the accession of power of the BJP government, which relies on the nationalists for its core support.

"Like China, Iran has been named by the Secretary of State as a 'country of particular concern,' one of the worst religious freedom violators. Baha'is, whom the government refuses to recognize as a religious minority, get the worst of it, but the situation is grim for Jews, Christians, Zorastrians, and dissident Muslims, as well.

"The State Department notes that in North Korea, 'genuine religious freedom does not exist.' The government imprisons, tortures, and sometimes executes religious believers, and suppresses all religious activity except that which serves the state interests.

"Nigeria is, like Indonesia, a country returning to democracy, struggling to survive against forces that would strangle it in the cradle. Moves to make Islamic Shariah law in several northern states amount to a crime and have exacerbated tensions between Christians and Muslims in the country, and led to thousands of deaths due to civil unrest.

"The government of Pakistan is clearly not doing enough to protect the country's religious communities. Ahmaidis are prevented by law from fully practicing their faith; religious minorities are jailed or worse under the country's blasphemy law; and a system of separate electorates for religious minorities politically marginalizes them."

"Freedom of religion in Russia remains threatened, with some 1,500 religious groups facing 'liquidation' for failing to meet a December 31, 2000, registration deadline. While the Putin government appears to be committed to the principles of religious freedom, it remains to be seen how vigorous it will be in addressing the nation's many religious freedom problems which occur mainly at the local and regional levels.

"The Commission has found that the government of Sudan is the world's most violent abuser of the right to freedom of religion and belief, and that it is committing genocidal atrocities against the civilian population in the south and in the Nuba Mountains. Tragically, the situation in Sudan has grown worse in the twelve months since the release of last year's Annual Report. The government of Sudan continues to commit egregious human-rights abuses, including widespread bombing of civilian and humanitarian targets, abduction and enslavement of women and children by government-sponsored militias, manipulation of humanitarian assistance as a weapon of war, and severe restrictions on religious freedom. The relationship between oil and the government's action has become clearer. Foreign companies doing business in Sudan that want to offer securities in U.S. markets should be required to disclose the full extent of their dealings in that country. Foreign companies involved in developing Sudan's oil and gas fields should be barred from the U.S. Stock Exchanges.

"In Vietnam, the government prohibits religious activity by those not affiliated with one of the six officially recognized religious organizations. Individuals have been detained, fined, imprisoned, and kept under surveillance for engaging in 'illegal'—in other words, unauthorized—religious activities. In addition, the government uses the recognition process to monitor and control officially sanctioned religious groups.

"Before I take questions from the press, I'd like to make one last observation. The terms of the present Commissioners expire in two weeks, on May 14. These Commissioners are a politically, religiously, and professionally diverse group of people. Yet for two years, they have worked harmoniously to present information to the current administration with recommendations for promoting international religious freedom. Their work has been invaluable; I'd like to thank them all for their commitment and hard work.

"And I'd like to make a final plea to the President, Senators Lott and Daschle, Speaker Hastert, and Representative Gephart, to appoint new Commissioners as soon as possible, so they can resume the work.

"Thank you, and now I'll take questions from members of the press."

The press rose to its feet, jabbing pencils, notepads, and tape recorders into the air, each member desperate to field the first question. Baron stood calmly, not saying a word. Elliot Abrams scanned the group and picked out Baron with a pointed finger.

"Yes, Mr. Baron."

The other members of the press stared at him in astonishment.

"Mr. Chairman, one brief question and I must take my leave. Over the past several years, I've compiled information to show that the atrocities occurring in the world will eventually, for the sake of peace, lead to some type of one-world government and religious system. Do you view the current world-wide religious persecutions as facilitators of this type of system?"

The Chairman tucked in his chin nervously, and addressed Baron's question indirectly. "I can only say that some type of religious uniformity in the world may help reduce the persecutions. As far as the persecutions leading up to some type of new world order... I have no comment on that."

The press lurched forward with a babble of questions. Baron noted the Chairman's comments, turned, and exited the room.

As he left the building, the nation's capital greeted him with a bright, beautiful day. His view of the dome of the Capitol Building was backlit by the late afternoon sun. He pulled out his cell phone, checked for messages, and found the one he was waiting for. Prichard had the documents. Baron dialed a number.

"This is Baron. Tell Prichard that he is to pass the information to you on the Capitol, and then come to where the foxes swim."

He ended the call and moved into the afternoon crowd.

CHAPTER 25

Montana.

A snowstorm had moved south from Canada, blanketing the western half of the state in a white cloud. As Prichard, Los Cruzado, Rachel, and Scott drove east on Interstate 90, the storm reduced their visibility down to 20 feet. Walls of wind and white powder surrounded them. Still, Prichard kept his foot on the gas, and they moved over the icy road at a 50-mile-per-hour clip.

The shock of what happened back in Seattle hadn't worn off. It kept replaying itself vividly in their minds. The brutal murder of the two detectives made them understand the evil they were up against.

Prichard broke the silence with a question.

"Hey, Rachel. You're the head doctor. How can we fight them?"

"Actually, I've been wondering why they haven't telepathically attacked us yet. I've read about a technique we might have to develop in order to prevent them from manipulating us with their minds. The problem is that no one has ever really tried it before; we won't know if it works until we have to use it."

"What is it? What's the technique?"

"It a method called *pushing*. When the mind of a subject perceives a telepathic message, the subject can render that message innocuous by a mental concentration technique, which reduces the volume of the message. From what I've read, it's like slowing turning down the volume on a radio. You mentally reduce the sound."

"Okay, but how do you do it? How does it work?"

"I'm not exactly sure. Theoretically, it hasn't been proven to work."

"Great. Maybe if we talk nice to 'em, they won't kill us before we can hand off this information."

Los Cruzado took his gaze off the white storm and spoke up.

"I believe nothing will defeat this evil except faith in Christ. Anything less than that is mere human folly."

"So what are we supposed to do, Father? We need some kind of real, tangible defense against this thing," Prichard retorted.

"There is no defense except belief in God. Man's lack of belief, and his false belief in his own ability, is precisely why we are in the trouble we face now. Soon, we will face even greater trouble."

"So, what am I supposed to do when these guys come at us? Kneel?"

"Exacto."

"Forget it. I'm gonna shoot first, and we'll invite 'em to tea afterwards."

"That will be your downfall."

"Yeah, well, it's kept me going so far."

They grew quiet as the snow thickened. Scott peered out the back window of the Blazer, watching an impossibly dense wave of snow cover the world. He saw a dim light emerge from the thickness, growing closer and brighter. Scott's heart thumped in his chest as he anticipated a visit from above. But the lights grew closer, and he realized they were headlights. Soon, the headlights closed the gap, and were only a few feet behind them. Scott barely made out the vehicle's dark shape.

The vehicle moved next to the Blazer in the right lane. Prichard glanced over at it, aggravated at the driver's ability to sneak up on them in the storm. The driver held his vehicle steady right next to them.

"Well, go ahead and pass us if you want," Prichard said, irritated. To his surprise, the vehicle lurched and lunged at them, bumping violently into the Blazer.

Prichard cursed as he struggled to maintain control of the Blazer on the slippery road. The Blazer swerved and skidded, nearly spinning, but Prichard fought with the wheel and kept them on the road. Just as he regained control, he felt two more bumps to the rear and right sides of the Blazer. Two more vehicles locked them in a box. Prichard's eyes lit up. The Blazer rapidly approached the back of a semi-trailer, which slowly emerged from the shroud of the storm, like a whale from the depths of the ocean.

Prichard slammed on his brakes and the rear vehicle slammed into them, pushing them along the slick road. He realized they were going to be shoved into the back of the semi. Prichard braced himself.

"Hold on, everybody! Hang on!"

The back of the semi filled their field of vision as they slammed hard into it. The Blazer did a 360 on the icy road. Prichard and the others screamed as the Blazer rolled off the road and down a steep embankment. It tilted awkwardly on its side, sliding down the hill, tossing up a plume of snow. Inside the Blazer, Prichard, Rachel, Los Cruzado, and Scott bounced and jostled in their seats. Finally, the Blazer came to a dead stop at the bottom of the embankment.

After a moment, Los Cruzado popped open his door and climbed out. Rachel also managed to exit the Blazer. She and Los Cruzado jumped down into the deep snow. Scott crawled out next, while Prichard fumbled for his gun. Scott could see a bloody gash across Prichard's nose as he reached his hand in to help him.

"Prichard, come on, man! Get outta there!"

Prichard reached up, bracing his feet against the seats and dashboard. Within seconds, he and Scott jumped down to the snow, joining Rachel and Los Cruzado. They comforted each other, Rachel being especially concerned with the cut on Prichard's nose.

"Steering wheel got me," he gasped.

Suddenly, Rachel screamed, startling the men. They turned to see a line of Illuminated Ones along the top of the embankment, appearing on the snow like ghosts. They moved steadily down the hill, their eyes glowing like fire.

"Come on!" Prichard yelled, and they raced off in the deep snow.

The Illuminated chased them, speeding down the hill. As they passed the Blazer, some of them, incredibly, leaped over it. They ran in a line, drawing swords from underneath dark coats.

There was a woodline ahead of them, and the four of them made a run for it. Scott was the fastest, and he entered the woods first. Prichard ran with Rachel, pulling her by the hand. While he ran, Prichard turned and opened fire; to his astonishment, an Illuminated One laterally dodged the bullet. Prichard's aim had been dead on, but the creature sidestepped it with an impossible agility. Prichard emptied his clip to no avail, and then ran full-force for the woods, dragging Rachel with him.

By the time they all entered the woods, The Illuminated were closing in on them. The four struggled to keep up their speed against the depth of the snow.

Scott slowed down to let the others catch up. A sound exploded from nowhere, and he turned to see a wall of snow pounding through the trees. The wall looked like an avalanche, at least 30-feet high and a half-mile wide, but it moved with the fluidity of the wind. Incredibly, it shifted directions and headed straight for them. Scott ran back for the others, who had stopped frozen in their tracks. The wall bore down on them. They saw that the line of Shadowed Men had also come to a stop. The four watched the wall of wind and snow descend upon them, its rolling wave washing over them. Prichard felt his feet lift off the ground, and soon he couldn't discern the direction in which he was being thrown.

The Illuminated Ones stood defiantly, but the wall hit them with a powerful force. It pounded and buried them. Within seconds, the wave dissipated and the sun broke quietly through the sky.

Scott found himself on top of the snow, unburied and amazed. He looked around and found Prichard, Rachel, and Los Cruzado, also unharmed. By rights, they should be freezing, but they weren't even cold. The group huddled closer together and looked each other over in disbelief. They realized they should be dead, but they were very much alive. They scanned the horizon behind them, but there were no signs of The Illuminated.

"I don't see 'em," Scott nearly whispered, stunned.

"Neither do I," added Rachel.

"They're gone, all of them," said Prichard. "Oh, my God…"

"Exacto," concluded Los Cruzado.

An hour later, they stood on the side of the interstate, flagging down a tow truck.

CHAPTER 26

Rachel silently said a prayer of thanks. They'd crossed the Illinois border hours ago and now they were entering the fringes of Chicago. Prichard objected to the idea of all of them staying at her home; instead, he opted for them to hide for the night in a non-descript hotel. Tomorrow, they would head for D.C. to hand over the documents to Sikes.

Prichard paid for a separate room for himself, and one for Rachel. Los Cruzado and Scott chose to share a room. Prichard tossed his backpack on his bed, stumbling into the bathroom. He turned on the faucet, splashing his face with cold water. He took a whiff of his underarms and winced. A shower was definitely in order. It had been a long, dangerous journey, but it was nearly over. He thought about what he'd do once they completed the hand-off. His mind went to Columbia and his squadron of Copes Commandoes. As much as he hated the thick heat of the jungle, he needed to get back there and back to work. The drug war seemed like an endless nightmare from which the world might never awaken, and deep down Prichard was a soldier. He knew where he belonged, and what he had to do.

Prichard unpacked some toiletries and a change of clothes. He found his gun and reminded himself that he needed to clean it. He dropped it on the bed. The one thing occupying his mind was the power of the evil they were facing. Prichard could hardly believe the ability of the Shadowed Men, and he wondered if he would be able to resist them when the time came. Then he considered the power that protected them, the same power that Los Cruzado, Rachel, and Scott prayed to. A God he tried all his life to deny, but could deny no longer. If there was such evil in the world, there had to be a

God to counter it. Prichard looked out a window as the rain fell from the dark sky.

"Are You really real, or what? Are You really up there?"

"He is real, Douglas. He is the most real of all things."

Rachel stood in his doorway, beautiful against a backdrop of falling rain.

———◆———

"When did you know that God was real?" asked Scott.

Los Cruzado gave him a look like a father might, smiling at him with a gentle warmth and patience.

"I think I knew when I was a boy. My people were very poor and we prayed often for the Lord to sustain us, eh? He always did. Sometimes in ways that were not always physically substantial."

Scott and Los Cruzado stood outside, Scott leaning his back against the railing of the balcony.

"How?"

Los Cruzado was poised, gearing up to tell a faith story.

"My father was a coffee farmer and one particular year we were not doing so well. One morning, my mother gave me a pig to take to the village butcher to slaughter for meat. I remember not wanting the animal to die. It was a runt, and had been through a difficult birth. I had grown fond of it, eh? Well, I was looking for a reason to spare its life; I prayed on my feet the whole way to the village. Soon, an old woman came along and was begging and pleading with me to help her. She was a peasant who had just lost her home in a mudslide. Her *familia* was now homeless, and had already been starving. I saw her plight as a way to get a good use of the pig. He would still have to die, but at least he'd die for a good reason. I gave the pig to the woman and went home, content that the Lord would look on me with favor.

"When I arrived, my mother was furious, and she beat me severely. I went to bed that night covered with welts and crying, but inwardly glad about what I'd done."

Scott shook his head. "So how did God reward you for what you did?"

"Well, at first He did not, and I did not expect Him to. We should never do a thing for God and expect Him to give us anything back; we should simply do what He asks. But, within a few months, my father's crop yielded a bounty bigger than any my village had seen in years. We did not hunger for many seasons after that. I was certain God was pleased with what I had done. From that day on, I was convinced that He existed, and I pledged myself to His service."

Scott nodded, feeling himself warm to the story and to Los Cruzado. "I can tell you when I first believed."

"When was it?"

"It was a few days ago. I was trapped in my townhome, with the police coming through my front door. They were convinced I had killed Biggsby. I didn't, obviously. I was praying, asking God to give me the strength to pull the trigger on the gun in my hand—to end my life. I knew I had no way of proving that I didn't commit the crime, so I was trapped. Prison is no place for me. I knew I'd die in there, so I figured I should save the taxpayers a few bucks."

Los Cruzado was absorbed by Scott's confession.

"I had the gun to my head, but I couldn't pull the trigger. I could hear the police at the door, and I knew I was going to prison. Then a light appeared, a powerful, bright, warm light. A man was standing in it, and he was smiling down on me. I dropped the gun and found myself first on my knees and then on my face, praying. The man said one word to me."

"What was it, Scott?"

"He simply said, 'Live'. That's all. The next thing I knew, I was standing on the street."

Los Cruzado crossed himself. *"En el nombre del dios.* Like Peter from prison."

"Who?"

"The great disciple, Peter. Once he was in prison, and an angel of the Lord rescued him."

"I don't know the story. There's so much about the Bible and God that I don't know, Father. I guess that's pretty pathetic."

Los Cruzado smiled and placed his hand on Scott's shoulder.

"I understand; we've all been in that place, eh? Don't worry. You do have much to learn, but then again, we all do. I'll teach you as much as I know."

Scott smiled at the man who would become his teacher. *"Gracias."*

"Tu bienvenido. You are very welcome."

———•◦•———

Prichard stood there absorbing Rachel's beauty. "Can I help you with something, Rachel? Is your room okay?"

"My room's fine. I just wanted some company, that's all."

Prichard shrugged his shoulders. "Come on in."

Rachel entered the room, but left the door open. A breeze wafted the clean, metallic smell of rain into the room. "I just wanted to see how you're doing."

"Ah, heck, I'm all right. This trip has been a lot more than I bargained for, though. I'm gonna rip Baron a new one when I see him. I had no idea what we'd be up against."

"I don't think he could have known, Douglas."

"Yeah, well… He knew more than we did. I mean…we could have used a little more information. He'll answer for it."

Rachel moved closer to him. "Can I ask you a question?"

"Ask away, pretty lady."

"Do you ever pray?"

Prichard was floored by her sheer loveliness, and by the sudden urge he felt to cross the room and kiss her. It had been a long time since he had been with a woman, and Rachel was among the most attractive he'd ever known. He wondered if she felt the same way.

"Prayer? I haven't had much use for it, Rachel, to be honest. I don't think God has much use for a war-hound like me, either."

She look at him sweetly. "You're wrong about that. God has a plan for each of us, but few of us take the time to discover it."

"Well, honey, I think it's as simple as this: Some of us are destined to know God and others are not. I must be one of the latter."

"Why do you think He chose you to go on this mission? Why do you think he chose any of us?"

"I don't know. Who knows why He does anything?"

"He has His reasons, Douglas."

"Well, I wished He'd clue me in."

"He has, but you won't listen."

"Yeah, well, I think He's the One Who ain't listenin'. I have prayed on occasion, Rachel. He's never answered a prayer of mine."

"God is not a genie, Douglas. It doesn't work that way. Sometimes, He answers our prayers in ways we don't understand or expect."

"Yeah, well, why all the mystery? You make a simple request, and He should grant it. What's the problem?"

"Well, let me ask you this. How much do you *believe* in Him? How much do you really believe that He *can* answer prayer? Too often, we ask God for things but in our hearts, we don't believe He will answer. And guess what? He won't."

Rachel felt attracted to Prichard, and she moved closer to him. Her heart raced at his nearness. She wanted to touch him, to somehow make this battle-scarred man see that God wasn't the only One who loved him. *She* loved him, too.

"Rachel, please. How can there be a God? Do you know how many friends I've lost in wars? Do you know how many people I've killed? If He does exist, how can He want anything to do with humanity? Look at how cruel and unjust we are to each other. Look at all the disease, poverty, bloodshed, and famine in the world. Where is God, anyway? What's He waitin' on?"

"How can you doubt God after everything we've seen? *You* can't explain the evil we've been up against. And as far as all the horrible things in the world, those things are happening because of our lack of belief. The amount of suffering and evil in the world is equal to the amount of disbelief. But God is waiting for something, Douglas. He's waiting for you. He's patiently, faithfully waiting for you to come to Him. One day, He won't wait any longer. Your chance is now."

Prichard felt the truth in her words, but ducked his head in shame. "Rachel, I know you mean well, but honey… He can't want me. He can't want me, after everything I've done."

"But He does. Do you know that Paul was a persecutor of Christians before God made him holy? Do you know that Moses killed a man? Do you know that Jesus saved a woman who was a prostitute? God saves and uses all kinds of people. You are no exception."

Prichard could barely look at her; his resistance to her was weakening. "How could He want me? After all these years… how could He?"

Rachel stepped up to him, only inches away. "How could He? How could I?"

Prichard was pleasantly shocked by her words.

"The answer is simple. Love. Because He loves you. Like…like I love you, Douglas."

He looked at her for just a moment more and then pulled her in, kissing her softly and deeply. The power of his feelings for her washed over every fiber of his being. Rachel embraced him and kissed him with a longing and an intensity that surprised even her. They kissed for a good long while before parting, and then didn't know what to say to each other. Prichard felt his love for Rachel growing stronger every minute, and it was all she could do to stop her heart from racing.

"Rachel, I didn't... I'm sorry, I..."

"It's okay. I wanted to."

"Yeah?"

"Yes."

"So what brought all this on? Was it the suit?"

She threw back her head and laughed. Prichard loved her laugh, and the wonderful sound of it soothed his ears.

"I always knew I had this affect on women, but..."

After another round of laughter, she regained her composure.

"That's pretty funny. If you must know, it wasn't the suit."

"Sure, sure. That's what they all say."

She couldn't stop gazing at the sparkle in his eyes.

There was a long pause between them, an awkward moment. Where would they go from here? Rachel decided to let God lead the way. The only other man she'd ever had feelings for was Captain Macon Ballard, but it hadn't worked out. Then along came this man, with all his complicated, bloody past and his uncertain future. How could she expect something good to come of a relationship with Prichard?

Rachel reached back and unfastened the chain that held the gold cross around her lovely neck. She placed it in Prichard's hand.

"Douglas, I'd like to pursue something with you, but I think you should know that my belief is strong. If you want to be with me, you'll have to get to know Him."

Prichard took the cross and stared at Rachel. Could it be possible? One of the things he had prayed for all these years was the love of a good woman.

"Thank you, Rachel. I'll think about it. I mean I'll... pray about it."

"Okay. I'm tired. I'm going to bed. Should we get up early tomorrow?"

"Yeah. I plan to get us outta here pretty early."

"All right. Good night."

Rachel left his room, taking a second to glance back at him before closing his door.

Prichard opened his palm, and stared at the tiny gold cross and chain. Something moved and shifted in his heart: the Spirit. With his other hand, he picked up his gun and weighed the deadliness of it. Somehow, the small cross held more power. The gun in one hand, the cross in the other, and him caught in the middle. For the first time since he was a boy in Virginia, Prichard knelt and prayed to God.

CHAPTER 27

Prichard looked at the reflection of his tired face in the shimmering waters of the Capitol reflecting pool. He wore a Washington Redskins ball cap and a Georgetown sweatshirt. He had a camera draped over his shoulder, looking like a model tourist. Prichard caught the glow of the morning sun as it bounced off the curve of the Capitol Building's dome. In a few minutes, he would hand off the documents to Sikes and be done with this thing. He couldn't wait for it to end.

He pulled out his cell phone and spoke with a crisp but worn-out voice. "Okay, everybody, let's get this over with. We've got a few minutes. I'm heading up the steps of the Capitol now. We're supposed to make the drop on the northeast side of the building. Is everybody ready?"

Scott was at the wheel of a gray van, parked on the northeast side of the Capitol. Los Cruzado rode shotgun while Rachel sat in the back, monitoring a portable GPS system tapped into Prichard's cell phone. A red blip on the screen showed Prichard moving toward the steps of the Capitol.

Scott put his own phone to his ear. "We're waitin' on you. Make sure you watch your back."

Prichard climbed the massive steps. "Son, that's somethin' that I'm definitely good at." Prichard looked around for any signs of The Illuminated. So far, he saw only surging pockets of tourists and the ever-present forces of security. Prichard knew this had better go smoothly; the odds of them escaping if something went wrong were slim to none.

Since the July 1998 shooting at the Capitol, in which two policemen were killed, the government had spent $126 million beefing up security inside and outside the building. X-ray machines stood at all the entrances now, and cast-iron posts were installed around the perimeter of the building, to stop any truck carrying explosives. The Congressional police, with its 1,200 members, had more powerful weapons, and better bullet-proof vests. They also carried night vision equipment and devices to detect chemical and biological weapons.

As Prichard moved past a Congressional police officer, he saw the brand new 40 caliber Glock automatic pistol in his side holster. Prichard whistled under his breath. Those guns were accurate and excellent weapons for defense. He wouldn't want to have to shoot his way past a cadre of men who wielded them.

Prichard didn't see anyone on the northeast side of the building. Three police officers stood talking on the southeast steps. Prichard took a photo of the dome, like a tourist. He pulled out his cell phone again.

"I'm in position now. No sign of Sikes yet. It looks like he's gonna be late. I'll give him ten, and then we cut out. We can take the information to Baron ourselves. He might not like it, but hey, times are tough all over."

Scott focused on Prichard from behind a pair of binoculars. "I got you. Sounds like a plan to me. By the way, that is the ugliest sweatshirt I've ever seen."

Prichard smiled. "Why thank you. I got you one just like it, Scotty."

Prichard saw a black Lincoln Towncar move into the massive parking lot from Capitol Street. The sleek car pulled to a stop about 20 feet from him. "Looks like this might be Sikes. Stand by."

Several doors opened on the car. A group of security men stepped out, looking menacing. Sikes moved through the group and walked over to Prichard. He was grinning like a buffoon. Prichard thought his face looked exactly like it had when he'd last seen him, in Colombia. He had often wondered why Baron insisted on working with a man as slippery as Sikes. Maybe he'd just answered his own question. Sikes did his job so well, and kept such a low profile, that he was the perfect operative. But, no matter how good he was, Prichard didn't like him. He always felt like he needed a shower after being in the man's presence.

"Well, well. Prichard, Prichard. Taking in the monuments today?"

"Shut up. Let's get this over with, so I can go home."

"Home? Where's that? Bogotá? Are you sure you're an American?"

"I don't have time to spar with you, Sikes. I've got the documents, but I didn't expect you to show up with a buncha meathooks. Is this what you call propriety?"

"Just a little insurance. Just in case you lost your head."

"You know, I don't trust you, Sikes. This information is important and the public needs to be informed of it. They need to know what's in store for them."

"They will. And as far as you not trusting me, I'm deeply wounded. I've always thought you and I had a very good working relationship."

"Yeah, well, we don't."

"That's too bad. I'm sorry you feel that way. Well, then, let's get on with it. Where are the documents?"

Prichard hesitated and then reached into his backpack and pulled out an manila envelope. Scott watched through the binoculars as Prichard handed it to Sikes.

"He's passing the envelope," Scott observed.

Sikes took the envelope and tucked it into a leather briefcase. Smiling, he looked at Prichard. "Thank you for all your efforts on this one, Prichard. As usual, you've done a man's job. You make it tough for us to do this, after such loyal service."

Prichard raised an eyebrow. "Do what?"

Sikes turned and walked away. When he was few feet from Prichard, he pulled a gun. Prichard saw it flash in the sunlight, and pulled his own .45.

"Sikes! Don't do it!"

Sikes spun clumsily on his heel, brandishing his pistol. Before he could pull the trigger, Prichard fired a shot into his right shoulder. The force of the bullet knocked Sikes off his feet.

Two security guards scrambled from the Lincoln and snatched Sikes from the parking lot, dragging him back to the car. A third opened fire on Prichard, who dove to the pavement, rolling to find cover next to a building service van. Bullets riddled the van, blowing out a tire. Prichard cursed as he realized he was under automatic gunfire. The Congressional police officers on the southeast steps ran in his direction. In a few seconds, the Lincoln pulled away and headed for an exit on Capitol Street. Prichard pulled out his cell phone.

"Scott, don't let 'em escape! Block the street! Block the street!"

Scott pulled the van up in front of the Lincoln just as it entered Capitol Street. The car stopped abruptly, then spun and headed to the southeast side of the Capitol Building.

Prichard rose to his feet, but stayed safely behind the service van. He watched the Lincoln speed past the Congressional guards and open fire on them. Two of the guards went down as the Lincoln rounded the southeast corner and disappeared.

Prichard raced around the northeast side, yelling into his cell phone. "They're heading around the other side of the building! I'm gonna try to cut 'em off! Meet me on the other side, on Pennsylvania!"

Scott revved the engine of the van, turned and raced around the northeast side of the building, toward Pennsylvania Avenue.

Prichard came around the northwest corner just in time to see the Lincoln bearing down on him. The tourists scattered in screaming droves at the rapid approach of the black car. Prichard took a stance and fired several rounds at the front grill of the Lincoln, a few bullets chipping crisply off the windshield. The Lincoln suddenly turned left, rumbling down the steep steps of the southwest side of the building.

"Jesus," Prichard said. He ran down the stairs, keeping up with the Lincoln as it slowly descended. Halfway down, Prichard leaned over the concrete railing and jumped, barely able to stay on his feet as he hit the ground. His ankle turned, but not enough to stop him from running to the bottom of the steps with the Lincoln in pursuit. Prichard aimed up at the car and fired rapidly. The bullets bounced and spider-webbed the glass on the windshield. Several arms with automatic weapons poked out the side windows and sprayed fire in his direction. Prichard dove and rolled to the ground as the bullets tossed dirt and bits of concrete. He grunted when a bullet burned into his left thigh. Prichard hit the ground as the Lincoln finally made it to the bottom, and raced across the grass toward the reflecting pool.

Prichard stood on his feet and chased the Lincoln as it sped around the reflecting pool and tore across the Mall. The bullet caused his leg to burn with an intense heat, but he ran limping, reloading his gun, and opening fire again. Bullets whizzed and bounced harmlessly off the dirt around the Lincoln as it sped farther and farther away. The car finally turned right, and recklessly entered Madison Street, racing past the National Gallery of Art before turning up Seventh.

Prichard stopped running, wincing at the pain in his leg. He turned just in time to see several dozen security and police officers pouring over the northwest and southwest steps of the Capitol. He limped on, but he knew they'd catch him soon. He pulled out his cell phone.

"Scott, I need an extraction on the Mall. You've got to hurry. It looks like every cop in D.C. is on me."

From the van, Scott could see Prichard moving ahead of the small crowd of officers. "We got you, Prichard. Keep runnin'."

Prichard limped across the grass as the van pulled up next to him. The security officers were right on him, but Rachel pulled open a side door and Prichard jumped in. Scott slammed on the gas and the van kicked up dirt as they hit Seventh and headed north. They found Pennsylvania, and drove west until they came to Interstate 66. They raced out of town, leaving behind a capital besieged with security and D.C. police.

Rachel attended to Prichard's leg as they sped along the interstate.

"Where to now?" Scott asked.

"The beach," answered Prichard, grimly.

Scott exited the interstate and they looked for a place to dump the van.

CHAPTER 28

The tide moved in on Smith Island as the sun set. The foxes in their beachfront burrows scrambled for dry land when the ocean poured into their underground homes.

Prichard, Rachel, Los Cruzado, and Scott stepped off the Maggie Brown and moved down the beach towards Baron's house. They'd come to the end of an incredible journey, unlike any adventure they'd ever known. The hand of God Himself manifested in their lives in ways they would have thought impossible just a few weeks ago. Now, it was time to talk to Baron and find out what their next move would be. The documents were gone, and it seemed likely that the proof in them would never see the light of day. They had many questions, and they would demand answers.

Baron's door was open when they entered; Prichard went in first with his gun drawn and ready, not quite willing for a cross to replace the security of a firearm just yet.

"Baron?" he called. "It's Prichard. Everyone's here; we need to talk."

No answer.

"All right. Let's split up and check every room. He's gotta be here somewhere." They all nodded and went their separate ways.

Prichard started to check Baron's massive library, but he was stopped cold by Rachel's scream. He raced out of the library, through the living room and kitchen, and up the steps, meeting Rachel at the top.

"What is it?!"

Rachel fell shaking into his arms, pointing to a bedroom. Prichard left her on the steps and entered the room, finding Baron's dog, carved and hacked to pieces. He stepped back from the room, trembling with horror.

"God almighty…"

As he reached Rachel, Scott called from downstairs. Prichard and Rachel raced down and headed outside by the front doors of the house. They found Los Cruzado and Scott standing together.

"Scott, what's going on?"

"Is that Baron?"

Scott pointed to a burned and charred body, still smoldering. Prichard moved over to the body and knelt. Indeed, it was his friend. Baron's nightmares had finally caught up with him. Another good man dead. Prichard suddenly felt his whole body snap to alert. This had just happened. All of them were in danger.

"Come on. Let's get out of here."

As they turned to leave, they saw them standing along the beach in a dark mass. The Illuminated Ones, at least a thousand of them, crowded the shoreline. Their eyes glowed like stars against a black velvet twilight. They were dabblers in the black arts and witchcraft, formulators of a dark alchemy. They had played with evil for so long they had become darkness itself, their very skin taking on the pitch of bleakness. The glowing eyes focused on the four who stood at the house, the four who had given them such trouble over these past few weeks. They gazed with an unmitigated hatred on those they would soon kill.

Prichard instinctively drew his gun and fired into them, but the bullets did nothing. "Inside! Everybody get inside!"

They all turned and raced back into the house.

"Block the doors and windows! Use the furniture!" They moved furiously, up ending couches and tables, turning over bookcases to block the doors. They knew these efforts would only delay the inevitable but it was all they could do. They gathered together, sweating and exhausted, in the center of the house, the kitchen. Prichard spoke as if they were about to go into battle.

"Okay, if we stay together, we'll do better against them when they come in. I'm the only one who's armed, so stick to me. Don't get separated."

The Voice suddenly entered the room like an unwelcome guest. They heard it just as if it was human.

"There is no defense against us, friends. Better for you to not struggle. Go on outside, and I promise they will be merciful to you."

They jumped at the sound, completely taken off guard. This was the first time they'd heard it together, and the terror of it was unsettling.

"You see, all your efforts are so small and futile. The time and energy you spent chasing after the proof of some world conspiracy was all wasted. The documents are being fed into a shredder as we speak. The world will never have the benefit of the knowledge of the coming order. We will take you by surprise. All your efforts make it even more satisfying for us, though, now that we have you. I imagine it must be like this for the wolf, when he feels the thrash of his prey within his fangs. Delicious."

Los Cruzado spoke up with defiance. "You are nothing, eh? Do you think you can defeat God? All *your* efforts will be crushed. In fact, He has already beaten the armies of darkness. You are simply too dense to see it!"

"Los Cruzado, Los Cruzado. You, and men like you. Such fires and passions for your God. The thing you fail to understand is that man will never be worthy of what the Lord offers. To men like Prichard, you are nothing more than a communist. Rachel, a woman of high regard and intelligence, is really just a simple whore. Scott, if you take away his awards and the prestige of his occupation, is merely ... a nigger. And Prichard, a murderer and a killer. A man hardly worth the love of Christ."

Los Cruzado became furious. "The thing you fail to understand, you foul coward, is that God does indeed love each and every one of us! The very reason for this battle is that He seeks to save as many as can be saved! But you will soon know the flames of damnation!"

"Perhaps, but not before I get to play my little game!"

Suddenly, the voices, millions of them, crowded into their minds. They cursed and cajoled, laughed and spat vile words and expletives. The physical pain of it brought Rachel to her knees. Scott reached for her, but he himself buckled at the pain of the mental assault. The Voice spoke over the din, catching Prichard's attention.

"Now, Prichard..."

"Get away from me," bellowed Prichard. "Don't come near me!"

"Now, now. Let's not be too hasty. Look at them, your so-called friends. Get rid of them. They are not worthy of a man like you. A man of such striking bravery and courage. Get rid of them now, so we can discuss your future with us."

"Get away from me!" Prichard fired several shots in the room, blasting holes in the walls, but nothing else.

"Kill them now! And then get rid of yourself!"

"No!" But Prichard was astonished as his gun hand started to rise on its own, drawing a line against Los Cruzado. His body shook as he struggled against the impulse and the power of The Voice. He felt his finger slowly squeezing the trigger.

"Yes! Yes! He is your enemy! A communist who has not had the interest of your great country at heart! Kill him first!"

"No! I won't!"

"Yes, but you will! And do you know the most frightening thing about it, Prichard? It's what you've wanted to do all along. It's what you've been trained to do. Kill the communist! You know it was us who was with you before. Now you must complete what you failed to do."

Los Cruzado fell to the ground under the assault of the voices, his eyes wide with pain as he watched Prichard move toward him, pointing the barrel of the gun to his temple. Prichard stood over him, pinning Los Cruzado to the wall with his gun.

"Do it! Do it now, Prichard!"

Prichard felt the power of evil surge within him and he realized there was nothing he could do to stop it.

Los Cruzado spoke. "The Lord is my Shepherd, I shall not want. He makes me lie down in green pastures, he leads me beside quiet waters, he restores my soul. He guides me in paths of righteousness for his name's sake. Even though I walk through the valley of the shadow of death, I shall fear no evil..."

Prichard felt his hand freeze as a warmth overcame him. The manipulative evil dissipated.

"No! No! He's just babbling! Achh! Shoot him! Shoot him!"

But Prichard couldn't. The room was suddenly lit with the light of God's power, hovering among them in undulating, shifting shape. The voices subsided and Los Cruzado called them together to hold hands and pray. The Voice shrieked in pain as Los Cruzado, Rachel, Prichard, and Scott prayed silently together on the floor in Baron's kitchen. The light that was among them turned into a powerful flame, growing in size and brightness. The light rose above them, then fragmented into shards of fire shooting out from the house. Outside, the Shadowed Men were hit by the fire that burst at a blinding speed from the house; it toppled them in waves along the beach.

Los Cruzado, Scott, Rachel, and Prichard fell apart from each other, their bodies exhausted after being used as conduits for the holy fire. They helped each other up.

Prichard turned to Los Cruzado, gratefully. "Thank you, Father. Thank you for remembering that prayer. That's what stopped me. That day in the jungle."

Los Cruzado touched the side of Prichard's face, smiling. "Yes. That is what stopped you."

"But it won't stop us!" shrieked The Voice.

The windows in the kitchen exploded inward as the bodies of The Illuminated came crashing through the glass. Prichard drew his gun, but they moved so fast he was blind to them. He yelped in pain as his wrist snapped, and the gun flew across the room. Prichard felt punched and kicked and he landed on the tile. Scott fared no better when a kick to his mid-section sent him reeling, knocking the wind from his lungs. Rachel felt the hot sting of a bony hand cracking her cheek. She was knocked back against a wall; she banged her head and fell. Los Cruzado stood there as three Illuminated Ones moved among them. He watched one of them draw a sword from underneath his black cloak. Los Cruzado barely felt the long blade cut through him, the cold of the steel mingling with the warmth of his flesh and blood. The Shadowed Man pulled back the blade, and Los Cruzado fell to the floor.

Rachel screamed. "Father! No! Noooo!"

The Voice was laughing now, as it entered their minds.

"Take them outside. Execute them."

The Shadowed Men dragged Scott, Rachel, Prichard, and a bloody Los Cruzado outside, into their midst. The others crowded around them as they were moved down the beach, close to the edge of the ocean. They dropped them there, surrounding them. The leader stood and spoke, but the words didn't come from his mouth. His skin shimmered and rippled with its darkness, blending him into the night.

"What prey has been brought before us this night?"

His voice was so loud, they grimaced at the volume of it.

"Death is the only thing worthy of our enemies."

The Illuminated One drew his sword and stood behind a kneeling Prichard to strike, when suddenly his fiery eyes caught the sky colored glow of a sphere of light, flying in over the beach. The Shadowed Men all turned their eyes to watch the light drifted over the ocean. Several hundred feet out over the water, the light stopped and hovered. The Illuminated Ones moved closer to the edge of the beach to gaze at the light. The radiance shifted then, and changed it shape; phosphorous drippings of it fell to the water, dissipating in plumes of steam. The light took the shape of a man, a man in a robe with a dark beard and scars on his hands and feet. The man hovered powerfully above the water. The Shadowed Men exploded in curses and bellows of hatred and anger. They recognized the King of their enemies. They screeched at the man, spewing forth their intentions to destroy him. The man did not move.

Scott recognized him. "It's Him. Jesus…"

Prichard, Rachel, and Los Cruzado joined him in his admiration of the One they knew to be the Son of God.

The lead Shadowed Man cursed orders to his troops, who formed an attack line along the beach. Several hundred formed the front line, with hundreds more backing them up. The lead Illuminated One raised his sword into the air. When he brought it down, the phantoms raced off across the water, running across the surface of it, heading straight for the Messiah. As they ran across the water, they let out a war cry from the depths of the hell from which they'd come. Rachel, Prichard, Scott, and Los Cruzado watched the Messiah wait. The Illuminated grew closer and closer to Him. When they were within 50 feet of Him, the Messiah raised his right hand in a gentle gesture. The waters in front of Him formed a wave, shooting several feet above their heads. The wave held there, then dropped with a thunderous crash on top of them, crushing them.

In an instant, no sign of them remained, as if they'd never been there.

The leader of the Shadowed Men and those remaining on the shore gave up a guttural cry of anguish and madness. The leader called up a new line and they formed on the beach. They, too, raced across the water toward the Messiah with a renewed hatred, their swords drawn. The Messiah allowed them to get even closer than the first had. Again, He made a simple gesture. The Illuminated were picked up and twisted off the water by a powerful, controlled wind. They were tossed several hundred feet in all directions, some of them landing on the beach, others landing far out in the ocean.

The Messiah looked directly at Prichard, Scott, Rachel, and Los Cruzado, smiling. He rose high up into the air, the wind flapping His robes. He vanished, absorbed into a cloud. As He disappeared, thunder rumbled across the sky.

The remaining Illuminated let up a victory cry.

In pain, Los Cruzado spoke. "We…We must move back. He is going to destroy them."

Prichard looked at Scott and Rachel, then around at the Shadowed Men, who had lost interest in them.

"Let's go." Prichard and Scott lifted Los Cruzado off the ground and dragged him away from the beach. Rachel followed in tow. They moved behind a high sand dune for cover. Los Cruzado choked and coughed on his own blood.

"Good. Now, look, my children; look upon the power of the Lord…"

In the sky above them, the clouds shifted and formed a massive blanket. The clouds turned blood-red, as they roiled and rolled overhead. Thunder cracked again and then the ground started to rumble, at first gently, then building in intensity. The earth shook with a violent quake; its tumult pounded the ground so loudly Prichard feared they might go deaf. The Illuminated Ones stumbled and fell into the buckling and cracking earth. Huge, gaping fissures opened and hundreds of the Shadowed Men disappeared. The sky suddenly brightened with the fiery intensity of God's power. Lightning burst between and underneath the clouds. The skies opened up, raining down a shower of sulphur and flames. The Illuminated scattered and ran, screaming like children as they were consumed by the fires of heaven. The rain of Godfire fell in thundcrous waves, torching the bodies of the evil ones. When the armies of God assaulted the beach with more firepower than all the human armies of the earth, their destruction was complete. The quaking subsided, and when the last Shadowed Man fell, the rain of fire stopped.

Prichard, Scott, Rachel, and Los Cruzado were the only survivors. They emerged from behind the dune and saw the beach littered with the smoldering bodies of the dead. The sky around them cleared, and Baron's house was burning.

A rain began to fall, cooling them and the beach. Los Cruzado stood to his feet. To everyone's astonishment, his wound was healed so completely that not even a scar remained. Prichard's wrist and leg were healed, as well. All their injuries were gone.

They turned their eyes skyward; there, now masked by the cloud, shone the blue fire, the glow of the power of Christ. They watched as the light receded and vanished several miles out, over the ocean.

"Men and women of earth. Why do you stand there looking into the sky? This same Jesus who has returned to heaven, will come back in the same way you have seen Him go into heaven."

They turned and saw Captain Smith of the Maggie Brown. The old sailor moved off toward the pier. After a moment, Scott, Rachel, Prichard, and Los Cruzado followed him.

EPILOGUE

The man stooped and dug the blade of a hoe into the earth. He worked feverishly, digging a long row in the dry ground, pounded by the heat of the Nicaraguan sun. He stopped as a group of children came up to him, laughing and kicking a soccer ball. The man stood and pulled back the hat from his brow. The man's name was Prichard, and he smiled down like a father on the children. He laughed and ran among them, playing and frolicking, feeling the most freedom he had known in his life.

Los Cruzado, Rachel, and Scott watched Prichard as the sun set over the mountain village. In a moment, they joined him and the children of *Corderilla Isabella.* They were together, and they knew God had great things in mind for them. The four friends smiled at each other, and focused their eyes and hearts on the horizon of their future.

The Christ stood on the edge of a stormy ocean. With a small gesture, He calmed the waters and cleared the skies. He moved across the waters where He paused and stood, until He rose into the air to take His place in heaven. He is the One Who sits at the right hand of God...

On his robe, and on his thigh, He has this name written: KING OF KINGS AND LORD OF LORDS.

VERNON BUFORD

is an active member of Far Hills Community Church. Also, he is the director of a youth club sponsored by a Christian-based organization called Harvest Youth Ministries. Vernon lives in Kettering, Ohio, and is currently working on *Legions Against the Temple,* the second book in the *Legions Series* trilogy.

Additional copies of this book and other
book titles from DESTINY IMAGE are
available at your local bookstore.

For a bookstore near you, call 1-800-722-6774

Send a request for a catalog to:

Destiny Image® Publishers, Inc.
P.O. Box 310
Shippensburg, PA 17257-0310

*"Speaking to the Purposes of God for This
Generation and for the Generations to Come"*

For a complete list of our titles,
visit us at www.destinyimage.com